2|23

Also by Michael Hartmann

A Web of Dragons

The Phoenix Pact

Michael Hartmann

KNIGHT

First published in Great Britain in 1988
by HEADLINE BOOK PUBLISHING PLC

First published in paperback in 1989
by HEADLINE BOOK PUBLISHING PLC

This edition published 1977 by
Knight an imprint of Brockhampton Press

ISBN 1 86019 6411

Typeset on 10/12pt English Times
by Colset Pte Ltd, Singapore

Printed and bound in Great Britain by
J. H. Haynes & Co. Ltd., Sparkford, Somerset

Brockhampton Press
20 Bloomsbury Street
London
WC1B 3QA

This one is for the women in my life:
Mel and Robyn, my mother,
Lesley and her daughters,
Debbie and Anne.
I love them all.

VIETNAM

September, 1968

Typhoon Tammy, that's what the weathermen called her. But the impoverished millions who had survived her devastation in the Philippines had a more appropriate name – Satan's Whore. Five hundred miles wide and black with rain, her spiralling winds flailed the ocean into great canyons and exploding peaks of foam. She had already claimed two hundred lives on Luzon and now she came howling out of the South China Sea bent on Vietnam.

Off the coast, the American aircraft carriers battened down. All sorties were cancelled. Even the B-52s flying out of Guam were grounded. Haiphong and Hanoi would experience a different kind of fury today.

To the north, in communist waters, the Gulf of Tonkin was crowded with ships – fishing junks, gunboats, Russian steamers – all bustling for shelter before the typhoon struck. As evening approached and the horizon heaved with giant clouds, so the Gulf emptied of all but a few stragglers . . . and behind those stragglers, caught in the first lashing rains, came a solitary junk.

It was a ratty little vessel, weather-beaten and unvarnished, its engine making a sluggish doem-doem sound as it ploughed through the running swell. It was built of

1

wood with filthy fan-shaped sails, the kind of junk that had been plying tea, opium and pork meat down the Pearl River for over two hundred years. It bore no name, just a number, and the flag of Red China was pinned to its mast.

The crew were Cantonese, especially recruited for this voyage. They were Triads, every last one of them, pickpockets and pimps who had hung the blue lantern with the Wo Shing Wo. Tattooed and disposable.

Only the captain and his mate possessed any air of authority. They were Chinese too but when they were alone and spoke to each other, the language they used wasn't Cantonese – it was English. And the accents were unmistakable. Because both men were Americans, born and bred.

Up in the wheelhouse, Ko, the older of the two, was beginning to panic. 'I don't believe we're doing this,' he kept repeating. 'I just don't believe it.' Ko was fat, built as squat as a bulldog, and the sweat was sluicing down his pink jowls. He was in a bad way. His eyes were blood-shot, throat raw, his belly stitched with cramps. For fif-teen years he had been an operative in the CIA but never before had he experienced this kind of awe-struck terror. 'Tell me you ain't scared, come on, Ricky, tell me that,' he said to Tang, burping with nerves.

But Ricky Tang, twenty years his junior, was made of different stuff. Face of a pop star, heart of a hangman – that's what they said about him in the pact. 'We're still running ahead of the typhoon. We're not going to sink if that's what's worrying you,' he said.

'It's not the typhoon,' muttered Ko. 'It's this whole damn operation. It's what we've got stuffed down in the hold. Jesus, Ricky, I can't believe we're doing this.'

Ko was a superstitious man. He believed in spirits, in

2

Yin and Yang, the balance of the elements. And in his mind the typhoon that howled at their stern was an omen, a warning from the Taoist gods. They had to stop now, pull back before it was too late. Because what they intended wasn't simply cataclysmic on a man-made scale, it was a betrayal of nature itself. 'We don't have to go through with this,' he pleaded. 'It's not too late. We can jettison the cargo in deep water, Ricky. We can explain to the others. It was the typhoon, that's all we have to say – '

Tang gave him a look of contempt. 'What's got into you? You've been in Phoenix from the beginning. You've always known what we intended. Don't funk out now.'

The junk nose-dived into a mountainous wave, every plank groaning, and an avalanche of spray splashed against the wheelhouse. Sea water spurted in through the joints, swilling around their feet in a salty froth.

'Have you thought how history is going to brand us, Ricky?' said Ko, his mouth hanging slack with terror. 'Have you ever thought of that? Mad dogs, that's how. Renegades.'

'It's too late for regrets,' said Tang. He was chewing hard on gum, working the muscles in his jaw. In comparison to Ko, who was all belly and baldness, Tang was slenderly built, well-muscled and tanned, with long, black hair that curled down the back of his neck. He could have been a pop star, just as they said about him in the pact, some teenage heart-throb. But those in the pact knew that his looks were deceptive. Because Tang was as cold as a cobra. Whatever had to be done would be done. 'Dedicated unto death' – those were his own words.

'When we get ashore, you'd better be on the ball,' said Tang. 'One fuck-up and we're all dead. Remember that.'

Ko shrugged, giving him a sullen look.

Tang could see that he was cracking up. Ko shouldn't have been recruited into Phoenix in the first place. He was a moral weakling, plagued by conscience. That was the problem with this war, he thought. Too many of the commanders were men like Ko, from the generals in Saigon right up to the President himself . . . weak-willed men terrified what history might make of them. Then to hell with history. Because Ricky Tang had memories. Oh man, he had memories that would blow your mind . . .

The Ia Drang Valley back in '65; struggling through waist-high grass, trees all around them as stark as gibbets. And suddenly all hell let loose. His friends screaming as they fell. The North Vietnamese coming at them from every direction, firing at them from the trees, scrambling out of camouflaged foxholes. The yells of pain, the terror and all his friends dying . . . he still shivered just thinking about it.

He had been in the 1st Air Cavalry then – before the CIA recruited him – just twenty years old and full of delusions about justice and the American way. Jesus, what a day that had been. When the medics had pulled him out from under a pile of corpses they said he was entwined in the limbs of a dead NVA sapper and they could still see the puncture marks where he had bitten into the man's jugular.

But what difference had it made, the nightmares that still possessed him, all his buddies wiped out in a single day? The North Vietnamese still came pouring down the Ho Chi Minh Trail like an army of ants. The Vietcong still controlled the paddies. More drastic means were needed. And America had those means, everybody knew it. All it lacked was the will.

Then damn the politicians, thought Tang. Thank God there were still a few men with the courage and foresight to do what was necessary. Oh, he knew what they would be branded, every one of them who had sworn allegiance to the Phoenix Pact, just as Ko predicted – mad dogs and renegades. But if that was the case, they sprang from a proud heritage . . . Napoleon, Churchill, MacArthur, men who seized the moment, men who had changed the world.

Tang knew they must be close to the North Vietnamese coast by now, about eighty miles south of Thanh Hoa. Peering through the rain-battered window, he caught a glimpse of calmer water ahead. 'There's the estuary,' he said, relieved that the first part of the operation was almost complete. 'Within the hour we'll be docked. We'll get the papers cleared and unload. What did I tell you? Easier than catching clap in a Bangkok brothel – '

And in that instant the first bomb fell.

All Tang felt was a vast, surging sensation that seemed to propel the junk out of the water, buckling its keel. Next to him, Ko was hurled across the wheelhouse, shrieking as he slammed into the chart table.

Then – out of nowhere – the rockets began to hit. The swirling edge of the typhoon made the fighters invisible but, as Tang felt the junk shudder with each successive explosion, he could hear the roar of their jet engines swooping overhead.

And incredibly, in that driving rain, the junk was burning. Bright flashes – white as starlight – sizzled and crackled as the phosphorous warheads incinerated the vessel. The junk was already beginning to list. Its stern was obliterated, the masts had come crashing down.

Ko was tugging at Tang's arm. 'We've got to get off. Oh jeez, Ricky, my ribs are all caved in.'

But Tang didn't hear a word he said. He was in a world of his own, his head spinning with questions. How did they find out about us? How did they pinpoint our position in this storm? There could only be one answer. Betrayal. So who was it? Who was the traitor in the Phoenix Pact?

Ko was screaming at him now, pulling hysterically at his arm. 'For chrissake, Ricky, we've got to get off!' And, coughing up red sputum, Ko staggered out of the wheelhouse.

Tang followed him, out into the wind and rain. He stood for a moment on the disintegrating deck, filled with a helpless rage as he watched the phosphorus spark and hiss around him. Then he plunged into the swirling water and swam for the shore.

Briefly, the rain lessened, held back by the buttress of the coastal hills, and then Tang saw it, the bulbous black silhouette of a helicopter sweeping in over the estuary. For a second he thought it must be American, a rescue chopper, and he experienced an irrational surge of hope. But then he saw its guns firing and knew it had to be North Vietnamese. The water ahead of him burst into a thousand tiny fountains. The helicopter was firing tracer and he could watch the scarlet streams of fire arcing in towards him, incomparably graceful, like two brilliant snakes curling in for the kill.

Glancing back, Ricky Tang saw the bow of the junk slipping below the waves. But his last emotion was not one of fear, only a profound regret. We were so close, he thought. Just a few more hours, that's all, just a few more hours . . . and the war would have been ours.

ONE

Hong Kong, eighteen years later

There were enough multi-millionaires in Gaddi's that August night to service America's national debt. But when Jacqueline O'Neill entered the restaurant, every head still turned.

She paused at the entrance, a little breathless, like Cinderella just alighted from her pumpkin coach. She was dazzling, tall and willowy, wearing a cocktail dress of shimmering sapphire blue. Her corn-coloured hair was made golden by the candlelight. She looked around, almost nervously, with bewitching child-like eyes. Then, with a soft, exquisite smile, she took Josef Rakosi's arm.

As the maitre d' escorted them to a table looking out over the lights of the harbour, the matrons of Hong Kong society, Chinese and foreign both, coolly appraised her. But there wasn't a man in that restaurant who didn't experience an instinctive sexual envy. Joe Rakosi knew it and that's what made the pleasure so sweet. Because he knew what they felt about him, the taipans and hongs sitting at their tables – a hustler, too damn sharp for his own good, crude and probably crooked too. But tonight all they felt was envy.

Rakosi had ordered champagne and a waiter opened

the bottle, pouring the Dom Perignon into tulip-shaped crystal glasses.

Coughing to clear his throat, Joe Rakosi lifted his glass. Why did he always feel so nervous when it was just the two of them alone? She was so beautiful he was almost in awe of her. 'Here's to us,' he said in that gravelly, indefinable accent that reflected his Hungarian childhood and working-class British youth. 'This is going to be our night, Jackie, a night to celebrate.'

Jackie O'Neill's fingers brushed back a wisp of hair from her eyes. She normally wore her hair down in a luscious golden cloud around her face. But tonight – for the occasion – some ultra-chic hairdresser in Central had done it up and Rakosi dreamed of how he would like slowly to take it down again . . . coil by golden coil. She raised her glass to drink to his toast but there was a look of uncertainty in those almond-brown eyes.

'Relax,' said Rakosi. He grinned, the grin that a veteran steeplejack gives when he sees a novice step out for the first time onto an iron girder fifty storeys up. 'You're not still worried are you?'

'Terrified.'

'Don't be. I told you, from here on it's plain sailing.'

She gave a skittish smile. 'That's what they said about the *Titanic*.'

He laughed but it was strained. 'Come on, what sort of talk is that? You trust my judgment, don't you?'

'Yes, of course I do. But you have to appreciate my position, Joe – '

Her voice, that California-blessed whisper, made her sound so vulnerable. One moment Rakosi wanted to protect her with his life, the next he wanted to ravish her.

'I've got an awful lot riding on this, Joe, more than you could ever imagine.'

8

'How much do you think I've got invested?' He smiled reassuringly. 'Believe me, Jackie, there are no icebergs out there. It's warm, clear water all the way.'

She smiled, reaching across the table to squeeze his hand, and he caught an intoxicating glimpse of honey-soft cleavage. 'You're a good friend,' she said. 'I don't know what Mike and I would have done without you.'

Rakosi gulped his champagne. A friend, yeah, great, he thought. A friend was the last thing he wanted to be. Just looking at her made his blood race. Damn the woman, what was it about her? He never bowed to anybody but in her presence he felt so goddam gauche.

Joe Rakosi was a proud man and successful – most would say brilliantly so – but about his own looks he had few pretensions. He was built big, too big, with a bull chest and heavily muscled shoulders. People never imagined him to be an international trader, a financier. More like some drunken Irishman mixing cement, he thought sardonically, especially with that flushed air he possessed, the gingery-red hair balding at the temples and the florid cheeks that made it seem he had a booze problem or caught the sun too easily.

'I know it's a good deal and I know I should trust you,' said Jackie, sipping her champagne. 'But these last few months have been hard, Joe. I don't seem to have the confidence anymore.'

'Don't worry,' he said, laughing a little too loudly. 'I've got enough of that for both of us.'

There was the shadow of a smile on her lips. 'You can afford the confidence,' she said. 'You've got the track record to warrant it.'

And Rakosi thought, yes, you're damn right I have. I might have the face of a Hungarian beet picker but in forty-five years, starting from nothing, worse than nothing, starting as the son of a refugee, I've carved out a fortune. And I owe it to nobody, just my own guts and resilience.

Joe Rakosi had been fourteen when he and his parents fled Budapest in 1956 after the Hungarian uprising had been crushed by the Russians. He still lived it in his dreams, scavenging acorns to eat, hiding in sewers, sleeping in ditches at night. He remembered all those months spent in an Austrian refugee camp; family 387, queuing up to receive flour in buckets like so many prisoners in a prison camp. Then arriving in England to that grey rain and sullen insularity with nothing, not even a knowledge of the language. But Rakosi had learnt his lessons well. There was only one ethic – power. The Russian tanks had taught him that. And only one morality – success.

The financial world, for all its high-flying pretensions, possessed as much conscience as a gang of cutthroats and that suited him just fine because at heart he had always been a back alley fighter. He liked to get in close and jerk up the knee. After all, the deal he had at hand, the one Jackie was so worried about, wasn't exactly kosher . . .

Three weeks earlier he had been contacted by an acquaintance, a New York brahmin by the name of Theodore Snow whom he had cultivated for his Wall Street connections. Snow had seats on a number of boards and one of them was a corporation called Oiltec. Twenty years back Oiltec had been quoted on Wall Street at ten dollars a share. But when Snow had contacted him three weeks ago those same shares were fetching fifteen cents – if anybody was foolish enough to buy them. Oiltec was the corporation, they said, that had put the junk into junk bonds.

Except – according to Snow's inside information – all

that was about to change. A Canadian property baron, Adolph Fleischman, hustling for acquisitions, was intending a take-over. Secret negotiations were virtually concluded and a major announcement would soon be made. Oiltec still possessed some worthwhile real estate on the Eastern Seaboard, patents and oil claims. With new management and new injections of capital, Oiltec – like Lazarus – was going to rise from the dead.

Snow's information offered Rakosi the opportunity for a quick, clean killing on the stock market and, using a nominee company based in the Cayman Islands, he had moved swiftly to purchase large blocks of Oiltec stock for both himself and Snow. But then, as events unravelled, he began to realise that the inside information he had been given presented the opportunity not just for a financial killing but for a killing of a very different kind . . . a conquest he had been dreaming about for nearly a year.

It was mad. It had been mad from the beginning. Jackie O'Neill was head-over-heels in love with Mike Keats, besotted by the man. They were engaged to be married for God's sake! And it wasn't as if Mike Keats was some stranger. Mike was probably his closest friend, one of the few men in the world he could trust. Mike held twenty per cent of the shares in Trident Enterprises, the weapons-dealing arm of his business empire. He was Deputy Chairman of the entire Good Hope Group. They were like brothers. And yet it meant nothing. If he had to trample over Mike Keats to get to her, Rakosi knew he would do it. Because he had been fantasising about Jackie O'Neill for months, just as besotted with her as she was with Mike Keats.

Rakosi had his own mistress, a Chinese woman, Tina Wai, half his age, one of the most dramatically alluring women in Hong Kong, or so everybody said. But it had got to the stage that he couldn't make love to her without dreaming of Jackie. When he brought his lips down to Tina's soft breasts, they became Jackie's breasts. When he moved inside her, the whispers of response weren't oriental, they were Jackie's purring moans. He had become so infatuated that in his darkest dreams he hoped that somehow Mike Keats might die, a car smash, a tragic illness, anything to get him out of the way. He knew he was hoping against hope, indulging in a senseless exercise. Or was it? Because suddenly events had begun to turn in his favour.

Jackie, who had been head-hunted in Los Angeles to work for a firm of Hong Kong commodity brokers, had decided she could do better on her own. So she and Mike Keats had resolved to go into business together. Mike Keats was going to learn the commodities trade, getting out of the arms-dealing business – which they both said they hated – into something more 'acceptable'. Mike Keats had put up his savings to meet the initial costs. Jackie supplied the expertise. But expertise alone wasn't enough in a push-and-shove bazaar like Hong Kong. You needed a healthy dose of luck in a place like this – joss, they called it. And joss was the one thing Jackie had in short supply.

In her first three months of business two deals had gone disastrously wrong. The Chinese government in Peking had back-tracked on a sugar contract leaving her with a full shipment – twelve thousand tons – which she had to sell at a loss. Then a cocoa bean consignment from Indonesia had arrived at its destination infested with insects. Her lawyers had begun litigation but Rakosi knew it was one of the immutable laws of nature in the Third World that if you couldn't bribe your way to justice you cut your losses and got out fast.

But following these two disasters had come another fortuitous turn of events. Mike Keats – only weeks away from resigning as Deputy Chairman of the Good Hope Group and relinquishing his shares in Trident – had been contacted by an oil sheikh whom he knew from his days flying helicopters in the Oman. Sheikh Faisal ibn Yasi was his name, a devout Muslim who believed it was Allah's will that he supply arms to the guerrilla fighters in Afghanistan. And he wanted Mike to act as his agent. The potential profits were enormous, too big to ignore. So, with the new commodity business on the ropes, Mike Keats had to forget his moral qualms and get on with the job. A month earlier he had flown to Pakistan and from there had trekked across the border into Afghanistan with a group of Mujahedin.

That left Jackie alone in Hong Kong sinking deeper and deeper into a financial morass, a woman who, for all her brains, demanded constant moral support. But there was no way she could contact Mike Keats, no way at all.

Suddenly it was all so easy, thought Rakosi, just a case of sympathy and concern . . . and ensuring that she fell deeply into his debt.

Jackie O'Neill was so close to bankruptcy, so emotionally battered, that it hadn't taken much to convince her. The value of Oiltec stock could increase by five or six hundred per cent in a matter of days once the take-over announcement was made. And those were the sort of profits she needed to save herself. So she had agreed. Somehow, she said, she would raise the necessary capital even if she had to beg, borrow or steal it. Then, just three days ago, she had come to him with two hundred and fifty thousand US dollars.

When he purchased the stock for her, Oiltec shares

had increased to sixty cents on a flood of rumours. But even at that price Jackie O'Neill could make herself a rich woman.

And tonight was the night. According to Theodore Snow, the official take-over announcement was expected in New York some time in the mid-afternoon, about one o'clock in the morning Hong Kong time. It couldn't be better. There was time enough for a long lazy dinner with plenty of champagne before they returned to his apartment. That's where they would receive the news on his telex. And after that, he thought, his cheeks flushing at the prospect, there would be the matter of his own personal reward.

Jackie had finished studying her menu and ordered Beluga caviar followed by cold salmon with watercress mousseline. Rakosi ordered a more substantial meal, the terrine of pheasant with Texas beef and oysters to follow. And more champagne of course.

The hors d'oeuvres had just been placed before them and the second bottle of champagne opened when the maitre d' came to their table, slipping a piece of paper into Rakosi's hand. 'A telephone message, monsieur.'

Rakosi read it and then looked across at Jackie, his face creased into a fleshy grin. 'Just part of the Rakosi service,' he said. 'While we were eating, I thought you would like to be kept informed of developments. It's the first news of the day from Wall Street.'

Her eyes, as liquid as honey, enveloped him. 'What is it? Tell me.'

'Rumours are flying thick and fast. Some of the merger brats must be passing tips to their old Harvard cronies.'

'But has it affected stock prices?' she asked anxiously.

Rakosi's grin broadened. 'Sure it has. Oiltec opened this morning at ninety cents.'

There was a look of utter astonishment on her face.

Rakosi spelt it out for her. 'Do you know what you've made tonight, just sitting here at this table? In round figures, close to eighty-five thousand dollars – tax free, cash in the bank. And the official announcement isn't due for another three hours yet.'

'Eighty-five thousand, my God!' She started to laugh, hardly able to believe it. And there were tears in those beautiful brown eyes of hers, tears of sheer relief. 'It's just incredible,' she said. 'How can I ever thank you enough?'

Joe Rakosi said nothing. But he could hardly contain his elation. You're mine, he thought. You're mine at last.

Every time he went into action his thoughts were the same. What in the hell am I doing here? I'm going to be killed and for what? This is meant to be a business venture, that's all. Never again, never. I've got to be out of my head. Please God, I'll do anything, just don't let me die. Let me get through tonight, that's all I ask. Mike Keats glanced down at the glowing green numbers on his watch face, trying to ignore his hammering anxiety. It was midnight. Time to move. His mouth was dry as ash.

They were high on a rocky promontory with a dry summer wind whipping up the dust. Above them in a clear black sky a crescent moon hung as bright as a Saracen's sword over the mountains of the Hindu Kush while below them, nestling in a valley, lay the village of Qishlaq Imir. From what Mike could see, it was a sad cluster of mud houses, one joined to the other, bleak and brown, the same tonight as it would have been seven and a half centuries ago. Except then it was the Mongol hordes of Genghis Khan who had laid waste to the land around it. Today it was the Russians.

The job at hand was simple enough, to get down into the village to rescue a woman. But there was a platoon of Spetsnaz – Soviet commandos – down there guarding her and that's what scared the life out of him. Because they were the best, not dumb farm boys from Tashkent conscripted into the rifle brigades.

One woman . . . Tajwar Karmal was her name, known in the Resistance simply as Halima; fifty years old, a widow and mother of seven sons, three of whom had already died in the Jihad. She was a legend, they said, a woman who could converse with kings and yet retained the common touch. She had come across the border on a short mission, walking in with a group of Mujahedin who had been ambushed. That's how the Russians had caught her.

To outsiders – Westerners – it may have seemed strange that in an archaic Islamic culture the very same men who relegated women to a life behind the veil should risk themselves for a woman, even such an important one. But then so few people truly understood the Mujahedin. Most were content with the misconceptions. And three weeks ago, back across the border in Pakistan, Mike Keats had despaired of them himself . . . their absurd, intrepid posturing like nineteenth-century bandits, all that talk about dying in the Jihad, about paradise and beautiful maidens. It would have been quaint if it hadn't been so arrogant. Sheikh Faisal ibn Yasi had sent him to study the Mujahedin operations, to assess what weapons and equipment they needed to fight the war. That was it, a cold, commercial operation. And that's why he had come across the border with Farouq Mohammadi.

But now that he had come to know the Mujahedin as men and not the story-book characters they pretended to be, now that he understood their cause, it went beyond mere dollars and cents. He hated the bigotry of their mullahs and shook his head at many of their medieval ways but he would never be able to forget them. He had seen children fighting T-72 tanks, trying to wedge stones in their tracks, and old men firing flintlocks at helicopters. It was the kind of foolish, breathtaking bravery that broke his heart.

The seconds were ticking by. Tension was building. He could see it on the faces nearest him. He looked across to where Farouq Mohammadi, the leader of the group, squatted under a ledge of rock. Why was he waiting?

Mike Keats double-checked the contents of his canvas satchel: the claymore mines, detonation wires, clamps. Everything was ready. Jesus, he thought, let's get on with it. Then suddenly he heard a sound, a hurried scampering of feet on gravel and quickly cocked his Kalashnikov AKM, an assault rifle taken off a dead Russian two days earlier.

The others heard the sound too and instinctively hunched down into the dirt. Only Farouq remained squatting, unperturbed.

A young boy appeared, clambering up over the rocks. Farouq went forward to meet him. The boy was wearing a tattered khaki shirt and baggy trousers with a pillbox hat made of grey karakul wool on his head. He was thin with one shrivelled arm and although he tried to look a man, Mike guessed he had to be about ten years old. His dusty face was streaked with sweat.

Farouq offered the boy water. 'Where are the Russians?'

The boy was out of breath. 'Some, just a few, are in the village with the woman '

'What about the rest?'

'They have pitched camp to the west, down by the karez.'

'How many are by the karez?'

'Twenty or more.'

Farouq turned to Mike Keats and his long, brown, handsome face was etched with a smile. 'Did you hear that? At least three quarters of them are down by the irrigation channel sleeping with the goats.'

'Have they dug in?' asked Mike in Pashtu.

The boy replied, speaking too quickly for Mike to understand.

Farouq explained. 'The boy says they're lying down by the water. They've dug a few shallow defensive positions, nothing more. They've been marching all day. They're exhausted.'

Mike Keats was surprised. He hadn't expected that, not from Spetsnaz troops. 'Good,' he said, a little dubious.

He saw the young boy gawking at him, trying to work out how a Mujahedin could speak such bad Pashtu in such an atrocious accent. It pleased him that the boy was puzzled because it confirmed that by now he was almost indistinguishable from the men around him.

He had the same build which helped of course; tall and lean, long-limbed like a marathon runner, with the same dark Mediterranean, almost Semitic looks. Being constantly on the move and existing on meagre rations had given him a gaunt, leathery appearance. He had grown a beard, jet black like his hair, which followed his jaw line. And he wore the same clothes too, the loose shirt falling to his knees, the baggy pants, the same swirling turban. With his smattering of Pashtu, Mike Keats knew that now – to a Russian at least – if the need ever arose, he could get by as an Afghan nomad innocently minding his sheep.

Farouq spoke quietly to the boy, and then addressed the fifteen Mujahedin and Mike who made up his group. 'Halima is being held in the mullah's house on the edge of the village. We are lucky that she hasn't already been airlifted back to Kabul. But in the morning that will certainly happen. So we must act tonight.' He turned to Mike. 'The boy will lead you down to the karez west of the village. You can deal with the Russians there. When you are finished, head back into the mountains. We'll meet at the cave, you know the place. Try to make it by dawn before their helicopters can track you.' He gave a wicked, white-toothed smile. 'Here's your chance, Salesman – hey, what do you say? – a chance to prove that the merchandise in your sack is worth the effort of dragging it all the way from Chitral.'

'Salesman' was Farouq's nickname for him which they had all adopted. It had been said with a certain derision a month ago but, Mike Keats hoped, was said with a certain affection now. 'How many men do I have with me?' he asked.

'We may have to fight house to house,' said Farouq. 'Two men, that's all I can spare.' He saw the look of concern on Mike's square-set face and hastily added, chuckling, 'But you have the claymores, Salesman, as lethal as ten men – or so you say.'

Twenty Russian commandos, maybe more, and he was being given two men plus one boy with a shrivelled arm. Mike Keats shrugged. What could he do? As Farouq himself had implied, the time had come to prove himself. 'Once we reach the village I'm going to need at least fifteen minutes to set up the mines,' he said. 'Remember that.'

Farouq nodded.

Mike Keats was a helicopter pilot by profession and helicopter pilots – the good ones at least – were notoriously cautious men, working on the basis that if trouble hadn't happened already it was bound to happen soon. That could make them difficult to deal with, perfectionists in almost everything they did.

'You and I will synchronise watches,' said Mike. 'If you open fire before I'm ready, it's going to be suicide.'

Farouq smiled. 'I understand.'

'Keep your men in check. I don't want them swaggering in there and blasting away just to prove how brave they are.'

Farouq chuckled. 'You seem nervous, Salesman.'

'Damn right I am.'

'But the Russians aren't good fighters, not even their Spetsnaz. Nikolai is built too big, like an ox. He is clumsy. He likes the vodka too much. Don't tell me he frightens you.'

'Everybody with a gun frightens me,' said Mike.

'Even us?'

'You most of all.'

And every one of them grinned. They liked that. The tension had been broken. Even Mike could relax a little. They were going to do just fine, he thought.

Joe Rakosi's apartment was on Magazine Gap Road, just below the mist line of the Peak. It was the penthouse of a ritzy new block called Celestial Mansions, an auspicious name for the Chinese. The fung shui was just great, he said. That's why he had bought the place for six million Hong Kong dollars. It stood on a small spur half way up the Peak, on the tail of a slumbering dragon. It had its back to the thick greenery of the mountain which was good and it looked out over the dazzling waters of the Fragrant Harbour which was even better. Good fung shui meant good fortune. The Chinese believed it implicitly, everybody from ship owners to hawkers selling chickens' feet. And, according to Joe Rakosi, the Chinese had to be among the smartest people in the world.

'Just look at that view,' he said as he ushered Jackie O'Neill through the door into the soft hum of the air conditioning. 'That's got to be worth a million dollars on its own.'

Jackie had to laugh. Joe Rakosi gave a value to everything. What would the Niagara Falls be worth to him? she wondered. One hundred million? Or the Grand Canyon? Fifty million more? But he was right in one respect, the view was superb. Soaring spires of light that rivalled Manhattan were all around them while on the far side of the harbour on the mainland she could see a kaleidoscope of electric brilliance that ran from Tsim Sha Tsui to the man-made finger of Kai Tak Airport.

Earlier today, facing the spectre of bankruptcy, Jackie had hated the place. But now, buoyant with the news from Wall Street, her head spinning from the champagne, it seemed suddenly magical again.

Joe Rakosi played some slow, smoky jazz on the hi-fi and uncorked a bottle of Bollinger that frothed over his hands. They laughed together, both of them a little drunk, and drank the amber liquid, cold and sharp.

Jackie was floating on air. 'It's been a beautiful evening.'

'It's going to get a lot better, I promise you that,' he answered. 'Let's check the telex to see how Oiltec's doing.'

Jackie followed him through to the study. Rakosi never entertained at home. This was the first time she had been to the apartment and she was surprised how magnificently it was decorated. She hadn't expected it from Rakosi whose charm lay in being a rough diamond, none too cultured and proud of it.

But when she complimented him, he just laughed. 'I couldn't put two white walls together and make them match. What you're looking at is twenty-five thousand in interior decorator's fees.'

'Twenty-five thousand – do you mean US?'

'I wish I did – no, sterling. I had to fly him from London, first class too. And put him up in a suite at the Mandarin.'

She giggled. 'I'm obviously in the wrong business.'

'Oh no, lady, not now you're not.' And, taking Jackie's hand, he escorted her to where the telex stood in the corner of the study. Ripping the sheet from the machine, he held it above her head. 'Okay, what do you think? Up or down? Bulls or bears?'

Jackie laughed tipsily. Her heart was pounding. 'I'm sorry, I'm just too nervous to think.'

'Then see for yourself.' And, drawing very close to her, putting his arm around her shoulders, he held out the sheet so that she could read the printing.

For a moment Jackie was unable to focus. But then, her eyes widening, she let out an enchanted gasp of disbelief. 'No, it can't be. I've got to be reading this wrong.'

'There's no mistake,' he whispered and his face was so close that Jackie could sense his hot breath on her neck. 'Read again. You'll see for yourself. Oiltec is standing at one dollar twenty. You've just doubled your investment, Jackie – a cool quarter of a million.'

'A quarter of a million! I don't believe it – '

'Clear profit.'

'A quarter of a million, oh my God!' And, half-laughing, half-crying, Jackie threw herself into his arms.

She had intended nothing more than a spontaneous gesture of gratitude. They were friends, the very best of friends. 'You're a genius!' she cried. But, as she reached up to kiss his cheek, Rakosi twisted her head violently, bringing his lips hard against hers.

At first Jackie was too astonished to resist. She felt his arms around her. It had to be the drink, she thought, the excitement of the moment. She tried to push away, laughing, trying to make a joke of it. But he held her tight.

Then – to her horror – she felt his tongue trying to push into her mouth and she heard him groaning deep in his throat. 'Oh God, yes. You can't believe how much I want you.'

What should she do? She felt paralysed. She tried to wriggle free but she could feel his fingers digging into her arms and the sudden alarming sensation of his erection pushing against her stomach. 'No, Joe,' she said. 'No, please.'

But Rakosi wouldn't give up. 'Please, baby, I've been dreaming about you for months.'

Jackie was panicking now and, pushing hard against him, managed to break free. 'Please, Joe, please, no. This is so wrong,' she stuttered.

Rakosi's face was flushed bright crimson. 'Come on, don't play coy.'

Jackie stumbled back into the doorway of the study, panting with shock.

'You knew what was going to happen when you came up here, especially tonight,' he said. 'Come on, admit it, you knew.'

Jackie half-laughed, still trying to keep this thing within bounds. 'But, Joe, we're friends. That's all we've ever been, you know that.'

'One night, that's all I'm asking,' he pleaded. 'Mike's a long way away.'

'How can you say that?'

'What he never knows will never hurt him.'

Jackie started to back down the passage. 'I'd better leave,' she said.

Rakosi's voice was cracking. 'What's the matter with you? You're not some simpering teenager. I bet you've been to bed with hundreds of men. Don't tell me Mike hasn't had you.'

She tried to remain calm. 'I'll get a taxi,' she said, heading for the door.

But he strode after her, grabbing her wrist. 'Oh no lady, you don't leave, not like that!'

'Please, Joe,' she murmured, 'don't make this worse than it is . . .'

'Quarter of a million dollars,' he said and there was spittle on his lips. 'Quarter of a million. I've saved your bloody bacon, Jackie. In my book that's got to be worth something.'

Oh God, she thought, feeling sick to the stomach, I should have realised.

Rakosi was breathing hard, his bull chest heaving. 'Remember one thing, I'm the one who's making you rich, not your precious Mike out there in Afghanistan.'

Jackie sensed the first stirrings of fear. She knew Rakosi had a short temper. She knew he could be hard and vindictive too. But she had never seen him like this before, not so mindlessly aggressive.

She tried to placate him. 'Look, Joe, if I ever gave you the wrong impression, I'm sorry. We're friends, that's all, just friends. Tomorrow we'll know it was the drink that's caused this scene. We'll both laugh about it. But now I'd better go before anything happens that we regret.' And, pulling her hand free, she made for the door.

'No!' he shouted after her. 'You stay!'

Jackie ignored him. She reached the door. She turned the handle. It was locked. Now the fear had turned into a boiling panic. She turned to face him, trying to sound unafraid. 'Please, Joe, just let me out.'

He was standing in the middle of the room on a Persian carpet, one hand holding a champagne glass, the other kept menacingly behind his back.

'Quarter of a million dollars, you bitch, and you won't even open your legs for me. What more does a man have to do? One night, that's all I'm asking.'

She shook her head. 'I can't, Joe, you know that.'

'Then damn you!' And in one blurred movement, hurling the champagne glass against the wall, Rakosi swung his right arm out from behind his back.

For an instant Jackie thought she had imagined it, that it must have been a glint of the light. But then she knew there could be no mistake. And with uncomprehending horror she stared at the knife in his hand.

Down they went, down through the gullies along precipitous goat paths, down into the valley until they crept into an orchard of mulberry trees on the southern slopes of Qishlaq Imir.

With Mike Keats at his shoulder, the young boy from the village crawled through the trees. He stopped, eyes darting, breathing hard, then sprinted across a small patch of ploughed land and went down on his belly in the dark shelter of the mosque wall.

Mike followed, bent low, running as hard as he could without making a noise, and squatted next to him. Sweat was dribbling down his face into his beard. His teeth were gritted so hard that his jaw ached. He looked back and saw the shuffling silhouettes of the other two as they emerged from the orchard. The first was young Abdul, married only a month, pale as paste with a long, hooked nose and always smiling. The second was the grandfather of the group, Malik Gailani, with his grey beard and patriarchal ways. He said he was born before the turn of the century but that was just boasting. He wasn't a day over seventy-five.

Mike watched them as they drew close and both men flashed him broad grins. Bloody hell, they were actually enjoying this!

Mike waited, listening. But the only sound was the raw whisper of the wind. It was the silence that he hated most. It made him feel so damn vulnerable. He rose to his haunches, about to give the signal to move on, when suddenly he heard a sound – a man's footsteps. It had to be a guard. But where was he?

All of them froze, not sure what to do, not daring to breathe. Then another sound intruded, so ludicrously mundane . . . the long warm hiss of a man pissing against a wall.

Abdul was the first one to spot him and, as silent as a ghost, his pale face shrouded by his turban, began to creep forward.

The guard, with his rifle slung over his shoulder, was enjoying his little game of cutting patterns into the baked mud of the wall. He began to hum a tune, the first three bars of something merry, at the exact moment that the wire looped over his head.

The garrotting was done with such precision that the only sound was an abrupt, bilious sigh. Abdul held the body tight as its nerves twitched. Then, when there was no more movement, he let it slowly collapse, the trousers wet with urine, until it lay just a crumpled bulge on the ground.

They moved swiftly now. Time was short. They followed the wall for fifty yards, crawling under mud windows, hearing the snoring of the villagers, until they reached a small copse of willow trees. Mike could smell the water, clean and cold, where it bubbled up from its underground caverns.

The young boy from the village touched his arm. 'The Nikolais are on the other side.'

Mike nodded. Easing the heavy satchel off his back, he slithered forward on his belly, parting the green sedge. His heart was thudding in his chest. Why in the hell am I doing this? he kept asking himself. I'm a helicopter pilot, a salesman, not a goddam commando. I'm going to get us all killed. Reaching forward with his hand, he felt the cold water. Gently, centimetre by centimetre, he parted the last of the green sedge. And there across the water – not more than fifty feet away – lay the Russians.

He could see them among the saplings, sleeping with their heads on their packs. Some shallow trenches had been dug, some rocks piled up and lines of fire hacked out of the dry grass. It was pretty sloppy. He hadn't expected anything like it, not from elite Spetsnaz troops.

Edging back to join the others, he carefully removed the claymore mines from the satchel. There were three mines in all. The first one he handed to Abdul, the second to Malik and the last one he kept himself.

Off to the right stood a poplar tree, precious in Afghanistan for its timber. Mike touched Abdul on the shoulder, pointing to it. Abdul knew what had to be done and, with the mine hugged to his chest, he slid off through the grass. To the left, hidden in the shade of a willow, was an old hitching post. Malik understood too what had to be done and set about the task. Mike looked up into the willow tree directly above him. There was a fork in the branches that was perfect.

Just three claymore mines, each aimed across the pool to where the Russians slept, each with their arcs interlocking. They were shaped like brake linings, large, solid things, and were designed so that they exploded outwards spraying thousands of metal pieces in a lethal arc that could dice a man like an onion. But securing them took time. With the Russians so close every movement had to be in slow motion, melting into the darkness undetected.

Mike checked his watch, praying that Farouq's men didn't blast off before the synchronised time.

Abdul crawled back, his pale features alight with excitement. Then old Malik, like a grey beetle, came crawling along the edge of the sedge.

Mike connected the wires joining the three mines. He was sweating so badly that it ran down his forehead, stinging his eyes. He checked his watch again. Just sixty seconds to go.

Not a Russian stirred. One of the sentries had squatted down, his head slumped forward. Another one, further back, lit a cigarette.

Forty seconds . . .

The last wires were connected. The detonator rested in the palm of Mike's hand. For these last few seconds he was lost in his own capsule of silence. His thoughts turned to Jackie. What was she doing tonight? How was the business faring? Please God, things weren't so bad. They were going to be millionaires one day, that's what she kept promising him. Not that he cared. That kind of money had never interested him. He smiled to himself, wondering what it would be like married to the world's most beautiful workaholic.

28

Twenty seconds . . .

He could hear two Russians talking. Poor bastards, he thought. He felt totally calm now. The sweat had dried on his forehead. His pulse rate was down. He was fully in control.

Just five seconds to go . . .

And suddenly, shattering the stillness, came a burst of rifle fire from the centre of the village.

Across the karez, the Russians started to jerk up, grabbing for their weapons. They began to shout at each other as they heard more shots from the village. In the distance a grenade exploded. A sergeant was on his feet barking orders and now they were all scrambling to their machine gun emplacements, the Spetsnaz training working in swift automation.

It was a frightening sight and Abdul shrank back, ready to run. But Mike, as calm as a monk in his cloisters, judged the moment to perfection.

The explosions boomed simultaneously and the Russians were hit by a blizzard of shrapnel so intense that they were hurled into each other, arms flailing. The mud wall behind them seemed to shatter into a thousand jagged crevices while the concussive echo of the explosions rolled over Qishlaq Imir like the backwash of some great jet that had broken the sound barrier.

Mike saw a Russian staggering to his feet clutching his belly. He saw another, desperately wounded, turning around and around. There were others on their knees, unable to rise. There were guttural cries for help.

After the initial, stunned shock, Abdul and Malik were firing now, nothing crazed, just single shots to put the wounded out of their misery.

And suddenly it was over. Not a shot had been fired back at them. There was just a terrible silence. The bodies of the Russians lay one upon another, limbs slowly twitching in death. Never in his life before had Mike Keats witnessed a scene of such concentrated carnage. He couldn't believe that he was the author of it. It was too terrible to contemplate.

Then next to him, with a blood-curdling yell, old Malik jumped to his feet and shouted out in exultation, 'Allahu Akbar! Allahu Akbar!' It was the war cry of the Mujahedin.

That broke the spell. Mike grabbed him by his arthritic leg, hauling him down. 'You'll get yourself killed, you bloody old fool!'

Speed was everything now. They had struck the decisive blow but there was still the sound of intense firing coming from the village and things up there could be different, very different indeed.

Joe Rakosi was a man possessed, lost in a trance of his own making. Hypnotically, he moved the knife from hand to hand. 'I'll use it if I have to,' he said, his voice low and tense, barely under control. 'Oh yes, I'll use it all right.'

He dimmed the lights in the room until there remained just a faint coppery glow around the walls. Then he went quickly to the hi-fi, bending over it. But no music came.

'Every door is locked,' he said. He drew close to her, telling her to undress. 'Slowly, slowly, garment by garment . . .'

And terrified of the knife, Jackie O'Neill obeyed. She fumbled with her clothes, her eyes fixed on the blade.

Rakosi gasped out loud when he saw her breasts fall free. 'Oh my God, they're beautiful,' he groaned. Then, in a grotesque parody of a striptease, he began to undress himself. He was fleshy but solid, built like a bullock. He smelt sour, part sweat, part eau de cologne. Thick ginger hair grew across the back of his shoulders and sprouted in tight curls on his chest, creeping down his belly until it joined the bush of his pubic hair. His engorged penis was short and thick, heavily veined, the colour of red mud.

He sighed, hesitating, as if he had to summon up the courage to say the words. Then he said in a harsh whisper, 'I want you to tell me things, Jackie . . . tell me that you want my body . . . tell me those secret things you tell Mike.'

Jackie remained silent. She was still so stunned that she could barely comprehend what was happening.

'Go on, say it. Say you want my body,' he demanded with the blade of the knife shaking in his hand.

'I want your body . . .' she murmured inaudibly.

'Louder dammit, say it like you mean it! Say it like there's some feeling there.'

Dear God, she thought, this can't be happening. 'I want your body . . .'

'Say you want to open your legs for me and stretch them wide. Go on, say it.'

'I want to open my legs for you . . .'

'Oh yes, yes.' There was a look of ecstasy in his bloodshot eyes. He came closer.

Jackie backed away, her legs almost buckling under her. 'Don't use the knife,' she stammered. 'Please don't use the knife.'

'Then be good,' he said and, with a sneering smile, forced her shoulders down onto the Persian carpet.

Jackie lay beneath him, drained of any will, shivering with fear. She felt him come down upon her. This isn't happening, she kept repeating to herself, this isn't happening. She lay, helplessly speared under his barrel of a body, washed with a mind-numbing terror. She could

31

hear him grunting phrases in a foreign language that had to be Hungarian. He was moving faster and faster, pounding at her, his body caught in a series of sweat-drenched spasms.

And beneath him, her eyes tightly shut, Jackie kept saying to herself, 'Oh God, why me? What have I done to deserve this?'

Mikhail Kazakov, attached to the 298th Independent Reconnaissance Battalion of the Spetsnaz, had just taken the woman out of the mullah's house when the first shot was fired. Spinning around, he saw the door of the mud-built dwelling blown open and a turbaned figure squirming in through the window. Thirty seconds earlier and he would have been caught in there like a rat in a trap.

His first reaction was one of incredulity. How had the bandits – the dushmen as the Russians called them – got into the village? How had they got past the guards? Then a rocket hit the building next to him, showering him with grit and, desperate for cover, dragging the woman, Kazakov flung himself into an irrigation ditch.

And it was at that moment, down by the karez, that the claymores exploded. Their concussive blast was so immense that it seemed to shatter Kazakov's eardrums. Huddled in the ditch, up to his chest in freezing water, he tried to stem his panic. Damn those bastards in Kabul. Why hadn't they sent in the helicopter before dusk as he asked?

Kazakov was a captain in the Chief Intelligence Directorate, the GRU, a powerful and secret organisation. He was a bright, ambitious staff officer. But he had never been caught in withering crossfire in the black of the night like this before with shells exploding around him and no idea who was friend or foe.

He could hear the dushmen – the bandits – shouting to each other as they ran from house to house. The Afghan woman, the one they called Halima, was hugging the side of the ditch and he grabbed her by the shoulders. 'What are they saying?' he demanded through gritted teeth. 'Tell me, you bitch!'

'They say I'm not in the mullah's house. They're sweeping through the village to find me.'

'Which way are they coming?'

She glared at him. 'This way, Russian, this way – '

Kazakov tried desperately to orientate himself. The ditch had to lead out of the village. But in which direction? He wasn't a front-line soldier. He was a desk man, an intelligence officer. Then he realised that of course it had to lead to the spring where the underground water came up, to the exact place where the main body of the Spetsnaz were camped. If he just followed the ditch he would find help. The water though was freezing his bones. 'Come with me,' he hissed, dragging the woman with him as they splashed along the narrow channel. Then he hesitated. Help might be this way but he knew that if they were caught down here in the ditch they stood no chance, no chance at all. He stopped, trying to clamber up the black, slimy bank but kept slipping back. He began to shake now with trapped terror. But he had no choice, he had to blunder on. 'Faster!' he shouted at the woman.

Then directly ahead of him, he saw the dense outline of trees. They were willows with their whip-like branches dipping down into the water. Yes, he thought, we can climb out there and, surging ahead, he reached the trees. He turned to the woman. 'Grab a branch,' he hissed at her. 'Now pull yourself out!'

Seizing a branch himself in a furious panic, he began

to scramble up the bank – and found himself staring straight into the face of a dushman.

For a second they both stared at each other. Then, with an hysterical yell, Kazakov hurled himself back into the water. He surfaced, using his AKM to fire blindly upwards. He was screaming incoherently, expending the full magazine in two or three mad bursts before he tried to flee, propelling himself through the water, half-swimming, half-running in a terrified frenzy like some cornered animal.

A single burst of fire hit him. And down he went, down below the surface, choking and gagging, down into the flurry of mud at the bottom of the karez. Every instinct in his body screamed out that he should surface. But somehow, caught in the terrible moment of that bewildering shock, his intelligence prevailed. He knew that if he showed any signs of life, any signs at all, they would finish him off.

And so, with his lungs bursting and his eyes wide in that black, icy water, he let his body rise slowly to the surface and bob over like a cork. With one small movement of his foot he was able to float lifelessly to the side of the bank and there he lay on his back, mouth slack, like a shot-torn corpse. He knew that a bullet had entered his back and another had shattered his right elbow. But he was still conscious, perfectly lucid, the shock dulling his pain.

The bandit who had shot him – a bearded man wearing a dusty red turban – was still crouched at the top of the irrigation ditch. Kazakov heard him call down to the woman in such slow, broken Pashtu that even he understood what was said. 'Are you the one they call Halima?'

The woman nodded, her eyes wide with fright. 'You're not Afghan.'

'No, but I'm with Farouq Mohammadi. We knew the Russians were taking you to Kabul. That's why we've come to get you.'

Then the woman replied in fluent English. 'Who are you? What are you doing with the Mujahedin?'

With a small laugh, the man replied in English, 'My name is Keats, Mike Keats. I'll have to explain the rest later.' And with a hesitant smile, as Kazakov watched, he reached down to take her hand.

Joe Rakosi looked down at her. 'Tears?' he said, brushing his stubby fingers across her cheek. 'It's not the end of the world you know. All you've done is pay your dues.'

Jackie sat up, her tear-stained face etched with dull defiance. 'Just let me get dressed and go.'

He used the hem of her dress to wipe the sweat off his forehead. 'Not just yet, my love.' Naked, he climbed to his feet and stepped across to the hi-fi. 'I want you to listen to something first.'

Listlessly, Jackie waited. She thought of trying to make a bolt for it but what would be the good of it? The doors were locked, he was twice as strong as her. But, most of all, he had that kitchen knife with its sharp serrated edge in his hand.

Rakosi finished rewinding the tape. He gave Jackie an oblique glance, smiling to himself as if he was holding back some special secret. Then he pressed the 'play' button and turned towards her.

Jackie heard a voice, a man's voice talking, and shook her head in disbelief. Because the voice on the tape was unmistakable. It was Rakosi's flat accent, half-cockney, half-Hungarian, crude and commanding, filled with lust. 'I want you to tell me things, Jackie . . . tell me that you want my body . . . tell me those secret things you tell Mike.'

'You're sick,' she murmured.

But Rakosi just stood there with a hard, fixed smile on his face. And the words continued . . .

'Go on, say it. Say you want my body.'

'I want your body.'

'Louder dammit, say it like you mean it. Say it like there's some feeling there.'

Jackie could feel the revulsion seeping through her body like a slow clammy poison. Rakosi had dictated those things to her so that he could record every obscene phrase, every last syllable and sound of the rape.

Rakosi twisted the knife in his fingers. 'I often make these recordings,' he said as if making polite conversation. 'Tina and I lie in bed at night and listen to how it was the night before.' He smiled. 'She didn't like it at first. You know what the Chinese are like, all this bourgeois coyness. It takes months to get through to them. But you're a Californian girl, a liberated lady.'

He could hear his own groans coming over the tape now and he began to shiver. 'Tonight of course the recording has an extra benefit,' he said, dry-mouthed. 'You know how easy it is to edit a tape. Cut out the commands and just leave the replies. No problem at all. Tell me, Jackie, how do you think Mike would react listening to this – after it had been edited, of course? Do you think it would turn him on?'

Jackie stared up at him, sickened to her stomach.

'I don't understand you,' said Rakosi jauntily. 'I mean Mike's a good guy. He's one of my best friends.' And he smiled. 'But if I hadn't given him his chance in the arms-dealing business, what would he be today? Just another helicopter hack bumming around the world.

What do you see in him . . . past the looks I mean?'

Jackie glared at him. 'Do you really want to know?'

He laughed. 'You're not going to give me that knight in shining armour crap, are you? We all know he's a nice guy. But, as the saying goes, nice guys come second. Admit it, Jackie, you're not so different from me. You want the same things I want. How long do you think you and Mike will stay together? You're poles apart.'

Frightened as she was, Jackie couldn't stand his taunting. 'He's twice the man you are, you bastard!'

'Is he now?' Listening to the tape, Rakosi could hear the increased tempo of his own moans and curled back his lips in a strange, piercing smile. 'Twice the man, you say. Well then, we'll just have to try again, won't we . . .?'

It was the instinct for survival that propelled him, knowing that the Afghans looted every Russian body they found. Slowly, like some crippled reptile, Kazakov dragged his mud-soaked body up the side of the ditch and slithered over the top into the dark protection of the trees.

The pain was excruciating but he daren't make a sound. His life depended on it.

Two bandits ran past him. They were loaded with stolen weapons that clanked and clattered on their backs. They were both laughing and one raised his fist to the other in a gesture of triumph.

Kazakov gritted his teeth. Laugh while you can, he thought. Because I'm going to crush you all one day . . . men, women and children . . . every last one of you bastards.

When eventually he was satiated, sheened in sweat like a

Sumo wrestler, Joe Rakosi flopped onto the sofa, the knife still in his hand, and said to her, 'I know what you're thinking. You're thinking that you're going to make me pay. You're going to see me rot in jail. Burn in hell!' And he laughed. 'If you want to report it to the police, go ahead. Subject yourself to the whole messy procedure – doctors and swabs, endless statements to the cops. Make yourself public property. Mike will be delighted.'

Ambling across to the bar, he took a frosted bottle of Dom Perignon from an ice-bucket and uncorked it, pulling back the gold tinfoil and drinking straight from the bottle.

'Before you set off to crucify me, just think what the jury will hear . . . sure we made love that night, I had just helped Miss O'Neill make a fortune on the stock exchange. We were drinking champagne and one thing led to another. I don't feel proud of it. She was engaged to a good friend. But these things happen. As for those wild allegations about the knife, sure I've got knives in my kitchen. Who hasn't?'

There was lipstick smeared across Rakosi's chin. He took a swig from the champagne bottle. Bubbling liquid spilled down his naked chest. He knew he was invulnerable.

Torpidly, Jackie began to dress. She didn't think it was possible to feel so degraded, so bruised and violated.

Rakosi played with the knife like a toy. 'Why don't we see how much you've made on your back over the last hour. It'll probably be the most profitable screw you're ever likely to have.' And, smirking, he led her through to the study.

As they entered the room, the telex was clattering out a message. 'The shekels roll in,' said Rakosi in a lazy, half-drunken voice. He ripped the completed message from the machine. 'Let's see, shall we . . .'

But almost instantly, as his eyes fell on the message, the complacent smile evaporated. He read the message once, his eyes flickering back and forth across the page. Then, muttering to himself, he read it again.

Now even Jackie was alarmed. 'What is it? What does it say?'

Letting out a stream of obscenities, Rakosi crumpled the message in his hand and threw it on the carpet. Then he reached for the telephone. 'What is it?' asked Jackie again. 'What's happened?'

'Read the fucking thing yourself!' Rakosi was punching out the international dialling code for New York. 'I'll kill the stupid shit, I'll kill him . . .'

Bending to retrieve the crumpled message, Jackie opened it and, with trembling fingers, began to read.

IMPERATIVE YOU SELL ALL OILTEC STOCK. SELL AT ANY PRICE. ELEVENTH HOUR CRISIS. FLEISCHMAN PULLING OUT OF TAKE-OVER DEAL. ONCE NEWS HITS WALL STREET WE ARE FINISHED. FOR GOD'S SAKE SELL. T SNOW.

Dimly, her head spinning, Jackie could hear Rakosi screaming down the telephone. 'How can the news be out so soon? A press conference? Oh for fuck's sake, why didn't you warn me? What do you mean, have I sold any of the stock? I've only just received your message. I'm not a bloody miracle worker!'

Jackie's nightmare had taken on a terrifying new dimension. The Oiltec collapse was going to be bad, she knew it.

Rakosi was bellowing. 'What's the price, Theo? Give me the damn price! Eighty cents. Christ, they're falling like a brick!'

All Jackie knew was that she had to get out of there. She had to do something to save herself. 'Where are the keys?' she demanded, half hysterical.

'What damn keys?'

'The keys to the front door, you bastard!'

'Behind the bar. Let yourself out.' Rakosi had forgotten about the rape now. All that mattered was his money.

Like a woman concussed, Jackie staggered back to the living room. She dressed in a daze. She grabbed the keys and stumbled out of the front door.

Out on the street it was hot, that summer Hong Kong hot, when even at night, the air is still and thick as treacle. Jackie ran along the pavement desperate for a taxi, the sweat pouring down her face. She had to get home. She had to get to a telephone. Because now she faced a crisis more immediate than the rape. Now she was fighting for her life.

The helicopter caught them at dawn.

All through the night they had been fleeing deeper and deeper into the arid wastes of the Hindu Kush towards the Pakistan border, pushing the pace until they were all near exhaustion, knowing how vulnerable they were. Young Abdul, married just a month, led the way, negotiating a dizzy ledge that wound around the eastern face of the mountain, while fifty yards back Mike Keats, Halima and old Malik followed, still lost in the long shadows of the southern face.

Mike heard it first, just the sullen throb of a five-bladed rotor cutting the air, and acted instinctively.

'Stay still, hug the rock face!' he shouted to Halima and Malik. He screamed ahead to Abdul warning him to do the same. 'For God's sake, don't move, any of you!'

Then the Russian chopper loomed around the mountain. Mike recognised it immediately. It was a Hind-D gunship, one of the most lethal multi-role helicopters in the world. It was camouflaged a speckled grey and cut through the mists of the morning like a shark in cold waters. Mike could see the 12.7 mm machine gun protruding from its nose. He could see the two stub wings providing rails for its Spiral anti-tank missiles and rocket pods. It was moving slowly, following the contour lines – hunting them.

Maybe Abdul never stood a chance. He was the most exposed. But, caught in the first watery light of dawn, pinned like a fly against the cliff wall, he suddenly lost his nerve.

Mike saw him start to run. 'No!' he screamed. 'They'll see you!' But the wind whipped away his words.

The Hind-D tracked him along the broken ledge, a great grey monster biding its time as he scrambled and fell and scrambled on again. Abdul ran for maybe fifty yards until he knew he was doomed. Then, in one final gesture of defiance, like a fox at bay, he turned. He wedged the Kalashnikov into his shoulder and shouted into the teeth of the wind – 'Allahu Akbar!' – before the first rockets exploded around him.

Mike Keats gripped Halima's arm. 'It'll come back now looking for us. Don't move, don't even breathe.' And, just as he had predicted, the gunship turned and made its way back through the granite peaks.

The deep resonance of its two turboshaft engines crushed out every other sound. Mike knew the chopper was equipped with night and all-weather sensors. He knew the co-pilot and gunner would be scouring every gully, every rock and ravine. And as each second passed so the light of morning grew brighter.

Next to him, his face hard against the cliff, old Malik murmured a Muslim prayer, preparing for martyrdom.

Mike was beyond hope. All he had left were ironic memories . . . those navy lectures with a silhouette of the Hind-D on the blackboard and a supercilious instructor saying: 'Learn the specifications, gentlemen. They might be important to you one day.'

The gunship came so close that it hovered directly above them, its downdraught flogging at their clothes. Mike closed his eyes, resigned, waiting for that burst of machine gun fire that would blow him off the mountain into oblivion . . . the last sound he would ever hear.

Every moment was an eternity.

He thought of Jackie. I'm so sorry, my darling. What a stupid way for it to end . . .

But then – amazingly – the Hind-D veered away. Mike didn't dare move, didn't dare so much as glance up until the deep throb of its engines was just an echo on the air. Then he let out a long, disbelieving sigh and smiled thinly at Halima who looked close to fainting. Only old Malik gave an incorrigible grin.

Later, as they moved on, they saw Abdul's body two hundred feet below them wedged in among some rocks. His skin was the colour of snow.

Halima stopped. She was fifty, dumpy and maternal, a woman who looked better suited to haggling over food prices in the bazaar than climbing these awesome mountains. But never once had she tired, never once had she asked for a respite, not until now so that, for a moment at least, she could remember a man. 'He is in Paradise,' she said. 'He has earned his reward.' Then, turning to Mike, she said with a nod, 'You gave us good advice, Mr Keats.'

'I was a chopper pilot myself. I know how it works.'

'Then you'll know that we must have missiles, the kind that a man – or a woman even – can carry.'

Mike gave an exhausted grin. 'Yes, I'm beginning to appreciate that fact.'

But Halima wasn't smiling. 'If we're going to win this war, Mr Keats, then we must have weapons – weapons that will blow helicopters like that all the way to hell.'

By seven o'clock that morning Jackie O'Neill knew the worst.

'We're just beating our heads against a brick wall,' said George Duncan, her New York broker, an old classmate from UCLA.

Jackie was beyond desperation. 'Get rid of them at any price, George, I just don't care.'

'There's a panic run, Jackie, you've got to understand that. At the moment Oiltec stock is about as popular as yellow fever.'

Jackie nodded, her face puffy, her eyes red. 'I appreciate that, George. But please keep trying, please . . .'

'What made you buy in so big?' he asked. 'The Oiltec take-over was touch and go from the start. You should have contacted me first, Jackie. Who in the hell recommended you get involved?'

And, appreciating the bitter irony of it, Jackie O'Neill replied, 'It was a friend . . .'

After she had rung off, Jackie limped to her kitchen, bruised and exhausted, to make coffee. She had never felt so desolate in her life, so totally alone. But out of that desolation a smouldering rage began to burn. The whole Oiltec scheme had been a ploy to get her into Rakosi's debt, that's all, a convoluted plan to ensure that, one way or the other, he could satisfy whatever sick lust he had been harbouring all these months.

But why should he get away with it, just dismiss her like some whore he had paid for the night? He thought he was invincible – with that facetious, filthy grin on his face – he thought he could do what he liked with impunity. Well, she would prove him wrong . . .

Seizing the telephone, she dialled 999, the Hong Kong emergency number, and heard the call ringing. But then, as she waited, Rakosi's words began to echo in her mind . . . 'If you want to report it to the police, go ahead. Subject yourself to the whole messy procedure – doctors and swabs, endless statements to the cops. Make yourself public property. Mike will be delighted.'

A woman answered the telephone, speaking in Cantonese.

Oh God, thought Jackie as the tears streamed down her face, what should she do?

The woman at the other end of the line was speaking English now. 'Please, you must tell me, what do you require? Is it the police, ambulance or fire brigade?'

But there was no reply, just a broken sob, as Jackie put down the phone.

It took them another hour to reach the rendezvous point, an ancient cave used by robbers in biblical times. Farouq and his men had made it there before them and, as the two groups came together, the greetings were effusive. Old Malik hugged everybody, relieved to see his comrades alive, telling them all how bravely young Abdul had died and how proud his widow would be. But the operation had been a success, that's all that counted. Even Farouq shook Mike's hand, grinning in fierce exultation. 'Salesman, my friend, what a marvellous night it's been!'

Breakfast had been prepared in the cave . . . green tea, broiled mutton and hot naan bread. But the food was incidental. What mattered now were tales of the battle.

'We killed three Nikolais!' shouted one of Farouq's men.

'Three – pah!' Old Malik, his white beard greasy from the mutton fat, had grabbed centre stage. 'What's a few stray lambs when I can talk about a whole flock!' And, with blood-curdling, dramatic gestures, he began expounding to them all the glory of what had transpired at the karez.

The excited displays of bravado were too fast and furious for Mike's limited Pashtu. He was exhausted; depressed too. There was no glory for him in other men's deaths. And so, taking a cup of green tea, he went and slumped down at the entrance to the cave.

Morning filled the sky now, a grand renaissance of pink and gold and high brush stokes of glacial cirrus. Mike loved this time best of all . . . sitting at the controls of his chopper, cutting through the first velvet thermals. For a few brief moments with the air as soft as down he could imagine that everything was right with the world.

He was sipping his tea, lost in his thoughts, when Halima came to the cave's entrance. She said nothing, just watched the morning light spreading its crystal brilliance over the distant snow-capped peaks.

Looking at her now in the daylight, Mike could see the lines of exhaustion etched into her brown and wrinkled face. It was a plain housewife's face, sturdy and patient. He could imagine her in Italy or Spain amid the olive groves, bustling her children to school, cooking pasta for the evening meal.

'They're making a great hero out of you in the cave,' she said eventually. 'According to Malik you must have killed at least a hundred Russians at the karez. The Lion of Qishlaq Imir, that's what they're calling you.'

Mike shrugged, smiling. 'Anything has to be an improvement on Salesman.'

'Yes, of course – Salesman – that's what they call you, isn't it?' She hesitated a moment then continued. 'Over the years I've dealt with a good many arms dealers, Mr Keats, but you don't fit the mould. What makes you come out here? Arms dealers are businessmen, not adventurers. Most I've met prefer red wine in a restaurant to green tea in a cave. What is it that motivates a man like you? Is it just profit or something deeper perhaps?'

'What are you suggesting?' he asked.

'Some men are attracted to war. It's a very ancient love affair.'

Mike just shook his head, too tired to grace the suggestion with an answer. He had learnt to fly helicopters in the British Navy. He had seen his first action in the Falklands War in 1982, three weeks of wind-lashed murder, picking up the wounded from the burning gorse of Goose Green and from the burning hulks of British destroyers hit by Exocet missiles. When he returned to England, he had discharged himself from the service, loathing that same violence – the blood, pain and senseless destruction – that Halima implied he was in love with.

There must have been a look of hurt in his dark liquid eyes because Halima said, 'I didn't mean to offend you. But there has to be some reason for you to risk yourself like this?'

'Yes,' he answered flatly. 'My terms of reference.'

'I don't understand . . .'

'It's basic enough . . . to know what the Mujahedin need to fight this war, first I have to know what sort of war they're fighting.'

She considered what he said and then answered, 'To a cynic that could sound like a sales pitch.'

'I don't need a sales pitch,' said Mike, refusing to rise to her bait. 'The man who employs me will pay for everything I recommend.'

Her puzzlement remained. 'But there was no need for you to take part in the attack on Qishlaq Imir. Why risk your life in that way?'

How did Mike answer? How did he explain all the conflicting emotions? 'Let's just say that when you live with men like these, when you cross the border with them and see what's happening, you come to understand their cause.'

She gave a sturdy smile. 'Good. So you're no longer neutral. You've taken sides.'

'There's a saying that the hottest places in hell are reserved for those who stay neutral in a crisis.'

She crinkled her eyes, teasing him. 'But I thought the hottest places had already been reserved for the arms dealers.'

Mike laughed. But it was only camouflage because what she said was far too accurate.

She climbed to her feet. 'You've had nothing to eat.'

'Tea was enough, thank you.'

'Nonsense. Eat while you can. Tomorrow it could be boiled grass.' And off she bustled, heavy-hipped and dumpy, the image again of a peasant woman who believed that all of life's cures came out of a cooking pot.

But the sting of her words remained . . .

Mike Keats often wondered how in the hell he had got into the arms-dealing business. It certainly wasn't by design. After leaving the navy, he had worked in London, insuring aircraft rather than flying them. But the boring predictability of it – constant schedules, papers, contracts – had driven him mad. So, after a year, he had answered an advertisement in an air magazine to fly Bell Hueys for the Sultan of Oman. At the time it had seemed harmless enough, two years in the desert with a fat gratuity at the end of it all. That's where he had met Sheikh Faisal ibn Yasi. The sheikh's eldest son had been his squadron leader and they had been in the same helicopter, flying an urgent sortie along the South Yemen border, when a sand storm had brought it crashing down. Mike had sustained head injuries which effectively grounded him for six months and the balance of his contract was spent in Muscat with both feet on the ground. The job they gave him was advisor to the Sultan on the purchase of military equipment – his first unintended step into the world of arms dealing.

Nine months later, on a business trip to Hong Kong, he had met Joe Rakosi and – as the cliché went – received an offer he couldn't refuse. Rakosi could be a persuasive man. 'I know you worry about the ethics of the business,' he had said. 'Hell, don't we all. But I promise you, Mike, we're going to be dealing with the nuts and bolts, that's all.' With the Iran–Iraq War engulfing the Middle East, the nuts and bolts turned out to be telescopic sights, range finders and turret motors for tanks – more than five million dollars' worth sold to Iraq. While at the same time he sold military software in the form of camouflage uniforms, webbing and boots to Iran.

The work involved constant travel. It was hard, secretive, depressing a lot of the time. Nobody was what they appeared to be. The art of survival ruled everything.

Monies moved through a maze of middlemen and off-shore corporations. It was a dirty business ruled by the desperate need of the buyers and the greed of the suppliers.

Mike had made money – good money, more money than he had ever dreamed of making – but living in a shadow of secrecy, sacrificing honour for cash and constantly compromising his moral values wasn't the way he wanted to live.

Then he had met Jackie.

She had hated his involvement, loathed it from the very beginning. It was a hell of a business, she had said, and she was right . . .

Maybe that was the real reason why he was out here with these men, sharing their hardships, fears and rare moments of triumph. Maybe it was a way of salving his conscience. But, whatever the reason, this was going to be the end of it. He was a commodity broker now. He dealt in cocoa not guns. He was committed to Farouq and his Mujahedin. He believed in their cause and would ensure they received the necessary supplies. But after that it was over. As Jackie had said, 'You and Joe don't cry all the way to the bank, Mike, you walk there over corpses.'

They found him when the sun was high and thought at first he must be dead like all the others. But Mikhail Kazakov clung tenaciously to life.

There were flies crowded on the black scabs of his coagulated blood, flies that lifted off in an angry swarm when they pulled him from the bushes where he had crawled to hide. As the medics lifted him onto a stretcher, Kazakov began to bleed again and they thought he would be lucky to survive the day. But they had not reckoned with the resilience of the man and, as they rushed him to the waiting helicopter, they could hear him mumbling over and over in a feverish litany . . . 'Keats, Keats, his name is Mike Keats.'

It had been a bad night, constantly tossing and turning, her dreams full of jealous imaginings. How could he do it to her? How could he treat her this way? Until five in the morning, when sleep was hopeless, Tina Wai had climbed from her bed.

With dawn rising and the first sounds of Hong Kong's traffic outside, she showered, letting the hot water steam away some of the long night's anger. Then she stood in front of the mirror in her tiny bedroom deciding what to wear. When she confronted Joe Rakosi she wanted to look her best. She would never admit how much he had hurt her, the loss of face would be too great. The greater the pain, the more open her defiance. And it was clothes – her startling good looks – that she used as her weapons.

Tina Wai was not beautiful, not in the traditional doe-eyed, delicate Chinese way. She transcended that. She had a broad, high-cheekboned face, almost Mongolian, and huge dramatic eyes as black as basalt. She was tall for a Chinese woman, bony but languid, the perfect ramp model. She had started her career as a model for Issey Miyake, one of Japan's top designers. 'There's something of the tiger in her,' Miyake had said. And at one time Joe Rakosi had been captivated by her in the same way.

Damn him, she thought, damn all European men. Did they really sell themselves on this myth that Asian women were submissive concubines, slant-eyed playthings without any emotion or pride? They were no different from women anywhere else in the world. They hurt the same and they retaliated with equal wrath.

Tina Wai wasn't prepared to forgive and forget. She had sacrificed too much for that. She came from a traditional Chinese family who forbade her to consort with a gweilo, no matter how rich the foreign devil might be. So Tina had broken with them and given herself totally to Joe Rakosi. What more did she have to prove?

Why had he done it to her? That's what she couldn't understand. Not once before – not once in their twelve months together – had he made such patently false excuses to keep her away from his apartment. Even when he had business meetings until the early hours he called her over afterwards. There had been times when he had come knocking at her door at three or four in the morning.

All she knew was that over the last few months he had been distracted. It was nothing he said, nothing he did. But intuitively she knew there was something wrong. And then yesterday, when she was in town and free, wanting nothing more than to spend the night with him, he had made every excuse possible to keep her away. It was an important meeting, he had said. Why didn't she understand? Hell, these things happened once in a while.

Why didn't she understand? Because he was feeding her lies, that's why. There was only one reason why he had dismissed her from his bed, that was to replace her with another woman. But he would pay for it. Oh yes, he would pay all right.

It was 9.30 am by the time Tina came out of her Mid-Levels apartment onto Conduit Road looking for a taxi. She wore a Miyake design in black and grey linen, a sombre, ultra-zen ensemble that would have looked gaunt and ungainly on a woman less imposing. But set against that backdrop of towering concrete buildings against a hazy grey sky and on her, with brilliant emerald green accessories, it turned every head.

When she reached the penthouse twenty minutes later, letting herself in with her own key, she could hear Joe Rakosi showering. He's late, she thought bitterly. It must have been a hard night.

Realising it was her, Rakosi yelled above the hiss of the water, 'Be an angel, make some coffee will you. The amah is sick, she says. I feel like death myself. How about some orange juice first? I'm dehydrated as hell.'

'What happened?' asked Tina, her voice dripping acid. 'Did your meeting go on all night?'

Rakosi grunted from behind the glass shower door. 'It was a bloody nightmare. I lost a fortune. Half a million, maybe more if I can't get rid of the shares. Bloody Snow, he's on the board of Oiltec, he should have known. The man's got the brains of a pea!' Rakosi stepped out of the shower with steam rising from his body. He hadn't been to the gym in weeks and was getting paunchy. His eyes were bloodshot and puffy.

Tina knew the signs. He had been drinking heavily last night. 'So who was here?' she demanded. 'Who was so special that I had to stay away?'

'What are you getting uptight about? Bloody hell – '

'Because I want to know. I'm entitled to know!'

'It was business, I told you. Just business.'

Tina glared at him with dramatic coal-black eyes. 'What sort of business do you conduct between the sheets?'

'What are you talking about? You're mad. Jackie O'Neill in my bed – '

'Jackie?' The breath caught in Tina's throat.

'Yes, Jackie,' snapped Rakosi with an air of injured innocence. 'And if you think I'm in trouble after Snow's cast-iron guarantees, Jackie's up to her neck in it . . .'

Tina blinked, her face flushed with humiliation. 'Did you have inside information?' she asked in a stuttering voice.

Rakosi growled back. 'Fat lot of good it did us. Jackie lost quarter of a million – that's about everything she owns and maybe more. I don't know how she's going to get out of it.'

'Oh God, what's she going to do . . .?'

'I'm worried about her,' said Rakosi, pressing a square of tissue on to his chin where he had cut himself shaving. 'You know how brittle she can be, what crazy things she can do. Get me that orange juice, will you?'

'Of course, yes, I'm sorry . . .' And Tina fled to the kitchen. She felt ridiculous, consumed with embarrassment. She had been convinced that Joe had manoeuvred her out of the way to get another woman into his bed. She had twisted every innocent explanation into a falsehood. Poor Jackie, she thought, starting a new business, Mike away and now this.

But, as her sense of foolishness dissipated, Tina was filled with an immense relief. She understood Joe Rakosi. He was self-centred; a rough, physical man obsessed with personal ambition. But ironically, his greatest attraction lay in those same faults. Tina herself was an ambitious woman, hard when the need arose, ready to fight to get what she wanted. And that's what she admired in Rakosi, the driving power, the charisma that surrounds a man who takes risks and beats the odds. The two of them were destined for great things.

And, at times, when the pressures of business were off, he could be a gentle man too in his own peculiar way. When he had first taken her, Tina had been a virgin, just twenty years of age. Since then she had been his woman, faithful to him in every way. She had suffered his ego, she had complied with his sexual ways that often repelled her. She had done so because – in her own way – she loved him. One day she would be his wife, she was determined about that. But first she had to learn to trust him.

Fussing with the napkins and silver cutlery, she poured the fresh orange, prepared hot croissants in the microwave and, leaving the coffee to percolate, took the tray into the bedroom.

Rakosi grabbed the glass of orange, gulping it down. 'Choose me a tie, will you?'

Tina took out an Italian silk tie in russet diagonals that matched his tan suit. She held it against his chest. 'Why are you getting dressed in such a hurry?'

'I'm late enough as it is,' he said gruffly. 'I'm meant to be having breakfast with a bunch of Kenyan politicians at the Peninsula to settle the final details on a chemical plant project. Phone down to the lobby will you, tell Chan to have the Rolls waiting. I hope he's not sick too like the damn amah.'

Tina did as he said. Then she brought him coffee which he gulped down as he chewed on a buttered croissant. They walked together to the lift and she reached up to kiss him goodbye. 'If you can get away from the meeting early, I'll be here.'

Rakosi shook his head. 'Sorry, babe, I've got appointments right through the day. I'm flying to Kenya tomorrow and everything is piled up.'

'What about tonight?' she asked in a low, husky voice.

He smiled down at her. 'Yeah,' he said, 'tonight will be fine.'

The lift doors closed and Tina walked back into the penthouse. Joe was hers again and she felt good. She had a free day today, no modelling, no photographic sessions. She might go shopping, buy herself a new outfit and later prepare a special dinner for when Joe came home. But first she needed a cup of coffee, just a few minutes to sit and let the pent-up tension seep away.

She turned towards the kitchen. But, as she did so, a small glint of light, something lying on the carpet, caught her eye. By the leg of a brass coffee table lay a small diamond earring. Puzzled, Tina picked it up. It wasn't hers. It had to be Jackie's. But what was it doing there on the floor?

She felt a sudden sense of unease. What exactly had happened here last night? Then she noticed that the red indicator lights on the hi-fi were glowing. But there had been no music playing when she arrived.

And a terrible, irrational realisation began to dawn. Oh God, no, she thought, it couldn't be. It was a manifestation of her jealousy, that's all. But she couldn't ignore it, couldn't dismiss it from her mind . . . and, feeling sick to the stomach, she walked across to the hi-fi.

She pressed the eject button to remove the tape, hoping that it would bear a label to show it had been commercially recorded. But it didn't. It had been purchased as a blank tape – one that Rakosi had recorded himself. She retched, tasting the bile in her mouth. Then, clumsy with nerves, she put the tape back into the hi-fi and pressed the rewind button.

Listening to the whir of the machine, she remembered all those nights here in this apartment with Joe trying to break through her shyness. 'Go on, baby, listen to it. Listen to those beautiful moans. That's you, baby, that's you.'

No, she thought, it couldn't have happened, not with

Jackie. But there was no way she could leave it, not now. One way or the other she had to know. And, trembling with apprehension, she pressed the button marked 'Play'.

For four days Jackie O'Neill had watched the price of Oiltec stock collapse to twelve cents. And only at that price was she able to sell. But by then it was too late. She was bankrupt. Ruined.

She had put up her Los Angeles condominium as collateral. That was gone. Everything she possessed was gone. Before Mike Keats had flown out of Hong Kong he had signed a general power of attorney in her favour which she had used to draw on most of his savings. So those were lost too.

If only it had stopped there, monies begged and monies borrowed. But it hadn't . . .

Slumped in her office, poring over the papers, Jackie found it impossible to believe that she could have done it. But there it was in black and white, all the proof anybody needed – cold, calculated theft.

As a child, raised in northern California, she wouldn't have stolen an apple off a neighbour's tree. But here in Hong Kong she had intentionally forged documents, putting them before a friendly bank official, so that she could draw on a buyer's letter of credit days before the vessel with its cargo of sugar reached port. More than half the funds from that LC had gone towards the quarter of a million dollars she had given to Joe Rakosi, funds she could never replace.

What would they do to her? she wondered. Both parties were major companies. There was no way of hushing it up, no way of paying back the money. A police investigation? A criminal trial? The prospect of it sent her into a wild panic. She couldn't face it. My God, the thought of going to prison – she would rather be dead.

But there had to be some way out of the mess. Hong Kong was built on money. The place was awash with cash. Somehow she would raise the money. A couple of days, that's all she needed. But, reeling from events and half-doped on tranquillizers, time had become a blur. Jackie O'Neill had let precious days – fatal days – slip by . . .

She received the call from the seller's agent late in the afternoon. She knew him well. He was a manager for Asia Trading, a charming man with two children. For him, of course, it was just routine. He had received the certificate of weight and quality from the general superintendent, he said. All his shipping documents were in order. He would be presenting them to the bank first thing in the morning to draw on the buyer's LC.

There was no way out now. Stunned, like a woman told she has advanced terminal cancer, Jackie locked herself into her office. She was a bright woman, brilliant in some ways. Problems on paper she could handle with consummate skill. But she lacked the strength in adversity to handle this kind of mind-numbing crisis. Mike was the only one who could help her now. Mike loved her, Mike would forgive her for what she had done. Mike possessed all the resilience in the world. Somehow he would find a way of getting her out of this mess. All she had to do was get him back to Hong Kong.

Stumbling to draft a telegram, hardly aware of what she was writing, knowing only that it was a desperate plea from the heart, Jackie took it to the post office by the Star Ferry and despatched it herself. Then she retreated to her apartment in Repulse Bay and prayed he would be in time.

*   *   *

Mike Keats received the telegram on his second night back in Pakistan. He had intended to remain in the little mountain town of Chitral, once a trading post on the Old Silk Road, for another week. He had to work out with Farouq Mohammadi and the other Mujahedin commanders the inventory of weapons and supplies they needed. Then he had intended to fly to the Oman to negotiate the finances. But one look at the telegram convinced him how bad things had to be:

> PLEASE MIKE YOU MUST RETURN. I HAVE DONE THE MOST STUPID AND TERRIBLE THINGS. WE COULD LOSE EVERYTHING. I FEEL SO ASHAMED. I DO NOT KNOW IF I CAN HANG ON. I FEEL SO FRIGHTENED MY DARLING. I DO NOT KNOW WHICH WAY TO TURN. EVERY HOUR COUNTS. JACKIE.

Mike's first concern was to telephone Hong Kong, to speak to Jackie and reassure her. But the antiquated exchange in Chitral was incapable of getting him through to Islamabad, let alone out of the country. So he was forced to despatch a telegram:

> RETURNING IMMEDIATELY. DON'T PANIC. ALL PROBLEMS CAN BE SOLVED. WE WILL SEE THEM THROUGH TOGETHER. REMEMBER I LOVE YOU. MIKE.

There were only two ways of getting out of Chitral, either a ten-hour road journey over murderous terrain or by air – if you were lucky enough to beg or bribe a ticket.

But Halima – who was respected by all the competing factions of the Mujahedin and worked to try and keep them unified – was a woman of great influence and it was to her that Mike went. Her office consisted of a couple of small, dingy rooms behind the bazaar. In the outer office a young girl of the Hazara tribe pecked away at an ancient Imperial typewriter and answered the telephone while Halima herself was closeted in the inner office bent over her papers. When she got up from the desk, Mike was amazed to see that she was wearing a veil.

Halima laughed. 'I'm expecting a delegation of the mad mullahs. But they support the Resistance so why antagonise them?'

But, in purdah or not, Halima operated with blunt, no-nonsense efficiency and within the hour had secured a ticket. 'Come back soon,' she said. 'There's work to be done.'

'As soon as I can, I promise.'

Halima smiled behind the black mesh of her veil. 'You can tell your fiancée one thing from me, tell her she's a lucky woman.'

Mike smiled, a little embarrassed. They had come to know each other well over these past few days and a cautious respect had grown into firm friendship.

'And get her to feed you,' she said. 'You're as thin as a stick!'

The following morning Mike caught the flight to Peshawar. From there he caught a connecting flight to Karachi and began a frustrating ten-hour wait at the airport before he could board a plane to Bombay where he would connect with a British Airways flight. Hong Kong, however, was still twenty-four hours away.

* * *

It was ten in the morning. Jackie was in her apartment, too frightened to leave, when her secretary
telephoned.

'A group of men came in,' said Ruby Lam, sounding
terrified. 'They were from Asia Trading. They said it was
about the sugar contract, something wrong with the buyer's letter of credit. I told them you weren't here, that
you were sick. But they demanded to see all the papers.'

'What did you do?'

'I didn't think there was anything wrong.'

'So you showed them . . .?'

Ruby started to cry. 'They had a lawyer with them. He
said all sorts of things – '

'It's all right, Ruby, it's all right . . .' What was the
purpose in getting angry with some poor Chinese girl
caught in the middle? Jackie took a deep breath. 'After
they had looked at the papers, what then?'

'They said they were taking them away.'

'What else did they say?'

There was silence from the other end of the line.

'What else, Ruby, what else did they say?'

And Ruby answered in a timid voice. 'They said the
police would have to deal with it now.'

At three thirty that afternoon, the British Airways flight
from Manchester and Bombay touched down at Kai
Tak. Mike Keats' only luggage was a canvas hold-all
which he had carried with him on the plane. So there was
no waiting at the baggage carousels and he was the first
through Customs into the main concourse.

Running to the public telephones near the police
counter, he telephoned Jackie's apartment. The number
was engaged.

He breathed a sigh of relief. He knew Jackie only too

well. He understood the manic depressions that sometimes seized her and he knew where they could lead. But
the fact that the telephone was engaged meant that
Jackie was using it. And that had to mean that she was
still hanging on. He waited a minute or two then tried
again. Still engaged.

That was when he telephoned the office. Ruby
answered. 'I received Jackie's telegram in Pakistan,'
said Mike. 'What in the hell has been going on?'

'The police have been here,' Ruby answered in a thin
voice.

Mike was shocked. 'When?' he asked.

'Less than an hour ago. There were two of them, both
detectives from the Commercial Crime Bureau.'

'Was Jackie in the office?'

'No, she's not well. It's her nerves,' stuttered Ruby.
'But I phoned her at the apartment.'

'What did she say?'

'She said the police could do what they liked. She
didn't care, that's what she said.' Ruby began to cry.
'She said that nothing mattered, nothing anymore . . .'

'Listen to me,' said Mike sternly. 'I want you to get
through to Jackie. Tell her I'm back in Hong Kong. Do
you understand? Tell her I'm driving to her apartment
now.' And, replacing the telephone, he ran out to the
taxi rank.

It took fifteen minutes to get through the Cross Harbour Tunnel and onto Hong Kong Island itself. From
there it was another fifteen minutes to Repulse Bay. And
all the time Mike sat in the back of the taxi cursing the
traffic that clogged the roads until at last he came around
the final bend on Repulse Bay Road and drove up the
curling concrete drive of Number 101.

Jackie's apartment was on the fifteenth floor of Block

B. Mike rang the bell but there was no response. He knocked, rapping the door with his knuckles, but there was still no response. Fumbling for his keys, he let himself in.

'Hello, Jackie, it's me!'

There was no reply. Everything was still. Too still.

'Jackie, where are you?'

Papers lay scattered over the lounge floor: accounting documents, bills of lading, receipts. Pens chewed at the ends, cups of half-finished cold coffee . . .

Mike strode down the passage towards her bedroom. 'Jackie, for God's sake!' The door was shut but he threw it open – and there she lay.

She was fully dressed, curled up on the bed, eyes closed. Her face was puffy, her make-up smudged as though she had been working too hard and had collapsed into a troubled sleep in the early hours of the morning. Pill bottles littered the bedside table. Mike stood for a moment, rooted to the spot. Dear God, he thought, she's dead.

He stepped closer and saw the telephone clutched in her left hand. Then he understood why the phone must have been engaged. Jackie had been trying to make one last desperate call before she was overwhelmed. As he stumbled to the bed, the tears beginning to sting his eyes, she looked to Mike like some poor waif huddled up, all afraid of the world, her beautiful blond hair in unbrushed tangles around her face.

There was a note on the bedside table. It was wet with spilt water, scribbled out in ballpoint and began – 'Oh, Mike my darling, I'm so sorry . . .'

But Mike wasn't interested in explanations. His only concern was to keep her alive. Reaching down, he felt for the pulse in her wrist. Yes, yes . . . the pulse was still there! Damn you, he thought, damn you, you're not going to die on me like this and, pulling the telephone from her limp hand, he dialled 999 for an ambulance.

He hauled her off the bed, shaking her violently, demanding that she stay alive. The tears were pouring down his cheeks now. He dragged her to the bathroom, pushing his fingers into her mouth, trying to make her vomit. And some bile did come up, dribbling out of her mouth. She was unconscious still but her pulse was fluttering. Mike poured cold water on her face. 'Don't give up on me,' he kept saying. 'Don't give up on me now.'

He lay her on the carpet, pumping at her heart. Then, opening her mouth, he breathed in, trying to force his own life into her lungs. And he pumped again at her heart. Then – for the first time – Jackie began to cough and more bile came up. And Mike cried out triumphantly, 'Yes, that's it, yes, yes, keep doing it!'

And in that way he continued massaging her heart, talking to her all the time, saying how much he loved her, pushing and pumping, trying desperately to keep her alive until at last he heard the wail of sirens approaching.

What Rakosi had done was beyond forgiveness. In China, thought Tina Wai, they would put a placard around his neck proclaiming to all the world that he was a rapist. Then they would put a bullet through his head. She had been betrayed and she would never forget.

When she had heard the tape in Rakosi's apartment, her immediate reaction had been to flee, to get as far away from the man as possible. But, despite her horrified shock, there remained a residual cunning, the first dark seeds of hatred, and before she fled the penthouse Tina had taken the first step in her revenge – she had made a copy of the tape.

Then, leaving a garbled message about some urgent photographic assignment, she had fled to a friend's cottage. The cottage was in the New Territories north of Fanling near the Chinese border where she knew Rakosi would never find her and where she could nurse her pain. For Tina the loss of face was absolute. There could be no greater dishonour. The mere fact that she had been in bed with a man capable of such things made her feel soiled and abused.

But, as she walked the duck farms and terraced vegetable gardens near the cottage, she began to appreciate how difficult it was to hit back. Rakosi was rich and influential but, unlike most men in his position, he had no reputation to maintain. He joked that integrity was an over-sold commodity. His greatest reputation, he said, was the fact that he had no reputation at all.

But, despite what he said, everything was finite; riches, power, even the extent to which a man like him, a so-called maverick, could withstand scandal . . .

Imagine a trial for rape, she thought with fierce glee. Imagine him sitting there in the dock knowing that every word on that tape, every filthy, perverted utterance, was going to be splashed across the newspapers. Convicted or not, it would destroy him.

But a trial for rape depended on Jackie O'Neill testifying, and so far – from what she had been able to learn – Jackie had done nothing. Tina understood her reasons of course. No woman willingly humiliated herself in that way. And with just her word against Rakosi's, there was no guarantee of conviction. But Jackie wasn't on her own, not any longer, because now Tina could testify with her. Now there was the evidence of the tape.

She knew it would be hard. But if they steeled them-

selves, they could do it. Tina Wai had sacrificed everything for Rakosi. She had been disowned by her family,
shunned by her friends. Revenge wasn't merely an
option, revenge was everything. But first she had to convince Jackie O'Neill. She had to let her know that they
were friends and that, giving each other the necessary
moral support, they could see this thing through to the
end.

It was late afternoon when she telephoned the office
and it was Jackie's secretary, Ruby Lam, who answered
the call.

'Can I speak to Jackie please?' she asked in Cantonese.
Ruby Lam tried to answer but her voice faltered.

'What's the matter?' asked Tina.

'It's just too terrible,' Ruby sobbed.

'What is it?'

'I only heard a few minutes ago. It's Miss O'Neill – '

'Why, what's happened to her?'

'She's in the hospital,' Ruby answered. 'They say she
tried to kill herself.'

At six that evening, flying first class, Joe Rakosi
returned to Hong Kong.

It had been a successful business trip, very successful
indeed. In two months' time a consortium of European
companies would begin to hack away the Kenyan bush
south east of Nairobi for the erection of a chemical
plant. The economic journals were already lauding it as a
symbol of international cooperation. It was all so much
horse manure of course. What the project amounted to
was a platform for making money and if it also helped
Kenya that was just a happy coincidence.

The financial package that he had put together was
impressive – two hundred million dollars' worth of

export finance incentives and government guarantees. And when the chemical plant was completed in two years' time, his commission for services rendered would be just short of twenty million. Money like that made up for a lot of Oiltec fiascos.

Rakosi had a saying: the hard part is getting the customer into your pocket, the rest is a waltz. And Malimbi was so deep into his pocket now that his head didn't even show.

Rakosi had dealt with Malimbi before, using nominee companies to buy central London properties on his behalf – 'coup d'état insurance', Malimbi called it. The two understood each other and that's why Malimbi had come to him when the World Bank's feasibility study recommended the building of the chemical plant.

Rakosi, in his turn, had gone to the Italians and the Germans knowing that their governments would provide export credit terms spread over ten years in return for the standard guarantees from the Kenyan Government. A chemical plant valued at two hundred million was not a difficult deal to sell and, for the companies that submitted quotations, built-in commissions followed as night follows day.

Rakosi had set up a Luxembourg corporation to act as broker. The corporation would negotiate the various quotations, add the customary twenty per cent – ten per cent each for himself and Malimbi – and then put them before the Kenyan Government where acceptance without question was assured.

Twenty million greenbacks, thought Rakosi as the Boeing 747 made its ponderous approach over the cluttered rooftops of Kowloon. There were men down there in the sweatshops and factories, coolies digging ditches and fishermen in their sampans who would slog out their lives for an infinitesimal fraction of that sum – the myth of honest labour.

Chan, his chauffeur, was waiting in the airport concourse. He took Rakosi's luggage and led him to where the Rolls Royce Silver Spirit was parked. Rakosi instructed him to drive first to his offices in St John's Building above the Peak Tram Terminus for a quick briefing from his management staff before he returned to his penthouse to sleep off the jetlag.

But he had only just settled into the back seat, pouring himself an XO cognac, when the car telephone chirped like a pampered cricket.

It was Tina Wai on the line.

He was delighted. 'Hi, babe,' he said. 'Where are you phoning from, the penthouse?' He had missed her. But when she spoke, her voice was cold and distant, filled with restrained malice. 'What in the hell has got into you?' he grumbled. 'What am I supposed to have done?'

She ignored the question. 'I'm phoning about Jackie.'

Rakosi experienced a sudden, sick sensation. 'What about her?'

'It's bad, I'm afraid.'

'How do you mean, bad?'

'She tried to kill herself.'

'Oh no,' he muttered, stunned by the news. 'When did it happen?'

'Just this afternoon. Apparently she took an overdose.'

'Is she going to make it?'

'It's touch and go. She's in a coma.'

Rakosi was dismayed. 'Which hospital is she in?'

'The Queen Mary,' said Tina. 'Mike's there with her.'

'Mike? When did he get back from Afghanistan?'

'Earlier today and thank God too,' she answered. 'He was the one who found her.'

'Okay,' said Rakosi, 'I'm on my way there now.'

'Yes,' said Tina, her voice filled with bitterness, 'I think you should.' But, before Rakosi could answer, she had rung off.

Fuck you then, he thought angrily. I've had enough of you blowing hot and cold. All over me one minute, spitting in my face the next. Bloody women, you never knew where you were with them.

He gave instructions to Chan to drive direct to the Queen Mary hospital. Then he sat brooding in the back of the Rolls Royce. If Jackie O'Neill had tried to kill herself, he knew damn well what her motives had to be – and that's what terrified him. What if she had left a suicide note? What if she had pointed the finger at him, written about that night and what had happened? Rakosi could feel the tension begin to squeeze at his temples. The back of his neck prickled with sweat. If she had – and if Mike Keats had found the note – then the whole damn world was about to blow up in his face.

When Rakosi came upon him, Mike Keats was in a corridor outside the Emergency and Accident Department leaning against a wall, arms folded, head down, lost in a world of his own.

Rakosi was shocked by his appearance. His clothes, just an open-neck cotton shirt and khaki slacks, were threadbare and bleached bone-white from constant washing. But it was the physical appearance which shocked him more. Since he had last seen him, Mike Keats had lost at least fifteen pounds and seemed gaunt and hollow-eyed. His black hair was wild and unkempt and he had grown a beard. He could have been one of those radical, existentialist writers that the French idolised. Or Che Guevara, he thought. All he lacked was the cigar. But he looked fit though, oh Christ yes. His face was tanned mahogany, the kind of hard-beaten, leathery tan that came from sun and dust. And Rakosi could see the sinew in his arms.

Every time they came together, it struck Rakosi how different they were . . . physically, emotionally, in every way possible. Mike Keats was self-contained, not easily given to outbursts of temper or emotion while Rakosi was profligate, hungry, demanding. Rakosi was an extrovert. It was a tool of his trade and he used it to great effect. He could be a man's best friend in an hour and forget him in a week. But with Mike Keats it was different. If you had his trust, he would be your friend for life. But if you betrayed him, God help you . . .

And thinking of that, Rakosi held back. This was stupid, he thought, like running between a snake and his hole. Mike Keats hadn't seen him. It would be safer to contact him later by telephone. Because if Jackie had left some garbled suicide note blaming it on him there could be a bad scene. He took a step back, half-resolved to sneak away. But then the decision was taken from him.

Mike Keats looked up and his face was set as hard as stone.

Oh God, thought Rakosi, faltering in mid-stride, he knows. 'Hello, Mike . . .' he murmured.

Mike Keats gave an exhausted smile. 'Hello, Joe. It's good to see you.'

For a moment Rakosi couldn't move, saturated with relief. Then, with an uncertain smile, he said, 'I heard on my way from the airport and came straight over.' He walked over, shaking Mike's hand and placing a sympathetic arm around his shoulder. 'How is she? Is she going to be okay?'

Mike stared down at the floor. 'She took a massive overdose. I just don't know . . .'

'Why would she do a thing like that? It's crazy.'

'It has to be the business. There's no other reason.'

'I knew a number of deals had gone sour,' said Rakosi. 'I tried to help as best I could. Not that it helped much. We both took a hammering on Wall Street last week. But if she needed help and you were away, why didn't she come to me?'

'I don't know, Joe, I just don't know . . .'

They were silent for a time, not sure what to say. Then Rakosi asked, 'Did she leave a note or anything?'

Mike nodded. 'Yes . . .'

Rakosi felt his mouth go dry. 'What did she say?'

Mike shrugged. 'Just how sorry she was. But nothing about why . . .'

Rakosi tried to disguise his relief. 'Do you think you can get some coffee in this place?'

Mike gave a tired smile. 'It was good of you to come straight over, Joe. But you've had fourteen hours in the air. Why don't you go home? The doctors say it's just a question of waiting now.'

'Yeah, perhaps you're right . . .' Rakosi hesitated a moment and then said, 'You're looking pretty burnt-out yourself. How did it go in Afghanistan?'

'I survived.'

There was another pause before he asked. 'And on the business side . . .?'

Mike shook his head, giving a despairing grin. 'You can't keep away from it, can you, Joe.'

Rakosi laughed. 'Does a leopard change its spots?'

Mike smiled. Rakosi was incorrigible. But at least he made no pretence about it. 'Yeah, the commissions are going to be fine,' he said. 'They would be a lot better though if we could lay our hands on some surface-to-air missiles. That's what the Mujahedin desperately need.'

Rakosi sucked at his teeth. 'Do you think your oil man, sheikh whatever-his-name-is, would foot the bill?'

Mike gave a tired shrug, half joking with him. 'Why, have you got some contacts in the CIA who would oblige?'

But Rakosi didn't joke about such things. 'If we can convince the Americans of the need, why not?' He turned to Mike. 'Do you think you can prove a need? Set it out on paper?'

Mike gave a wry laugh. 'When you've been pinned to a cliff face like a fly on a wall with a Russian gunship hovering above your head, that's when you learn all about the meaning of need.'

Rakosi looked impressed. 'So you came that close?'

Mike nodded. 'Close enough . . .'

'All right,' said Rakosi. 'Leave it to me, I'll see what I can do.'

They fell silent again, watching young Chinese interns in their grubby white jackets bustling past patients who lay on iron beds parked end to end down the corridor. Public hospitals in Hong Kong resembled casualty clearing stations; overcrowded, claustrophobic, constantly frenetic.

A doctor edged his way down the passage towards them. He was Chinese, plump-faced and wearing glasses. 'There's no change,' he said. 'Why don't you go home, Mr Keats?'

Mike shook his head. 'Thanks. But I'm happy to wait for the time being.'

Rakosi glanced at his watch. 'I'd better get back.'

'I'll phone if there's any change,' said Mike.

Rakosi climbed to his feet. 'Don't worry, she's a tough lady. She'll pull through.'

But they were just words, a smoke screen to hide his true feelings. Because, as Rakosi left the hospital, pausing a moment to stare out over the pewter-grey waters of the Lamma Channel, he knew that his survival depended on only one result – like an unwanted problem, Jackie O'Neill should slip quietly away.

And in truth the prognosis for her had never been good. Jackie had been brought to the Queen Mary in a comatose state, the drug levels in her system critically high. An immediate stomach pumping had been ordered but she had overdosed on Mandrax so there was no way that dialysis could assist. There was nothing for the doctors to do but monitor the level of consciousness, the pulse rate and the blood pressure . . . and wait.

Jackie's condition had stabilised within a few hours. She had been hauled back from the brink of death. But the fight wasn't over. Within forty-eight hours disturbing signs began to manifest themselves. Her state of consciousness deteriorated. A lung infection set in. The doctors feared anoxic damage to her brain. An encephalogram was ordered so that the wave patterns of the brain could be measured. The results were virtually conclusive. The damage appeared to be irreversible. It was a sad fact that if Jackie O'Neill survived, she would spend the rest of her days as a vegetable.

The doctors were pragmatic in their advice. If Jackie was flown back to California and hospitalised near her parents, she could live for years. But here in Hong Kong they didn't give her more than a few months. Hong Kong air was so polluted and germs so rife that she would quickly fall victim to hypostatic pneumonia. But what was the purpose in flying her back to America?

'Mercy killing, is that what you're suggesting?' said Mike.

'No,' they replied. 'Just letting nature takes its course.'

Mike, however, couldn't view it in such a cold-blooded light, letting her lie there until some virus carried on Hong Kong's hot, humid air completed the work of the Mandrax. There had to be some hope; other doctors maybe or an improvement with time. It had happened before. But it wasn't his decision alone. Jackie's parents had to be consulted. They were the ones responsible for the final decision. So Mike contacted them and they agreed that she couldn't be left in Hong Kong. She had to be flown back to California as soon as possible. But Jackie's parents weren't wealthy people. Her father ran a small hardware store, her mother was a school teacher. The astronomical costs of American medicine would cripple them both within a month. So Mike agreed that he would meet all the medical expenses – just as he agreed to clear Jackie's business debts.

It would have been simple for him to shelter behind the corporate shield of their bankrupt company. But that wasn't Mike's way. Jackie had suffered enough. He didn't want her name besmirched with a prolonged criminal investigation. In addition it was his company too. His name was on the letterhead. So he approached each creditor with the proposition that if they dropped all police involvement, he would personally guarantee that every last dollar was repaid.

When Joe Rakosi heard, he thought Mike was mad. Protecting a lady's financial virtue had gone out with the bustle. Survival was the name of the game not misplaced loyalty. But for Rakosi personally, the news was good. Because now – up to his neck in debt – Mike Keats was unable to make the break he had been threatening from Trident Enterprises. It was a neat irony, thought Rakosi. Personal honour had brought Mike Keats back to a business which personal honour had made him leave.

And for Joe Rakosi that couldn't be better. Because, despite his avowed dislike of the business, Mike Keats was a bloody fine arms dealer. He was a master of the technical intricacies. He understood international finance. He engendered trust among his clients and, most important of all, he was willing to put himself in the firing line along with his hardware.

Over the past year Mike Keats had made Trident the most profitable company in Rakosi's Good Hope Group. Now it seemed he would ensure the profits continued.

And it was those two things – the news that Mike Keats was staying and the lure of profits – that motivated Rakosi to try and obtain the missiles so desperately needed by the Afghan rebels.

Invariably, high-tech hardware, such as surface-to-air missiles, was only sold at the highest political level, government to government on the basis of properly authenticated end user certificates. At least that was the way it was said to be. But Joe Rakosi knew that what was said and what was done was purely coincidental. Missiles were no different from chemical plants in Kenya. They were simply items of trade.

But if the missiles were going to be obtained honestly, without breaking the laws of half a dozen states, they had to come from a country already supplying moral and material support to the Afghan guerillas. That meant the US Government and, effectively, that meant the CIA.

But why should the Central Intelligence Agency want to sell high-tech weaponry to a relatively small Hong

Kong based corporation like Trident? Rakosi knew the answer. Because the CIA liked to work that way, that was why.

It was common knowledge in intelligence circles that the CIA used thousands of private sector businesses to help in its intelligence-gathering activities. CIA cargoes were flown by private airlines. CIA monies were channelled through independent off-shore corporations. Washington policy makers argued furiously about the implications of using private, profit-making corporations in sensitive intelligence work. Apart from the obvious security risk, there was the continual chance that businessmen co-opted into operations would convince CIA agents to accept options designed more to increase profits than further the needs of national security. One Director of the Agency had described it as 'the private sector tail wagging the CIA dog'. But, despite the misgivings, private companies were still used for the very sound reason that in the modern world they provided the best of all covers.

Joe Rakosi knew enough of the business to know that if it was to the CIA's advantage, it would have no hesitation in supplying the missiles. But first he had to make contact, first he had to put his case.

The US Consulate General in Hong Kong, a dull three-storey building set behind iron railings, was situated directly across Garden Road from St John's Building where Rakosi had his offices. Rakosi preferred to deal face to face. Things got done a lot quicker that way. So he simply crossed the road and walked up to the reception desk. It took less than ten minutes to be ushered through to somebody who could deal with his query – a sensitive intelligence matter, as Rakosi expressed it. He sat with the official for an hour, giving him enough information to whet his appetite. Then he left, satisfied that the wheels would start turning.

Two weeks passed without him hearing anything. But Rakosi knew it would take at least that long for the CIA to carry out its preliminary checks, to ensure he was a force to be reckoned with and not some jelly bean outfit hustling for a piece of the big time. Then, eighteen days after his visit to the Consulate, he received a call from the official with whom he had spoken. Two special representatives were flying out from Langley, Virginia . . . and they would very much like to meet him.

Rakosi contacted Mike Keats immediately. There was work to be done, he said, papers to be written. But, while Mike was prepared to help with the necessary planning, he made it clear that he wouldn't be able to attend the meeting. Arrangements had been made, he explained, to fly Jackie back to California.

Rakosi pleaded with him, piling on the pressure. Couldn't it wait? Just a day or two, that's all? What harm could a day or two make? But on this one thing Mike Keats was adamant. When Jackie was flown out of Hong Kong, he would be on the plane with her. Rakosi would have to handle the CIA on his own.

The meeting took place in a small front office of the Consulate looking down at the long lines of Chinese patiently queuing for their American visas. Joe Rakosi preferred to conduct such meetings over lunch. Two or three bottles of vintage Burgundy tended to soften even the toughest opposition. He suggested the Mandarin Grill, just a short walk down the hill. But the two men from Virginia politely declined, sending out instead for Diet Coke and curried noodles. And the meeting proceeded right there.

Rakosi presented a dossier to each man, mainly prepared by Mike Keats.

'There it is, gentlemen, the full breakdown – details of the Mujahedin missile requirements, suggested shipping arrangements, proof of our financial integrity, even individual profiles on the Mujahedin commanders.'

The two Americans studied the dossier.

'My partner, Mike Keats, has been into Afghanistan with the Mujahedin,' said Rakosi.

Yes, they said, they knew.

'He knows a number of the commanders well, especially Mohammadi.'

Yes, they said, they knew that too. They were polite. They appeared interested. But, no matter how hard he tried, Rakosi couldn't pin them down.

The younger of the two was a lanky Mid-Westerner with an old-fashioned crew cut and steel-rimmed glasses. His name was Larry Pike but Rakosi dubbed him the 'Idaho Technocrat'. He had an engineering degree and had been a fighter jock in his day. He could fly 'anything with wings on', as he put it, and was studying for his MBA. Probably played scratch golf too, thought Rakosi. Larry Pike was one of nature's achievers – aggressive, bright and cocksure of himself.

The elder of the two – clearly the one in charge – introduced himself as Chuck Baldwin. He looked to be in his early fifties, built short and stocky and thick around the waist with what seemed like a beer paunch. But Rakosi was certain it was as solid as a bag of wet cement. At first glance Baldwin had an amiable look with a round face, curly grey hair and bright blue eyes. But then the scars became apparent, not just physical ones, the scars of experience too. It was obvious that Baldwin had spent a lot of hard times doing a lot of hard drinking in some of the world's most dangerous places. He was one of those rough-edged individuals whose best friends are foreign correspondents, war photographers and bandits. He probably knows Beirut better than New York, thought Rakosi.

Talking to him, it soon became obvious that Baldwin wasn't there to enter into serious negotiations. He and Pike were on a scouting expedition, that's all, getting the lie of the land so they could report back to their superiors.

Baldwin, while appearing to play it straight, did just the opposite. He was a master of the Delphic answer. Everything he said was capable of at least three meanings. He was altogether a dangerous bastard, thought Rakosi, who knew that if he had any hope of securing those missiles, it was Baldwin he would have to convince. But, behind that blue-eyed, amiable smile, Chuck Baldwin seemed singularly unimpressed.

Rakosi's assessment of what Baldwin thought of him was correct.

'I wouldn't trust him to feed my dog,' Chuck Baldwin said later that night as he and Larry Pike took a taxi along Queensway.

'But he's shrewd,' said Pike, 'shrewd as hell.'

'What's that got to do with it? So was Stalin and he shot ninety per cent of the people who ever shook hands with him.'

They climbed out of the taxi on Lockhart Road opposite Police Headquarters and walked east towards the heart of what Chuck Baldwin and so many other US servicemen used to consider the heart of Hong Kong – Wanchai . . . bars, cheap booze and beautiful little rice-paddy whores dressed in red satin.

'Don't dismiss Rakosi that easily,' said Larry Pike.

'I go on gut reactions.'

'You should know a bit about him first . . .' Larry Pike loved recounting other people's success stories, the big stings and megabuck deals. 'Rakosi originally came to Hong Kong as a two-bit trader,' he said. 'He bought and sold . . . cheap denim, digital watches, some early military stuff in the way of uniforms and boots. But he could see he was going nowhere. He needed one big hit to set him up.'

'Big hit? Sounds like a bank robber.'

'All businessmen are – of a kind.'

'Some more than others though . . .'

Chuck Baldwin had fond memories of Wanchai from his Vietnam days when he would escape to Hong Kong to snatch a weekend's R and R. It had been one hell of a place then – bars every step of the way, music blaring, kids selling fake watches, neon signs thick as laundry and those beautiful little Suzie Wongs bright as butterflies. But, walking along, he could see that the area was now a shadow of itself, tired and shabby. Places were no different from people. They grew old and died. A few disinterested doormen, sitting on fold-up stools, invited them into topless bars. 'Happy hour. First beer very cheap. Enjoy a nice girl, sailor.' But the places were dives.

It made him feel middle-aged. So they got off the street, climbing some narrow stairs to a small Thai restaurant that served ice-cold Singha beer and tom yam soup hot enough, as Larry Pike expressed it, to leave the afterburn of an F-16.

'So what was this one big hit of Rakosi's?' asked Chuck Baldwin.

Larry Pike's eyes lit up. 'Oh, a very cute deal.'

'Fraudulent?'

'Aren't they all?'

Larry Pike took a long gulp of beer. 'Let me begin at the beginning . . . Rakosi, the shrewd carrot-topped Magyar that he is, saw that the property market in Hong Kong was about to rocket. So he forms this corporation see, Good Hope Ventures – it's still his flagship – and uses it to purchase a fancy piece of real estate in the heart of the financial district. He puts ten per cent down while the balance is on repayment terms that would cripple Brazil. But it doesn't matter because a month later – wham bam, thank you mam! – along comes this Hong Kong family, the Chans, shippers and sheep stealers as far back as the Ming Dynasty. And they want Rakosi's building so bad that they're prepared to give Rakosi a fifty per cent profit on the deal.'

Chuck Baldwin scooped pale green chicken curry out of a clay pot. 'So where's the catch?'

'Simple. The whole deal was a sham, just a book entry. Rakosi had already given the Chans an irrevocable undertaking to buy the property back at the same price within six months.'

'Where's the percentage in that?'

Larry Pike was loving it. 'Because on paper – for a few months at least – Rakosi's company has now made a profit running into millions.'

'So?'

'So suddenly it's red hot. And Rakosi is a whiz kid.'

'So big deal, what does it mean?'

'It means that every bank in Hong Hong is busting down the doors to lend Rakosi money, that's what it means.'

'Loans have got to be repaid.'

'Sure,' said Pike excitedly. 'But in the meantime, he's got twenty-five million of other people's money. And the guy's a chess player, I mean he's six moves ahead before he even begins.'

'Okay, so what does he do with the twenty-five million?'

Larry Pike attacked a plate of fried squid. 'Rakosi has developed a close relationship with this Australian, see. And this Australian is on the board of a corporation that owns some huge iron ore claim way out in the outback. There's no great deal in that – '

'Except?'

'Except for the fact that the corporation has entered into a long term contract with the Japs to mine the ore and ship it out, prices guaranteed.'

'So the twenty-five million was shunted down to Australia to buy shares?'

'You've got it – ten days before the official announcement of the contract. Within a month the stock had increased thirty per cent.'

'And that's when Rakosi sold?'

'Took his profits and ran,' said Pike enviously, swilling back his beer. 'He shared half with the Aussie who had given him the insider information, paid the Chans a hefty sum for their cooperation, got rid of the Hong Kong real estate that had been the basis of it all and deposited his profit – a cool six million – into the hallowed vaults of the Hong Kong and Shanghai Banking Corporation.'

Chuck Baldwin ordered more beers. 'It was a dangerous manoeuvre.'

'That's the sort of guy he is. Rakosi's a high roller.'

'Do I detect some boyish admiration?'

'We can rely on him, Chuck. He's not some crazy idealist. He's a businessman.'

'What are you saying, that profit is more reliable than patriotism?'

Larry Pike grinned. 'A lot of the time, yeah.'

Chuck Baldwin heaped boiled rice onto his curry. 'Then God help us all,' he said.

The Headquarters of the Central Intelligence Agency is situated in Langley, Virginia, a few miles south west of Washington DC. The headquarters building itself is nicknamed the 'Toy Factory' and inside the marble and glass reception area there is carved one of those biblical inscriptions that is intended to imbue a sense of higher purpose:

And ye shall know the truth and
the truth shall set ye free.

But Chuck Baldwin, a confirmed cynic with five years to go before retirement, knew that truth in the Toy Factory was what they wanted it to be. Which is why, when the Rakosi matter was considered, he expected his report to be ignored.

James Dexter, Chief of Operations, Far East Sector, sat in his office on the sixth floor with the report in front of him. With him in the office were Olley Flynn, Chief of Operations for the Near East, and Saul Larousse, a young hot-shot from the State Department.

Thomas Delaney, Director of the CIA, was meant to chair the meeting. But Delaney was a sick man. It was common knowledge at executive level that it was cancer; terminal apparently, although Delaney was battling it to the end. Radium treatment kept him from the meeting, which was why the job of chairing it fell on James Dexter.

Sucking at his unlit pipe, Dexter, a tall man, well over six foot, angular and thin, with a slow, sometimes infuriatingly cautious manner, opened the report file. 'Baldwin is none too complimentary,' he said in his dry Vermont manner. 'In his opinion, the man is a crook. Let me quote – "I suspect that Rakosi's only concept of the word trust is that of a legal gambit for avoiding tax." '

Olley Flynn, a big, physical man, hard-drinking and stubborn, gave a derisory laugh. 'So Rakosi is a son of a bitch. He's not the first one we've dealt with and he won't be the last. The fact is, he's the right man in the right place at the right time.'

'You mean he fits our purpose?' said Dexter.

'Yeah, that's exactly what I mean.'

James Dexter turned to Saul Larousse. 'We keep hearing the Soviets talk about cease-fires and pull-outs. But how far can we trust them?'

Larousse was the youngest there; brilliant, ambitious and self-aware. 'It's our opinion that the Kremlin genuinely wants to get shot of Afghanistan. The Soviets are bogged down. They've lost too many men. It's an embarrassment to them now, even at home. But, just as we weren't prepared to pull out of Vietnam without some kind of workable settlement, they're not going to pull out without one either.'

Dexter lit his pipe. 'So you believe their peace initiatives are genuine?'

'Absolutely,' said Larousse.

'And what's our official position?'

'We must be seen to support any initiatives to end the fighting. Act as honest brokers.'

'In the past we've supplied Stinger and Redeye missiles quite openly to the Mujahedin,' said Dexter. 'How's that effected?'

Larousse shook his head. 'No, I'm sorry, right now

it's all too delicate. The Soviets keep telling us that if we're not prepared to show good faith, how can we expect good faith from them? Politically, to supply missiles at this time would be an unwise provocation.'

Olley Flynn glared at him. 'What are you suggesting, that we drop them like a hot potato? Let the Mujahedin go out and punch the commies to death?'

'We're not suggesting any such thing, Olley. But the fact remains – '

'The fact remains that at long last we're getting some co-ordination among the rebel groups,' said Flynn aggressively. 'This man Farouq Mohammadi is a born leader. The number of men under his command has trebled in the past year. The other leaders listen to him. If we fail to give him the support he needs, we all deserve our butts kicked.'

'The State Department doesn't want to abandon these people,' said Larousse patiently.

'Then what do you want?' demanded Flynn.

'Be surreptitious, that's all. We can't be seen to be prodding and pushing the Mujahedin towards the conference table and at the same time arming them to the teeth.'

'Use middlemen, is that what you mean?'

'If you have to, yes. Just don't wave the Stars and Stripes and don't supply American-made weapons.'

Olley Flynn was satisfied. 'That's easy enough. The Israelis are sitting on a fat stockpile of SA-7 Grails that they captured off the Syrians in Lebanon. It's the Russian equivalent of our Stinger, an updated version of the old Strela.'

'How simple is it to operate?' asked Dexter who was a lawyer by training.

'Like all commie weapons,' said Flynn. 'A kid of six

could use it. The operator simply aims the launch tube at his target and takes the first pressure on the trigger. That brings on a red light. The instant the seeker has locked onto the target the light turns green. Apply full pressure on the trigger and boom – the missile accelerates to one and a half times the speed of sound. Easy to carry, even easier to use. It'll bring a chopper down like a stone.'

'How many do the Israelis have for sale?' asked Dexter.

'Several hundred.'

'But I have to emphasise that we can't be seen to be involved in the deal,' said Larousse, 'not in any way.'

Flynn assured him. 'Israeli agents will deal direct with Rakosi. Apart from making the initial introduction, we'll have nothing to do with it.'

'That would be acceptable,' said Larousse. 'But if you have doubts about Rakosi's honesty, why use him?'

'Rakosi is basically irrelevant,' said Flynn. 'He just happens to head the business. It's his partner, Keats, who counts. He's built up a good relationship with the Mujahedin, especially Farouq Mohammadi. Keats is a competent operator, quiet, tough, honest. Not one of your average bar room heroes. The rebels trust him and I think we can trust him too.'

'To be discreet, I hope,' said Larousse.

'He's a professional,' replied Flynn flatly.

'Good,' said Dexter, tapping the ash out of his pipe. 'Then it seems we are agreed. It will have to be cleared by Tom Delaney, of course, but that will be our recommendation – honest or not, Rakosi is the man we use.'

Mike Keats was in London buying telescopic sights when he received the call from Hong Kong.

It was Rakosi on the other end of the line. 'Thirty-six

launchers!' he shouted excitedly, ignoring security. 'And that's just the first consignment, Mike. It could be double that, treble even!'

Mike was incredulous. 'How many missiles per launcher?'

'A minimum of six.'

Even a quarter of that number had been beyond Mike's wildest hopes. 'It's fantastic,' he said. 'How did you do it?'

Rakosi was laughing, delighted with himself. 'Charm, Mike, pure charm!'

'Where are we getting them from?'

'Certain Middle Eastern gentlemen who have made a number of trips into the Lebanon.'

'The Israelis?'

'You've got it. Capturing them off Syrian Muslims to sell them to Afghan Muslims – but what the hell, Mike, trade is trade.'

Now Mike Keats was laughing too. 'It doesn't matter where they come from. All that matters is what they can do. Farouq is going to be over the moon. It's incredible news!'

'Not bad news for the bank balance either,' said Rakosi. 'In fact, it's already been okayed by the accountants – I'm awarding bonuses. You're in the money, Mike.'

'How much?'

'Plenty of zeros – one hundred thousand US.'

Mike let out an amazed whistle. 'My God . . . thanks Joe, that's going to solve a lot of problems.'

'No more than you deserve,' said Rakosi grandly. 'Anyway, Mike, what are friends for?'

One hundred thousand dollars – he had never received a

single payment anywhere near that sum before. And it made him feel good, there was no denying it, damn good indeed.

Mike Keats wasn't a boastful man. The last thing in the world he wanted to do was shove his success down anybody's throat. But even so, it was a time to celebrate, a time to be sharing . . . to buy a present for a woman he loved without saying why, to take her out for a good meal and maybe to the theatre afterwards.

Sitting there in his hotel room, Mike realised that success celebrated alone was no success at all. But who could he share it with? The few good friends he had were scattered all over the world, either with the British navy still or flying helicopters in the Oman. It was the price he paid for being a gypsy. But there was one person, one woman, who meant more to him than the world. That was why, a few minutes after Rakosi's call, Mike telephoned California. And that was when he received the news.

It was Jackie's father who spoke to him. 'It was better this way,' said the old man.

Mike's eyes misted. 'She wasn't in any pain, any distress?'

'No, no, she just slipped away . . . they said she didn't feel a thing.'

Mike felt the hot tears begin to sting his eyes. He had known all along that this was how it must end. But, even so, it was almost unbearable.

'She died at ten o'clock this morning,' said her father. There was a long, heart-rending silence. Then, his old voice breaking, he said, 'She was such a beautiful girl. Oh God, Mike, she had so many friends. Why did it have to happen?'

TWO

Russia

The first snows of December were falling out of a raw white sky. Icy flakes, more like hail, pockmarked the snow banks along the side of the road and crackled against the windscreen of the car before its wipers swished them away. The Chaika limousine appeared to be all alone in that bleak landscape, one tiny black beetle crawling through the folds of an endless shroud of glaciated hills and frozen lakes.

In summer when the hills were green it was different. Then every dacha was occupied. Families picnicked among the silver birches and rowed boats on the lakes. But now, blanketed with early winter gloom, nobody stayed in their country homes. Nobody, that is, with the exception of Grigori Kirilenko.

But that was only to be expected, thought Mikhail Kazakov as he sat enfolded in his greatcoat in the rear of the vehicle, because Colonel-General Kirilenko, the Deputy Head of the GRU, had been at odds with the world for as long as he could remember.

They passed the sign that told them they were fifty kilometres north of Moscow. The Chaika rounded a bend, its tyres crunching on the compacted snow, and there ahead stood the ruined church of St Basil which marked the turn-off to Kirilènko's dacha. The GRU chauffeur knew the route well and swung off the road, following a forest track through the pines.

Kazakov took a bottle of spiced vodka from his pocket, unscrewed the cap and drank straight from the bottle. The burning liquor served a dual purpose, first as a protection against the cold but, more importantly, to give him Dutch courage. He had been preparing for this meeting for over three months, using the long days in hospital to draft and re-draft his notes, spending endless hours rehearsing what he would say. As winter came and he grew stronger, he had gathered more information, checking his facts and re-checking. Because today would be one of the most important of his life and he had to be prepared.

The Chaika followed the track through a thicket of birch trees, snow falling from their boughs, and then pulled up in front of the old wooden dacha. From inside, where it was warm, a dog began to bark. Lights went on. Kazakov took one last mouthful of the vodka and climbed out of the car. The subzero temperature bit at his face.

Kirilenko appeared. He was a tall man, so tall that he had to stoop in the doorway. He was silhouetted against the buttery light of the interior, his face a long wedge of brooding shadow. He said nothing, hardly moved, just stood there with his hands plunged deep into the pockets of an ancient army jacket.

Kazakov struggled through the snow carrying his briefcase of documents. He climbed the wooden steps of the dacha and made his formal greetings.

The Colonel-General gave a curt nod. 'Come in, come in,' he said. He closed the door against the arctic wind and with that stiff, corseted gait of his – the result of an old injury – led Kazakov through to the main room where a log fire was burning.

His dog, Gagarin, a great wolf of a thing named after Russia's first man into space, had slunk back to its rug in the corner where it sat watching Kazakov with luminous green eyes. Kirilenko had lived alone for nearly twenty years since the break-up of his marriage. He was a crusty old bachelor who had no time for women. Generally, in fact, he preferred his own company. In the GRU they said that Gagarin, the dog, had only one friend – Kirilenko. And Kirilenko himself had only one friend – the dog. But that was the way the ignorant spoke, the ones who didn't understand.

The old general helped Kazakov to remove his great-coat. 'So a bullet shattered your right elbow did it? Never mind, we must all cope with our handicaps. It's good discipline learning to be left-handed.'

Kirilenko returned to his brocade-covered armchair by the fire. 'Those bandits taught you a thing or two at Qishlaq Imir. But you've paid for the lesson, a useless right arm and a bullet through the lung. Have you profited from it though, Misha, that's more important, have you profited from it?' Kirilenko lit a cigarette, a cheap Bulgarian brand. With his access to the special shops, he could smoke any cigarettes he wished. But he would never touch anything that came from the West. Although he stood apart from other men, he strove hard to be one of the proletariat. He sat for a time, deep in thought. Then, getting up from his armchair, stiff-backed and awkward, he walked to the kitchen door. 'I'll bring some vodka,' he said.

Remaining in the room, Kazakov was suddenly aware of the smells. It was the smell of the dog mainly, that thick-furred smell that dogs give off when they're wet.

But there was the smell of herrings in open jars too, of Ukrainian bread and tobacco, musty furniture, ink, books . . . and, strangely, the distinct undertow of Kirilenko's own body odours. Kazakov had known the General since he was a boy but Kirilenko had always been such a distant man, so patrician and aloof that he never associated him with smells. He remembered a young GRU officer saying of him once: 'He drinks without getting drunk, eats without getting fat and farts in silence. What sort of man is that?' A master tactician, that was the answer; a brilliant chess player, a philosopher, a soldier. The General was a man with a purpose in life. And that purpose was to plan great plans.

Most junior officers in the GRU saw him as a secretive, elitist figure, a man who wielded immense power in one of Russia's most powerful organisations. But Mikhail Kazakov saw him in a different light. Because the ageing General was not simply his superior, he was a close blood relative, an uncle on his mother's side. As a boy, he had sat at Kirilenko's feet listening to him talk of Russia's great struggles. That's when the real bond had been forged, in those early years . . . teacher and student, prophet and disciple.

Kirilenko had directed his path into the GRU and thereafter had despatched him to every place possible where decisions were measured in the consequences of life and death, not simply scores on an examiner's sheet – to the endless tundra of the Chinese border, to Vietnam and Cambodia, to Poland and Berlin and then, finally, when the time was right, to the mountains of Afghanistan. But by then, when he landed in Kabul, Kazakov had been entrusted with Kirilenko's one great secret.

The General returned from the kitchen clutching a

bottle of Polish vodka. 'So, Misha,' he said, 'you have seen Afghanistan from the lowest level – with your face in the mud and a bullet in your back. How does it look?'

Kazkov drained his vodka. 'You continue to see it from the walls of the Kremlin, Uncle. How does it look to you?'

'The perspectives may be different but what we see is the same – a disaster.'

'So you see no hope through conventional military means?'

'Do you?' Kirilenko stared at him over his beak of a nose. 'Twenty years ago when I was in North Vietnam we used to heap scorn on the American GIs. Look at them, we used to say, soft, venal men trying to win a war with machines, a war they're too weak to fight man to man. But tell me, Misha, are our own troops in Afghanistan any better? You've seen how many take drugs. What are we coming to? Where's our old spirit? You've seen how many shoot off their toes to go home.'

'But what about our political initiatives?' asked Kazakov.

Kirilenko gave a scornful laugh. 'In Moscow they talk continually about it being "our Vietnam". We must pull out our troops and leave more of the fighting to the Afghans, they say – the same suicidal formula employed by the Americans in Vietnam.' Kirilenko was unable to hide the bitterness in his voice. 'I tell them to remember the patience of the Russian bear. Our one great virtue is our endurance, I say. We proved it against Napoleon, we proved it against Hitler. And how do they react? They look at me as if I'm some old fool on a park bench mumbling to myself.'

'But Soviet policy is clear,' said Kazakov. 'We cannot allow a communist regime on our own borders to be

93

overthrown. That has dictated our policy for decades. To go against that would be disastrous.'

Kirilenko gave a cynical smile. 'Words, Misha, all they need is words. And then everything is altered and yet nothing is changed. Words for defeatists are a wonderful thing.'

A long silence ensued.

Kazakov was drinking too much vodka. He coughed nervously. 'So there have been no encouraging developments?'

'No.'

'Then it seems we have no choice.'

'No choice at all . . .' For a long time Kirilenko gazed at the glowing embers of the fire. Then he said in a low voice, 'Those Yankees chose the name well, Misha. The Phoenix . . . the mythical bird that rises from the flames of its own funeral pyre. What a wonderful symbol that is. Hope out of despair. Victory out of defeat. They were traitors, each and every one of them. But now, all these years later, I can sympathise with their desperation. And if we embark on this course then, in the eyes of those fools who govern us at least, we'll be traitors too. Does that disturb you?'

Kazakov replied clumsily. 'There are times when the word traitor describes a higher form of patriot.'

Kirilenko gave a sardonic chuckle. 'Who says you have no poetry in your soul? That's a fine sentiment, Misha. If we fail, you can quote it to your GRU executioners as they drag you to the furnace.'

Kazakov went ashen.

Kirilenko saw the transformation. 'Do you frighten so easily?'

'No, no, of course not . . .' But Kazakov's lips were grey.

The old General gave a scornful laugh. 'Within the Chief Directorate of Intelligence I make the rules and I break them, Misha, you should know that. I am a power unto myself. So don't worry, nephew, we are fireproof.'

Kirilenko lit another of his cheap Bulgarian cigarettes. The smell of them was like old rags burning. He regarded Kazakov sternly. Then he said. 'So you think you have found someone who can raise the Phoenix for us?'

'I hope so, yes.'

'And who is this man?'

Kazakov raised his shattered elbow. 'The one responsible for this.'

Kirilenko frowned. 'You're not motivated by revenge, are you?'

Kazakov immediately protested. 'No, no.'

'Because that would be foolish, Misha, very foolish indeed.'

'That's not it at all, revenge is irrelevant. But when I came across Keats, he was deep into Afghanistan working with the bandits. Naturally I investigated the man.'

Kirilenko nodded solemnly. 'And what was the result?'

'Keats and his business partner are exactly what we have been looking for.' Kazakov smiled. 'They're the perfect solution, Uncle.'

There were wolves out that night. Kazakov could hear them in the pine forest high above the dacha howling at the moon. It was four in the morning but he couldn't sleep. He could hear music, the lyrical cadences of Tchaikovsky's *Swan Lake*, coming from the main room and occasionally Kirilenko's muffled cough. So the old General was still in his armchair by the dying embers of the fire, still smoking his cheap Bulgarian cigarettes as he studied the papers.

Shivering from the cold, Kazakov wrapped the bed quilt around him and sat on the edge of the bed. The howling of the wolves, coming like a death wail out of the frozen darkness, turned his blood cold. His insides were churning. He had no delusions about the plan he had devised. But what other choice did they have?

Sitting on the edge of the bed, he could see his pale reflection in the wooden-framed mirror that hung on the wall. He had a round face, chubby like a child's. He had a small mouth with dimples in both cheeks. Even his hair, the colour of wet sand, fell over his forehead in a juvenile fringe. The image he so desperately wanted of himself was that of a resolute man, square-jawed, stern and unforgiving. But the truth, he knew, was reflected more in the soft, sagging lines of that face.

For weeks now, as he had painstakingly placed each block of the puzzle into place, he had been gripped by an irrational fear. He kept telling himself that it was an aftermath of Qishlaq Imir, running wildly down that irrigation ditch like a child fleeing from ghosts. But his fear wasn't for the past, it was for the future.

Perfect plans designed with chessboard precision were only found in text books. In real life they were shot through with risks. And Kazakov's scheme, based so totally on subterfuge, played out in the shadows, was fraught with terrible dangers.

The crucial link, the kingpin, was Nguyen Thanh Xuan, a general in the PAVN, the People's Army of Vietnam, and its Director General of Political Affairs, effectively the Chief Political Commissar of the entire Vietnamese armed forces. He and Kirilenko had worked closely together in Hanoi back in 1968 and had remained close friends. He was the only man they could trust – or so Kirilenko swore. But many years had passed since they had worked together, two much younger men in a war-ravaged country, and Kazakov knew that loyalties, like men, grew old and feeble. But even if they could trust him implicitly, Nguyen couldn't function in a vacuum. False papers would have to be prepared, officials deceived. And webs of deceit were too easily broken.

What if reports began to filter back from Hanoi to some other Directorate of the GRU? Then they themselves would end up as the hunted ones, traitors . . . no different from those CIA renegades who had first conceived of the Phoenix Pact. Because, despite what Kirilenko said, Kazakov knew that nobody in the GRU was fireproof, not even Kirilenko himself.

The GRU had no mercy for those who betrayed it. Rank was irrelevant. When he first joined the organisation, along with the welcoming handshake, that certain knowledge was imparted to him – there was no mercy for traitors, only the inevitability of a terrible end. And it would haunt Mikhail Kazakov until the day he died . . .

The interviewing officer had been a small weasel-eyed Muscovite who spoke in a self-opinionated whisper. 'The Glavnoye Razvedyvatelnoye Upravlenyie – the GRU – is a secret brotherhood, Lieutenant, never forget that. If you want to join the KGB, that's a simple matter. Just enter any regional headquarters in any provincial town. Just ask your leader in the trade union. It's easy. The man on the corner who sells you chestnuts is an agent. The pretty girl who dances with the band is a volunteer. The KGB is all around us. That is its strength. But nobody knows the GRU – and that is ours. The KGB polices the nation. The GRU defends Mother Russia. We have a saying, Lieutenant . . . to join the brotherhood may cost you an arm but to leave it will cost you your head. There's only one way to leave us and that's through the chimney of the crematorium that you can see through the window.' He had smiled then, a sharp little smile full of malice. 'Before you make your final decision to join us, Lieutenant, let me show you a film. It will only take a minute or two. Sit back, please. Smoke if you wish. Relax.'

It had been a black and white film with no sound, just the burr of the film as it threaded itself through the projector. A room could be seen, a high vaulted room like a boiler house with bare concrete walls. In the centre of the room were the doors of a furnace and they swung slowly open to reveal white hot flames, an incandescent vision like the face of the sun. Kazakov could sense the heat burning out through the film. Jerkily, the camera panned to one side until it focused upon a plain pine coffin lying on a trolley. So this was the crematorium. But what was the purpose of the film? It made no sense – until then, in a sudden, blurred close-up, a face was seen.

The cameraman adjusted the focus and the face emerged into stark clarity. It had been the face of a young man, blond and handsome. But now it was the face of a terrified, demented animal. Kazakov stared, horrified, at those eyes darting wildly around the room, the face bathed in sweat, the spittle dribbling from between his bruised and bloody lips. Then the cameraman pulled back into a wide angle. Oh no, for pity's sake, it couldn't be . . . but there was no mistake. Because only then did Kazakov see that the man was tied with thick steel cord to a stretcher and the stretcher itself was propped up against the wall facing the furnace doors.

Two attendants dressed in white boiler suits came

over, moving slowly like morticians, and picked up their burden. The man trussed to the stretcher screamed but they took no notice. They lay the stretcher on the rails in front of the furnace. The man writhed and screamed so loud that – although there was no sound – the veins in his neck seemed ready to burst. Then one of the attendants pressed a button and slowly, slowly – like a descent into hell – the stretcher trundled towards the flames.

Kazakov could still remember retching so badly that he had to hold the bile in his mouth and swallow it again in order not to disgrace himself.

'He was a colonel,' the interviewing officer had said. 'He had a bright future with the GRU. But he disobeyed orders. He thought he knew better. He thought he could do things his own way. As I said, we all leave the GRU through the same chimney, Lieutenant. Most of us leave with honour but a few – like that man – depart in shame.'

Kazakov was woken by a hand tugging at his shoulder. It was Kirilenko who stood above him, ramrod straight, holding two glasses of hot tea. 'You're right,' he said. 'The key to the plan is Rakosi.'

Kazakov sat up, yawning. He had fallen into a drugged half-sleep wrapped in the quilt. 'So you think the plan could work?'

Kirilenko turned and with a stiff gait walked across to the ice-frosted window. 'Keats, of course, is vital because of his close links with the Afghan bandits. But we must be careful with him, Misha. From what I read, he's an idealist set adrift and such men are like unexploded bombs. Give him a chance to guess at the truth and he might be difficult to handle. No, we must concentrate on Rakosi, he's our man.'

'But what about Rakosi? What do you think?'

'Ah, Rakosi . . .' Kirilenko's brooding features broke into a hawkish smile. 'I have read your profile on Rakosi several times. He comes from a poor background, the only child of Hungarian refugees. As a boy he was a street brawler mixing it with every hooligan who made fun of his accent. He left school early and went straight into finance. He's a man of great ambition, Misha. He's also a man of considerable greed. He's amoral and he's a gambler. I don't think we could hope for a more perfect combination.'

'So you think we can manipulate him? Get him under our influence first and then lead him where we wish?'

Kirilenko gave a derisory laugh. 'The man's unrestrained ambition is like an iron ring through his nose, Misha. All we need is the necessary rope.'

Kazakov was fully awake now, fascinated. 'How do you propose to get him under our influence?'

'We must offer him something worthy of his vision. No other way would work.'

'But such men have no limits to their vision.'

'Exactly,' said Kirilenko.

'What were you considering?'

'I was thinking of a country perhaps . . .'

Kazakov was amazed. 'An entire country? But is that possible?'

'Very much so,' said Kirilenko. He pondered for a moment, staring out at the grey dawn rising. Then, with the faintest smile, he said, 'I think Mozambique would be ideal.'

They met in Bombay.

Chuck Baldwin was heading towards retirement. Mike

Keats was just thirty-five. There was a generation between them. But from the moment they first shook hands in the opulent lobby of the Taj Mahal Hotel, they were friends. Neither was out to impress the other. Chuck Baldwin was too long in the tooth for such idiocies while Mike Keats had never cared. So there was no display of egos, no manoeuvring for the inside edge. Mike recognised that Chuck Baldwin was a professional, a man with a lifetime's experience in the CIA, while Chuck had heard of Mike's scrupulous honesty and commitment to the Afghan cause. But more than that, in plain terms, they enjoyed each other's company.

They had a light lunch together in the first-floor lounge of the old wing. Chuck Baldwin ordered a hamburger and beer. Mike Keats had coffee and cake. They talked while a Sikh pianist played a medley of Cole Porter tunes and Maharajahs sipped tea around them.

'The units left Israel yesterday,' said Chuck Baldwin.

'Where are they now?' asked Mike.

'Cyprus.'

'Any change in the scheduled timings?'

'They'll be landed in Islamabad tomorrow at noon.'

Mike was relieved. So far so good.

'What arrangements have been made to get the units up to the Afghan border?' asked Chuck Baldwin.

'It'll have to be by vehicle,' said Mike. 'North across the Indus River and then a twelve to fifteen hour haul up through the mountains to Chitral.'

'Are the roads still open?'

'The snows have held off so far.'

'Good, that makes it easier. What about security?'

'Security will be tight, I can promise you that.'

'Who's in charge?'

'One of the Mujahedin leaders, a woman – '

'Tajwar Karmal, is that the woman you mean, the one they call Halima?'

Mike nodded.

'Tough lady I hear.'

'Competent too,' said Mike.

Chuck Baldwin devoured his hamburger, washing it down with cold beer. 'She's got the top men back in Washington shaking their heads. Nobody is too sure what to make of her. A woman so high up in an Islamic revolutionary movement is pretty rare.'

'The exception that proves the rule,' said Mike.

'Then I look forward to meeting her.'

'Good, so you're coming up to the border?'

Chuck called for another beer. 'Officially, we're on your books, didn't you know that? Trident field managers. Hired and paid.'

Mike smiled. 'Yeah, Joe Rakosi told me.'

'That way we can check out the hardware after it has been delivered, see that it's in working order. Instruct the Mujahedin on maintenance and tactics . . .' Chuck grinned. 'After-sales service the Trident way.'

'But why the subterfuge?'

'Part of the game,' said Chuck with gruff irony. 'We're meant to be keeping a low profile. It's chicken-shit of course. The Russians have more spies along the Afghan border than Paris has bidets. Within the week they'll know all about us.'

'Cover or no cover, I'm glad you're going to be there,' said Mike. 'At least that way you'll get to see first hand what their real needs are.'

Chuck raised a hand. 'You're preaching to the con-verted, Mike. If I have any say in matters – which is doubtful – there's going to be a lot more missiles on the way.'

Mike said nothing, but he couldn't hide his satisfaction. Chuck Baldwin was going to be more than a friend, he was going to be an ally.

They paid the bill and left the hotel, criss-crossing the road between the teeming yellow-and-black taxis to where the Gateway of India stood. It was an ornate triumphal arch built of brown stone at the height of empire to serve the single purpose of glorifying the British Raj. At one time the Viceroys of India landed there. But now it was a place where tourists took photographs and beggars plied their trade.

Beggars surrounded them, touching and pleading with mute eyes. They gave twenty rupees to a young boy with a baby in his arms then shooed the others away. It was either that or be swamped.

'I was sorry to hear about your girlfriend's death,' said Chuck Baldwin.

Mike shook his head, smiling. 'I should have realised you would do a check on me.'

'We understand that a while back you intended getting out of the arms business.'

'There's been a lot of water under the bridge since then,' said Mike. 'Why, what makes you raise the matter?'

'A question of continuity, that's all. We like to know we're going to be dealing with one man, somebody we can trust.'

'Don't worry, I'll be on the scene until the last stocks have been delivered.'

'And after that, what do you reckon you'll do?' asked Chuck Baldwin.

Mike shrugged. 'Impossible to say. . . I'd like to get out of the business but it has a way of sticking to you.'

Chuck Baldwin grinned. 'Yeah, I know. Like shit to a blanket.'

There was a blind man who was selling peanuts roasted on a tiny charcoal brazier; two rupees for a paper cup. 'Feel like any?' asked Chuck Baldwin.

'No thanks. Do you?'

'Last thing I want. But what the hell, I'm built for comfort not speed.' He purchased a cup, and then they left the Gateway of India, walking through the crowded streets towards the Prince of Wales Museum.

'Do you want some gratuitous advice from a guy who in thirty years has made just about every wrong move in the book?' asked Chuck Baldwin.

Mike laughed. 'Sure, why not?'

'I've been dealing with arms dealers since the Bay of Pigs, Mike, and you don't fit the mould. I go on gut reactions and my gut tells me this isn't your business. You want to stick it out until you've finished your dealings with the Mujahedin, that's good. You're committed to them. But when it's over, you'll have more cash in the bank than I'll ever see. Don't get greedy, Mike, that's all I say. Take the money and move on.'

Mike replied amiably. 'That's a pretty sweeping statement from somebody who's only known me a couple of hours.'

Chuck Baldwin laughed. 'Don't believe it, I've got a dossier on you in my hotel room that's thicker than *War and Peace*.'

Mike laughed too. 'You're right,' he said. 'I should get out of the business. But, as I said, it's not that easy . . .'

'It was when your girlfriend was alive. How has it changed?'

'Joe Rakosi has been good to me. He gave me the start. We built up the business together.'

'Rakosi? If it suited him, he would toss you overboard tomorrow.'

'You don't mince words, do you?' said Mike, surprised.

'I don't like the man,' said Chuck Baldwin bluntly.

'He's been brought up the rough way,' said Mike, trying to excuse him.

'So was I but that doesn't make me a snake.'

Mike laughed, embarrassed. 'Did you two argue?'

'No,' said Chuck Baldwin with an edge of distaste in his voice. 'But I've met his type before, Mike, I've met them too often.'

As Chuck Baldwin had promised, the units arrived in Islamabad on schedule – thirty-six SA-7 Grail launchers each with six missiles.

They had been designed and manufactured in the Soviet Union. They had been given to Syria and captured by Israel. From there, with Trident Enterprises acting as agent, they had been sold to the Afghan guerrillas with just one purpose in mind – knocking Soviet helicopters out of the sky. In Israel they had been carefully sealed and crated into wooden boxes marked: Full Circle Machinery Limited – a name invented by an agent with a strong sense of the ironic – and were designated on the customs documents as 'tractor spares'.

They were cleared through customs in Islamabad without a hitch, loaded onto lorries and then driven north over bleak and mountainous terrain to the ancient trading town of Chitral.

Two days later letters of credit were negotiated in London and the following day commission in the sum of two million Swiss francs was deposited into the account of Trident Enterprises in Zurich. Joe Rakosi was a contented man.

* * *

But on the Afghan border, where Mike Keats was now waiting, commission in a Swiss bank was the last thing on his mind. Farouq Mohammadi's men had been due back from their area of operations east of Charikar ten days earlier. But there was still no sign of them. And the rumours filtering out of the war zone were ominous, rumours of long and bloody battles, rumours of a massive offensive by the Russians to try and break the back of the Mujahedin . . .

The first of the wounded limping back across the border confirmed it. They spoke of desperate hand-to-hand fighting. They spoke of their dead comrades lying thick among the stones while down in the valleys, new Russian tanks clanked past the burnt-out hulks of the old.

Larry Pike had flown in to Chitral to join Mike Keats and Chuck Baldwin and drove up to the border with them to wait for further news.

They watched Mujahedin reinforcements climbing past them into the stony wastes of the Hindu Kush; grim-faced men, each with a blanket slung over his shoulder, each carrying his Kalashnikov.

'Bloody Russians,' said Chuck Baldwin. 'One minute they're talking about pulling out their troops, the next they're putting an extra fifty thousand men into the field.'

'They want to cripple the Mujahedin before they have to negotiate with them,' said Mike. 'They've tried it before. It didn't work then and it won't work now.'

'How long will it take these guys to get to the fighting?' Chuck Baldwin asked as another column of Mujahedin climbed past them.

'Six or seven days,' said Mike. 'They'll walk continuously, stopping for three or four hours in every twenty-four, just time enough to eat some bread, brew green tea and snatch some sleep. Then they'll march on for another twenty hours non-stop.'

'What sort of shape will they be in when they get there?'

'Some will be in a bad way. Their feet will be swollen all the way up to their knees. They'll have lost five or six pounds in weight. If the snows come early, some might have frostbite. But don't worry, they'll give as good as they get.'

'Always put your money on a fanatic,' said Larry Pike. 'They feel no pain.'

Mike looked at him. 'If the Russians invaded America, started blowing up your houses and refusing you the right to worship the way you wanted, then maybe you'd be shooting a few yourself, Larry. Except you'd call yourself a patriot I suppose, not a fanatic.'

Larry Pike shrugged. He cared as much for the Mujahedin as he did for a tribe of Borneo head hunters. This was just another job. He was the technical man. What counted were the mechanics. 'You were a chopper pilot, weren't you?' he asked Mike Keats as they made their way back to their tent to sleep.

'Yes I was.'

'They say you flew in the Falklands War?'

'That's right.'

'That explains it,' said Larry.

'Explains what?' asked Mike.

'You guys are just different, that's all. You get kind of close to things. Eat out of mess tins and shave under your rotor blades. Always in there shovelling shit with the infantry. You tend to get involved, if you know what I mean.'

Mike knew exactly what he meant. Chopper pilots weren't blue sky boys, fancy fighter jocks. Yes, they did get involved which meant that most of the time they had to put people before machines.

It was a long night with the wind buffeting the tents. In the first cold grip of dawn Mike slipped from his sleeping bag and walked away from the camp. He climbed higher into the bleak lunar landscape, as arid as a desert, until the Afghan border was only a hundred yards from him, an invisible contour line that curled through the barren crags.

He found a vantage point and waited there until the sun had risen. He was beginning to despair when suddenly he caught a glimpse of a distant figure. Then he saw another, a turbaned figure toiling along a stony ridge. Another followed, hobbling. Then another . . . and another . . . Mike waited, his excitement mounting. He could see the rifles slung across their shoulders. Yes, they were Mujahedin!

Now they had noticed him too and the lead figure, a tall man swathed in a tattered blanket, began to stumble towards him. Mike saw him wave his arms and shout out at the top of his voice in broken English. 'Salesman! Salesman, my friend! Allah be blessed, you're here!'

Farouq Mohammadi had returned.

More than a third of Farouq's men had perished in the bitter fighting. Farouq himself was wounded, just a flesh wound. But others were not so lucky. And one of these was old Malik Gailani, the greybeard.

Amazingly, despite a stomach wound and shrapnel in his arthritic legs, he had walked unaided from the battle-field, a distance of over fifty miles. But it had finished him. He was near collapse, consumed with fever.

Mike Keats rushed back to camp. Stretchers were found and the badly wounded driven to the nearest clinic, a small mud building ten miles to the south east on the road to Chitral. It was run by a volunteer group, mainly Scandinavians, who called themselves Liberation Medicine. The facilities were primitive but the professional care couldn't be bettered.

They took old Malik first because he was the most grievously wounded. For nearly an hour they worked on him while Mike waited. But then the surgeon came out. 'I'm sorry,' he said. 'There's no hope. Infection has set in and it's irreversible.' The surgeon gave a long, bitter sigh. 'With a clean bandage and a simple drug like penicillin, he would have survived. It's absurd . . . they're fighting battles with computer-controlled artillery and laser-guided bombs, imagine it – and yet they don't carry so much as an aspirin!'

'Then why can't they be trained?' asked Mike. 'Why can't they be taught what drugs they need?'

'They know what drugs they need. They beg me for drugs every time they cross that border!' said the surgeon angrily.

'So it's just a question of money?'

'Isn't it always . . .?'

'But surely medical equipment must be a top priority?'

The surgeon gave a despairing shrug. 'Bullets or penicillin . . . kill one of them or save one of our own . . . I know how I would decide, Mr Keats. But I'm not fighting this war.'

Mike left him and went through to the small cot where Malik lay. They had cleaned his wounds and given him pain killers to ease his suffering. There was nothing more they could do.

When Malik saw him there was a look of joy on his sunken features and he grinned fiercely, showing his brown, broken teeth. 'Remember Qishlaq Imir, Salesman, remember that night?'

'Yes,' said Mike, smiling. 'I remember it.'

'We fought a great fight then. I often think of it. And I tell all the new fighters too. I tell them how glorious it was.' He reached out and gripped Mike's hand. 'It's good to see you again, Salesman . . .'

Mike could hardly talk. 'It's good to see you too,' he whispered.

Malik looked up at him and for the first time there was a shadow of concern on his ancient, wrinkled face. 'Tell me,' he said. 'Do you think my children will remember me?'

Then he said nothing more. He closed his eyes, slipping into a coma and within three hours he was dead. The official cause of death was given as peritonitis.

Malik was seventy-five years old. He had three wives, a dozen sons and more grandchildren than he could remember. He had been the pride of his race, a warrior and a friend . . . and he had died for the lack of a clean bandage.

For days afterwards Mike was filled with an angry despair. He grieved for Malik but the old man was only one of hundreds whose lives could have been saved if they had received rudimentary first aid on the field of battle. In the spring, after the winter snows had melted, there would be new offensives. Something had to be done before more lives were wasted.

'There's no glory in dying from peritonitis,' he said. 'It's just a tragic waste. That's what makes me so angry.'

Halima sat opposite him in the small, dilapidated office where she worked in the narrow lanes of Chitral. There was a look of stoic resignation on her dumpy features. 'You know our problems,' she said.

'What if I can raise the money?'

Halima smiled. As much as she admired Mike's energy, she often despaired of his naivety.

'But what if I can, will you give me the men to train as medics?'

'Of course we will.'

'Good,' said Mike defiantly. 'Then it's settled. I'm flying out tomorrow.'

At nine o'clock the following morning Mike was at the airport waiting for the one flight out.

Bearded and tanned, dressed in boots, jeans and a quilted anorak, sitting patiently on his rucksack and reading a dog-eared copy of Umberto Eco's *The Name of the Rose*, he looked more like a mountain trekker than a businessman. But that's the way he preferred to be.

Sitting there in that tiny airport on the edge of the world, it struck Mike how clearly the extremes of Islam could be seen. The men passengers walked around as they wished, drinking tea, reading or talking. But the women were banished to purdah, a claustrophobic room from where they could only gaze out at the airstrip through the black mesh of their veils. Mike felt a great pity for the Afghan women. And a great admiration for them too. They had fled into Pakistan from the mountains and deserts of Afghanistan, nomads most of them, and only a few wearing the veil out of choice. But in all wars there are extremes and now, while their menfolk were away, they lingered in the refugee camps humbled and veiled by their priests, the 'mad mullahs', as Halima called them.

The flight was delayed which was nothing unusual for Chitral. But by three that afternoon Mike had landed in Peshawar and was settled into his room at Dean's Hotel engaged in the frustrating business of trying to make contact with the outside world.

It was evening in Hong Kong when he eventually got through to the office and Rakosi answered his private line.

'Ten minutes later and you would have missed me,' he said. 'I'm flying to Europe tonight. How are you doing up there? Rather you than me!' And he laughed.

The line was terrible but through the crackle of the static Mike was able to explain that over the next few weeks he intended to concentrate on the supply of medicines and medical facilities to the Mujahedin.

Rakosi saw no problems. 'Pharmaceuticals are easy to obtain and even easier to ship. Profits are good too.'

'No, Joe, there's no profits, not this time.'

Rakosi grunted, unable to believe he had heard correctly. 'It's like trying to talk under water on this bloody line. What did you say?'

'I said no profits, Joe.'

'Are you crazy? Why not?'

'Because we've made enough money out of them already.'

'What's the matter with you? That's what we're in this business for. They make war, we make profits. Don't start getting sentimental on me.'

'You can call it what you like, Joe. I just think it's time we started giving a little instead of constantly taking.'

'We're not taking, we're selling – there's a difference you know. And whose time are you going to be doing these "good works" on?'

'I'll take leave if it will make you any happier,' said Mike sharply.

'No, it won't make me any happier. You're letting your heart rule your head, Mike.'

Mike kept his patience. 'I've got my reasons, Joe.'

'What about charging expenses at least?'

Mike was to the point. 'No, Joe, no charges of any kind.'

Rakosi stifled an angry outburst. He could sense that Mike's mind was made up and once he was set on a course it wouldn't be easy to shift him. 'All right,' he said grudgingly. 'It's your ballgame. You know what's going to make them happy. Two weeks, that's it – not a day longer.'

Mike was astounded. Well, well, he thought, so Chuck Baldwin was wrong. Joe Rakosi had a heart after all.

But what he couldn't know was that Rakosi had lost all interest in limited profits, the kind to be obtained from the supply of bandages and pills to a few ragged guerrillas. He was doing little more than going through the motions. Because now he had his sights set on far grander things – the kind of profits that dwarfed anything he had made in the past.

A few minutes after Mike Keats' telephone call, as Joe Rakosi sat in the back of his Rolls Royce en route to Kai Tak to catch the flight to Zürich, he used the car telephone to settle one final deal. It was an early Christmas present to himself – a sixty-foot cabin cruiser which he intended to call *Good Hope*; sleek and white, less than a year old, luxuriously outfitted and purchased with a permanent Chinese crew of three.

Joe Rakosi knew nothing about sailing but he knew all about status. And why shouldn't he be entitled to all the trappings of success? He had worked damn hard. He deserved it. All his life he had striven for recognition and now he had received it. That was why he was flying to Europe . . . because at long, long last he was about to join the ranks of the great international brokers.

* * *

It was below freezing when the Swissair flight landed in Geneva; no snow yet but so cold that it hurt the lungs to breathe. The hired car was waiting, a Mercedes 500 SE with an English-speaking chauffeur, and Rakosi settled in for the drive.

He had dealt with Swiss financiers before . . . dry, secretive men, dull as dumplings; reliable, yes, like their currency, but lacking flair. That had been his experience of them and that's the kind of man he expected to meet this time. But Jean-Paul Delacroix – as he soon discovered – defied classification of any kind.

Delacroix didn't reside in Geneva or Zürich, the centres of Swiss banking, but lived instead in the old Catholic town of Fribourg south west of Bern. There was no wood panelling in his offices, no portraits of long-dead merchants wearing whiskers and wing collars. On the wall behind the reception desk hung a Byzantine ikon of the Virgin flanked by two black and white blow-ups of starving Ethiopian refugees. While on an opposite wall, above a black leather sofa, hung an Andy Warhol silkscreen of Coca Cola bottles that must have been worth enough to feed those refugees for the rest of their lives.

Rakosi prided himself on being very much his own man but he preferred others to conform. Disturbed, he took a seat, expecting to meet some egocentric whiz kid who had made his first million financing pop concerts or condoms. But Delacroix surprised him again.

The man who came out to meet him was in his late thirties wearing a conservative business suit and tie. 'I hope you had a good trip,' he said in softly accented English. 'Thank you for coming all this way. I'm sorry if it caused you any inconvenience.'

Delacroix had a strong Slavic look: a sharply-boned face with high cheekbones and a thick mane of chestnut hair that fell over his eyes. He reminded Rakosi of a Russian ballet dancer, the kind they swoon over in the West; part Cossack, part poet. But if Delacroix's looks suggested a tempestuous character, his manner did not. He was amiable, polite and urbane.

Delacroix's personal office was decorated in the same style as the reception area; black leather furniture, chrome and glass, a Thai buddah, African sculpture hewn out of serpentine. But morning coffee, Rakosi noticed, was served in delicate white Rosenthal cups.

There was a cluster of photographs arranged on one side of Delacroix's desk. 'My wife and sons,' he said, pointing to the photograph of an attractive dark-haired woman posed with two young boys.

'Nice-looking children.' Rakosi's confidence was returning. Normality was reassuring in a financier. He noticed another photograph, this one of a young man wearing the black cassock of a priest. 'A relative?' he asked.

Delacroix smiled. 'No, that was me many years ago.'

'You, a priest?'

'I was a Jesuit for over ten years.'

Caught totally by surprise, Rakosi laughed. 'What made you leave?'

Delacroix smiled politely, pushing back the hair from his eyes. 'Faith is a fragile thing, Mr Rakosi. Unfortunately I grew tired of continually picking up the pieces. But don't worry, God doesn't balance my books.'

'Does he give you stock market tips at least?'

'Only when the company has a Catholic chairman.'

Rakosi chuckled. He was beginning to like the man. Before flying to Switzerland, he had checked out Delacroix's credentials and, although he had learnt nothing about his early days in the priesthood, had discovered he had a first-class reputation as a 'maker of deals'; nothing small-time either, only major international projects. He was a brilliant financier, they said. Maybe that was why he could afford his eccentricities.

A secretary entered the office carrying a number of files which she placed on the desk. They were professionally bound, each a couple of inches thick, like schedules prepared for a building contract. Another, slimmer, file was handed personally to Delacroix and Rakosi saw the title *Good Hope Group* typed on its cover.

'When we spoke over the telephone, you asked if I would be willing to represent certain national interests,' said Rakosi. 'But you never said which nation.'

'As I explained, it was not a matter which I could divulge over the telephone.' Delacroix relaxed back into his leather-padded chair. 'But, of course, I can tell you now – it's the country of your birth, Mr Rakosi.'

'Hungary?'

Delacroix smiled. 'You seem surprised.'

'I'm bloody amazed! I fled Hungary when I was just a kid. My father was in the '56 uprising. He threw Molotov cocktails at the Russian tanks. What in the hell does Hungary want with me?'

'You don't resent the country do you?'

'I don't resent it, no. I'm just grateful I got out.'

'You speak Hungarian fluently?'

'When I have to, yes . . .'

'Then isn't it logical, Joe? You don't mind if I call you Joe, do you? If Hungary needs representation in the West, who better to seek out than a man like you, an entrepreneur with Hungarian blood, a man who speaks the same language? Especially one who has been so successful. The way you managed that chemical plant project in Kenya was most impressive.'

Rakosi remained silent. The Kenya deal had been a platform for screwing commissions, nothing else. It was a dangerous example.

'And prior to that, when China was first opening its borders, there was your joint venture in Canton for the manufacture of ceramics. Most impressive too.'

Rakosi relaxed. The ceramics joint venture had been one of his most successful. 'In what capacity does Hungary want me to represent them?' he asked, beginning to warm to the idea.

'Initially as a buying agent,' said Delacroix. 'But of course if the Hungarians are satisfied with your services . . .' He leaned forward, speaking more confidentially. 'I was in Budapest less than a week ago talking to their top government officials, Joe. Hungary is indebted to Western banks for billions. They need hard currency to service the debts and yet they don't have the expertise to sell their products on the world market at competitive prices. They're looking for men like you, Joe – good aggressive traders, men who can sell their steel for them, their machinery, their coal.' There was the trace of a smile on his lips. 'The commissions could be considerable.'

Considerable? Christ, that had to be the understatement of the year! Rakosi's pulse was racing. With just a fraction of that trade he could be earning commissions worth millions of dollars each month. But, more important still, he would be rubbing shoulders with statesmen, exerting influence at international level – what he had always dreamt of doing.

Delacroix refilled their coffee cups. 'The prospects are bright, Joe, but I'm sure you appreciate that oak trees must grow from acorns.'

'So where do we begin?' asked Rakosi in a brisk, business-like fashion.

Delacroix patted the pile of files on his desk. 'Right here,' he said.

'What are they, schedules of items to be purchased?'

'That's right.'

'What sort of figures are we talking about?'

'Over the next four to five months, I'd say between forty-five and sixty million, perhaps more.'

'And my commission on that?'

'It varies . . . anywhere from two and a half to five per cent. But, as I say, Joe, prove yourself on this contract, prove to the Hungarians that you have a highly motivated, efficient management team and I can promise it will be worth your while.'

Rakosi allowed himself a satisfied nod. 'Who is the stuff intended for, Hungary itself?'

'No. It's a little complicated, Joe. There are other communist bloc countries helping with the finance. But essentially it's an aid package for a Third World ally.'

'What sort of aid?'

'Ninety per cent of it, of course, will be coming from the communist bloc itself. So you won't be involved in that side.' Delacroix began to leaf through the files. 'Basically, Joe, you're being contracted to obtain from the West the items they can't supply from their own resources . . . spares for Western-built machinery and vehicles, tools, radio equipment, computers, US and Canadian grain . . .'

Rakosi nodded. 'Yeah, I get the picture. So the recipient is some impoverished Marxist state up to its dictatorial ears in debt and starvation, am I right?'

Delacroix smiled. 'Absolutely.'

'And what's the name of this little Shangri-la?'

'Mozambique,' said Delacroix.

* * *

So that he knew what he was dealing with, Delacroix gave Rakosi some background information on the country. Rakosi sat and read it and then commented. 'If the world ever needs an enema I can tell you where to insert the syringe.' Joe Rakosi had a genius for reducing complex issues to their lowest common vulgarity. But not even the country's most fervent supporters could deny that Mozambique was in dire straits.

Clinging to Africa's south eastern coastline, it had been colonised by the Portuguese as far back as 1505. But it was not a country blessed by nature. It possessed no mineral wealth, no great forests and no rich farming land. Mosquitoes controlled the coastline while inland there was little but dry thorn scrub and tsetse flies.

In 1964, as the winds of change blew down Africa, a war of liberation erupted in the country. The Portuguese fought it for ten long years until in 1975 its colonial empire collapsed. Portuguese imperial rule was replaced by a militant Marxist regime. But it didn't end there. Within months an anti-communist guerrilla campaign had flared up in the east of the country. Renamo, as they called themselves, were supplied and armed by neighbouring South Africa. So the fighting dragged on year after year with no end in sight.

It was the kraal dwellers who suffered most, the impoverished black peasants who made up ninety per cent of the population. With no clean drinking water, no roads, no work and the highest infant mortality rate in the world, they were shot for not being communists and hanged if they were.

Not that Joe Rakosi cared too much. One man's chaos was another man's fortune, hopefully his. But Delacroix was visibly upset when he spoke of the situation.

'There was an analysis published earlier this year,' he

said as he and Rakosi made their way to a nearby restaurant for lunch. 'It was called the *International Index of Human Suffering*. And do you know which country was rated as the most comfortable in the world?'

Rakosi turned up the collar of his overcoat against the bitter wind. 'No idea, the United States maybe . . .'

'No, it was right here – Switzerland,' said Delacroix. 'And do you know which country was placed at the very bottom of the index, the home of the world's worst human misery?'

'Mozambique, I suppose.'

'That's right. Ironic, isn't it.'

Rakosi shrugged. The irony escaped him.

Under the gothic spire of Fribourg's Cathedral of St Nicolas, they came to the restaurant. It was warm inside, filled with the sharp tang of Kirsch and the rich aroma of cheese fondues bubbling. They sat at a corner table while Delacroix ordered a bottle of crisp white Neuchatel.

'I noticed that those schedules in your office referred to military communications equipment,' said Rakosi.

Delacroix nodded. 'But it's not just a purchasing exercise, Joe. It involves a technical study first to see if the present systems can be integrated. You'll be paid for the study and then earn commissions on any equipment you recommend buying.'

Rakosi looked puzzled. 'You say they've got an integration problem. What do you mean?'

Delacroix explained. 'When the Portuguese abandoned Mozambique back in '75, they left most of their communications equipment behind – radios, teleprinters – and that's still the mainstay of the Mozambique army. Four or five years after independence, however, the French sold the new government several squadrons of armoured cars. But naturally enough, considering the sale was being made on a long term, low interest basis, and considering they were looking after their own interests first, the French insisted they contain French radios. Then later the Russians compounded the problem by supplying old T-55 tanks with Russian radios. And none of them are compatible!'

Rakosi laughed. 'Yeah, I can believe it!'

'They just don't have the technical expertise to integrate the systems, Joe. So now, when they go into action against Renamo rebels, the only way the armoured commanders can communicate is by sticking their heads out of the turrets and waving different-coloured flags at each other. Skirmishes there look like boy scout jamborees.'

Rakosi smiled, shaking his head. 'The wonderful world of Walt Disney . . .'

The wine was served and both men ordered the restaurant's winter speciality: the Berner Platte, mixed boiled meats served on a bed of young french beans.

'I notice that some of the items have to be landed in Mozambique within six weeks,' said Rakosi. 'Why the urgency?'

'Because the situation is critical, Joe. Renamo are gaining ground every day. For the communist bloc to lose a close ally like Mozambique would be humiliating, especially one on the borders of white-ruled South Africa. Something more than a little Marxist-Leninist dogma is needed – like food in people's bellies for example. Otherwise the government out there could collapse within the next six months.'

'So long as it isn't paying my charges,' grunted Rakosi.

Delacroix laughed. 'Don't worry, Joe, the finance is guaranteed. And the level of your commissions takes into account the degree of urgency.'

Rakosi frowned. 'There's one aspect of the contract that bothers me, Jean-Paul. And that's having to buy the items in my own name. If I'm acting as an agent why do I have to make the purchases as a principal?'

'Politics, Joe.'

'I'm a businessman not a politician.'

Delacroix gave a shrug and a little wave of his hand. 'At this level we're all politicians, Joe. You see, Hungary doesn't want it openly known that it's on a shopping spree in the West, especially for a Marxist ally. It's what you would call in Hong Kong, a matter of face.'

But Rakosi remained dubious. 'I can tell you now,' he said, 'being perfectly blunt about this – there's no way you can expect me to be liable for forty-five or fifty million. In a couple of years maybe, yeah. But at the moment I just don't have those kinds of reserves.'

Delacroix assured him. 'All you have to do is supply me with certified invoices, Joe, and you'll have your money within thirty days.'

'No disrespect,' said Rakosi, 'but communists are notoriously bad payers, especially ones already strapped for hard currency.'

Delacroix gave a knowing smile. 'As I said, Joe, the finance is guaranteed.'

'What's that supposed to mean?'

The smile flickered. 'It means that I'll be holding it in trust. Every last cent will be secured in escrow.'

Rakosi looked happier. 'In which country?'

'Right here, Joe, Switzerland. In a Fribourg bank.'

And Rakosi smiled. 'In that case, Jean-Paul, we might just have a deal.'

'I'm delighted, my friend.' Delacroix lifted his glass. 'Then here's to Mozambique.'

'And to double-quick payment,' Rakosi replied.

* * *

The deal looked good, said Rakosi. But obviously he would have to study the terms first, work out cost factors with his people in London and Hong Kong.

Delacroix emphasised the urgency of the matter. Decisions couldn't be delayed. He must know within the week. Otherwise he would have to look elsewhere. But later that afternoon when Rakosi climbed into his hired Mercedes, well oiled with alcohol, Delacroix had no doubt that he would sign.

'Cheers!' Rakosi said a little too loudly, his cheeks flushed from the final cognac. 'I'll telephone from London before the end of the week.'

As Delacroix watched the car drive away, the first flurries of snow began to fall. But he remained there on the narrow Rue de Lausanne, lost in his thoughts, letting the snow flakes melt on his cheeks. There was no way he could go back to the office, not now. Instead he walked up a tiny street called the Ruelle des Macons until he reached the steps of a medieval wooden walkway scaling the side of the hill. Pensively, he climbed the steps until he came out by the grounds of the College St Michel.

Delacroix had been a pupil there, taught by Jesuits, and knew every inch of its imposing sandstone buildings. He walked through the silent gardens and entered the stone-flagged ambulacrum. The pupils had all gone home. Climbing the stairs, he came to a small chapel on the third floor, the chapel he had known as a boy, and knelt on a cushion at the altar rail.

Above the altar hung an oil painting, darkened now with age and countless layers of varnish. In the centre of the painting St Ignatius, founder of the Jesuits, lay dying surrounded by his priests. The Holy Ghost hovered above him in the form of a black dove, while to one side the gentle Jesus, merciful in a robe of crimson, his hand held out, waited to receive his soul . . . just as one day He would receive the soul of Jean-Paul Delacroix.

Delacroix remained there at the altar rail looking up at the painting for a long, long time until the gloom was thick around him. Then, with tears sparkling in his eyes, he whispered aloud. 'So I begin again, Father, a little evil for the greater good. Guide me please, forgive my sins . . . and give me strength.'

Immediately he arrived in London, Rakosi's top priority was to contact Mike Keats. He telephoned Hong Kong, both the office in St John's Building and Mike's bachelor apartment overlooking Deep Water Bay. He contacted Dean's Hotel in Peshawar and even sent a telegram to Halima way up beyond the Khyber Pass in Chitral. Damn the man, where was he? There was work to be done.

Joe Rakosi employed managers to run his New York and London operations. But they were accountants and economists, office creatures. Their turf was Wall Street and the City, not the African bush. Out there in Mozambique, amid the filth and flies, trying to get things done knowing that around the next bend in the road you could be blown to bits on a landmine . . . that was another world entirely. That was Mike Keats' turf.

And at last he found him, not in the Far East or along the Afghan border but in the Persian Gulf, in the Oman. 'I need you back here, Mike,' he shouted down the phone. 'We're working to deadlines. It's important.'

Mike answered calmly. 'So is this, Joe.'

'What are you doing there anyway?'

'I spoke to you about it before you left Hong Kong.'

'You mean the free medical supplies?'

'That's right.'

124

'I'm sorry, Mike, but in business charity starts at home. It's just going to have to wait.'

'A few days, Joe.'

'I'm up to my neck in it here. How many days?'

'A week – '

'A week? Are you crazy? Have you got any idea of the potential of this contract?'

'I'll be back before the week's out, I promise.'

'You're a stubborn son of a bitch.'

Mike replied evenly. 'Just an amateur in comparison to you, Joe.'

'All right,' growled Rakosi. 'I'll just have to push ahead until you get here. But a week at the outside – that's it. Then I want you here in London. Because if this deal in Mozambique goes right for us, it's going to open up the doors of Fort Knox. Within five years, Mike, they'll be listing us in *Fortune* magazine's top hundred.'

'That's what you always say,' commented Mike with sceptical good humour.

Rakosi burst out laughing. 'But this time it's true, you cynical bastard. This time it's true!'

Another of Rakosi's megabuck deals. They came with the monotonous regularity of English rain these days. And if Rakosi wanted him so badly, there could only be one reason . . . the arms trade.

Mike wondered what the moral gymnastics would involve this time. Purchasing civilian helicopters in the United States perhaps . . . very easy business, being wined and dined by the salesmen, hard days on the golf course; no need for end user certificates, no need for congressional okays. The trick was having them shipped to Brazil where they could be electronically re-outfitted and then despatched to Africa as killing machines. Or mortars from neutral Austria: he had purchased those before. The end user certificates would show they were destined for Libya but the instructions would be printed in Shona or Swahili, African languages only spoken two thousand miles to the south. Nobody queried it. But then the Austrians were obliging people. Where there was a will there was a way. All you needed were the morals of a dog.

Chuck Baldwin had been right, thought Mike, the business wasn't for him. Joe Rakosi had a way of steam-rollering objections and dangling golden carrots. It was too easy to keep saying: 'Just this one last time'. But that was the kiss of death and Mike knew it. It didn't matter how good the Mozambique deal might be, he owed it to himself and he owed it to Jackie's memory, he would never deal in arms again.

The stony wastes of the Rub' al-Khali, washed crimson by the sun, were suffused into a panorama of space that encompassed the evening sky and then the sea beyond. There seemed to be no horizon, no distance, no sense of time. The past was a myth, the future was a legend. Only the present existed. Mike Keats was fascinated by the desert . . . the great empty spaces, the endless sky. He could understand how Sheikh Yasi, despite his enor-mous wealth, loved nothing more than to be out there with his kinsmen and to lie down at night under the stars.

When Mike was brought to him that evening, the Sheikh had pitched his tents twenty miles south of Muscat on a rocky peninsula overlooking the silver waters of the Gulf. A traditional meal of boiled lamb and rice had been prepared. Mike's hands were washed in water poured from a brass jug. Then he reclined on cushions in the ancient way to partake of the meal.

Sheikh Yasi was in his sixties but could have been twenty years younger. He was a simple man at heart, a Bedouin. But he was a man who enjoyed life too. 'You're looking older, Michael. I detect a few grey hairs. And still no wife I suppose?'

'No,' said Mike with an enigmatic smile, a sudden image of Jackie in his mind. 'Still no wife.'

'You need a woman. She'll fatten you up.'

Mike shook his head. 'Too busy, I'm afraid.'

'Nonsense. I'm as busy as you and I keep seven of them happy.'

They both laughed, both men who had respect for each other.

Using his right hand – according to Bedouin custom the left never touches food – Sheikh Yasi took a piece of tender lamb, squeezed rice around it until it made a moist ball and then popped it into his mouth. 'You said you had a request, Michael.'

'I'm afraid I come with a begging bowl.'

Sheikh Yasi smiled. 'I know it's not for yourself. You're too proud for that. So it must be for the Mujahedin.'

Mike nodded.

'Tell me about it.'

And Mike began, explaining the desperate need of the Mujahedin for medical supplies. He told the story of old Malik who had fought countless battles and seemed indestructible until the simple – preventable – infection of a wound had killed him. He explained how men bled to death when they could be saved, how small wounds turned gangrenous, how diseases like typhus wiped out entire villages. The Mujahedin already fought against staggering odds, he said. Why should they be burdened with this one too?

'You say they have nothing in the way of medical supplies?'

'Very few of them . . . what they have they steal off Russian corpses.'

Sheikh Yasi was a devout man. He spurned the ostentation of so many other sheikhs in the Persian Gulf. He had no palace with fountains running rose water, no Boeing 707 to fly his wives to Europe. Conforming with Islamic law, he wore no silk nor gold. Faithfully, he bent to his prayers five times a day. He believed that the greatness of the Muslim peoples lay in their simple faith and their simple courage. And to him, of all men, the Mujahedin most symbolised those virtues. That was why he had felt compelled to assist in their struggle and that was why he listened so intently now.

When Mike had finished, coffee was poured from a long-beaked pot. Sheikh Yasi sat for a time sipping the sweet, black liquid. Then he said simply, 'Thank you, Michael, for telling me these things. I'll see what can be done.'

Seeing what could be done took exactly forty-eight hours. Sheikh Yasi may have been a simple Bedouin, a son of the sand. But oil and faith made a potent combination.

Fifty Mujahedin, carrying papers identifying them as Pakistani servicemen, would be flown to Saudi Arabia to train as medics with the Saudi army. The government in Riyadh would meet all necessary costs and when their training was completed, another fifty would follow. Jordan would take a further fifty, the lame and the wounded who couldn't fight, for training as hospital orderlies.

As for medicines and medical equipment, a private

trust was to be created in London for the specific purpose of purchasing and supplying everything necessary to the men in the field. Sheikh Yasi had contributed the first two million while another four million had been contributed by certain concerned individuals who, for political reasons, preferred to remain anonymous. Six million dollars – it was a fantastic beginning. And more monies were promised.

'So that old warrior, Malik, didn't die in vain,' said Sheikh Yasi with an impish smile. 'He's in Paradise now looking down at us, no doubt very pleased with himself too. And so he deserves to be. It's not every day a man has a multi-million-dollar trust named in his honour!'

When Halima heard, she burst into tears of excitement. Even Chuck Baldwin, the world-weary cynic, couldn't hide his pleasure. 'That's good,' he said. 'Damn good.'

'How are things going up there?' asked Mike.

'Larry and I have checked out the hardware and finished instructing. We're all set to fly out. Miami here we come – except the goddamn airstrip is six foot under snow.' He laughed. 'If we can find somebody foolhardy enough to take us, we're going to try and hump it out by road.'

'Any fighting rumoured?'

'Not unless the Ruskies have brought in a regiment of Eskimos. The Hindu Kush is all snowed in.'

Halima came on the line. 'Make sure we have the medicines by spring, Mike, that's all that matters. They must be here by spring.'

'You'll have them,' said Mike. 'That's a promise.'

But if Mike was to keep the promise, speed was of the essence. The trust had to be set up and functioning. Staff had to be employed. Supplies had to be purchased and shipped.

The following morning he flew to London, arriving at Heathrow just after ten. His one crucial task was to set up the Malik Gailani Trust. But he was also aware that Joe Rakosi was waiting for him and, knowing that Rakosi possessed as much patience as a rampaging bull elephant, he telephoned direct from the airport.

'Where are you?' shouted Rakosi.

'Heathrow.'

'We've got to talk. Thrash things out. How about lunch?'

'Today?'

'Of course today. Come to the offices here in Holborn. I'm going to take you to a little restaurant on the Thames that I've discovered. It's run by two French brothers. Old-style French cooking, just brilliant. None of this nouvelle cuisine rubbish – two carrots, a piece of trout and a blob of sauce made to look like a poor imitation of a Picasso. This is real food, Mike. It costs an arm and a leg, but we deserve it.'

'This deal has got you excited hasn't it?'

'It's not this deal, Mike – it's the promise for the future. I tell you – and no bullshit this time – you and I are on the verge of great things.'

The restaurant was superb, one of those essentially English establishments, despite the fact that it specialised in French cuisine; a converted Victorian house on the banks of the Thames, with green lawns that rolled down to a small jetty. The weather was miserable, a persistent cold drizzle that was typical of December in England. But it was warm inside with a log fire burning.

Champagne cocktails were served at their table. 'They

give you a good kick-start,' said Rakosi, flushed and ebullient. He glanced at the menu, decided on the consommé Celestine followed by fresh salmon and then the roast baron of lamb, put the menu aside and said, 'Let me come straight to the point, Mike. I need you in Mozambique running that end of the operation. And I need you there yesterday.'

Mike was silent for a moment. Then he said quietly, 'I can't leave until the trust has been set up, Joe. I told you that on the way here.'

'Christ, that bloody trust!'

Mike remained impassive.

Rakosi tried to hide his irritation. 'Yeah, okay. A week, is that enough?'

Mike sipped his cocktail. A week would suffice. 'Exactly what am I going to be dealing with in Mozambique?' he asked.

'The first thing is military radio equipment – '

Mike shook his head. 'Sorry, Joe, the answer is no.'

Rakosi raised his eyebrows. 'What do you mean, no?'

'I've made it clear before – no more weapons, no more arms dealing.'

'Who said anything about arms dealing?'

'Where else is this leading?'

Rakosi shook his head, as if offended. 'Just listen a moment. The only thing even remotely connected to the colour khaki is radio equipment. That's it, I promise. And when did you hear of a radio killing anybody, unless it fell on some poor bastard's head?'

'Then what else is in this deal?' asked Mike.

'Still sceptical, is that it?'

'To be frank, yes . . .'

Rakosi sucked through his teeth. 'In which case you wouldn't want to know, Mike. Because it's vicious stuff – vehicle spares, tools, electronic equipment, filthy capitalist grain to stop them all starving to death. Sinister as hell.'

Mike smiled. 'If that's what you're shipping, why do you want me?'

'Because I need a man who knows how to operate at the sharp end.'

'No guns, no mortars?'

'None at all.'

'You want me there as a field manager, that's it?'

'That's it exactly,' said Rakosi. 'I was in Mozambique last week, Mike, and you're going to love it. Sunshine, blue skies – a total bloody shambles.'

The waiter came and they placed their orders. Joe ordered a St Émilion to accompany the meal. 'Good times deserve good wine,' he said. 'Sounds like an advertising slogan.' And he laughed happily. 'The corner store days are over, Mike.'

Mike was grinning too. 'Okay, what's it all about?'

'We've been asked by a government to represent their interests, that's what it's all about, a whole damn government! Would you believe it? We've made it, Mike. We're in the league of the great international traders.'

But Mike wasn't that easily impressed. 'Which government?' he asked.

'It's ironic . . .' Rakosi gave a small laugh. 'I wonder what my poor old father would think if he was still alive?'

'Why do you say that?'

'Because the country we're representing is Hungary, that's why. Land of my birth, Mike.'

Mike sat bolt upright. 'Hungary?'

'Yes, Hungary. What are you looking so amazed about?'

Mike let out an angry sigh. 'Because it's a recipe for disaster, Joe.'

'What are you talking about?'

'Don't you appreciate the ramifications, for God's sake?'

Rakosi was genuinely puzzled. 'What ramifications?'

'Bloody hell . . . in one breath we're selling missiles to the Mujahedin to shoot down Soviet aircraft and in the next we're acting as commercial agents for one of Russia's closest Warsaw Pact allies.'

'So?'

'So something has got to give, Joe. Something has got to come unstuck.'

'Why?'

'What do you mean, why? It's obvious why!'

Rakosi laughed, splashing wine into his glass. 'You know your trouble, Mike? You see everything face on. You're too direct. You need to be more devious. Self-interest, that's what makes the world go around.'

Mike was trying to control his anger. 'Self-interest? Conflict of interest, you mean!'

'Rubbish.' Rakosi was grinning, trying vainly to camouflage his mounting annoyance. 'We're not supplying missiles to Mozambique, we're supplying humanitarian aid. I thought that was what you wanted.'

'The fact remains, Joe – '

'The fact remains that we're getting the best of both worlds. And if we can, why not? How do you think governments act, like convent school teachers? They're pragmatists. If I'm the best man for the job, they'll use me.'

'But why you specifically, Joe, why?'

'Because I'm Hungarian.'

'That can't be the only reason.'

'Because I'm the right man in the right place. Because my face fits. Because blood is thicker than water. God knows why. The fact is that I've got the contract. That's all that matters.'

Mike shook his head. 'I don't like it.'

'Why? Tell me.'

'It's too pat, too convenient . . .'

'What are you talking about? Mozambique and Afghanistan are the other side of the world from each other. What do you think we're involved in here, some kind of sinister international conspiracy? Come on, Mike, wake up. Ding ding – this is reality ringing your door bell.'

Mike said nothing. He couldn't find the words to express the vague but pressing disquiet that he felt.

'Enjoy your lunch,' said Rakosi expansively. 'I'm not paying these prices for you to get heartburn.' He swallowed more wine and then said, 'Look, I understand that you've got close emotional ties to the Afghans, and the Russians are the bogeymen right now. But we're dealing with Budapest, Mike, not Moscow. It's the same as dealing with Paris when you've got the hell in with Washington. We're businessmen, that's all. Little guys. We're putting grain into people's bellies. How bad can that be?'

Mike gave an unwilling smile. Despite his misgivings, he knew what Joe was saying made sense. He leaned back in his chair. That was the problem with the armaments business: you began to believe that everything had a political edge, some malevolent motive. 'All right,' he said, 'when do I fly out?'

The relief was evident on Rakosi's flushed features. 'I'll book tickets for us both for today week.'

'That's Christmas Eve.'

Rakosi laughed. 'What's the problem? We're free agents. Both bachelors, both without family ties. Free as birds, Mike.' He was in good humour now. 'Don't worry, you won't miss out on Christmas. I'll buy you a plum pudding in Maputo.'

Mike spent the next week commuting between the Holborn offices of the Good Hope Group and the Chancery Lane offices of Humbel Hatchard and Finken, the solicitors briefed to prepare the trust deeds and oversee the hiring of staff.

In Mike's opinion, lawyers had to be the single most fatiguing group of professionals in the world. Their indigestible language, their constant quibbling over commas and colons, their rapacious hunt for fees exhausted him. His mother, before she died, had wanted him to be a lawyer. 'Such a good career, my dear, so solid and respectable.' But Mike knew that within a year it would have driven him into a lunatic asylum. It was taxing enough just dealing with them for a week.

But within that time the trust deeds had been prepared at least and he was present at the interview when the trust manager, a man with experience in pharmaceutical sales, was hired. The Malik Gailani Trust, he was confident, would fulfil its expectations.

Mikhail Kazakov flew into the Mozambique capital two days ahead of Joe Rakosi and Mike Keats.

With him were three GRU specialists, ex-Spetsnaz commandos who had worked for Kirilenko in the past and had the ability to do a job, no matter how messy, without any questions asked. The diplomatic papers they carried identified them all as technicians from the Black Sea port of Odessa.

Maputo was one huge, sprawling shanty town. Nothing it seemed had been painted or repaired since the Portuguese had fled more than ten years earlier. Roads were filled with potholes. Ditches of stagnant water bred mosquitoes. There were shops of a kind but no goods in them, bread queues but no bread. Children begged on street corners oblivious of the flies crawling around their eyes. Western diplomats had called Maputo a 'hardship posting' for years. But so did the communists these days. For Mikhail Kazakov, however, ensconced in the Russian embassy, it was a matter of indifference. Once the job was done, he would never see the place again.

His first task was to gain information on the arrival of the two ships carrying Rakosi's cargoes. But that presented no problems. Russian technicians ran Maputo's port. All it took was a phone call.

The two vessels were both due to dock on Christmas Day itself, a full twenty-four hours ahead of the ships bringing cargoes from Hungary.

The first, a Panamanian-registered merchantman, carried vehicle spares, tyres, tools, dies, electronic parts, computers and machinery. The second brought Canadian wheat.

The unloading of the cargoes would be completed by the afternoon of the 26th, Boxing Day. The cargoes would be held in bond overnight and then officially handed over to the Mozambique Government.

In round figures, the value of the cargoes was ten million dollars. Rich pickings, thought Kazakov. And how easily it was all falling into place.

To gain access to the docks was just as easy. They had come to Mozambique as marine technicians and were taken on a tour of the port by the deputy harbour master, himself a Russian. Kazakov and his three men were dressed identically in grey slacks and white short-sleeved shirts, each of them carrying a bulky, black briefcase. They took great interest in the cranes and chains and paraphernalia of the docks. They had tea and cake, shook a lot of hands and even watched a tribal dance performed by stevedores.

Nobody had checked them when they drove into the docks and when they departed nobody noticed that their briefcases had been left behind.

That night Kazakov sent a coded message to Kirilenko at GRU Headquarters in Moscow. The message was for Kirilenko's eyes only and when decoded, it read:

THE NUTCRACKER SUITE HAS BEEN CHOREOGRAPHED. THE DANCERS ARE READY.

And the reply came back:

SHOW THEM THE BEST OF SOVIET CULTURE.

It was raining on the night of Boxing Day, a fat tropical downpour with bullfrogs out on the roads like a plague and broken palm fronds littering the mud verges.

In the Polano Hotel, where the foreigners gathered, the air conditioning had broken down. But the ceiling fans churned the wet air as guests crowded the bar. Most of them were already drunk and intent on getting drunker. What else was there to do in this godforsaken town?

Mikhail Kazakov sat alone at a corner table with a glass of Slivovitch and a complimentary bowl of cashew nuts. He glanced at his watch. It was nearly time . . .

He knew that his men would do the job swiftly and efficiently, leaving only those few subtle signs to mis-direct the blame. They would have cut through the wires already, retrieved the explosives left in the briefcases, planted the devices, set the timers and made good their escape. There would be no mistakes. They were profes-sionals. They did the job and asked no questions. But even so, the tension was gnawing at him. It was on occa-sions like this that his elbow ached badly, the right elbow – or what remained of it – the one that had been shattered at Qishlaq Imir.

And that in turn explained his presence at The Polano. It was against orders. He should have been waiting at the embassy, not mixing with these drunken Westerners. But a morbid fascination had dragged him there, a compul-sion to see the man whose bullets had shattered his elbow and pierced his lung, to look into his face and say to himself: so you're the one. He had assured Kirilenko that there was no element of revenge in the plan he had devised, and on one level that was true but deep down in the dark labyrinths of his mind he wanted very badly to make Keats pay. And before this thing was over, if all went according to plan, he *would* pay too – with his life.

Mike Keats was standing at the bar: tall, slim, with that dark beard cut to follow his jaw line. Kazakov would have taken him for an Israeli or a Greek, not an Englishman. He wasn't drunk like the others or, if he was, he hid it better, quietly nursing a beer. Kazakov didn't know why but he had expected more . . . a feroc-ity of expression perhaps, the merciless, uncompromis-ing look of a mercenary, a man dead behind the eyes. But he exhibited none of these things. Keats was nothing very special, he thought.

Josef Rakosi didn't look too special either. Glistening tracks of sweat were dribbling down his ruby-veined cheeks and collecting in big drops on his chin. He was well and truly gone, swilling back the whisky and laughing loudly at his own jokes.

It was nearly midnight. He would have to leave. But Kazakov desperately wanted to be there when it occurred, to see the look on their faces. He glanced down at his watch again. He would give it a couple more minutes, he thought, just a couple – and then it happened.

From a long way off there came a deep booming sound, its resonance so strong that the walls shuddered. It was one of those eerie, unforgettable sensations like the first shudder of an earthquake.

A silence fell on the bar.

Then came another boom, a low, growling explosion, followed by another . . . and another. The windows rattled.

'What in the hell is happening?' somebody shouted. The guests began to mill about in confusion. An Australian, who had barged out onto the terrace, shouted, 'Strewth, the whole bloody sky is lit up!'

In the distance a siren began to wail and rifle shots could be heard.

'It's got to be Renamo!' somebody exclaimed.

Kazakov smiled to himself.

A man ran into the bar. 'It's the docks!' he shouted. 'They've hit the port area. Everything is burning.'

Kazakov looked across at Rakosi and saw him standing there, open-mouthed. There was a hurried conversation between him and Keats and then Rakosi began to push his way through the crowd with Keats following.

Kazakov watched him rush out of the hotel and smiled sardonically. The Nutcracker Suite had been choreographed just for this – the dance of the Sugar Plum Fairy.

All through the night the sky was filled with a glowing orange aurora as the fires burnt. Initially the rain gave some hope of quenching the flames but at three in the morning the rain passed and the fires raged on unabated.

Joe Rakosi and Mike Keats rushed down to the docks and remained there throughout the night. But there was nothing they could do, only stand by and watch in despair.

By dawn, concentrating all of the city's fire-fighting resources, the conflagration had been contained. But by then – for Rakosi at least – it was too late.

A pall of noxious smoke hung over the port. Cranes had buckled and collapsed in the heat. Ships' containers had melted. Wood crates piled one on top of the other had been seared into instant charcoal that shattered at a touch. And everywhere, ankle-deep, lay pools of soot-slurried sea water from the fire hoses.

'It's like a goddam battlefield,' said Rakosi as he surveyed the destruction.

The State radio blamed the Renamo rebels for what it termed 'this economic atrocity'. Renamo propaganda found at the fence and snatches of camouflage clothing snagged on the wire took the matter beyond doubt.

'Ten million dollars up in smoke,' said Rakosi, shaking his head in exhausted bewilderment. 'What in the hell do they hope to gain? Tell me that.'

Mike Keats, his clothing grimed with smoke, could only shrug. 'What helps the government, hinders them. So they destroy it. It's as basic – and as blind – as that.'

'Amazing isn't it,' said Rakosi bitterly. 'We bust our guts to get here ahead of schedule, to show the Hungarians we can do the job, and look what happens. We get blown to hell, while out there at anchor – a full day later than us – the ships bringing the Eastern bloc aid sit safe as houses. Where's the bloody good in bothering?'

With shoulders hunched, he looked around at the devastation one last time. Not a thing had been saved, not even the grain. Then he said, 'I can tell you one thing, Mike, I'm not going to lose out on this bloody fiasco, not a single damn cent!'

News of the Maputo sabotage had been broadcast over BBC radio and by the time Rakosi got through to his London office – operating for the first day after the Christmas break – it was in turmoil.

Rakosi spoke to his London manager, an ex-banker called Simpson. 'Have you checked our insurances?'

'I've just finished speaking to the various companies. I've been on the phone all morning.'

'Are we covered? That's all I want to know.'

Simpson hesitated. 'I'm afraid we've got troubles.'

'What do you mean, troubles?' barked Rakosi, refusing to accept it. 'How can we have troubles?'

Simpson could be heard taking a deep breath. 'All the goods that we shipped to Mozambique were purchased here in Europe CIF Maputo. That means the costs of freight and insurance were paid by the suppliers and included in the overall purchase price. You've got to understand that it was the suppliers' responsibility to take out insurance, not ours.'

'You don't have to give me a lecture on what CIF means,' growled Rakosi. 'Did you stipulate to the suppliers that the insurance be warehouse to warehouse, that's all I want to know. Was the stuff covered in bond?'

'Yes, of course.'

'Then what's the problem?'

'Your fax from Hong Kong was clear,' said Simpson. 'We were only to make two stipulations to the suppliers. First, that the policies be warehouse to warehouse. Second, that the cost of freight and insurance shouldn't exceed twenty per cent of the purchase price of the goods.'

'Of course,' said Rakosi, trying to contain his temper. 'The Hungarians weren't going to reimburse anything over twenty per cent. So why pay out of our own pockets? Get to the point, man – '

'The point, Mr Rakosi, is that the suppliers didn't take out "all risks" cover.'

Rakosi felt the breath catch in his throat. 'What are you trying to say?'

There was a momentary silence. Then Simpson said in a dry voice, 'I'm trying to say that none of the insurance policies covered the risk of loss by war or riots.'

'But that's a standard clause. It has to be!'

'I wish it were, Mr Rakosi . . .'

Rakosi was stunned. 'So the stuff has been blown up, burnt to hell, and we've got no cover, no cover at all? Is that what you're telling me?'

'The cost of "all risks" would have taken us way above the twenty per cent. Nobody thought there would be any sabotage in the port area. It's never happened before . . .'

Rakosi's knuckles were white as he gripped the telephone. 'What about the suppliers?' he asked. 'Have they been paid yet?'

'Let me check.'

Rakosi waited, trying to control the rage that was about to explode in his chest like a grenade. On the other end of the line he could hear Simpson shuffling through papers.

'All documents have been presented to our bankers,' said Simpson.

'So when was payment made?'

'The LCs – the letters of credit – fell due on Christmas Eve. We negotiated thirty-day letters of credit with the suppliers,' said Simpson defensively. 'You agreed to that, Mr Rakosi. It's quite usual. I've got your signature on the memorandum – '

'Fuck my signature!' Rakosi let out a grunt of disbelieving fury. 'So the goods are destroyed, we've got no insurance cover and we're into the banks for ten million . . . is that what you're telling me?'

There was silence at the other end of the line.

Rakosi was desperately searching for a way out. 'What about Delacroix?' he snapped. 'This is his problem, not ours. We're just acting as agents for the Hungarians. They're the principals. They have to bear the risk. Did we submit certified invoices to him?'

'Yes,' said Simpson. 'We received his cheques.'

'When are they due for presentation?'

'This morning.'

'Then why haven't they been presented? Get down to the bank, for God's sake. Have them urgently cleared.'

'I'm afraid that's not possible.'

Oh God, thought Rakosi. He hesitated and then he asked, 'Why not?'

'Delacroix telephoned from Fribourg first thing this morning, immediately the office opened.'

'What did he say?'

'He said he very much regretted having to take such drastic action but he had no choice . . .'

'No choice how . . . ? What's he done?'

And Simpson answered. 'He's stopped payment on all the cheques.'

Like so many entrepreneurs greedy for vast fortunes, Joe Rakosi had learnt to be an audacious juggler. Balanced precariously on top of his corporate pole he kept eight or nine deals spinning in the air at a time. It was brilliant to watch, the mesmerising stuff of business legends, but all it needed was one mistake and the whole lot could come tumbling down.

Rakosi was a rich man. His businesses made money. But profits earned were reinvested, not left fallow in banks. So while, on paper at least, his total corporate wealth may have been twenty-five million or more, to find nearly half of that in cash in a matter of days was almost impossible. Yet that's exactly what he had to do because ten million dollars was due to the banks to cover the letters of credit they had honoured on his behalf.

He could negotiate short extensions perhaps, borrow part of the money from other banks, guillotine projects he had under way, but that was dangerous . . . blood in corporate waters. Other creditors – like sharks – would smell it and come homing in.

Yet somehow Rakosi had to find the money. The banks kept him alive. If they called in his overdrafts, if they cut his lines of credit, he was finished. Delacroix, he knew, offered his only avenue of escape . . .

And Delacroix was waiting.

'Try and see my side of it,' he said when Rakosi telephoned in a black rage that night. 'What else could I do, Joe? The terms of the contract are clear. Risk in the goods remains with you until they are handed over to the

Mozambique Government. And that includes the time they're in bond.'

'There's no way I'm going to be saddled with a ten million dollar loss,' said Rakosi. 'The principal is liable. That's Hungary, not me. I'm just the agent.'

'That's not what the contract states, Joe.'

'You gave me an undertaking, you bastard. You said you were holding the monies in escrow.'

'And so I am, Joe. But my hands are tied. I can only pay out in terms of the contract, you know that.'

But Rakosi was past reason, swinging blind punches like a boxer staggering up from the canvas. 'That's bullshit. I've been on to my lawyers. You've got seven days to pay. If you don't, you're going to have the biggest bloody lawsuit you've ever known.'

'Come now, Joe, litigation won't solve anything. Instead of threatening each other over the telephone, why don't we get together and discuss this problem rationally, try and work out some suitable compromise?'

Through the red haze of his anger Rakosi knew it made sense. 'Where do you want to meet, in Switzerland?'

'I'm sure Mr Keats can handle matters in Maputo.'

'Yeah, well, it'll take a few days,' he grumbled.

'But you'll come?'

'Yes, I'll come.'

'Good,' said Delacroix. 'Believe me, Joe, the Hungarians have a great deal of faith in you. This is a hiccup, that's all. I still see a very bright future for us.'

The small apartment overlooking Gorky Park reverberated with the rich cadences of a tenor voice. Moussorgsky's glorious peasant music, his songs for solo voice and piano, the *Sunless Cycle*, had been playing all morning as the snow silently fell on the streets of Moscow. Grigori Kirilenko had learnt a long time ago that when he needed to bring his intellectual faculties to bear on the complex cross tangents of a scheme, he did so best on a tide of music. Music for him was not simply an emotional thing. Music induced a special clarity of mind.

The ashtray next to his chair was filled with stubbed-out cigarettes, the cheap Bulgarian brand that he knew Mikhail Kazakov disliked so much. He lit another, letting the acrid blue smoke curl around his face.

So far, he thought, the scheme had gone well, better than expected.

Like a good workman he had used the tools that lay to hand. Details of massive and urgent aid relief to Mozambique had been known to him at the time Kazakov first proposed his scheme. Russia was assisting too. He had also known that a commercial agent was needed in the West and it had been simple enough to ensure that Rakosi was appointed as that agent. His counterpart in Budapest was an old and valued comrade, more than happy to comply.

He had gambled of course – a risky gambit – that in the rush to meet the deadline, to get the goods purchased and shipped, Rakosi, who knew next to nothing about conditions in Mozambique, would either overlook the need to protect against sabotage or – like so many other shippers who were only responsible for landing the goods – consider the risk too negligible to warrant the extra costs involved, especially when those costs had to come out of his own pocket. That was why Delacroix had been instructed to make the contracts so niggardly when it came to the question of insurance allowances.

And the gamble had paid off. But even if he had mis-calculated this time, there would have been no loss, simply a delay until he found another way of subjecting Rakosi to his will.

For all his brains and ambition, Rakosi was no different from a million other capitalists. Look how many of them lost fortunes when the stock exchanges crashed, ignoring all the signs, obsessed by money. How easy it was, he thought, to manipulate greedy men running so fast that they failed to check the way.

He looked up at the clock on the mantelpiece, the one next to the silver samovar. His driver would be collecting him soon for the flight to Leningrad. Kirilenko disliked flying. But Delacroix was in Leningrad on some business to do with the fur trade and it was essential they meet.

It was three thirty in the afternoon, already dark, when the Aeroflot flight landed at Pudvolko, Leningrad's airport. The city was in the tight grip of winter. Kirilenko's Chaika limousine drove along the banks of the Fontaka, one of the three rivers that flow through the city. Pack ice, broken and grey in the gloom of the water, could be seen drifting out towards the Gulf of Finland.

There was a bottle of vodka waiting in his room at the Leningradskaya Hotel. Kirilenko took a warm, welcoming slug and felt better. The bureaucrats complained about the Russian liking for vodka: a nation of Soviet Socialist drunks, they said. But they might as well complain about an Englishman and his tea. In this frozen climate vodka didn't slow people down – it was the only thing that kept them going.

He had agreed to meet Delacroix for dinner and at seven thirty prompt, after a warm bath to ease the constant ache he felt in his lower back, he made his way down to the hotel dining room.

Delacroix was already at the table sipping a drink that

obviously wasn't vodka. He looked far too well-groomed to be Russian, so obviously a product of Western riches. He was an enigma, thought Kirilenko, one of those men whose motives are simultaneously obvious and mystifyingly obscure . . . a lapsed priest, a capitalist and a communist spy. Each aspect should have grated against the other, like that pack ice floating down the Fontaka.

Yet Delacroix always appeared contented and assured, not a man of contradictions at all. Not that he had always been that way. Kirilenko thought back to the time when he had first dealt with him, all those years ago in Nicaragua . . . a young priest hiding in the slums of Managua, disgusted with the corruption and injustice of the world. He had been prepared to kill then. And he had killed too – in God's name – just as he had smuggled guns into the hills and consorted with lepers and whores. He had been a fire eater then. But even now, behind the camouflage of the silk shirt and elegant ways, Kirilenko could sometimes detect hints of the old passion and guilt. Why else would he be doing this job? Despite the expensive suit and gold watch, Delacroix remained God's revolutionary.

Stiff-backed, Kirilenko sat at the table. 'You're looking well, Jean-Paul.'

They exchanged pleasantries for a time; discussing world politics, Delacroix's business in Leningrad, the bitter winter, until Kirilenko came to the reason for their meeting.

'I've heard rumours,' he said, 'that Keats, the helicopter pilot, Rakosi's associate, has started to work independently for the Afghan Resistance. Is there any truth in it?'

'He's been raising money for medical supplies, yes. But it doesn't go any further than that.'

'How well has he done?'

'I don't know too much. He's raised a fair amount in the Middle East. Oil money, of course. Some sort of charitable trust has been formed.'

'To benefit whom, the refugees or the bandits?'

'According to my information, it's essentially for the troops.'

'The men crossing the border?'

Delacroix nodded. 'Yes, the fighters.'

'Good, yes, that's excellent . . .' Kirilenko's hawkish features broke into a broad smile. He looked across the table at Delacroix and began to chuckle. 'It reminds me of Napoleon, Jean-Paul. The story goes that he was looking for a new general and his marshals were lauding the skills of a particular officer, what a brilliant soldier he was, what a great tactician. Napoleon listened until they had finished and then he asked just one question: "But is he lucky?" Because Napoleon understood, you see. Fate favours some men.'

Delacroix was puzzled. How was fate favouring Kirilenko? How could the supply of medicines to the Mujahedin be of any benefit to him? But he didn't question it. He worked for the General on a strict need-to-know basis. It rested more easily with his conscience that way.

'I'd like you to find out more about these medical supplies,' said Kirilenko. 'How is the money gathered to pay for them? Who organises distribution?'

'Apparently it's done through some private trust.'

'Then find out the name of it. Where are its offices, who runs it . . . everything you can.'

'Of course.'

'I need the information as soon as possible.'

'It shouldn't be difficult to obtain.'

Kirilenko gave a dense, inward smile. 'Medicines . . .

who would believe it.' And for a moment he was lost in his thoughts.

More chess moves, thought Delacroix.

Kirilenko took out a pack of his Bulgarian cigarettes. 'But don't approach Rakosi about it. Say nothing to him, not yet.'

A waiter came to their table. Kirilenko ordered for both of them: good Russian fare; first, shchi, a thick cabbage soup, followed by a herring salad. Delacroix ordered wine and Kirilenko ensured it was Russian; a sturdy red from Georgia.

'I understand you have arranged to meet with Rakosi,' said Kirilenko.

'Yes, in a couple of days.'

Kirilenko knocked ash from his cigarette, missing the ashtray. 'How was he when you spoke on the phone?'

Delacroix smiled. 'How did you expect him to be? Like a raging tiger caught in a trap.'

'So much the better . . . raging tigers are blind.'

'What do I do with him now?'

Kirilenko considered the matter. 'Financially, what sort of state is he in?'

'Precarious.'

'Will he go where we prod him?'

'If the bait is tempting enough.'

'So you think it's time to act?'

'I think so, yes. Before he regains his balance.'

Kirilenko leaned across the table. 'Well, then, Jean-Paul, if we already have the tiger in the cage, let's feed him the bait with the poison in it, shall we? Let's feed him Vietnam.'

Forty-eight hours later, on a snow-driven afternoon, Delacroix drove to Zürich Airport to meet Joe Rakosi.

Jet-lagged and jumpy, Rakosi was living on his nerves. There were bags under his eyes from lack of sleep. He smelt of whisky and, to compound it, had caught a bad cold in London.

'I had hoped you could join my family and I at our ski chalet in Zermatt,' said Delacroix as they climbed into his Porsche. 'But the weather is too bad, I'm afraid.'

'Suits me,' said Rakosi, snorting into a handkerchief. 'I want to get this Mozambique mess sorted out, not slide down mountains on my backside.'

They took the N1, the Zürich–Bern autobahn, heading for Fribourg. Snow flurries beat against the windscreen but in the cramped interior of the Porsche there was a toasted warmth.

'Have the Hungarians reconsidered their position?' asked Rakosi in a flat, nasal voice.

'I'm afraid not, Joe. On a strict reading of the contract they insist the loss is yours.'

'Yeah? Well, I've taken legal advice too.'

'All this talk about litigation, Joe . . .'

'I don't intend to be the loser in this thing.'

Delacroix gave a conciliatory smile. 'But you don't have to be. In fact, you could profit handsomely.'

Rakosi grunted. 'You keep making these veiled suggestions.'

'Very well . . . put simply, I can arrange to pay off the banks for you.'

'What are the terms of the loan?'

'No, Joe, not a loan . . .'

'What then?'

'Shall we call it an advance to be set off against future profits.'

Rakosi blinked. It sounded too good to be true. 'But we're talking about ten million dollars,' he said suspiciously. 'How are you going to swing that?'

Delacroix chose his words carefully. 'There are certain individuals in the Hungarian Government, Joe, men who hold the purse strings – very powerful men – who would like to help you.'

'Oh yeah,' said Rakosi, frowning. 'There's a saying – beware of Greeks bearing gifts. Why should they want to help me?'

'Shall we say that these individuals are interested in a certain opportunity that presents itself in the Far East.'

'Yeah, I can imagine – some nice little rip-off to line their private pockets.'

Delacroix shrugged. 'The West doesn't have a monopoly on corruption, Joe.'

'So they want me to be their front man, is that it?'

Delacroix nodded. 'Bureaucrats in Budapest don't enjoy the same freedom of movement as you, Joe.'

Rakosi glared out at the snow-shrouded landscape. 'Let me get this straight . . . I swing this deal for them – whatever it is – in the Far East and in return they pay off the banks for me. But the payment is only an advance against future profits. So what they're offering me is a short term solution . . . "we help you over the crisis, Joe, but in the long run it's still ten million out of your own pocket". Great!' Rakosi shook his head like an angry bull. 'From where I sit, Jean-Paul, that looks like a fat loss, not a handsome profit.'

'But it can be a profit, Joe.'

Rakosi snorted. 'How do you work that out?'

'Because the deal you're doing for them is directly linked to another deal, one that will benefit you personally.'

'What sort of deal?'

'I'm talking about arms, Joe . . . rifles, tanks, even jet aircraft.'

Rakosi raised his head, suddenly interested.

'Believe me, if you can swing it, this could be big.'

'How big?'

Delacroix smiled. 'The arms deal of the decade, my friend.'

Mike Keats was north of Maputo in the small coastal town of Beira when he received Rakosi's telex. It informed him that Simpson, the London manager, was flying out to take over the Mozambique contract. Mike was needed in Hong Kong. There was more urgent work for him to do.

Mike had hardly been able to clear away the rubble of the sabotage and he was already being pulled off the project. But at the end of the day Mike was a minority shareholder in the companies. Joe Rakosi was the boss and it was difficult to ignore a telex which ended with the words –

TRUST ME MIKE, THIS IS A MATTER
OF CRUCIAL IMPORTANCE. YOU'RE
THE MAN FOR THE JOB. JOE.

It took more than forty-eight hours to return, slogging along Mozambique's dirt roads past the rusted hulks of vehicles which had hit landmines, crossing the border into South Africa and then catching a flight from Johannesburg across the full breadth of the Indian Ocean to Hong Kong.

Mike had spent so little time in his apartment over the past few months that when he got back it felt like a stranger's place, musty and still.

Rakosi telephoned early in the evening arranging to meet the next morning for a cruise on his new yacht.

'Thanks for coming back so promptly,' he said. 'Tomorrow we'll be able to talk. I knew you wouldn't let me down, Mike. You're a good friend.'

The following morning they met at the Aberdeen Marina Club. Joe Rakosi was in fine spirits, not the angry, cornered individual who had surveyed the burnt-out wreckage of the Maputo docks. They had coffee on the patio while they waited for Rakosi's latest girl friend, a Cathay Pacific air hostess called Betty Wu.

'What happened to Tina?' Mike asked.

'Ancient history, Mike.'

'Pity.'

'No rhyme, no reason, just fell by the way.' Rakosi gave a locker room chuckle. 'Coudn't take the pace.'

'I liked her,' said Mike. 'Tina had a lot of style.'

Rakosi muttered, 'Yeah, well there's plenty more where she came from.'

Betty Wu, the air hostess, arrived as they finished talking. She was short and curvaceous, breasts bouncing under her tee shirt. Rakosi got up, kissing her and placing a protective arm around her shoulders as if to say: this is my new woman, forget the old one.

The *Good Hope* was waiting at the jetty; a sixty-foot-long cabin cruiser, sleek and white, every inch a millionaire's plaything. Champagne was served by one of the crew as they stepped aboard.

Mike stood at the wheel next to the Chinese captain as the *Good Hope* pulled away from the Marina. Slowly, its huge engines purring, it wound its way through the harbour past endless rows of green-hulled fishing junks moored together; laundry hanging from their rigging, piebald dogs asleep in the bows. There must have been a thousand vessels of every shape and size crowded into that harbour . . . sooty little sampans, pleasure junks, flatboats, water taxis with old women at the rudder, brine-encrusted barges piled high with dried fish. Along the shoreline, in the shadow of the housing tenements, there were painters and masons and carpenters at work. Fishermen in vests sat under sailcloth awnings playing mahjong. This was the Hong Kong that Mike loved, a chaos of colour and smells that he had experienced nowhere else in the world.

They cruised past the five huge chimneys of the Ap Lei Chau power station. Then they hit the open water, heading east past Repulse Bay. The intention was to do a circumnavigation of Hong Kong Island itself and then head for Lamma for a long, lazy seafood lunch at one of the scruffy Chinese establishments on the quay there; prawns in chilli sauce, green crabs and squid, some of the best food in Hong Kong.

It was a soft, grey day with the sky a winter lilac and Mike went forward to the bow, enjoying the spray against his cheeks. But it wasn't long before he heard Rakosi calling to him. Rakosi was sitting in the master cabin sipping champagne. 'Help yourself,' he said, pointing to a magnum of Dom Perignon in a silver ice bucket. But Mike preferred coffee at this time of day.

Rakosi relaxed in a leather armchair. 'It's time to talk, Mike, to explain why I brought you back. So where do I begin? Yeah, Maputo. Where else? It's a balls-up, Mike, total and absolute . . .' He went on to spell out the consequences. 'So you see, nobody else is liable, just us – and we're into the banks for ten million.'

'When is it due?'

'Yesterday.'

'Can you pay?'

'Sure. I can jump off the top of tall buildings too.'

155

'But there's got to be a way,' said Mike.

'There is one, yeah, just one. The Hungarians have offered me a rescue package. Delacroix says they'll pay off the banks.'

Mike was surprised. 'The full ten million? If they don't admit liability, how do they explain that?'

'An advance against future commissions, that's what they're going to call it.' Rakosi gave a cynical grin. 'Made in the interests of the state.'

'And what do they want in return?'

Rakosi got up from his chair, pouring himself more champagne. 'To be totally frank with you, Mike, Delacroix tells me that the offer is the brainchild of two top men, one of them a Government Minister. And what they want in return is . . . well, personal rewards.'

Mike sighed. 'How much? And which Swiss bank?'

Rakosi laughed. 'But that's the crazy part about it, Mike. They're not after money. You won't believe this but they're talking about treasure – sunken treasure.'

Mike laughed too, not because it was funny but because the whole idea was so bizarre. 'Treasure? You mean Spanish galleons, pieces of eight, that kind of thing?'

'Hang on a second,' said Rakosi, 'it's not as ludicrous as it first appears. In fact, Mike, it could be a very simple way out for us.'

'Okay,' said Mike sceptically. 'Explain it.'

'We've got to go back nearly twenty years, to the days of the Vietnam War,' said Rakosi, sipping his champagne. 'It's when the Americans were bombing the North. Operation Rolling Thunder, they called it. Appropriate too. Factories were flattened, docks, bridges . . . you name it. Can you imagine what it cost to keep North Vietnam on a war footing? The country was so desperate for hard currency that it resorted to any means available – and that included drugs for gold. Bullion and white powder, Mike, two of the staples of world trade. Chinese drug traders would sail junks to North Vietnam loaded with gold and collect opium in return.'

Mike could see where it was leading. 'One of the junks went down loaded with gold bullion, is that it?'

'The North Vietnamese sank it by mistake in a storm. The wreck is lying just off the coast in shallow waters.'

'But how do the Hungarians know about this?'

'According to Delacroix, one of his two men in Budapest was in North Vietnam at the time. All the commie countries were giving aid and sending specialists. He was a financial expert . . . rendering assistance with certain clandestine operations.'

'Drugs for bullion, you mean?'

'Yeah, he and a young North Vietnamese officer.'

But Mike was profoundly suspicious. 'Why haven't they raised the gold years ago? Why wait until now?'

'Because at the time they were too junior, Mike. How could they organise it without giving the game away? But over the years – along with their paunches and varicose veins – they've climbed the ladder. The Hungarian is a Minister now and the North Vietnamese officer is some big shot, a general or whatever.'

'But why do they need us to raise the bullion for them?'

'Because they can't appear to be directly involved,' said Rakosi. 'Otherwise questions are going to be asked. We're their cover, Mike. The junk was neutral, remember, from British Hong Kong. The North Vietnamese sank it in error. Morally, they can't claim cargo they sent to the bottom. So all we need is a few documents of convenience – some old company papers and registration certificates – to show that we have some claim to the cargo and we can go ahead quite openly and salvage it.'

Mike gave Rakosi a dark, disbelieving look. 'So we're going to start forging documents now?'

'Nobody is going to forge anything, Mike. Plenty of junks were sailing to North Vietnam at the time, plenty went down. All we've got to do is acquire the papers to one of them and put them before the North Vietnamese authorities.'

'I don't like it,' said Mike. 'It's corrupt and it's dangerous.'

'But Delacroix has assured me there'll be no problems. You'll have your visas, you'll have papers authorising you to dive.'

'No,' said Mike, angrily. 'There's got to be an easier way out of our troubles.'

'But we get fifteen per cent of the gold to cover our costs and there's got to be nearly a tonne of the stuff down there. For God's sake, Mike, it's a fortune!' There was an edge of desperation creeping into Rakosi's voice. 'But that's not the extent of it, Mike. That's only the beginning – '

Mike turned towards him. 'What are you getting at?'

'If we help them, Mike, they'll help us.'

'But they're already helping us – that's what you've been telling me – with advances against future commissions.'

'That's just bailing us out of trouble. But they're prepared to go further than that . . . to help us make money – big money.'

'How?'

Rakosi smiled, knowing that he had captured Mike's attention. He drained his champagne glass. 'You've been in the arms business long enough to know that the hard part is not getting the customers, Mike. Once you've got your lines of communication, that's easy. Getting the stock to sell – that's the hard part. Stocks come from the aftermath of wars. Each new conflict creates a new surplus. That's where we get seventy per cent of the stuff to sell.'

Mike said nothing. He didn't like the drift of the conversation.

'But there's one exception to the rule, Mike, one lot of surplus that never came onto the market, one huge, puzzling enigma. You know what it is?'

Mike nodded. 'What happened to the American weapons left behind in South Vietnam.'

Rakosi grinned, his eyes suddenly alight. 'Eight hundred thousand M16 rifles, a hundred self-propelled guns worth a million dollars each, five hundred tanks. Even seventy-three Northrop Tiger Fighters still packed in their crates. And that's just what the Pentagon *admits* was left behind.' Rakosi began to laugh, a low, throaty chuckle filled with avaricious expectation. 'But none of it has come onto the international market, Mike, not so much as a firing pin . . .'

Mike had been listening intently to every word and, although his face was hard set, the effect on him had been obvious – surprise mingled with disbelief. 'What are you trying to say, Joe, that after all these years – out of the blue – the Vietnamese are going to give you the chance to sell the American arms for them?'

Rakosi's expression was one of triumph. 'Yes, Mike, that's exactly what I'm saying.'

'I'm sorry, I just don't believe it.'

'Why not? They've got the weapons, so why not sell them? Vietnam is creeping back into the twentieth century again. It needs the cash, Mike. And if it's going to sell, why shouldn't we be the buyers? That's the deal – we raise the gold for them and they swing the arms deal our way. We scratch their backs and they scratch ours.'

Mike let out an angry, frustrated sigh. 'And you want me in Vietnam to check out the weapons and negotiate prices.'

'You're the best man for the job, Mike.'

'I don't want it, Joe. I'm not interested.'

But Rakosi was anticipating him. 'I'm not asking you to sell them, Mike. I know how you feel about that. Go there and make an assessment, that's all. Report back to me . . . what's worth buying, what's not, what are the prices they're asking.'

Mike shook his head. 'Why me, Joe? Go hire some ex-general in California, some weapons buff. He'll do the job just as well.'

Rakosi threw up his arms. 'Please, Mike – think about it for a second. This is a delicate matter, a question of trust. They're prepared to deal with you and me because we're part of the overall picture – Hungary, Mozambique, the gold bullion, the weapons – they all mesh together. But they're not going to deal with out-siders, not at this early stage. Surely you can understand that? This Vietnamese general is having to tread pretty carefully as it is. How do you think he'll react if we blow in with some gungho three-star general from San Diego?'

'You know how I feel about this, Joe. I've made myself clear.'

'But it has to be you, Mike, there's nobody else.'

Mike looked at him. 'Then it's just too bad,' he said and, without a further word, left the cabin to go up on deck.

But Joe Rakosi followed him. 'I swear to God, Mike, this is the last time I'll get you involved.'

'Don't you understand, Joe? I'm sick of it all.'

Rakosi looked at him in amazement. 'What's the matter with you. Mike? There's millions in this, millions for the both of us. We could be two of the richest men in the world!'

And that's when Mike's temper snapped. 'Money! God, it's like a drug with you, Joe, a craving that makes you blind to everything else. I don't want a fancy boat like this. I don't want to fly around the world buying and selling people's lives. For chrissake, don't you know me well enough by now?' Mike stormed to the bow of the vessel and stood there, his knuckles white as he clutched the railings, his black hair wind-tossed around his face.

The *Good Hope* slowed in the water as it approached the old fishing jetty of Lamma Island. Mike could see the sea-food restaurants along the waterfront; gaudily advertised, rough and ready under their corrugated iron awnings.

Mike let his temper subside. In his opinion, the Vietnam deal stank. But if it was Rakosi's only lifeline, the only way of extricating himself from the crushing losses in Mozambique, then it was his only lifeline too. Because if Rakosi sank, Mike sank with him.

Joe Rakosi came up and stood next to him at the bow. He gave a hesitant smile. 'I'm sorry, Mike, I know I come on too hard sometimes. But this Vietnam venture could just be the turning point of our lives. You're Deputy Chairman of the Group and you've got to realise that gives you responsibilities. The Hungarians are prepared to bail us out but we've got to play ball. We've got to raise that gold for them. If we don't . . .' He shrugged. 'Well . . . it's as good as committing commercial suicide.'

'And the weapons?'

Rakosi kept very calm. 'You're going to be there, Mike, you're going to be on the spot. You're going to have a chance to inspect several billion dollars' worth of armaments, perhaps the biggest stockpile in the world. It's the opportunity of a lifetime. And I know you, Mike, you've got the patience, you've got the diplomatic skills to pull it off.'

Mike said nothing. He was caught in two minds, undecided.

Then in a low, flat voice, Rakosi said, 'I think you have to appreciate something else too, Mike. Because, you see, this Vietnam project goes further than just the two of us.'

'What's that supposed to mean?' asked Mike suspiciously.

'It means that another party has a keen interest in you making an assessment of those weapons.'

'Which other party?' asked Mike with blunt suspicion.

Rakosi stared out across the green water. 'The CIA.'

Mike swung on him. 'How in the hell did the CIA get involved in this?'

Rakosi shrugged. 'We've used them to supply the Afghan guerrillas with missiles, Mike. You've been up on the border with two of their agents. This Vietnam project relates to American arms, American interests.'

'So you went ahead and reported to them?'

'I thought it was essential they knew.'

'And what did the CIA say?'

'You're the representative of Trident Enterprises, Mike. You're the one who should go.'

'Well, to hell with them.'

Rakosi said nothing for a time but, as the *Good Hope*

came in close to the jetty, he said in a low voice, 'The CIA have sent an agent to discuss matters with you, Mike. There are certain conditions, you see . . . a trade-off.'

Mike stared at him under furrowed eyebrows. 'What kind of trade-off?'

'I think it's best if you speak to the agent himself.' Rakosi pointed to the jetty. 'He's waiting for us there now.'

Mike saw him immediately, standing by the concrete steps; the unmistakable, grey-haired figure – short and chunky – of Chuck Baldwin.

The *Good Hope* moored alongside the jetty and Chuck raised a hand in greeting. But he looked uneasy.

Mike jumped down from the launch and went across to him. 'What in the hell is going on here, Chuck?'

Deep embarrassment showed on Chuck Baldwin's amiable features. 'I had nothing to do with this. I've been pulled in to speak to you because we're friends, that's all. But you've got to understand, Mike, this Vietnam thing could be important to us, too damn important to ignore.'

James Dexter, Chief of Operations, Far East Sector, sat in his office on the seventh floor of CIA Headquarters methodically refilling his pipe.

He was not a man much given to emotion. As dry as a well mixed martini, that's how he saw himself. But there were times when a quiet sense of achievement made the job worthwhile and he had to admit that he was pleased with the news.

For years now the CIA h d been trying to discover just how many US weapons th Vietnamese still held. What condition were they in? What kind of spares did the

Vietnamese possess to service them? Just how big was the stockpile? Some estimates reckoned they still held enough to outfit an army – a revolutionary army perhaps in some other part of the world. The Libyans exported their arms to terror groups. The Vietnamese could do the same.

The art of intelligence was the art of gathering strategic information and now he had a man going openly into Vietnam to obtain information the Agency had been denied for more than a decade.

It seemed strange that Keats, an arms dealer, should have moral scruples about obtaining the information. Apart from anything else, if the arms – or even a small percentage of them – were genuinely for sale, he stood to make a great deal of money. But whatever the situation, the intelligence potential was too important to let one man's qualms dictate the day.

Keats was known to have a great emotional attachment to the cause of the Afghan Resistance, especially to Farouq Mohammadi's faction. So the trade-off presented to him couldn't have been simpler. If he went to Vietnam, Mohammadi would be guaranteed a regular supply of ground-to-air missiles. If he refused, the supply would cease.

It was a bluff. But Baldwin, who had conveyed the terms of the trade-off, wasn't aware of that. Baldwin had been in the Agency long enough to know that factions like Mohammadi's had been sacrificed in the past and could be sacrificed again. So he had been more than convincing.

It was a pity of course that Keats required such active persuasion. Blackmail, in whatever guise, was distasteful. But then it was Keats' own partner, Rakosi – a crude individual with venal motives – who had suggested it would be the only way to convince him. And Rakosi had been right.

Siberian winds moaned through the hills, gusting the snow like dust. There was not a person to be seen out there, not a living thing. A raw day, achingly cold, was descending into a dark, mournful night.

Sitting in the back seat of the Chaika limousine as it drove along the deserted road, Mikhail Kazakov was a frightened man. It was such an obvious connection and he had missed it. How could he have been so careless, so stupid? Now everything was teetering on the brink of disaster. He wondered what Kirilenko would say. Would he abandon it or proceed and take the risks?

Kazakov huddled deeper into his army greatcoat. He had never felt so cold; frozen to the marrow. Why didn't Kirilenko remain in his Moscow apartment? Why did he insist on coming out here every chance he got, into this frozen wasteland? Was he in quarantine from the world or keeping the world in quarantine from himself?

The car reached the snow-shrouded ruins of the old orthodox church and turned off the road, up into the inky black expanse of the forest. When they came to the clearing there was smoke curling from the chimney of the dacha. The carcasses of two wolves, skinned and gutted, their blood turned to a crimson frost, hung from meat hooks on the veranda.

Kazakov climbed from the car, hurried to the door and hammered on it with a gloved fist. Inside he could hear Gagarin set up a thunderous barking. He heard Kirilenko calming the beast and then his footsteps creaking on the boards. The door was opened and Kazakov barged in. 'I've got bad news.'

'Calm down and then tell me,' said Kirilenko. 'Don't panic. You know I despise panic.'

Kazakov slumped into a chair by the log fire. His voice was high strung with nerves. 'Just as you suggested, I carried out an in-depth check on the divers Keats has hired for Vietnam. But there's one couple, a husband and wife, Australians called Seager . . .'

Kirilenko handed him a glass of vodka. 'What about them?'

'The records show they flew in to the Caribbean island of Grenada just two days before the Americans invaded in 1983. They were seen diving in the harbour area and questioned. They were obviously checking for underwater obstacles, clearing the way for the invading forces.'

Kirilenko relaxed back in his chair, his eyes half-hooded. 'And where does that lead you, Misha?'

'They work for one of the American security agencies – at least on a part-time basis – probably the CIA.'

Kirilenko nodded. He appeared to be totally unconcerned.

'But don't you see,' said Kazakov, 'that means the diving team searching for the junk will be infiltrated by the CIA.'

Kirilenko smiled. 'Of course it will.'

Kazakov was amazed. 'And doesn't that worry you?'

'Why should it? They're on a sightseeing trip, that's all. A chance to look and see and report back. The story we fed Rakosi is true. There were junks bringing gold bullion to North Vietnam to trade for opium. And there is evidence that some of them went down. Don't be so concerned, Misha. Nobody knows what we're really seeking, not even the CIA.'

Kazakov was bewildered by Kirilenko's lack of foresight. 'I'm not suggesting they know now but when the divers find the junk, what happens then? Then they've got to know!'

'They'll find containers, Misha, watertight containers encrusted with barnacles. There'll be no indication what they contain. Why shouldn't it be gold bullion? The divers will raise them for us and then their job will be done.'

But Kazakov wasn't convinced. 'I'm sorry, Uncle, I think it's an insane risk.'

The General got up from his chair, rubbing his back, and stood in front of the fireplace. 'When a man has to lift a weight that's impossibly heavy, Misha, how does he do it? There is only one way. He uses levers . . . ropes and pulley and poles. And we are doing the same thing – except our levers are people. There are two of us, just you and I. How else can we proceed with this great and burdensome scheme unless we use people?'

'I understand that, Uncle. But once the CIA are involved – '

'How can the CIA touch us? Assuming for a moment that they discover the true contents of the cargo – which they will not – you and I are three or four times removed from any risk. Consider it, Misha . . . it was the Americans who first conceived of Phoenix. So if it comes out into the open, it's an American problem, not ours – more especially if they've had CIA divers looking for it. The whole scheme will look like a CIA plan, not ours at all. Every step of the way, somehow, the Americans will be involved, Misha, even into Afghanistan itself. And at any time, if the true nature of the cargo is discovered, it will be the Americans who move heaven and earth to bury it again.'

For the first time Kazakov smiled uncertainly, beginning to comprehend.

'Don't you see, that's the pure beauty of it, Misha. If there's any error on our part, if anything is discovered, it will be the Americans who have to hide it for us. Either that or take the blame.'

'Yes, I see now.' Kazakov laughed, drunk with relief. 'Yes, I see!'

Kirilenko walked to a side table where his pack of cigarettes lay. He lit one, inhaling deeply. Then he said in a low voice, 'I know you have nightmares, Misha, dreaming of those furnace doors opening in the GRU crematorium, that instant of unspeakable agony as you feel your flesh melting. And certainly, if we are caught, that's what we can expect. Because we are traitors, Misha, you and I, never forget that, traitors to our own kind. And it matters not one blink of an eyelid that they are greater traitors . . . traitors to the ideals of world communism, traitors to Mother Russia itself. Yes of course we run a risk, a very grave risk. But the more we use others, the less we do ourselves, the greater our protection.'

Kazakov remained silent. The reminder of how vulnerable they were terrified him. Kirilenko was right. The image of those furnace doors clanking open haunted his dreams.

Kirilenko put another log on the fire. Then, walking in that awkward fashion of his, he returned to his chair. Outside, the wind moaned eerily around the corners of the dacha.

'I was in Vietnam when I first learnt of the Phoenix Pact. I still remember the day when we discovered the American agent, Tang, lying like a drowned rat on the shore and began to interrogate him. Oh I despised him then and everybody who had conspired with him. They were animals, I thought. How could men contemplate such a thing? No doubt our captors will think the same of us too if we are ever caught. But, as the years passed, I came to understand, Misha, even to sympathise . . .'

He fell silent for a time, staring into the fire. Gagarin came across and lay at his feet. Kirilenko smoked his cigarette, deep in thought. 'I think about them a great deal these days, Misha . . . the men of the Phoenix Pact. I can imagine them gathering together in Saigon or Manila or Hong Kong, whatever place it was. It would have been hot and humid with the sound of insects at night, a world away from this snow. But they had watched their dreams evaporate, just as we do, Misha, and they agreed to that one final desperate plan, just as we have done. They were a secret brotherhood, driven on by an impossible patriotism, Misha, just as you and I are driven. Because, you see, we have all become brothers in that same pact. We are their mirror and they are ours. That's the perfect symmetry of it. Vietnam is Afghanistan. The Ho Chi Minh Trail is the Hindu Kush.'

Kirilenko puffed at his cigarette, letting the ash fall down the front of his woollen jacket. 'The Phoenix, Misha, such a perfect symbol . . . out of the ashes of defeat we strive to change history and – American or Russian, it doesn't matter who – that mythical bird shelters us all under her wings.' He laughed very quietly, as if indulging in a private joke. And then he turned to Kazakov and said with a strange kind of affection, 'Destiny, Misha . . . it always comes on wings of fire.'

THREE

Vietnam

Nguyen Thanh Xuan had always known this day would come, a day when the debt was finally called to account.

As the chauffeur-driven Skoda, a gift from the USSR, rattled its way along the dirt road, he glanced at his old colleague seated next to him in the back of the car. He had admired Grigori Kirilenko as a man and loved him as a brother for the best part of twenty years and never once in all that time had he been given cause to doubt him – until now.

Who was right, who was wrong? Were his own doubts a sign of weakness or proof of a sanity which Kirilenko, in his obsession, had thrown to the wind? Nguyen had made many hard decisions in his life. He had been just twelve when he had stepped over his first body, a French paratrooper lying in the dust of Dien Bien Phu and since then the course of his life had been marked out by bodies: South Vietnamese, American, Cambodian, Chinese. But he had never questioned the need for death or the price of killing before – not until now.

The Skoda came round a bend in the road and there was a roadblock ahead. Nguyen saw the small squad of soldiers hurriedly assembling into a ragged line. Word of his arrival had preceded him. A full general was almost unheard of in these backwaters of Nghe Tinh Province and the Director General of Political Affairs, a man just one step away from the thirteen-member Politburo, was a rare and awesome creature. The roadblock commander stepped forward and saluted. The boom was lifted and the Skoda drove on. It was less than a mile now to Con Cuong.

Nguyen stared out of the window. The end, they said, always justified the means. Even so, if the request had come from anybody else – anybody at all – he knew what his answer would have been. But Kirilenko was not 'anybody else'. Grigori Kirilenko held a special place in his heart, very special indeed . . .

It had been a day much like today, he remembered. They had driven out of Hanoi together up into the Western hills. Except their destination then had been a little village resting among the terraced paddy fields. It was called Phu Qui where he had been born, the son of a peasant, and where his wife and two children lived. The date was indelible in his memory: 28th October, 1968; a crisp, clear day, he remembered, full of autumn promise.

His wife had prepared lunch outside their stone cottage under the banyan tree that he had climbed as a boy. There was pork on the table together with brown rice and beer. Being in Hanoi, Nguyen missed his children badly. They seemed to be growing so quickly and he was seeing so little of them. But they were safer in the country. He remembered that he had his daughter, Thi Lao, sitting on his lap while his son, Teo, all of eight years old and, in his absence the man of the house, sat solemnly by his side. He was proposing a toast in French, the one language he and Grigori shared. 'Here's to an early victory in the south and an end to the war,' he had said.

And it was at that moment that his son had looked up and said as simply as if he was pointing to an ox in a field, 'Look, Daddy, a Yankee aircraft crashing.'

It was coming in low, skidding over the hills, an F-4 Phantom trailing brown smoke. It was obviously trying to reach the border, to get across into Laos before the pilot had to eject. He remembered shouting at both his children, 'Quick, get into the house. It's coming this way.' His wife had gathered Thi Lao into her arms while Teo, knowing the drill, had sprinted into the cottage to open the trapdoor to their small cellar.

Seeing that his children were safe, he and Grigori had grabbed their rifles, running for the high ground like amateur duck hunters, scrambling up the hill, firing wild bursts hoping to bring the bird down. That was why they didn't see the second jet.

It came in from the east, protecting its crippled buddy, swooping low over the paddies, and the first they knew of it was the cannon fire that exploded into the side of the hill. Instinctively he had thrown himself down the slope, crashing down through the undergrowth. He heard the deafening screech of its engines as the second Phantom swooped overhead . . . and then – so stupid – his ankle caught in the roots of a tree and he heard it snap like a twig. He lay for a moment filled with a sense of foolishness.

He never saw the bomb falling, never dreamt it could happen, not to such an insignificant village . . . and he was still sitting there when the napalm exploded.

He heard it first, the huge rumbling *whoosh* of energy being released and oxygen exhausted, sensed the blinding flash of flame and then felt the bursting wave of its heat. Staggering to his feet, hacking an opening in the undergrowth, he looked down the hill with disbelieving eyes.

Because it seemed as if the whole of Phu Qui was lost in a rolling ball of fire.

He tried to run then, filled with terror for Thi Lao and Teo, but his ankle gave under him and he fell. 'Grigori!' he shouted. 'Please, my children!'

Then he saw Kirilenko sprinting down the hill, bounding over rocks. Flames – a searing brilliant yellow – rolled like an avalanche over the roof of the cottage. But Kirilenko didn't flinch.

Having to crawl most of the way, sobbing with the effort, Nguyen propelled himself down the hill. And all the time he was praying to a God he had long forgotten: let them live, please God, let them live. But he could see it was hopeless. The cottage was engulfed in flames. The air inside must have been roasted. It was blistering his face even there on the hill.

But then, like an apparition, he saw Kirilenko come staggering out of the cottage. He was hurt badly. His legs were on fire. Smoke was swirling around him, but there in his arms he held little Thi Lao, protecting her from the flames with his body bent over her. And he staggered with her, half-running, until he knew she was safe and only then did he lay her down.

Stepping back, Nguyen saw him beating at the fire on his body. It was napalm, napalm that smoked and hissed and ate into his flesh. Nguyen remembered crying out, 'My friend, my friend!' But Kirilenko appeared to be in a trance. 'Teo is inside,' he said. And he turned back to face the conflagration. Nguyen tried to hold him, saying that he should go himself. But Kirilenko pushed him away. 'You'll never make it,' he said in an emotionless voice, 'not with that broken ankle.' And, like a wounded gladiator, still shrouded in smoke, Kirilenko lurched back into the cottage.

There was nothing Nguyen could do but wait there, cradling Thi Lao in his arms. He saw the roof of the cottage collapse. He saw great showers of sparks flying into the air. Trees were burning. Smoke was everywhere. And in the distance he could hear the terrified bellowing of oxen being burnt alive.

And then, like some giant, as tall as a tree, he saw Kirilenko emerge from the cottage. He held Teo over his shoulder with one arm while the other was around Nguyen's wife, dragging her with him. Kirilenko pulled them both clear. He laid them both down. Then, with blistered cheeks, he tried to smile . . .

Later the doctors said that the burning napalm had hit him full in the chest as he rushed into the cottage, adhering to his clothing and eating like acid through his skin. There were third-degree burns to his chest and stomach, to his groin and thighs. He was in great pain for many weeks but he bore it all with courage. Six months later, back in Russia, skin grafts lessened the hideousness of the scarring. But one injury could never be healed. Nobody knew about it, only the surgeons. Kirilenko kept it a close secret. But in Hanoi Nguyen had access to every file and that's how he learnt it from the doctors. As his friend – his brother – had carried his children to safety, the napalm had burnt so deeply into his groin that Grigori Kirilenko would never father children, never enjoy the natural fulfilment of sex again.

Later, when he learnt of the break-up of Kirilenko's marriage, although nothing was said, Nguyen knew what one of the root causes had to be. As the years passed and his friend grew more and more reclusive, spurning the company of women, he understood. Every step that Kirilenko took with that stiff, awkward gait was a reminder of the scar tissue and atrophied muscle beneath the clothing.

Thi Lao, the rose of Nguyen's life, was now a doctor, married with children of her own. Teo was advancing well in the army, a fine son of whom any father could be proud. Nguyen's wife was a dear and trusted companion.

Nguyen had always believed that there were certain debts that could never be repaid, debts of such abiding gratitude that a man would have to take them with him to the grave. But for this one debt at least a form of payment had been found and Kirilenko – to whom Nguyen had pledged his conscience – had come to collect.

Con Cuong, like a leper colony, lay torpidly on the floor of a deserted jungle valley near the Laotian border. It was not big, not by the standards of the 'bamboo gulag', that long bead of camps stretching the length of Vietnam. It held just a thousand inmates. But to those invisible bureaucrats in the Ministry of the Interior who managed the camps, Con Cuong was notorious because only the worst of the hardliners were kept there, those who owed a blood debt to the people, and none of them – no matter how passively they accepted the new order – would ever see freedom again.

There was a committee of senior officers waiting for them at the main gates. The camp commander made a speech saying how honoured Con Cuong was by the presence of General Nguyen and 'our Soviet comrade in socialist solidarity, General Kirilenko'. Lime juice was served to wash away the dust of the journey and then the camp commander escorted them towards his office.

They passed long lines of bamboo huts with earthen floors and roofs of palm leaves. There was the smell of defecation in the air, the buzz of flies. An old woman, her eyes white with cataracts, swept the dirt with a twig broom. But otherwise the camp appeared deserted.

'Your man has been held back from his working party,' said the camp commander.

'It is a pleasant day,' said Nguyen. 'We thought perhaps we would speak to him outside.'

'If that's what you would like. We have a garden which is tended by the inmates. Catholic priests mainly – they make the best gardeners.' The camp commander smirked but neither Kirilenko nor Nguyen smiled.

'We wish to speak to him alone,' said Nguyen. 'No guards please.'

The supercilious smile evaporated from the camp commander's face. 'Very well,' he answered, knowing that his integrity had been impeached. 'I'll take you to the garden direct.'

It was a small place, fenced in by a high bamboo wall and shaded by trees. There was an ornamental pond which Kirilenko noted had been built in the shape of a crucifix. Lotus leaves floated on its jade waters and next to it stood a wooden bench.

'If you would care to wait here,' said the camp commander curtly. Then he left.

After he had gone, Nguyen walked across to the pond and stood with his hands behind his back. He was a handsome man, strongly built but trim with a military bearing. His black hair, receding just a little now, was brushed back from his forehead and he wore a moustache. He was a quiet man by nature, not given to shouting orders; polite, enigmatic, decisive. He looked down into the pond, searching for the deep golden glimmer of carp. Then he spoke in French. 'I must ask you, Grigori, one last time, please reconsider this.'

Kirilenko admired the roses that grew in one corner. 'Have you ever known me to make a rash decision, Xuan?'

'I'm not saying that . . .'

Kirilenko hid his sarcasm in a smile. 'Not rash but wrong, is that it?'

'You're acting all alone Grigori, an outcast, a lone wolf, even in the GRU. And you're asking me to be the same.'

'Because others are blind, must we be blind too?'

'But consider the devastation, Grigori, think of the terrible implications.'

Kirilenko cast him a hawkish look. 'I've considered all the implications, Xuan . . . moral, political, tactical. I'm not some mad dog, you know that. We've worked closely together for years. I'm a rational man. But you must appreciate that what I'm doing is not just for Russia. Because, if we lose in Afghanistan, then the world revolution loses too. Then everything you and I have striven for – the messianic ideals of Marxist-Leninism – will be set back fifty years. And for what? It's madness – a ragged horde of feudal bandits who enslave their women in hoods. No, Xuan, there's simply no alternative.'

Nguyen turned, looking directly at Kirilenko. 'All I have to say is no.'

Kirilenko gazed back at him. 'That's true. But we are brothers, Xuan, you and I, we have always said that. Not biologically, not by some random division of genes, but in spirit. Deep down in your heart you know I'm right in what I must do.'

Nguyen turned his face back to the pond. He had been wracked by indecision since Kirilenko had first contacted him months earlier. Through the trees, coming across the parade ground, he could hear the shuffling clank of chains. The prisoner was being brought to them. Now was the moment. He couldn't prevaricate any longer. The decision had to be made. But what did he say? How did he bear the burden? He had always thought the cargo would be left on the sea bed, left there just as they had agreed all those years ago; unmarked, unspoken, an obscenity left to the silence of the tides. Surely there was some other way?

In his mind he could see the dead of the future, thousands upon thousands of them littering their mountain hamlets. The barren winds of the Hindu Kush were whispering through their bones. But then he saw his own children, he saw the orange flames rolling over Phu Qui, he saw Kirilenko with Thi Lao cradled in his arms. 'We are brothers, Xuan, you and I . . .'

The bamboo gate that led into the garden creaked open. 'Well,' asked Kirilenko. 'What is it to be, Xuan? What is your final decision?'

Nguyen stared up into the sky, hesitated a moment, breathed deeply, and then replied. 'Very well, Grigori, I will support you.'

Behind him, he could hear Kirilenko's sigh of relief. 'Thank you, Xuan.'

But he said nothing. The decision was made and now he was part of the subterfuge too. The Phoenix Pact envelops us all, he thought bitterly.

The clank-clank of the prisoner's chains were muffled as he walked onto the grass. They heard the voice of a guard. 'I will wait outside.' Then the bamboo door creaked shut.

There was silence, broken only by the soft drone of a bee among the roses. Then, as one, Nguyen and Kirilenko turned to face the prisoner.

Both of them had to contain their shock. The man before them looked ancient yet they knew he was in his early forties. He was so emaciated that the handcuffs on his wrists seemed like a great weight that bowed his shoulders. A diet of two tiny bowls of rice and sorghum a day had kept him alive these years but only just. Bare chested, with his ribs protruding like the bars of a cage, he was a pathetic sight. But even so, after the first shock of the transformation, the stubborn arrogance in the eyes was still discernible, that same air of unbowed cockiness he had displayed even under torture.

Kirilenko stepped towards him. 'Hello, Ricky,' he said. 'How are you?'

And Ricky Tang replied. 'So it's you . . . I had hoped you would be dead by now.'

Mike Keats had been blackmailed into the Vietnam project and he was an angry man, so angry that for a time he had considered turning his back on it all.

Chuck Baldwin was under pressure himself – 'caught between a rock and a hard place', as he expressed it – and just as disgusted as Mike. But, in the end, his common sense prevailed.

Mike was not being asked to do anything out of the ordinary; commit acts of sabotage or contact agents. He had the opportunity to see things in Vietnam that interested the CIA, it was as simple as that. When he returned he was going to write a report anyway, so all he had to do was walk from his offices across Garden Road and deliver a carbon copy to the US Consulate. The best thing was to get on with the job and get it over with. And that's exactly what he and Chuck Baldwin did.

Chuck had moved first by putting the diving team together, recruiting five Australians and one New Zealander. The leaders of the team were Podge and Patti Seager, both South Australians, who had flown up to Hong Kong for an early briefing.

Podge Seager who, as his name implied, was short and round, a happy-go-lucky individual, constantly smiling, had studied the charts. 'It's a big area,' he had commented. 'Isn't there some way we can narrow it down?'

Mike's information had been sketchy at that time. 'I'm told we'll have more exact bearings when we get there.'

'What sort of wreck are we looking for?' Patti had asked.

'A Chinese junk.'

'Wooden?'

'Mostly, yes.'

'Then it will have broken up within a few years,' Podge had said in his flat, South Australian drawl. 'Microscopic organisms will have eaten it away. With tidal action, the few metal parts will have been scattered over the sea bed. There might be no discernible wreck at all, just bits and pieces. That could make electronic position-fixing pretty hit and miss.'

But Patti, who stood nearly a head taller than her husband, blond and statuesque with a honey-brown Barrier Reef tan, had been more optimistic. 'An ocean-going junk has to have engines, big ones too. They won't have shifted and nor will the gold.'

Podge Seager had smiled. 'I still say it's not going to be easy.' Then he had turned to Mike. 'Unless you want to turn this into a lifetime's work, Mr Keats, we're going to need better bearings.'

'We'll just have to wait and see,' Mike had replied.

Podge Seager had laughed. 'Yeah, well, we should have time enough. It'll probably take ten years to get our visas through!'

But he was wrong. Just as Joe Rakosi had said, the

visas came through within a couple of weeks, almost suspiciously fast.

Contracts were signed, equipment purchased. An air cargo company was hired to ferry the divers and their gear. Then, as Chuck Baldwin put it, it was time to get the show on the road.

The old '55' series DC-8 that took off from Kai Tak carried a load of twenty-five tonnes and seven passengers. Mike was amazed at the bulk of it all . . . the largest items were two six-metre inflatable boats with rigid fibreglass hulls, each fitted with twin 50 hp outboard motors. But around them were stashed generators, compressors, sonar equipment, a full decompression chamber, boxes of rations, tents, tables, a gas-powered refrigerator, wetsuits, masks, diving cylinders and rescue gear.

It was a short journey to Hanoi, less than an hour and a half, and they touched down at noon. The date was 15th February. In Afghanistan blizzards gripped the high passes of the Hindu Kush. But in Vietnam it was 27 degrees Celsius, a fine hot day under a china-blue sky.

Mikhail Kazakov stood in the shadow of a hangar watching the DC-8 being unloaded. Now that events were moving faster, reaching their first critical stage, he was finding it hard to keep his nerve.

But Kirilenko, who stood next to him, treated it all with an irrational calm.

Kazakov knew he should keep his mouth shut. Every time he spoke it revealed his nervousness. But he couldn't help himself. 'Do you really think Tang can be of any use to us after all these years? How can he possibly remember where the junk went down? There was a typhoon that day. And he was badly wounded you say.'

'Despite his wounds, it took us forty-eight hours to capture him,' said Kirilenko in a toneless voice. 'Never underestimate him, Misha. Tang was – and remains – a man of great tenacity.'

'But how could anybody remember?'

'Because he took bearings, Misha. Transits, they call them . . . lines through permanent landmarks, crossing at the spot where the junk went down. When Nguyen and I interrogated him, right at the end, when he was under the influence of drugs, he told us . . . a line of seventy degrees through the hill he called Stallion, a line of one hundred and twenty degrees through the outcrop he called Phallus. It's all in the transcripts that I kept and took back to Russia.'

'Then why do you need Tang at all?'

Kirilenko explained patiently, as he had explained before. 'Because we never tried to pinpoint the wreck, Misha. The few of us who knew the truth at that time made a decision that it should be forgotten. "Let it be washed away on the tides" . . . those were Nguyen's own words. So you see, we never went down to the estuary, we never discovered what hill he called Stallion, which rocks he named Phallus.'

'But now he has agreed to point them out?'

'After some persuasion, yes.'

'Torture, you mean?'

'Some men demand it, Misha, almost as a penance for what they will admit. He's down at the coast now with Nguyen. Don't worry, Misha, we'll raise the Phoenix soon enough.'

Kazakov watched a squad of Vietnamese troops march past the hangar. He felt very vulnerable here in Hanoi. 'I can't help it,' he said, 'but I keep asking myself: who else knows about the Phoenix?'

'Nobody knows – just the four of us. Just you and I, Nguyen and Tang.'

'But there must have been others at the time?'

'Of course there were others,' said Kirilenko irritably. 'But they are dead now, every last one of them. They were the ones who made the final decision, Misha . . . what lay at the bottom of that estuary was the work of a small group of madmen, they said. To let it be known that the war could be escalated in such a terrible way, to point the finger of blame, might place the Americans in an invidious position. That in itself could force an escalation. Nobody knew where it might lead or where it could end. So, you see, no papers were kept, no written record. The decision was made to wipe it from history. The Phoenix was an event which had never occurred.'

An official came across to inform Kirilenko that his plane was ready to depart. Picking up his briefcase, he and Kazakov walked out into the bright Asian sunlight towards the huge Antonov transport that would fly him back to Moscow.

'Tell me one thing,' said Kazakov. 'If the Phoenix was to be treated as an event which never occurred, why did you keep Tang alive? What was the point? Why not shoot him in the back of the head and shovel him into an unmarked grave?'

'Because spies make valuable bargaining counters, Misha.'

'Then why wasn't he exchanged?'

Kirilenko paused at the steps of the aircraft; a tall, stooped figure. 'Oh we tried, we tried several times. We thought we could do well with him. Overtures were made through the French Secret Service direct to Washington.'

'Then what happened to prevent it?'

'Something we had never considered, Misha . . . the Americans didn't want him. No, it went even further than that – they denied all knowledge of him.' Kirilenko gave a hawkish smile. 'Ironic isn't it, just as we resolved that the voyage of the Phoenix had never occurred, so they resolved that Tang had never existed.'

Mike drove alone that night, down to the pebbled cove where the two inflatable boats were moored. A sharp wind was blowing in with the tide and Podge Seager had suggested that he check they were properly secured. 'Bloody disastrous to lose them on our first night here,' he had said.

The shore line along the estuary was more rugged than they had expected with black basalt cliffs, steep ridges and ravine-lacerated jungle. So they had been forced to pitch camp on high ground nearly a mile from the sheltered inlet of the cove. The distance would make life inconvenient. But they had been able to hire a jeep at least – a rusting relic of the Vietnam War – to make the grinding journeys up and down each day.

Climbing from the jeep, Mike walked to the water's edge where the two boats swayed on the fast lapping tide. There was a full moon that night, pale as opal, seen one moment and then lost behind white clouds that scudded in from the sea. The wind rustled the trees. Wading into the water up to his knees, Mike checked the ropes that secured the two boats.

In some ways he was looking forward to the next two to three weeks with the diving team. Podge Seager and his divers were an amiable crowd who had promised to teach him enough about scuba diving and searching for wrecks to make him a professional himself by the time this was over.

With a practical sense of Aussie priorities, they had got the gas-powered refrigerator operating before anything else so that the beers would be ice cold and now they would be cracking the first cans of the night as they warmed the meat pies. Mike returned to the jeep. It had been a long, hard day and he was feeling worn out. Not as young as I used to be, he thought ruefully. A few cans of lager with Podge, Patti and the boys and he would hit the sack.

Clambering into the driving seat of the open jeep, he checked the time. It was eleven forty-five. He switched on the ignition. Fireflies floated in the headlights. He swung the jeep around in the tall feathered grass and headed back up the hill, rattling along the jungle-fringed track.

But if the next two to three weeks out in the sun, diving during the day and drinking beer at night, sounded pleasurable, what was to follow thereafter – the weapons side of his time in Vietnam – would be a long, hard grind.

He had received a written message earlier that evening from some Vietnamese general. The name at the foot of the note was indecipherable but no doubt he was Delacroix' and Rakosi's 'man on the take'. The note, in surprisingly good English, said that after the junk had been located and its cargo raised, the general would personally escort Mike on a tour of the armouries where the US weapons were stockpiled, a journey that would take them from Hanoi in the north as far south as the Mekong Delta. But one thing was clear – the gold first, raised and secured, and then the weapons after.

Mike could imagine what it would be like . . . dimly lit subterranean warehouses stacked with M16s, the stink of grease, guns under canvas, boxes and inventories and endless hours haggling over prices. How in the hell had he allowed himself to be cajoled into it? Despite the potential for vast profits and the interest of the CIA, he had no interest in the weapons deal at all. But then, with a bit of luck, he thought, the diving team might not be able to locate the bullion and the whole deal would probably self-destruct. That would solve his problems . . .

And in that way, Mike drove up the hill, half dreaming, lost in his thoughts, when suddenly – Christ!

All he caught was the glimpse of a figure before he slammed on the brakes, being thrown forward so violently that his chest smashed into the steering wheel. He looked up, his heart thudding. The figure of a man was caught in the glare of the headlights. He was standing there in the middle of the track only a couple of feet in front of the jeep. Stupid bastard, he could have killed him!

Mike expected the man to come forward, to shout, gesticulate, even run. But he didn't say a word, didn't move. He just stood there, glaring into the lights, frozen like some mesmerised animal. Mike blinked. Dear God, he was so thin. He looked more Chinese than Vietnamese and his head was shaven; the face of a living skull. But it was those eyes, those huge, haunting eyes . . .

Who was he? What did he want? Then he saw the drab grey tunic soaked in sweat, he saw the blood-smeared scratches on the man's face, the thorn cuts and lacerations. And instinctively he knew. He was a Vietnamese prisoner, an escapee.

Without a word, the man came around to the passenger's side of the jeep. He was breathing in short, shallow gasps. Mike could smell his sweat, smell the mortal desperation. And all the time his eyes were fixed on Mike, seeming to bore right through him. Mike had never seen a man so thin. He could almost hear the bones grating under his skin.

The man raised a stick-like arm to show that he was holding a weapon. It was a long, rusted machete. Then, in a rasping voice, he spoke. 'Are you part of that diving team?'

Mike couldn't believe it – it was English, a thick American accent! 'Yes, yes I am . . .' he stammered, totally amazed.

His answer galvanised the man. 'Okay, get moving.' And, suddenly all energy and quivering sinew, he scrambled into the front-passenger's seat. 'I knew your boats were at the cove. I saw you earlier, from a distance. I was trying to get down there, to leave a message in one of the boats, anything . . . just to warn you.' He pushed at Mike's arm. 'Put your foot on it! Hurry, we've got to get away from here!'

Bewildered, Mike shoved the gear shift into first. 'You speak English. Who are you?'

'Just get moving,' muttered the man. 'Get off this hill. Head north, away from the estuary.'

'This is my first day here. I don't know the tracks, I don't know which way . . .'

'Then find the goddam way!'

Mike was reeling – not from fear, he knew he could overpower the man if he had to – but from the sheer disbelieving shock of it all. 'Who are you?' he asked again. 'Why have you stopped me? How come you speak English?'

'My name is Tang, remember that – Ricky Tang. I might have a Chinese name, Chinese face, but I'm American. Don't let them tell you otherwise. Did you hear that? American!' Tang was staring ahead, eyes darting from one side of the track to the other. 'Are you diving for that junk in the bay?' he demanded.

'The junk? Yes, yes, we are . . .'

'And what are you meant to find?'

'Gold bullion, that's what we've been told.'

'Oh the motherfuckers,' he exclaimed. He stared at Mike, those huge black eyes exploring every reaction. Then he said, 'So you really don't know. You're not part of this thing.'

'Part of what thing?'

'Bullion? Shit! Is that what they've sold you? You haven't got the first idea!'

They reached a junction in the track roofed over with branches and tangled vines. Tang pointed to Mike's right. 'That way, yeah, that way – go north.'

Through the thick miasma of his shock, Mike was trying to grasp what Tang was saying. 'But if it's not bullion, what are we diving for? What's down there on the sea bed?'

Tang gave him a mad, emaciated glare. 'Shit, you really don't know, do you?'

'I keep telling you, we've been told it's bullion.'

'Bullion? Fuck you, man – it's doomsday, that's what it is. Doomsday!'

'Doomsday? What are you talking about?'

'I was on the junk when they sank it, that's what I'm talking about. I'm CIA, man, do you understand that? CIA! I'm a ghost from the Vietnam War.'

And suddenly all of Mike's pent-up suspicions, the profound doubts he had been harbouring about this whole Vietnam project, found their voice. 'What were you carrying?' he asked, determined now that he had to know. 'What was the junk's cargo?'

Sweat was pouring down Tang's skeletal face. 'Oh Jesus, man, how do I explain this thing? How do I explain it and let you sleep again? It's an instrument of war, that's all I can tell you. But like nothing you've ever known. It was during the war, terrible times, man, a kind of dream-world then. But you've got to get the word out. Do you hear me? You've got to warn people. Because if the commies use it . . . Blackmore, yes, he's the one. You've got to contact Earl Blackmore. Have you got that name?'

'Blackmore, yes, Earl Blackmore.'

Tang was nodding his head, muttering to himself. 'Yeah, yeah . . . he's the only one who'll do anything, the only one with the guts.'

'But who is he? Where do I get him?'

'He's CIA. He knows.'

'But what do I tell him?'

Tang was searching for the words . . .

'What do I tell him?' Mike was shouting. 'What do I tell Blackmore?'

'Tell him this, just this,' said Tang. 'Tell him they're trying to raise the Phoenix.'

'The phoenix, the bird?'

'Yeah the bird, man, the bird!'

'But who is trying to raise it?'

'The Vietnamese, the Russians – I don't know. They're the same men who interrogated me back in '68. They know me but I've never known them, not their names. Shit, man, if you don't know, how should I? God knows why they want it. But just the fact they want it, man, that has to be enough.'

They reached a shallow, rock-strewn stream and bounced across it, axle-deep. A flock of white birds screeched out of the trees, blurring the moon.

Tang gripped Mike's arm, his fingers digging into the skin. 'You believe me, don't you? You've got to believe me, man. Every last word I'm telling you is the truth, I swear to God.'

Mike looked into his face. He saw the half-crazed look, the huge, terrified eyes. Tang was on the edge of insanity, staring death in the face. But yes, he believed him. He believed every word he said.

Jamming the machete down between his knees, Tang began frantically to pull a ring from his finger. 'Take this,' he said. 'I've had it all these years. Never know why they didn't take it off me in the beginning. But since then I've hidden it . . . down between my buttocks, under my tongue – all these years. Because it's proof, you see, the only tangible proof. Blackmore will recognise it. We were all given one. It shows the phoenix, man, the phoenix with a dragon in its claws.'

'Why the phoenix?'

'The Phoenix Pact. This nucleus of us, the group – '

'But who gave it to you? Where? When?' Mike didn't understand – couldn't understand – what Tang was saying but instinctively he knew had to keep firing questions. Later, when this nightmare was over, then he could try and piece it together.

Tang was clutching his head. 'When? It was '68, yeah, that was the year – 1968.' He shoved the ring down into Mike's shirt pocket. 'Don't lose it, man. Because that's the only proof.'

'But who gave it to you, who was he?'

'It was Chan Chi-Wai, he gave us the rings. Tell Blackmore that, he'll remember – '

'Who was Chan Chi-Wai?'

'Wo Shing Wo – '

'The Triad Society?' It was becoming more insane by the moment.

'Yeah, the Wo Shing Wo. He was a big boss, a white

paper fan, a red pole . . . Christ, I don't remember. But show Blackmore the ring – it's all the proof you need.'

The engine of the jeep was shrieking as Mike hauled it up a rocky incline. 'Come on, come on,' Tang was urging the vehicle beneath his breath. They reached the top of the rise and came over the ridge. And Tang was the first to see it –

'There's a roadblock ahead!'

Mike slammed his foot on the brake pedal. The jeep slewed then jerked to a sudden halt at the side of the track.

Lights came on at the roadblock, blinding searchlights that scorched into their faces and lit up the jungle. Voices were shouting.

Tang tumbled out of the jeep, the machete in his right hand. He scrambled a few feet, bent double like an animal, then he turned back to Mike. 'Tell them I kidnapped you. But if you say anything about the phoenix, if you say anything about the junk, they'll kill you. As God's my witness, man, they'll kill you.'

Then he was gone.

Mike sat slumped in the jeep, his hands shaking on the wheel. He was drenched in sweat. The jeep had stalled. He saw soldiers come running down the track, a dozen or more. He saw them crashing into the jungle, pursuing Tang.

But other soldiers surrounded the jeep and one of them grabbed him, hauling him from the vehicle. And they were all screaming at him in Vietnamese, a mad tirade of abuse. Mike put his hands above his head. 'I don't understand Vietnamese. I don't understand . . .' A rifle butt smashed into his back, sending him toppling to the ground. He covered his head. They began to kick him. Boots pounded into his ribs. They were all around him, kicking and spitting and he could hear them screaming in pidgin English. 'Yankee bastard! Pig! We shoot your filthy brains out!'

It was an officer who pulled them off him, the same officer who had ordered the assault.

Bleeding from a kick to his jaw, close to losing consciousness, Mike had to stand with an AK automatic jabbed in his belly as the jeep was ransacked. Then he was escorted to the roadblock and his own body was searched. They made him strip naked, tearing at the seams of his clothing, searching every pocket. They ran their hands down his body, prodding and grunting. Every last item he had in his possession . . . his wallet, passport, watch, the ring Tang had given him . . . they were all taken.

Mike asked for water but they ignored him. They made him squat, naked, at the side of the track and there he waited for nearly an hour until a lorry arrived. Only then did they let him dress.

It took half an hour to reach the village. The lorry pulled up in front of a low concrete blockhouse, some sort of police station or army post, and Mike was taken inside. A soldier pointed to a dark, dank corner and that's where he was made to squat again.

An hour passed, longer . . .

The waiting was a device, he knew it, no different from the beating and the humiliation of being kept naked. It was intended to shatter his confidence, soften him up for the interrogation that lay ahead. And Mike was frightened, there was no denying it. But all the time Tang's words kept ricocheting around his mind – the Phoenix Pact, the CIA, the doomsday weapon . . .

* * *

Out there in the night Ricky Tang could hear his pursuers barking to each other like hounds on the scent. But he could go no further. His starved body just wouldn't carry him. He slumped down by some rocks. This was as good a place as any, he thought. And, taking the machete, stolen from a farmer's hut after he had escaped, he wedged it by the grip into a cleft of rock, testing that it was firmly held.

There was no way he would be made to answer any more of their questions. No way he would be tortured again. No way he would be dragged back to Con Cuong. At long last he felt at peace. Everything was a void. There was no fear, no pain, no hope any more.

Okay, Englishman, he thought, whoever you are, sorry buddy but it's up to you now.

He looked at the point of the blade. This was the way Roman generals used to do it, he thought. The honourable way. And, with a final smile, Ricky Tang fell upon his sword.

It was two in the morning when Mike was eventually taken into the room. A man in uniform – mid-to late-fifties, trim, wearing a moustache, obviously high ranking – rose up from his chair behind the desk.

'Please take a seat, Mr Keats.' Nguyen Thanh Xuan introduced himself and then said politely, 'You will appreciate there are some questions I have to ask.'

Mike had decided that it was best to be aggressive from the outset, to attack rather than passively answer his questions. 'I was assaulted by your soldiers,' he said. 'I'm a British citizen. I want to contact my embassy in Hanoi immediately.'

'You were helping an escaped criminal, Mr Keats, a very dangerous man . . . mentally deranged.'

'He had a knife at my throat. What was I supposed to do?'

Nguyen gave a thin-lipped smile. 'What were you doing on the road that late at night?'

'I had driven down to the cove to check our diving boats, to make sure they were secure, that's all. I was on my way back to camp when he jumped out onto the track in front of me.'

'But why did you stop? Why didn't you drive on?'

'Because I would have run him over. What was I supposed to do? I didn't know he was an escaped criminal.'

Chinese-style tea was brought into the office and a porcelain cup placed in front of Mike.

'Didn't he tell you who he was?' asked Nguyen.

Mike gulped the tea, desperate for liquid. 'He didn't tell me anything, not about his identity.'

Nguyen's face was a mask of scepticism. 'Are you sure?'

'I've just told you.'

'He's a schizophrenic, Mr Keats, normally desperate to tell people about himself . . . a man full of wild obsessions.'

Mike poured more tea. 'He said nothing about himself.'

'Then what did he tell you?'

'Just to drive north, that's all.'

'What language did he use?'

'English.'

'Did you notice anything about his accent?'

'It sounded American.'

'Didn't you find that strange?'

Mike shrugged. 'The Americans were in Vietnam a long time. An English accent would have surprised me more.'

'But you must have been puzzled . . . a man jumping

out of the jungle at you like that, a man who spoke fluent English. Didn't you ask him any questions?'

'I had a machete at my throat . . .'

Nguyen gave a deferential smile. 'Then if you didn't ask him anything, what else did he tell you?'

'I want to speak to my embassy,' said Mike. 'I don't have to answer these questions.'

A cold shadow fell over Nguyen's face. 'You may be involved in criminal matters, Mr Keats. Remember, this is not England. There is no such nonsense in Vietnam as the right to silence. Crime is a serious matter with us, not a game. You will remain here as long as it takes to answer. Now let me put the question again and I suggest you answer. What else did he tell you?'

Mike looked him straight in the face. 'Nothing that I can remember . . . directions, demands for money, that's about it.'

'Did he say anything about that sunken junk you are searching for?'

Mike's pulse began to race. 'No.'

'Anything about weapons of war?'

Mike assumed an air of puzzlement. 'Weapons? Why?'

'As I said, Mr Keats, the man is subject to delusions. He lives in a fantasy world.'

'No, nothing about weapons.'

Nguyen paused a moment. 'Anything about a secret pact?'

Mike's mouth went dry. 'A secret pact?' He tried to smile. 'You're right, the man must be mad . . .'

'No mention of any bird, a mythical bird of some kind?'

'I've told you already, he gave me directions and made demands for money, that's it.'

'Nothing else? Nothing at all?'

196

'Nothing that I can remember.'

Nguyen took a small white cotton bag from a drawer of the desk. 'Do you own a ring, Mr Keats?'

'Yes,' said Mike with icy calm. 'A signet ring.'

'Is it engraved with any design?'

Desperately, Mike tried to remember back to what Tang had told him. But it had been such a confused rush of words. 'It shows a bird with a dragon in its claws . . .'

'What sort of bird?'

Mike hesitated. 'A phoenix.'

'Why would you have such an engraving, Mr Keats?'

Mike coughed, giving himself time to think. 'I used to be in the British Navy. The phoenix was our squadron emblem.'

Nguyen smiled. 'And what is the significance of the dragon in its claws?'

Mike smiled too but his mind was whirling. 'That goes way back to the Korean War where the squadron served. The dragon in the claws of the phoenix is Red China.'

'Not North Vietnam perhaps?'

'What are you trying to get at? If that's meant to be some kind of accusation . . .'

Nguyen opened the cotton bag. Mike's passport, watch, wallet were placed on the desk together with the keys to the jeep. And the ring was there too. Nguyen held the ring in his fingers. 'Is this it, Mr Keats?'

Mike took it from him, studying it for the very first time. The heraldic design had lost its sharp edges, worn down with the years, but he could see the phoenix clearly: a bird like an eagle with wings of fire. And beneath it, impaled in its claws, its mouth twisted open in defeat, hung the dragon.

Mike studied the band of the ring and the underside of it too. But there were no words, no initials, nothing else he would have to explain. 'Yes, this is it,' he said casually.

'Good,' said Nguyen. 'Put it on please.'

Mike felt the blood drain from his face. He had never worn a signet ring in his life. Would it fit? Which finger did he use? Fumbling with the ring, he put it on the little finger of his left hand and pushed it up, his hands clammy with sweat. But the ring wouldn't go over the finger joint. He pushed harder. Come on, damn you! But there was no way, just no way it would go.

Nguyen's face was a bland mask. 'It doesn't appear to fit, Mr Keats.'

Mike shrugged, as if it was a matter of no concern. 'That's why I don't wear it. Speak to those men of yours, the ones who beat me up. They'll tell you it was found in my pocket, not on my finger. I carry it as a good luck charm, that's all.'

'Come now, Mr Keats, why are we sparring like this? The ring was given to you by the convict, isn't that the case?'

'I've told you,' said Mike, knowing how feeble it all sounded. 'I've had it for years.'

'Then why didn't you have the ring enlarged so you can wear it?'

Mike feigned an easy grin but he knew that with every answer he was digging his grave another foot deeper. 'Never got round to it, I suppose. Typical bachelor, just not organised with that sort of thing.'

Nguyen nodded. 'Yes, I see.' But all he saw was the fact that Mike Keats was patently lying. The ring was Tang's, there was no other explanation. Somehow he had managed to keep it during all his years of imprisonment. And if he had given it to Keats, there could only be one reason.

Nguyen got up from his chair. 'Thank you, Mr Keats, you've been most helpful. I'm sorry about keeping you here so long. There may be a few more questions but we can deal with them at another time. You can have your things back and I will arrange for you to be driven to your camp.'

Mike took his wallet and passport. He strapped on his watch and, as confidently as possible, scooped up the ring, pushing it into his shirt pocket. But he felt sick inside. Nguyen had seen right through him. Nguyen knew that it was Tang's ring. He knew that Tang had told him about the Phoenix Pact.

As he followed Nguyen out of the office, Mike tried to look unconcerned. But it was impossible to control his rising terror. What in the hell was going to happen now?

Standing there in the blackness, Nguyen watched his three most trusted subordinates escort Mike Keats to the open jeep. They had been told that Keats was an American agent, a saboteur. They were simple men but fiercely loyal. America was the imperialist paper tiger so they knew what must be done. Nguyen regretted having to make the decision. But events had forced it upon him.

It still amazed him how Tang had escaped, a half-starved prisoner who could barely walk. His guards were at fault. They had become lax with him, ignoring the fact that, even after eighteen years, the man retained an iron will. When he had them hauled up, they protested that they didn't know how it could have happened. One second Tang was there, they said, and the next he was gone. It was impossible. The fools. Well, the impossible had happened and they would pay for it.

Tang must have known that he stood no chance of staying free. He had only one reason for escaping – to intercept somebody from the diving team to warn him of the junk's real cargo. And Keats, the one he had found, clearly believed everything Tang had told him. So what choice did he have in the matter? To leave Keats alive would be inviting disaster.

In any event, it was only bringing the inevitable forward. Keats would meet a tragic accident now rather than in three weeks' time as originally planned.

Sitting in the back of the open jeep as it jolted along the track, Mike was filled with confusion. One voice inside him – the rational voice – kept saying: 'Okay, so you're in trouble. But keep calm, you're being taken back to the camp, that's all. Nothing is going to happen, not tonight. Nguyen is an intelligent man, too damn intelligent. He's not going to murder you out of hand.'

But another voice – raw instinct – kept yelling at him: 'Every one of Nguyen's questions meshed in with Tang's story. So Tang had to be telling the truth. Remember Tang's last words: as God's my witness, they'll kill you. And if you're just being escorted back to camp, if it's all so innocent, why send three soldiers with you, each of them armed? There's only one reason – they are going to kill you.'

The jeep increased speed, driving past a turn-off that led up into the hills. Mike jerked his head around. He had only been along it once before but he recognised the rotted bamboo fencing. It was the track that led up to the camp. Why had they driven right past it? And why were they increasing speed?

Then suddenly he knew. Like a man punched hard in the solar plexus, Mike sucked for air. His instinct had been right. They were going to kill him.

He recognised the track now. It was leading down to the cove where the two inflatable boats were moored. His mind was racing. They wouldn't shoot him. They needed an accident they could explain away. But what kind? A crash? No, he thought, the jeep couldn't go fast enough, not along this track, not fast enough to turn over and kill anybody. But they were heading towards the cove, getting closer every second, and the boats were there, the sea – oh God, he thought, they're going to drown me!

Terror, like a cold venom, paralysed his nerves. He was being taken to his own execution. But he couldn't die passively like this, just sit here and let them kill him. He had to do something and he had to do it now. Once he was out of the jeep, with the three of them around him, he was as good as dead. He took a deep breath, gritting his teeth. Oh God, he prayed, please help me – and, with a scream of cornered rage, Mike suddenly swept out his right arm.

The soldier next to him barely had time to open his mouth before the hard edge of Mike's hand smashed into the bridge of his nose. Bone cracked, spraying blood. The man gasped in astonishment. But, before he could react, Mike had chopped down hard again, this time into the side of his neck, bruising deep into the artery. The man slumped to one side and Mike grabbed the Kalashnikov, hauling it out of his senseless hands.

But the soldier in the front seat was turning now, shouting at the driver to stop. Mike felt the jeep skid as the driver braked, throwing them all sideways. The soldier in the front seat had lost his balance but was screaming in rage, trying to grab Mike's arm. Mike tried to push him away but every movement seemed so slow, so clumsy. Oh God, he thought, I'm never going to make it. They're going to kill me here.

And with a despairing lunge, he jabbed the Kalashnikov into the soldier's face. He felt the point of the

barrel rip open the skin of the man's cheek, he felt it
bouncing off the bone. He saw the soldier hurl himself
back, howling in pain.

And then Mike jumped.

Crashing into the undergrowth, he dived forward as
the first bullets shredded the leaves around his head. He
was on his belly now, crawling, panting, squirming
around the trees.

They were firing from the track . . . short, staccato
bursts that threw up the dead mulch around him. He
could hear their shouts of anger. But thank God for the
night. Because they were blind, all of them blind. And
staggering to his feet, zig-zagging wildly, crashing
through the black undergrowth, Mike fled. He didn't
care about direction, he had no plan. All that mattered
was staying alive.

Nguyen received the news with dismay. First Tang, so
starved that he could barely walk, and now Keats. Two
escapes in almost as many hours, one disaster compounding another . . .

A platoon of troops was despatched by lorry to the
scene to help in the hunt while a second platoon waited to
be airlifted there by helicopter. Keats had to be found
and he had to be found fast. 'Don't let him get inland,'
he instructed his officers tersely. 'The coastline is more
open. Keep him pinned against the sea.'

There was no neutral border, no sanctuary. He was alone
out there and slowly, methodically, they were boxing
him in.

Mike was toiling up a ridge, using the Kalashnikov he
had seized from the guard as a club to beat his way through
the undergrowth, when he first heard the helicopter. He

dropped down under a wet, moss-covered tree, and watched it come in from the north. Troops were disgorged onto a dirt track five hundred yards inland and then it lifted into the air again, an Mi-14, big enough to carry twenty-eight men, a great ugly dragonfly that clattered off over the wind-swept hills.

Troops were pursuing him from the north, troops were deployed as a stop-line to the south . . . and now more were coming in from the west. They were pinning him against the coastline, content to hold him there until dawn. And then, Mike knew, when they possessed the advantage of daylight, they would sweep through the hills until they found him. Wiping the sweat from his eyes, he checked his watch. It was 4 am. There were just two more hours until dawn. Then what did he do?

Dispirited, Mike climbed to his feet. But so long as it remained dark he had the edge and somehow – somewhere out here – he had to find a way of using it. Hunched low so that his silhouette wouldn't be seen against the skyline, Mike crawled the last few feet to the top of the ridge and peered down the other side to the sea.

The waters of the Gulf of Tonkin spread out before him like a vast black mirror, as empty as eternity. Never in his life before had he felt so crushed by the odds.

But then, far below him, nestled on one side of a small bay, he saw the palm-thatched roofs of a village. He could see fishing boats too, rows of them with their sails furled, silent black wedges on the silver-sheened water.

Yes, a boat, of course . . . the sea – why hadn't he thought of it before? And he felt a sudden, elated surge of hope. The plan forming in his mind was risky, desperately so, but it offered him a chance at least, something more than the sweat-drenched inevitability of being brought to bay like some hunted animal here in the jungle.

Mike knew he had to contact Podge Seager or one of his diving team. They were his only hope, the only people who could help him. But he knew too that their camp site would be ringed with troops and so would the cove where the two inflatable boats were moored. But if he could just get down to one of those fishing boats, if he could steal a conical hat and fisherman's clothes, if somehow he could drift close to the diving team when they were out on the estuary . . . yes, that had to be it. There was no other feasible way.

Frantically, he tried to work it out in his mind. They couldn't hide him indefinitely but they could smuggle water and rations on board one of the inflatable boats. The boats had two outboard motors and rigid hulls. Yes, that was the way . . . with enough petrol, he could strike out at night, head for international waters and take his chances. It was a crazy scheme with one chance in a hundred of being successful. But one chance was better than none at all. And, summoning the last tatters of his courage, Mike began the slow, painful descent.

It took him a full thirty minutes to get down into the dense tangle of banana fronds and mango trees that fringed the village. He knew there would be dogs and that worried him most. Their sudden barking in the stillness of the night could awaken the entire village. But, as he skirted the huts to get close to where the fishing boats were moored, Mike was alarmed to see that the village was already awake.

Through the web of vegetation he noticed the yellow glow of lamps being carried. He heard a sharp order in Vietnamese and then the soft sobs of a woman. Oh no . . . there was a sick sensation in his gut. So the troops were already there. They had to be searching the place, waiting for him. Mike lay for a few moments trying to fight off the despair. But he had to press on, he was committed. And, keeping to the cover of the trees, he crawled around to the far side of the bay away from the village.

Tall coconut palms led down to a small, sandy beach. Mike fell to his belly and leopard-crawled the last few feet until he came to the very edge of the palms. Then he looked across the water.

At first he couldn't tell what was happening. He could see a group of people but they weren't soldiers. And some hope returned. But who were they? It looked as if they were being prodded and pushed down to the jetty. Some were carrying baggage, some had babes in their arms. But it was confused, difficult to see. Until slowly, in the dramatic chiaroscuro of black night, silver moon and lamp glow, the scene emerged . . .

A straggly line of men, women and children – twenty or more – was being led down to the jetty where they waited in a timid huddle. They were clearly strangers. Mike heard a dog growling at them and one young village lout ran forward to throw a stone. But nobody retaliated.

A vessel was moored at the jetty, bigger than the fishing skips but not by much. It was built of wood, an ugly, unpainted hulk lying low in the water. There was one mast but the only superstructure consisted of a makeshift canvas awning towards the stern under which Mike could make out the bulk of an engine.

There was a man on the vessel wearing the straw pith helmet that was standard head gear in Vietnam. He was taking baggage from the group and tossing it into the well of the boat, one item thrown haphazardly upon another.

205

A group of village youths brought white plastic drums
and dumped them on the jetty. There was some ill-
tempered haggling, some shouts and waving of arms.
Paper money was refused. Some other form of exchange
was handed over – Mike couldn't tell what – and then
the drums too were loaded aboard.

It was obvious that the ill-assorted group on the
jetty – the strangers – were preparing for a voyage. But
why would they be leaving in the small hours of the
morning like this? Mike watched as the first of them
stepped aboard; the old folk first, followed by the
women with children. The boat sank deeper in the water,
swaying from side to side. It was a wood-rotted river
craft, not a vessel meant for the open seas. And with all
that baggage on board it was made doubly precarious.

And then suddenly it all fitted together, clicked in like
the parts of a puzzle. They were refugees! Yes, of course,
that had to be it.

That's why they were departing at this unearthly hour.
That's why there had been haggling over drums of water.
That's why one of the village boys had thrown a stone at
them knowing they wouldn't – or couldn't – retaliate.
Because they were political pariahs now . . . ethnic
Chinese or bourgeois merchants, the comprador class,
people too sick to work in the paddies, half-castes and
deviants . . . people to be exploited for every last ounce
of wealth they possessed.

Yes, thought Mike excitedly, it all made sense. And if
they were refugees, that meant they had to be heading
out into the South China Sea, out into the international
shipping lanes, to Malaysia, the Philippines or even
Hong Kong. It was a golden opportunity. He would
never get another chance like this again. If he could just
get onto that boat. But how? And he knew there was only

one way; no subterfuge, no scheme, he had to risk everything – he had to get into that water and swim.

The refugees were almost all aboard. They would be casting off any second. Hurriedly, Mike looped the sling of the AK over his head so that the rifle lay across his back. He kicked off his canvas jungle boots, leaving them in the grass. Then, like a turtle, he slithered across the sand on his belly and disappeared head-first into the inky water.

The refugee boat drifted away from the jetty, its engine making a sluggish bubbling sound. One of the villagers shouted a final insult.

With his eyes just above the water, his lank black hair and black beard camouflaging him, Mike swam as fast as he could without making too many waves or too much sound to give his position away.

He saw the vessel turn lazily, its propeller frothing up the water at its stern. And he began to swim faster, kicking hard. The breath was hissing between his teeth. Everything hung in the balance. Damn the bloody rifle; it was weighing him down, making him heavy in the water. Why had he slung it over his back? Stupid, he thought, stupid . . .

He was so close now that he could see the number painted in peeling white on the hull of the boat: *JU2*. But it was turning towards the open sea. A deeper, throaty sound came from its engine as it increased speed.

Mike swung at an angle, trying to intercept it. He swallowed water and choked. But the boat was gaining on him. If he missed it, if he missed this one last chance . . .

Nothing mattered now – not caution, silence, nothing – just speed. And like a swimmer in a race, Mike jutted his head forward into the water, propelling himself with hard frog kicks, scooping the water back with his arms.

He could just make out some netting hanging over the stern of the vessel, trailing in the water. He knew it was his only chance, if he could just reach it . . .

But the refugee boat was moving faster every second. He was never going to reach it. The rifle, the bloody rifle was dragging him down. He was sinking, ploughing through the water, spluttering salt water.

The bow of the boat cut through the water ahead of him. He could see the refugees huddled together, staring towards the village. But he was too far away, just inches, inches. Oh God – and with one last despairing lunge, Mike flung out an arm.

He felt his fingers catch twine. He gripped hard at the netting. His arm was jerked as it took the strain. And then, with a long, blissful sigh, he rolled on his back, staring up at the stars, as his body was pulled silently through the water.

He remained that way, held tight against the rough wooden hull, as the vessel chugged out of the bay and away from the village. But the minute it hit the open sea and the swell slapped hard against the bows, Mike knew he had to make his move.

His body weight had pulled the net deeper into the water, giving his bare feet a toehold, and, using the net like a rope ladder, struggling against the rush of the sea, Mike hauled himself up. His face appeared first – black-bearded, dripping sea water, like some marauding savage – and the refugee nearest to him, an old woman, shrieked.

There was immediate consternation as everybody scrambled to get away from where he clung to the side of the boat. Children screamed, an old man fell. Mike shouted out above the whip of the wind, trying to pacify them. 'It's all right, I don't want to hurt you!' But in a strange, foreign language, his shouts just added to the pandemonium.

Hauling himself over the side, Mike flopped sodden into the well of the vessel and looked around him, grinning. He had done it. He was aboard.

But to the refugees, cowering together, the Kalashnikov strapped to Mike's back meant only one thing – terror. Mike raised his open palms, smiling. 'It's okay, it's okay.' But they remained wide-eyed, staring at him.

'Does anybody here speak English?' he asked and thought immediately, as he looked into their simple, peasant faces, what a stupid bloody question.

But, amazingly, a woman's voice replied from the bow of the vessel, 'Yes, I speak English.'

Mike sat up as she came towards him. She was wearing a simple white blouse and black, peasant-style trousers. She looked young, petite, and her long, ebony hair was wind-tossed around her face. The others on board looked to be ethnic Chinese but he couldn't be sure with her. She stepped through the tangle of arms and legs until she drew close to him. She was not afraid like the others, Mike could see that. Ready for trouble, yes, puzzled perhaps, but not afraid. 'Who are you?' she asked. 'And what are you doing aboard our vessel?'

Mike replied, 'My name is Keats, Mike Keats. I'm English.' And still grinning stupidly, amazed that he had made it, he said, 'As to why I'm on board your boat, I don't think you're going to believe it. To tell the truth, I can hardly believe it myself.'

Nguyen had two helicopters deployed with more than two hundred troops on the ground. But even so it could take hours, maybe days, to find him. A hunt of this size couldn't be kept secret. Word would soon leak out. In

Michael Hartmann

addition, Keats was a foreign national. Reports would
filter back to Hanoi.

If things went wrong, Keats' disappearance could
cause acute diplomatic embarrassment. And recrimina-
tions would follow. Nguyen knew there was only one
way to deal with potential trouble, that was to pre-empt
it. So that same morning he telephoned Hanoi.

If he had followed standard procedures, he should
have gone through military channels or direct to the
Secretariat for Foreign Affairs. But in times of crisis
Nguyen also knew that just as important as the content
of any report was the man to whom it was reported. And
in this instance he chose his man with care.

General Do Muoi was Commander of the Western
Highlands Region which bordered Laos and Cambodia.
He was a full Politburo member, Vice-Chairman of the
Council of State and, therefore, a key member of the
ruling elite. But more important still, he was a man with
an almost pathological mistrust of the West.

As a general of the People's Army of Vietnam himself,
Nguyen was put straight through to Do Muoi's office.
The two men were old comrades.

Nguyen outlined the bizarre series of events and then
concluded in a voice that hinted of perplexed innocence,
'The criminal, Tang, was discovered late at night driving
with the Englishman, Keats. So Keats could well have
been an accessory to Tang's escape. Messages might
have been passed between them. Obviously Keats had to
be interrogated. I must tell you too that when I questioned him, he was evasive. But I didn't arrest him. I
thought I should investigate further. He wasn't threat-
ened in any way. In fact, he was being escorted back to
his camp when he tried to kill one of my guards, stole his
rifle and fled. His motives are a complete mystery –

unless, of course, he had something to hide.'

Do Muoi replied in a caustic voice. 'It's notorious that men like Keats, these arms dealers, operate on the fringe of the international underworld, often in close contact with fascist intelligence services, the Americans or British. Surely you appreciate that, Xuan? Has Keats ever worked with the Americans to your knowledge?'

'It's possible, yes, he may well have done so . . .' said Nguyen ambiguously.

'And this prisoner, Tang, ethnic Chinese no doubt, what were his crimes?'

'He was a henchman of the old Saigon regime.'

'An American collaborator?'

'More than that, an American-trained agent.'

'Well then, Xuan, I fail to see the mystery.'

Nguyen smiled to himself. 'Do you think Keats may be a US agent?'

Do Muoi's voice dripped vitriol. 'Innocent men don't steal rifles and flee into the jungle. Of course he's an agent. Don't concern yourself, Xuan. No blame can attach to you in this matter. I'll handle things here in Hanoi. The Americans amaze me. They never give up. They're like gnats constantly buzzing around our faces trying to destabilise the new revolutionary order. Keats is part of the pattern, that's clear . . . another bothersome insect. And insects, Xuan, you squash against a wall.'

There was one further matter which Nguyen had to deal with and early that afternoon he flew to Podge Seager's camp site by helicopter. As he came out of the Soviet-made Mi-14, bent low to stay well under the whirling rotors, Nguyen was in his general's uniform carrying a black leather valise.

Podge Seager, on the other hand, as dumpy as a brown

egg, balding just a little, was bare-chested. He wore canary-yellow boxer shorts and joggers. And all he carried was a can of cold beer.

Nguyen smiled sociably. 'Please excuse the dramatic entrance. But I bring apologies from Mr Keats.'

Patti Seager, in a faded tee-shirt and bikini bottoms, came across to join them. 'We've been worried sick about him,' she said. 'He just disappeared on us. Is he okay?'

'It was urgent business,' said Nguyen. 'Nothing to be concerned about.'

'He could have left a message,' said Podge Seager. 'Nothing's that urgent. And what happened to the jeep? We've been stuck up here all morning twiddling our thumbs.'

'The jeep is on its way,' said Nguyen.

'So when can we expect Mike back?' asked Patti Seager, offering Nguyen a mug of tea.

Nguyen accepted the tea. 'That's difficult to say . . .'

'No doubt he'll come winging back in his Learjet when we find the gold,' said Podge Seager with amiable sarcasm. 'If we ever find it, that is. On the information we've got at present we'd stand a better chance of finding sharks in the Himalayas.'

'I think I may be able to help you there,' said Nguyen.

'You haven't got those bearings, have you?'

Nguyen smiled.

'Well then, great, we're in business!'

'I have the new charts with me,' said Nguyen and the diving team gathered around the camp table as he spread out the first of them. 'The information came from the only crew member to survive. Immediately he got to shore, he took bearings. But you have to appreciate, he was badly injured at the time.'

Podge Seager grinned. 'We'll take all the help we can get, sport. Any chance we can speak to this crew member?'

Nguyen shook his head. 'Regrettably that's impossible. You see he died rather suddenly.'

The *JU2*, the only name it bore, wallowed and yawed its way through the South China Sea groaning in the white-topped swell like some cantankerous old camel burdened with too heavy a load. A few of the refugees were already turning the complexion of sour oatmeal and groping for the side. But on the faces of the others an uncertain kind of hope was glimmering. So far they hadn't been intercepted by the Vietnamese navy, they hadn't been looted or turned back to shore, and now at last they were on the edge of international waters.

There was a stiff wind at their back which enabled them to use the canvas sail. It was the texture of sun-cured tobacco and looked as if it had been a nest for rats but it carried them at a fair speed which was all that mattered and was more than could be said for the engine. The engine had broken down three times already. It was a miracle, thought Mike, that it worked at all. And with a couple of rags, some grease and a spanner, he settled down to try and repair it.

One of the refugee children, a boy of four or five who, because of his big Spanish eyes, Mike had called Pepe, came and squatted next to him, chatting away in Vietnamese. To children of Pepe's age friendship was never handicapped by a different language. In fact it seemed that all of the refugees – initially so terrified when he had risen out of the sea – were delighted to have him aboard.

The woman who spoke English, the petite one with the

long, shining ebony hair, was called Li Mei-ling. And once Mike had convinced her, she explained to the others how he had been wrongly accused by the military of helping an escaped convict, arrested and forced to flee.

So he was a victim of Vietnamese injustice too. But of more practical importance was the fact that Mike was the only one who understood engines and, even without instruments, just using the sun and stars, could keep the boat on a rough course of east north east.

And on top of that, a matter of wonderment to them all, was the fact that he came from Hong Kong. Because Hong Kong was the destination that had been agreed upon. Hong Kong was going to be their resting place, their first taste of freedom, the key to their future lives in America, Canada or Australia one day. It was that magic place that the poor of China still called The Golden Mountain Where Men Eat Fat Pork . . . and where all dreams came true.

But, as Mike sat working on the engine with little Pepe next to him, he understood the realities of what lay ahead. If they ever reached Hong Kong – and that was far from certain – there would be no taste of freedom, not for the refugees. They would be met by police and immigration officials; questioned, tagged and then trucked to a closed camp. And that's where they would remain. Freedom would be an eight-foot-high wire-mesh fence. It would be a bunk that an entire family shared. Those who were qualified might get out early, within eighteen months or so. But for the rest it would mean years of frustrated waiting; no work for the men, charity for the children. Some might never be resettled. Some might even die there.

But what purpose would be served in disillusioning them now? The days ahead were perilous enough. Destroy their hope, he thought, and he destroyed their courage. And without courage every last one of them was doomed.

Li Mei-ling understood the realities too. She was more educated, more sophisticated than the others who were mainly small traders and artisans. She hadn't left Vietnam seeking a land of milk and honey, she had left because life there had become intolerable and anything, even a closed camp, would be preferable. But it was obvious that she too was determined not to destroy the hopes of the others and the more they tried to use her as an interpreter to quiz Mike about their future, the more she gently deflected their demands. 'Why should he know the answer?' she would say. 'This is his first time as a refugee too.'

And they would laugh, the young women giggling behind their cupped hands, casting Mike friendly, almost affectionate glances. Within a few hours he had become one of them.

Although Li Mei-ling was not yet thirty years of age and although there were men on the vessel, a couple of whom had served in the army, it was apparent that everyone accepted her as the one who would speak for them and shepherd them through any crises that lay ahead. Mike was fascinated by her. She was a highly perceptive, highly intelligent woman. And a very beautiful one too.

As the little boat ploughed its weary way through day into night, the two of them sat and talked. Her grandparents, said Mei-ling, had come from Guangxi Province in China close to the Vietnamese border. They had not been Han, ethnic Chinese, but had belonged to the Zhuang, a minority group loosely related to the Thais.

Maybe that explained her tantalisingly sloe-eyed looks, thought Mike, the broad face, the generous mouth and especially that dusky, nutmeg skin; darker, more

sensual than the alabaster complexion of most Chinese.
Because she could so easily have been Thai or even
Indonesian. She was slim and small-breasted but there
was nothing girlish about her. Without a touch of
make-up and wearing those simple, ill-cut clothes, she
was still one of the most sensuous women Mike had ever
seen.

But for Mike the attraction was more than purely
physical. Despite the rolling of the boat and the crying of
the children, despite the constant crowded huddle around
them, he found that they could talk for hours – about
anything and everything – as if it was just the two of them
there, all alone. Mei-ling's English wasn't fluent, his
Vietnamese was non-existent. But with French words to
fill in the gaps, with mimes and gestures and a lot of
smiles, they understood each other perfectly.

She told Mike that her grandparents had been merchants who had prospered under French colonial rule.
Her father had been a doctor, trained in France himself,
but a radical, a socialist who could accept nearly everything from the West except one thing – its dominance.
He had fought against colonial rule and, during his years
in the hills, had even treated Ho Chi Minh, 'Uncle Ho',
himself.

Mei-ling said that she was a doctor too, trained in
Hanoi and Paris, a specialist in pediatrics. And, like her
father, she had always been a determined socialist. She
would have been happy to live all her life in Vietnam, to
work for the common good. Material things weren't vital
to her. But dignity was, a sense of purpose and, yes,
freedom too.

But now all those things had been lost. Vietnam was a
police state, she said, an imperial power. Poverty in
Vietnam wasn't a condition to be combated any more,

poverty had become a state of mind. 'Something is rotten in the state of Denmark,' she said, breaking the seriousness with a quick smile. 'You see, even in Hanoi we learn Shakespeare.'

Her elder brother, she said, had been in the North Vietnamese Army, just eighteen and one of the last soldiers killed before the fall of Saigon. As a result her family had been awarded the honorary title: Family Of Soldiers Killed For The Country.

But it had done no good, not the politics, the patriotism, not even her brother's death. Only one thing mattered in the end – the fact that they were Chinese.

In 1979, after the border war with China had erupted, three hundred thousand ethnic Chinese had been expelled from the North, simply deported, towed out to sea and set adrift, often with a few criminals in the boat to rob them. But because her father had been a doctor and because doctors were in such short supply, the family had been spared. But it was only delaying the inevitable.

'My father could never believe it,' she told Mike. 'I think it broke his heart. He was such a compassionate man, he had worked so hard for a just and decent society. He spoke out but it only made matters worse. They let him continue to work but only as a doctor in the prisons, not much better than a prisoner himself. And last year he died.'

'What happened to you?' asked Mike.

'Things got gradually worse for me too,' she said. 'They removed me from the hospital where I worked. I was a bad influence on the children, they said. I was a "bourgeois intellectual" . . . that was the term they used, another way of describing a Chinese who can read and write.'

'Were you able to work after that?'

She shook her head, making a joke of it. 'Not even in the prisons.'

'So how did you live?'

She smiled, sighing a little. 'I bribed officials for ration cards. I looked after other Chinese who were in the same position as me. We helped each other.'

'But how did you get this boat? How did you get permission to leave?'

Then she laughed but it was razor-edged with irony. 'Oh that was no problem. They wanted us to leave. That's all they ever wanted – provided we had the price to pay. Because you must understand, Mike, that in the great proletarian society I once dedicated myself to, gold will purchase anything . . . a boat, a life, anything at all.'

She pointed to the other refugees huddled under a tarpaulin to protect themselves from the wind. 'Each of us paid a tax of five taels of gold. Not Vietnamese currency, not dongs. Gold. This boat cost twenty taels and another five to repair. Just the water and rations that the villagers sold us cost three.'

Mike asked her, 'But where did you get so much gold?'

And she smiled sadly. 'We sold everything. We borrowed from family and friends. No doubt some of us stole. It's better to be destitute with hope, you see, than rich with none.'

Mike looked into her eyes. He could keep the truth from the others but not from her. 'You know they'll put you into a camp in Hong Kong. That you won't be allowed to work . . .'

She nodded. 'Yes, I know.' Then she fell silent for a time.

Pepe and a little girl left their parents, coming across to play with Mike. Mei-ling put out her arms, pulling them close. The children giggled and kicked. And Mei-ling said, 'Even if we grow old in the camps, even if there's nothing for us, for these little ones at least there's got to be a future. There just has to be, I won't believe otherwise. And that alone will make it worthwhile, Mike. Because you see, so long as one of us benefits then we all do . . .'

Mike could find no answer. How many millions of refugees over how many centuries had felt the same as her?

But Mei-ling never remained maudlin. That was her great strength. Nothing defeated her. And, climbing to her feet, she gave a bright smile. There was work to be done, she said. Food had to be prepared. And, while Mike finished repairing the engine, she supervised the evening meal.

Darkness fell on the sea. It was a crystal-clear night and the wind clapped in their one ragged sail. Slowly, one by one, the refugees fell asleep, huddled against each other.

Mei-ling sat next to Mike. She was exhausted too, struggling to stay awake. Mike was shy with women but the first physical advance was easier this time and he placed his arm around her shoulders. 'Rest your head,' he said. 'You might as well be comfortable.'

She looked into his face with those almond eyes, very serious for a moment, seeking out his true feelings. Then she smiled contentedly and snuggled into him.

After she was asleep, Mike gazed out at the green-black translucent waves, aware in every nerve of his body that she lay next to him. She was so slender. Her skin was soft, her body was warm, as warm as a child's.

Experiencing a sudden, irrational guilt, he tried to picture Jackie in his mind. But Jackie came from another lifetime now, another world. Events had crowded out the past, scouring his emotions. As much as Mike honoured her memory, his love for Jackie was something distant, blurred, a part of history. He had come too close to dying to live for the past. All that mattered now was the present and, God willing perhaps, the future . . . .

Nguyen knew that he should refer to Mikhail Kazakov who was waiting in Hanoi, that was the arrangement. But he didn't trust the man. There was a shiftiness about him, a disturbing lack of grit. If Kazakov was in a line of soldiers under fire, Nguyen knew he would be the first to panic and run. And panic could kill them all. So he bypassed him and went direct to Moscow.

As expected, Grigori Kirilenko accepted the news with equanimity. 'How long has he been gone?' asked the old General.

'Nearly forty-eight hours.'

'So he could still be in the hills, still hiding?'

Nguyen agreed but qualified it. 'I've had more than two hundred men combing the area and they've found no sign of him yet.'

'Then perhaps he got through the net, Xuan, made his way south down the coast or back to Hanoi?'

'A bearded Englishman alone in the Socialist Republic of Vietnam not speaking a word of the language? Tell me, Grigori, how long would it take for you to receive reports of a seven-foot negro hitch-hiking through Siberia?'

But Kirilenko didn't laugh. 'Then what do you think is most likely to have happened to him?'

'It's just possible he got on board a boat.'

'What kind of boat?'

'They tell me that several refugee boats left that same night, one from a nearby fishing village.'

'Have they been intercepted?'

'By the time I learnt of them, they would have reached international waters. To organise an air and sea search that far out, Grigori, would have involved too many people . . . too many questions to answer. Just too dangerous.'

Kirilenko understood Nguyen's predicament. 'What are his chances do you think?'

'They tell me the boats are very old, barely seaworthy. More than half of these refugee vessels go to the bottom.'

'And if the one he has boarded makes it to safety, what then?'

'If he makes public accusations, gives stories to the press you mean?'

'Yes.'

'Then we're still protected, Grigori. I try not to leave my belly bare.'

Kirilenko gave a soft laugh. 'You never disappoint me, Xuan.'

Nguyen explained the steps he had taken to pre-empt trouble. He told Kirilenko of the report he had made to Do Muoi, planting the idea in his mind that Keats was an American agent. 'That's now the official Politburo attitude to the matter,' he said, 'and the British Embassy have been informed accordingly.'

Kirilenko was pleased. 'Then how bad can it be? There's a fair chance that Keats will never be heard of again, lost at sea. But even if he makes dry land, what public harm can he do us? He's an arms dealer – disreputable characters at the best of time – a lackey for the CIA, a man already branded as a foreign agent.'

'The public harm doesn't concern me,' said Nguyen. 'It's the private information he passes on – that's what worries me. The CIA must still have files on Tang.

They'll know Keats is speaking the truth. And they'll have to act.'

'How?' asked Kirilenko. 'Their hands are tied, Xuan. They can't act, not openly. To do so would be to admit to the world that they know what the junk contains. No, they won't do anything, it would be rash in the extreme . . . not until they can be certain the junk has been discovered with its cargo intact. They'll watch, as best they can . . . and wait. That's all they can do.'

'And if we locate the junk, if we raise the cargo – what then?'

'At that time everything will be in our favour. The Americans will have no idea what we intend to do with the cargo, whether we intend to keep it in Vietnam or move it.'

'But what about the divers?'

'You know what we intend for the divers.'

'And the cargo itself?'

'It will disappear, Xuan.' Kirilenko began to chuckle deep in his throat. 'It will fly like the phoenix and be lost in the sun.'

Nguyen, a practical man, had little time for Kirilenko's flights of imagery. 'So you want the diving operations to continue?' he asked.

'Yes, of course.'

'They're already beginning to attract attention, you realise that. We can't carry on indefinitely, especially now. What happens if the Americans try some covert action?'

'Don't fret, Xuan,' said Kirilenko casually. 'The divers will find the wreck in the next few days, long before the CIA can try any Hollywood stunts. I can feel it in my bones.'

Nguyen was becoming angry. 'I don't remember you

making decisions in the past based on how your bones felt.'

Kirilenko was stung by the remark. 'Don't tell me you're having second thoughts?'

'I've never stopped having second thoughts. I'm just amazed you have none.'

'We've talked about this before,' said Kirilenko gruffly. 'You're still going through with this, aren't you? You're not going to let me down?'

'I gave you my word,' said Nguyen flatly, making it clear that he was only proceeding with profound reservations. 'But there's one thing I don't want any misunderstanding about, Grigori. If that cargo is salvaged, I want it out of Vietnam within twenty-four hours. Do you understand me? I don't want it here a minute longer. I'm not prepared to take the risk.'

'Of course,' said Kirilenko hastily, 'that's always been the plan. Don't worry, Xuan, I'm a thorough man, you know that. Arrangements are in hand.'

But Nguyen was determined to make his point. 'Twenty-four hours,' he repeated. 'And even that's too long.'

The arrangements that Kirilenko spoke of were in fact being made that same day in another South East Asian country. It was part of Kirilenko's complex plan that, on its migration west, the phoenix must roost in Thailand and it was to Thailand – shaped, some said, like the head and trunk of a sacred elephant – that he despatched Jean-Paul Delacroix.

A place had to be found where the necessary preparatory work could be done; a reasonably large complex too, not some mildewed shed on one of Bangkok's klongs, its endless network of canals. Yet, for safety's sake, the place had to be isolated. 'Close enough and yet remote enough', had been Kirilenko's cryptic instructions. And that was why Delacroix took the highway out of Bangkok down the trunk of the sacred elephant, south through Phetchaburi towards Hua Hin.

There were a number of properties that he had been recommended but ten miles north of Cha-Aam he found what he wanted.

Turning off the highway, away from the sea, he drove through flat, alluvial lands; a patchwork of paddy fields, bamboo stands, broken bush and tall sugar palms. He passed through a small farming village, the houses built on stilts in traditional Thai style and a mile further on down a cinder track came to the factory.

It was an abandoned rice mill, an ugly conglomeration of crumbling wooden structures with corrugated iron roofs surrounded by an eight-foot-high wall made of concrete blocks. Nobody worked there and, apart from the manager's residence, a small box painted garish pink and green, the nearest houses were back in the village.

The manager, a thick-set mechanic called Pansomchit who was retained to keep the machinery in running order, confirmed that the electrical power remained connected. Nor was there any problem with labour. Men and women could be hired from the nearby villages for a day, a week or a month at a time.

Delacroix inspected the buildings, satisfied himself that they met Kirilenko's requirements and then made the three-hour journey back to Bangkok. That same evening he contacted the owner of the mill and agreed a short-term lease of six months. The tenant, said Delacroix, was a Hong Kong based corporation, one of the companies in Mr Josef Rakosi's Good Hope Group.

*   *   *

Disaster struck on the afternoon of the third day – savage, elemental. Mike saw it first, just a blurred white speck on the blue haze of the horizon. It was another vessel, the first he had seen. But, as it emerged from the haze, he saw it was coming fast and it was set directly on a course to intercept them.

It wasn't a navy vessel, it wasn't a merchantman. But whatever it was, it had powerful engines. It was set low in the cobalt water, cutting a long lethal wake, and, as he watched it, Mike's initial feelings of concern turned into open alarm. He called to Mei-ling. 'Quick, the rifle – the Kalashnikov – get it for me!'

Mei-ling looked at him, sudden alarm in her eyes too. But she didn't question his command and, seizing the rifle, immediately passed it to him.

The refugees, who until now had seen the approaching vessel as a source of excitement, witnessed the rifle being passed. They saw Mike's face set as hard as stone and the smiles withered on their faces.

The vessel was slapping hard and flat over the waves, doing twenty knots or more. Mike knew there was no way on earth he could outrun it. 'Get everybody down,' he told Mei-ling. 'Get them out of sight.'

Mei-ling's face was clouded with fear but she remained calm. 'What is it?' she asked. 'Is it Vietnamese?'

Mike shook his head. 'I can't be sure. It's still too far away. Hurry though, you must get everybody down. You mentioned that a couple of the men had army experience. Quick, bring them here.'

Over the past three days Mei-ling had learnt to trust Mike, trust him with her life if necessary, and, although she didn't understand why, she knew they had to be in terrible danger. Quickly and calmly, she asked the men who had done army training to identify themselves and go forward to Mike. The others she told to get down and keep low.

But panic was inevitable. Was the approaching boat the Vietnamese Navy? Were they going to be shot? What was happening, were they going to die? Mei-ling tried to keep the refugees under control, to get them to lie with their children and stay there but the babble of hysterical questions wouldn't stop, and she turned to Mike, beseeching him, 'Please, you have to tell us, what is it?'

'I told you I can't be sure,' said Mike, his jaw muscles tight. 'But we can't take any chances. Because if it's what I think it is – '

But he said no more. Facts, figures, images were bursting in his imagination. He remembered the countless horror stories he had heard about the boat people in Hong Kong, the newspaper articles, the endless photographs. Over half the refugees who set out in small boats drowned. A hundred thousand had perished that way, maybe more. But for some, the fate they met was worse than drowning, horrendous beyond words . . .

Because with every mass migration there were wild dogs running at the flanks, pulling down the strays. And here, so close to the Gulf of Siam, to the thousand and one islands of the Indonesian Archipelago, those wild dogs hunted aboard vessels – powerful vessels, low and fast – just like the vessel bearing down on them now.

Three of the male refugees – the three with army experience – crouched close to him. Their weather-beaten faces were grim as they waited for instructions. Mike looked anxiously around him for some makeshift weapons they could use. There were bottles in a card-board box, a dozen or more of them containing cooking oil. That was it, nothing else. But they would have to suffice and Mike shouted to Mei-ling. 'Tell them to empty the bottles, tell them to pour the oil over the side and fill them with petrol. Do you understand? And then get rags, soak them in petrol too – '

But Mei-ling needed no further instructions. She understood exactly what Mike intended and spoke quickly to the men in Vietnamese.

There was an atmosphere of cornered desperation on the little boat now. The women huddled low with their children. An old man was silently weeping. The three refugees emptying the oil bottles were fumbling in their haste. A woman began to wail, certain they were going to die. 'Shut her up,' shouted Mike. 'For God's sake, shut her up!' And Mei-ling went across, trying to soothe her.

Mike knew that if they stood any chance of survival, it rested on his shoulders. He had only one magazine on the Kalashnikov so he would have to fire single shots. Surprise was their only advantage. That meant he would have to stay hidden until the final, crucial second. But how? What in the hell did he do? Then he saw a sheet of tarpaulin and dragged it to the stern next to the engine, covering himself with it. The tarpaulin stank of grease and urine and sour rice, so old it was as stiff as board. But it gave him cover at least and through its open folds Mike watched the other vessel drawing inexorably closer.

It was an ancient patrol boat of some kind, fifty foot long, with big open engines at the stern that smoked and growled, churning up the waves. It bore no markings, it had no flag. It was painted drab olive green, splashed with rust and engrimed with filth. There was an open bridge and in front of it, on the foredeck – as black and obscene as a whaling harpoon – stood a 60mm machine gun.

All of Mike's darkest apprehensions had proved themselves. He turned to Mei-ling, hissing from underneath his tarpaulin cover, 'I was right, they're pirates.'

She was too stunned to answer. Pirates . . . anywhere else in the world it was a word out of history – except here in the South China Sea. Because here it remained an everyday word, a word steeped in horror.

'Pass the message,' hissed Mike between gritted teeth. 'Tell everybody that they must just sit. Let the other vessel come alongside, let their crew come aboard if necessary. But nobody does a thing – not until I act.'

Mei-ling's skin was chalky-white with fear but in an unhurried voice she relayed Mike's instructions.

Mike saw that the three men had finished preparing the bottles. A petrol-soaked rag was jammed into the neck of each bottle and each man had taken four. Mike gave them the thumbs-up sign and they nodded back, indicating that they each carried a box of matches. Good, thought Mike, good.

Little Pepe wanted to be with Mike under the tarpaulin. He thought it was all a game and, grinning from ear to ear, his olive-pip eyes merry with amusement, tried to scamper across. But his mother grabbed him, tears streaming down her face, and wrenched him back. Mike smiled at the child and Pepe smiled back.

The other vessel was less than fifty yards from them now. There were a couple of men on the bridge, four or five on deck. They were short and brown-skinned with black hair, Thai perhaps or Filipino.

A couple of them wore jungle camouflage with the sleeves cut away from the shirts and the buttons undone showing their chests. One wore no shirt at all. His bare chest was covered with a tattoo; some kind of swirling dragon in mortal combat with a snake, and there was an MI6 slung across his shoulder. Another man – so fat that he had breasts, with a belly on him like a barrel – stood watching the refugee boat with a fixed grin on his face. He wore a red bandana, was smoking a cigar and carried a rifle too.

All of them looked to be hard men; ignorant, savage, the kind of men who relished their cruelty and their bizarre clothes. They looked like vultures, lived like vultures. They smelt of dead flesh.

One of them stepped towards the hand-rail. He wore a torn tee-shirt with the old Marine joke on it: 'Yea though I walk through the valley of the shadow of death I shall fear no evil – because I'm the meanest sonofabitch there'. He glared at the bobbing refugee boat for a few seconds and then shouted across the water in a rough sing-song language that Mike didn't understand.

From under his tarpaulin, Mike whispered to Mei-ling, 'What's he speaking?'

'It's Thai. I can't understand it all. But he's asking if we have any men on board.'

'Okay, tell him.'

Mei-ling climbed to her feet and in a clear voice called across the water.

The man in the tee-shirt shouted back.

'What's he saying now?' asked Mike.

And without looking down at him, her eyes still fixed on the other vessel, Mei-ling replied. 'He says they're coming aboard.'

Hunched under his tarpaulin, Mike was filled suddenly with an icy calm. So long as he remained hidden, they possessed the tenuous advantage of surprise . . . the mouse turning. But how long would that last? A couple of seconds at best. Then what? So this is it, he thought with a quiet sense of stoicism that surprised him. So this is where I die.

There was a sudden bump as the bigger vessel banged against them. Mike could hear voices shouting and through a tiny crack in the tarpaulin saw the fat man, the one with the cigar, jump aboard. He landed with a heavy thud, grabbing one of the refugees to stop from falling. Then, with his tiny eyes lost in pouches of flesh, he looked around him, sniffing.

A second sprang aboard, the bare-chested one with the tattoo on his chest. Then a third . . .

The fat man gestured to Mei-ling and she stepped towards him with her head bowed. He reached out with a puffy hand to push the hair from her face and then studied her as a man might study a slave he intended to purchase. He looked around the boat again and then he muttered, 'Thong . . . thong.'

It was the Thai word for gold, one of the few words Mike understood. Yes, that would be the way. Rob the refugees first, move the booty across, pick out the most desirable women and then get on with the worst of it.

'Thong,' muttered the fat man again. But Mei-ling didn't reply.

'Thong! Thong!' shouted the one with the tattoo on his chest.

Mei-ling hesitated, looking anxiously at the other refugees. But then she pointed to some wooden crates that stood only a foot or two from where Mike was crouched under the tarpaulin.

The fat man coughed, spitting a slimy globule of tobacco spit and phlegm onto the deck. He slung his M16 over his shoulder and, with the cigar clenched between his teeth, stepped over to the crates.

All Mike saw was the gut bulging over the pants, so

close he could touch it – and he fired the first shot straight up into the man's belly.

The bullet exploded out of the man's back, shattering his spine, hurling him backwards across the deck, mouth open in a gagging death stare.

The surprise was more devastating than Mike could ever have hoped. For a second – a precious, desperate second – the scene was a tableau, everybody frozen. And, still hidden beneath the tarpaulin, he fired at the second man, the bare-chested one. He hit him in the head and saw the body spin over the side into the sea. The third man at the bow gawked with stunned incredulity. Unable to tell where the shots were coming from, he reached out, trying to grab one of the refugees to protect himself. But Mike fired again, two shots this time, and heard him scream.

It was all happening in slow motion, reactions numbed. Mike was operating like an automaton: take aim, don't waste shots, take full advantage of the surprise. Casting the tarpaulin aside, pressing himself against the hot metal of the engine, he brought the Kalashnikov to his shoulder. The next shot was critical. If he failed, they were all dead. And, facing towards the other vessel, he fired. The man holding the machine gun – an instant away from firing it himself – threw up his arms and fell. He was hit, Mike didn't know where, didn't care. He was hit, that's all that mattered, and the machine gun was silent.

'Grab their rifles!' Mike shouted to Mei-ling. 'Give them to the ones with army training. Tell them to fire back. For God's sake now, do it, do it!'

He fired more shots himself, two aimed at the open bridge, and saw the two men there throw themselves down. There was pandemonium on the other vessel now as everybody dived for cover, men crawling for the hatches firing blindly back.

'Light the bottles!' screamed Mike. 'Throw them across, throw them now!' And he saw Mei-ling grab one, light the petrol-soaked rag and send it cartwheeling through the air. It hit the side of the bridge, smashed open, spraying petrol and with a bright *whoosh*, burst into flame.

One of the pirates made a daring rush for the machine gun and Mike fired at him, a fast, furious burst that flew wide but still sent him scurrying back on his hands and knees.

For a few more seconds Mike knew they held the advantage. The pirates were dismayed. Nobody had ever turned on them before, not like this. Now there were four guns firing at them. And bottles came spinning through the air – lethal Molotov cocktails – smashing on the deck, bursting like napalm in brilliant yellow flares.

'Throw them towards the stern!' Mike shouted. 'Mei-ling, tell them to throw them into the engines!' Mei-ling screamed instructions and two of the bottles, spinning streamers of brown smoke, burst into flame where the engines were housed, sending up great sheets of flame.

Now was the time to disengage, thought Mike. They couldn't fight them man for man. They were in a tiny boat, crowded together. It would be a massacre. And he shouted to Mei-ling. 'You have to get away! Put the engine at full speed. And keep everybody down, keep them on their bellies. It's their only chance!'

She looked up at him. 'What about you?'

But Mike was already on his way. Ducking around the engine, he jumped for the other vessel. He grabbed the rusted hand rail and scrambled over the top. It was a risk, he knew it, an insane risk. But it wasn't just for the others, a purely selfless deed. Unless that 60mm machine gun was disabled, they were all as good as dead.

Four of the petrol bombs had exploded on the fore-deck against the bridge and their blinding, intense heat gave him a few vital seconds. He reached the machine gun, swinging it a full ninety degrees so that it was facing directly at the bridge. Then, very calmly, almost casually, as if somehow this was all a dream, he checked the safety catch was off, braced himself and squeezed the trigger. The heavy-calibre weapon shuddered in his hands, puncturing great holes in the bridge. Mike raked the fire back and forth, aiming almost at his feet so that it sent great splinters up from the deck and then criss-crossing the bridge again.

Glancing to his right, Mike saw the stern of the little refugee boat as it set off in flight. It was thirty, forty yards away already and nobody was firing at it.

Mike squeezed the trigger of the machine gun again, pumping the last of the 60mm shells into the bridge. He ripped off the magazine box and tossed it overboard. Frantically, he jammed some rag into the firing breech. And then, with a wild sprint, he flung himself over the bow into the sea.

He stayed underwater, terrified that if he came to the surface too early he would be a sitting target, swimming with slow rhythmical strokes until he felt his lungs were going to burst. And only then did he kick for the surface. He broke the water in a great gasp for air and through the salt water that stung his eyes, he saw the pirate vessel burning furiously, crippled in the sea fifty yards from him. Damn you, he thought, hating the ship and everybody on it, damn you to hell.

Turning in the water, he looked for the refugee boat.

Then, as he was carried up on the peak of a wave, he saw it a hundred and fifty yards away due east. Good, he thought with grim satisfaction, it's getting out of range.

Then, taking a lungful of air, he dived down under the water again. And he swam that way, staying underwater for as long as he could, until all he could see of the pirate vessel was a smudge of brown, oily smoke in the sky. Only then did he feel secure enough to stay on the surface.

For another hour Mike swam until he saw the refugee boat wallowing in the water, waiting for him. Mei-ling was at the stern waving her arms. He was exhausted now, dragging himself through the water, swimming a slow, muscle-aching breast stroke. But even so there was an elation in him, the fierce joy of survival. They had fought the odds – staggering odds – and they had come through. It was unbelievable.

Mei-ling reached out to take his hand and Mike hauled himself aboard. 'This is getting to be a habit,' he said with a grin. He looked around him, expecting to see broad smiles on the faces of the refugees. But instead they were staring at him, ashen-skinned, their mouths tight shut.

Mike looked up at Mei-ling. 'What is it?' he asked.

And she answered in a hollow voice, 'As we were escaping, they fired at us. They had another machine gun, Mike, one on the bridge.'

Mike took a deep, shuddering breath, afraid to ask. 'How many casualties?

'Seven . . . three dead, four wounded.'

'Any children?'

She nodded. 'One little girl is dead.'

Mike shook his head. 'Oh Jesus, I'm so sorry . . .'

* * *

234

The mother of the little girl was hysterical, they all said so. She didn't know what she was saying. She babbled things and glared at Mike and her eyes were wild-set with grief. At first Mei-ling didn't want to tell Mike what she was accusing him of, but Mike insisted. The mother, she said, blamed Mike for the death of her child. All the pirates had wanted was gold and, if they had been given it, they would have sailed away. That's what the mother believed. It was Mike – the foreigner, the alien among them – who had started the shooting. He was the one responsible.

The moon was rising, a luminous blue-white orb as lovely as life itself, when they consigned the bodies of the dead to the sea. Mei-ling had told Mike to ignore what the woman said. It simply wasn't true. But, as Mike stood with his head bowed, he could hear the mother's inconsolable sobs and he was crucified with guilt. What would have happened if he had waited? Had he fired too soon? Was it true perhaps, would they have taken the gold and gone? Maybe the mother was right, maybe he was to blame.

But early the following morning, before the sun gave its warmth, they came upon a vision of what they might have been.

It was the skeleton of a sampan burnt black, half-filled with water, half-afloat, a suspended dream in the dawn-grey stillness of the sea. There were bodies inside. It was impossible to tell the exact number . . . five, maybe six or seven. The women were naked. The men had been bound with rough hemp. The little craft had been doused with petrol and then set alight. The faces of the bodies, washed with sea water, stared emptily up, strangely vacant as if they had never felt emotions or shared experiences. Their hair, eyebrows and eye lashes had been scorched away.

The mast of the sampan, blackened with flame, remained and fixed upon it was the final display of cruelty. A man, the master perhaps or one of the men who had resisted, had been decapitated and his severed head was now impaled upon it. The head didn't look human any longer, simply a wax replica: staring eyes, throat bulged out of shape. It was a totem, a figurehead, a warning.

The woman who had screamed at Mike the night before began to weep. My God, thought Mike, what a way to make her understand.

Mei-ling was standing next to him, barely coming up to Mike's shoulder. She was past anguish now. All that remained was a dreadful emptiness and her face, always so bright, so full of feeling, was expressionless. They were all of them mute, every living soul on board. They had been seared to the soul and nothing would ever be the same again.

Mike remained silent. It was a moment beyond intrusion. Slowly the sampan drifted away until it was no more than a silent wreck receding on the dip and rise of the waves. And only then did he break the spell. 'All right,' he said briskly. 'Let's get the sail up. Let's get things sorted out. Mei-ling, what about the rations and the water? Some of the water drums have been holed. If we don't sort out the water, we're going to be in trouble.'

Mei-ling nodded. 'Yes,' she said in a distant voice. 'Yes, you're right.'

'Then let's get moving!' And, clapping his hands, Mike began to bark orders.

As if dragging themselves from a dream, the refugees lethargically responded. But Mike kept at them. The bullet holes were corked. Sea water sloshing in the well of the boat was bailed out. Mei-ling tended to the wounded while two of the women checked the water supplies. The sun rose high, wintry but warm, and the constant chug-chug of the engine added an air of sturdy normality.

At noon rice was boiled with a little salted fish and there was a mug of water each. Mike was bent over his engine when he felt a hand touch his shoulder. He turned. It was the mother of the little girl who had been killed. She had collected his food and water and demurely, her eyes still wet with tears, she offered it to him.

Nguyen was waiting, pacing along the shingles, when the two inflatables returned to the cove that evening. 'How did it go?' he asked, unable to hide his anxiety.

Podge Seager lifted some diving cylinders from the boat and lugged them to the jeep. 'No luck, I'm afraid.'

'But it's been four days now . . .'

'Just a question of plodding on, sport.'

'No trace of the wreck at all?'

'Not yet.'

'I see . . .' And, without a further word, Nguyen returned to his vehicle.

Patti Seager joined her husband. 'What was that about?'

'The usual progress check.'

'He's worse than an expectant father.'

'A funny bugger though. Can't make him out.'

'What do you mean?'

Podge Seager shrugged. 'Probably just me misinter-preting it . . . but every time I report we've drawn a blank, he doesn't look disappointed at all. If anything, he looks pleased.'

*   *   *

Mike sat cross-legged in the stern of the boat watching Mei-ling as she worked. She was kneeling next to a young boy who had been wounded, changing his dressing. The boy was in pain and clearly frightened but Mei-ling spoke quietly, joking with him, until he began to laugh, his fear and pain forgotten. Mei-ling had a special way with children. She should have children of her own, thought Mike. And then, with a sudden, startling realisation, he thought – yes, our children, hers and mine.

It was the first time he had admitted it to himself and at first it shocked him. He was normally reticent when it came to women, overly cautious. And here the obstacles – objectively – were enormous. He and Mei-ling came from different worlds, different cultures. What did they really know about each other? Next to nothing. They had been thrown together with no choice in the matter. Any trust they shared was built on necessity. What kind of foundation was that? Be realistic, he kept saying to himself. But the more Mike tried to distance himself from his emotions, the more certain of them he became.

And Mei-ling felt something similiar, he was certain of it. He had noticed her watching him and then quickly lowering her eyes or turning away when their eyes met.

It amazed him, the pure physical desire he felt for her. No one, not even Jackie, had evoked the deep, driving passion that Mei-ling ignited. It was crazy, he thought, how could he feel this way? Look at them. Look at the situation they were in . . . on a water-logged boat not knowing whether they would survive another day. Both of them were hungry, filthy, past the edge of exhaustion. And yet when Mike looked at that broad, bright face he saw a beauty and a resilience that dazzled him.

Mei-ling finished with the young boy, packed her

small leather bag of medical kit, stashed it safely, and then came to the stern to sit next to Mike.

They had talked about everything over the past four days . . . their lives, their philosophies, what they had done in the past, all the little incidents and comedies of their lives. But somehow – frightened perhaps of what they might learn – they had avoided that one central issue that Mike couldn't avoid any longer. He wanted the question to come out naturally, just part of their conversation, but it never worked that way, not for him. 'I want to ask you something,' he said, wincing inside.

She tilted her head. 'What is it?'

'Are you – were you – ever married?'

She replied with a shy smile. 'Studying to be a doctor took up all my time.'

'But there must have been boyfriends?'

She teased him. 'The revolution didn't approve of Western-style romance.'

'None at all?'

She laughed to cover her embarrassment. 'There was one man, yes, a doctor in Paris when I was studying there. It was very romantic but it didn't last long. I was called back to Hanoi as soon as my studies were finished and since then, well, you understand, it was just my father and I.'

Mike said nothing. But he was delighted and couldn't keep the smile off his face.

'And you?' she asked. 'You must be married, I suppose . . .'

Mike shook his head. 'No,' he replied and was going to leave it at that. But then an image of Jackie came to mind. 'There was a woman though,' he said, 'I think I should tell you about her . . .'

*   *   *

Bottles of XO Cognac stood on the boardroom table acting as paperweights for the balance sheets. Joe Rakosi was having a late meeting with his accountants when the call came through.

It was Jean-Paul Delacroix on the line, calling from Thailand. There were certain business matters that needed to be discussed, he said, and suggested that Rakosi fly to Bangkok the following day.

Giving his apologies to the accountants sitting around the boardroom table, Rakosi transferred the call to his private office and went through. As he picked up the extension, he was expecting the worst. 'What's the problem? Don't tell me it's Mozambique again.'

Delacroix replied with that smooth, continental way of his. 'Everything is fine in Africa, Joe.'

'What is it then, Vietnam?'

'Yes, I regret there are problems.'

'How bad?'

'Bad enough to make it essential we talk.'

Rakosi let out a long, angry groan. 'I'm up to my neck here. I've got end-of-year accounts, a barter deal that I'm trying to negotiate with the Chinese. Can't you come here?'

'I'm afraid that wouldn't be convenient, Joe.'

'What's that supposed to mean? The mountain never comes to Mohammed . . . ?'

'It means simply that I would rather we discussed matters here.'

'And I would rather we discussed matters in Acapulco – but it's not possible!'

Delacroix remained calm, almost amused. 'I should explain, Joe, that it's not just Vietnam we need to discuss, it's Thailand too.'

'What in the hell has Thailand got to do with this?'

'All in good time, Joe . . .'

He's playing me like a bloody fish on a line, thought Rakosi.

'There's a Cathay Pacific flight that will get you into Bangkok in the late morning, Joe. I am booked into the Shangri-La and have taken the liberty of booking a suite for you too. Why don't we meet for lunch on the terrace . . . say one thirty?'

'What do you think I'm running here,' demanded Rakosi, 'a two-bit take-away?'

The Swiss financier was unperturbed. 'I appreciate your difficulties, Joe, but it really would be best.'

Rakosi's initial reaction was to tell him to go to hell. But for some reason he held back, puzzled at first and then deeply concerned. because he began to realise that, beneath the diplomatic veneer, Delacroix wasn't requesting his presence in Bangkok at all – he was ordering it.

Mike awoke with a jolt as if wrenched out of his sleep by a bad dream. He rubbed his eyes, muzzy-headed, and sat up, careful not to wake Mei-ling whose head rested in the crook of his shoulder.

It was dark still but dawn was approaching; that silent, half-way time when the first watery smudges of a distant day were seen more by the senses than the eye. The boat, lying dangerously low in the water, groaned as it pitched and rolled on the waves. Everybody on board seemed to be asleep, oblivious of the grey-green water sloshing around their feet. Even the man at the wheel had his head slumped forward, snoring.

What had awoken him? It was more than a dream. It was a sense of something very tangible out there in the last folds of night. Mike climbed to his feet, hearing

Mei-ling's slumbering sighs of protests, and looked around.

And there it was, as big as a skyscraper. Mike began to wave his arms, shouting at the top of his voice, 'Here we are! Yeah, yeah, come and get us! Oh you beauty, you gorgeous great thing!' He would never have believed that a merchant ship could look so good.

They met for lunch on the terrace of the Shangri-La Hotel overlooking the busy river traffic of the Chao Phya.

Jean-Paul Delacroix had spent the morning browsing in the city's antique shops, negotiating for some rare Khymer statuary. He looked every inch the debonair continental; chestnut hair a little windswept, slim, poised, relaxed, wearing a moss-green sports shirt creased enough to prove it was pure cotton, sand-coloured slacks and calf-leather shoes.

Joe Rakosi, on the other hand, had just battled in from the airport; a two-hour drive through the chaos of Bangkok's polluted streets. Thailand had three seasons – hot, hotter, hottest – and the air conditioning in his hired Mercedes had broken down. He had undone the top button of his shirt, revealing a red chafe mark, while his tie dangled around his neck like a noose. Rakosi's mood matched his looks. He shook Delacroix's hand, noticing it was dry while his own was clammy. Damn the man, he thought, somehow he always gets me at a disadvantage.

Delacroix gave an urbane smile. 'It's good to see you, Joe. What would you like to drink?'

Rakosi ordered a beer shandy, a full pint, while Delacroix asked for a Perrier with a slice of Thai lime.

'So what's screwed up in Vietnam? What's so bad we couldn't talk about it on the phone?' asked Rakosi with belligerent bluntness. He disliked being summoned, no matter how diplomatically.

Delacroix gave a small grimace. 'I'm afraid that your associate, Mr Keats, has caused us all a great deal of trouble, Joe.'

'What kind of trouble?'

'It seems that when Mr Keats got down to the coast with the diving team, he became involved with an escaped convict – it's a little uncertain how – and ended up helping the man.'

'A local Vietnamese, you mean? A criminal?'

'Very much a criminal, Joe, an ex-officer from the South Vietnam regime.'

'Oh Christ!' Rakosi flopped back in his seat, staring skywards. 'Are you sure about this?'

'I'm afraid there's no doubt.'

'So what's happened?' It was just the kind of idiotic thing Mike Keats would do, thought Rakosi. Bleeding bloody liberals – sap hearts, damn them all. 'Has he been arrested?'

'He was taken in for questioning, yes. But then he acted even more rashly, just compounding our problems.'

Rakosi held his hands up to his face. 'I don't even want to hear.'

'On his way back from the police station he attacked a guard and escaped.'

Rakosi was dumbfounded. 'He's got to be mad! Have they caught him? I don't believe this . . .'

'It seems he's still at large. But an extensive search is being conducted.'

Rakosi was clenching and unclenching his red-knuckled fists, trying to control his temper. 'So what happens to this arms deal, the inspection of the weapons? Is there any way we can salvage it?'

Delacroix shook his head. 'It was always a delicate matter, Joc, I made that clear at the beginning.'

Rakosi let out a groan. 'Why I ever sent Mike Keats, God only knows. I need my head examined!'

'Trust was essential, Joe. Secrecy and absolute trust. Mr Keats has been posted as an enemy agent. The British Embassy in Hanoi has been informed accordingly. With the best will in the world, you can't expect the Vietnamese to deal with enemy agents . . . or their associates for that matter.'

'So the opportunity is blown?'

'I'm afraid so . . .'

'There's no way I can speak to them perhaps, try and set matters right?'

'Our Vietnamese contact has washed his hands of the entire sale of weapons proposal. He wants nothing more to do with it. It was risky enough at the outset. But to deal with your organisation now would be suicidal. I'm sorry, Joe, I really am. But there's nothing either of us can do to retrieve the situation. I just hope your partner appreciates the damage he has caused. He has tossed several hundred million into the wind.'

'Not that he could care a stuff,' muttered Rakosi, boiling with pent-up frustration. The drinks arrived and he gulped furiously at his shandy.

'The best you can hope for now is a share of the gold,' said Delacroix with the mournful tones of a stockbroker advising a near-bankrupt client.

'Oh yeah, great. Fifteen per cent. And what will that bring me, supposing they ever find the stuff? Enough to cover costs.'

'At least the exercise won't have put you deeper into debt.'

'Cold bloody comfort you are.' Rakosi was scarlet-faced, his blood pressure soaring. 'How could he do it to me? How could he have got himself into a mess like this? The stupid bastard, he'll find himself in jail, that's what will happen. He'll be an old man before he gets out and I tell you now, I couldn't give a damn! He's only got himself to blame. He's like a bloody child!'

Delacroix waited until Rakosi's temper had subsided a little. 'There's nothing we can do for Keats now,' he said. 'He's the author of his own misfortunes, Joe. We have to consider our own positions. The important thing is to ensure that the gold is found quickly and flown safely out of Vietnam.'

Rakosi gave a distracted grunt. 'Are they still diving?'

'Yes. Their work hasn't been prejudiced – not yet at least. They'll find the wreck, I'm sure of it. And when they do, we must ensure everything runs smoothly. Because that gold is the quid pro quo for the ten million paid to your bankers, Joe. It's your insurance for a healthy profit in Mozambique. If we fail the men in Budapest on this one, it could be disastrous.'

'You don't have to preach to me,' muttered Rakosi. 'I know how the cards are stacked.'

Delacroix continued. 'It's been decided that when the gold is found, it will be flown here to Thailand first.'

'Why not fly it straight to Europe? Get it into some bank vault, that's the safest place.'

'It needs to be uncrated first. Rendered innocent, Joe. Checked, weighed and, if necessary, melted down into some new form. Flying it direct to Europe is too dangerous.'

Picking up a slim, crocodile-skin briefcase from next to his chair, Delacroix clicked open the combination locks. There were some papers inside which he handed across the table. 'The originals are in Thai script. But there's a certified English translation on top.'

Rakosi studied the translation. 'This is a lease agreement.'

'For the factory where the gold will be stored.'

'Why is one of my companies the tenant?'

Delacroix gave the slightest smile. 'That was our agreement, Joe. You and your corporations provide the necessary profile.'

'Act as patsies, you mean.'

'Nothing will go wrong, Joe.'

'Oh yeah?' snorted Rakosi. 'At the moment I get the feeling that your first name shouldn't be Jean-Paul, it should be Jonah.'

Delacroix gave a thin smile. 'Setbacks are inevitable.'

Rakosi just shook his head.

The lunch menus were placed on the table. Both men picked them up and there was an electric-charged silence as they studied them.

Delacroix decided on a salad and then said lightly, 'Oh yes, there is one detail concerning the gold which I should mention. Although I have already dealt with it on your behalf.'

'What's that?'

'I'm sure you'll agree it would be a pity to run into difficulties with the Thai Customs and Excise authorities.'

Rakosi jutted his head over the top of his menu. 'So what have you done?'

'I've spoken to a couple of gentlemen who may be able to assist us.'

The question shot out like a punch. 'Offered them bribes, you mean?'

Delacroix laughed. 'It doesn't appear to be too difficult here.'

'Probably why you chose Thailand in the first place.'

Delacroix nodded. 'Possibly, Joe . . .'

'And whose money is being used?'

'It's a book entry, no more.'

'Christ, why can't you say anything straight? Just yes or no. My money, is that what you mean?'

'Don't be concerned, the amounts are not substantial.'

Rakosi scowled, shaking his head. 'So I pay for everything – even the bloody bribes.'

'Don't look so down in the mouth, Joe.' Delacroix gave a sarcastic laugh. 'The lunch is on me.'

Joe Rakosi was considering an appropriate answer when a waiter came over, asking if there was a Mr Rakosi at the table. He identified himself and was told that there was an urgent telex waiting at reception.

Rakosi returned to the terrace a couple of minutes later with the telex in his hand. 'It's Mike Keats,' he said. 'He's been found!'

Delacroix cast him a quick glance of surprise. 'Where, in Vietnam?'

'No – in the middle of the South China Sea. Somehow he got onto a refugee boat and was picked up by a passing ship. I'm as dead as a dodo and he's okay. I don't believe it, he's got the luck of the bloody devil.'

The ship that rescued them was named the *Asia Windward*. She was a container ship, registered in the United States and manned by an American crew.

Seeing the little boat in the water, dangerously close to sinking, the master of the *Asia Windward* had obeyed the international laws of the sea and pulled around. The scramble nets had been lowered and the refugees, some with babies strapped to their backs, had climbed to safety – and to a new life.

247

Once aboard, there were hot showers for everybody. The rags they called clothes were discarded while the crew dug out jeans, shirts, jerseys, track suits, anything the refugees could wear. Their first meal – breakfast – was a feast: waffles with maple syrup and whipped butter, canteloupes, frankfurters, french fries, eggs sunny side up, beans and brown bread and more steak than the refugees had seen in their lives. It was a dream. The children sat in their outsize clothes watching Mickey Mouse movies while the adults sat back, safe at last, unable to believe it was true.

For Mike and Mei-ling only one thing clouded the moment – the knowledge that they were going to be separated, that Mei-ling and the refugees were bound for closed camps, a life behind wire that could take them years to escape. But that evening, after dinner, they received news that stunned them both.

The captain of the *Asia Windward* was a nuggety little Texan with the face of a boxer; rubbery nose, split eyebrows and a voice that sounded like grit being dumped on concrete. But he was the one who had insisted the refugees be cared for so well. And when he called Mike and Mei-ling to his cabin, he showed the full extent of his concern.

'I've radioed our Hong Kong agents to inform them we've picked you up,' he said. 'They've been on to the US Consulate and I've just received their reply. Everything is fine and dandy. A letter of guarantee has been signed.'

Mike looked blank. 'I'm sorry, I don't understand.'

'Nor do I,' said Mei-ling . . .

'Haven't either of you heard of RASRO?'

From the look on Mike's and Mei-ling's faces, the answer was obvious.

The captain beamed. 'Then you're in for a happy surprise.' He lit a cigar – like a proud father – and offered one to Mike. 'RASRO is a scheme operated by the United Nations High Commission For Refugees. Hell of a mouthful but it stands for Rescue At Sea Resettlement Offers.'

There was a glimmer of anticipation on Mei-ling's face. 'What does it mean?'

'It means, my dear, that once we've picked you up, you're our responsibility.'

'The shipping line?'

He laughed, puffing smoke. 'Good God no! Something better than that – the US of A, my dear, America! That's why I've been on to our agents. You see, Hong Kong will only let us dock if the US Government provides a written guarantee that you'll all be resettled within ninety days.'

Mei-ling looked like a woman who had just been told she had won a million dollars. 'But resettled where?' she asked in a voice struggling between elation and disbelief.

'In the United States – if nowhere better takes your fancy of course.'

Mei-ling's face was wreathed in smiles. 'But are you saying all of us?'

'Every last one. Grandpas to toddlers.'

Mike was amazed. 'Just incredible . . .' he murmured.

The captain chewed on his cigar. 'May I personally recommend Texas. It's a very fine place.' But then he added a word of caution. 'It's ninety days remember. We don't fly you there tomorrow. There's paperwork, red tape. And you're going to have to spend that time in the refugee camps, a full ninety days.'

But what was ninety days? It was a moment, that's all. A prelude. Just a breath in time. 'Oh, it's wonderful news,' said Mei-ling in a voice floating with exhilaration. 'Do you mind if I tell the others?'

The captain smiled like a fond uncle. 'You go right ahead.'

And off she went.

Mike remained with the captain after she had left, finishing his cigar.

'A little redeye?' asked the captain.

Mike accepted. He was delighted with the news but puzzled too. 'Tell me,' he asked, 'what would have happened if we had been in a bigger, more seaworthy boat?'

'If you had made Hong Kong under your own steam, you mean? Just sailed into the harbour . . .?'

'Yes.'

'Then those refugees would have been on their own. No preference, no help. Certainly no RASRO scheme.'

'Ninety day resettlement?'

'Nope.'

'Just a closed camp?'

'It's ironic,' said the captain, sipping his bourbon neat. 'But those Thai pirates might just have done you a favour. Because if that boat of yours hadn't been shot up so bad I would problably have left you to fend for yourselves. Dropped a little food and water on board and that's it.'

'Then, even if we had made Hong Kong, the refugees wouldn't have been looking at the United States?'

'Not within ninety days they wouldn't. Maybe not within ninety years.' He puffed deeply on his cigar. 'Nobody said life was equal, Mr Keats. Just lucky for some.'

After he had left the captain, Mike walked past the cabin where Mei-ling was gathered with the refugees. But it was not a time to intrude. They were together as a close-knit group for possibly the last time. They had risked everything and they had won through. And they deserved their good fortune, thought Mike, every last one of them.

The following morning, shortly after dawn – six days after Mike Keats had escaped from Vietnam – the *Asia Windward* cruised into the breathtaking grandeur of Hong Kong harbour. Mike was on deck with the refugees and he could sense the awe they felt. A soft breeze was blowing, humid and warm, and the lights of the city were still on, ten million of them glittering on the hills of Hong Kong Island and across the water in Kowloon. It was a magical moment.

An hour later the ship docked at Kwai Chung Container Terminal. Kwai Chung was the world's busiest terminal and even at this early hour the cranes were working, the lorries were queuing and everywhere, as far as the eye could see, were acres and acres of containers; blue, green, rusty brown, some stacked as high as tenement blocks.

Hong Kong . . . for all its dirt and congestion, it was his city. This was home and being back here, alive and free, filled him with jubilation.

Just as he had anticipated, a team of immigration officers and marine police were waiting on the dockside to process the refugees. The gangway was lowered and they came aboard.

Mei-ling, who was standing with him, watched the other refugees – excited yet nervous, uncertain of what lay ahead – collect their meagre belongings and start to file away. 'I must go with them,' she said. 'They need my help.'

Mike nodded, as slow as an ox. Just when he wanted to

say so much to her, he couldn't say a thing.

But Mei-ling was more direct. She bent to pick up her scuffed leather medical bag and then she asked him, 'Will I see you again?'

Prompted, Mike replied, 'You can bet on it.'

She gave a gentle smile. 'In which case I hope it will be soon.'

He grinned, besotted by her. 'Sounds good to me. How about this afternoon?'

And the two of them burst out laughing. Because suddenly all their private doubts were blown on the wind. Even if this afternoon was impossible, they knew now that there would be other afternoons, hundreds of them. This wasn't the end at all, only a new beginning. And, before Mike knew it, he was hugging Mei-ling close and saying, 'You're never going to get rid of me, you realise that. I'm going to stick to you like glue.'

And she was laughing as she said, 'Oh I hope that's true.'

The breeze was ruffling her hair and her lips were moist. Mike didn't care about the others on deck, the sailors and officials and the other refugees. He took her in his arms, pulling her close. She felt the hardness of his loins, felt how much he wanted her. And she rocked against him, slim as a sapling. He bent his head –

'Li Mei-ling, come forward please!'

Mike ignored the guttural shout.

'Li Mei-ling!' boomed the immigration officer.

Little Pepe was pulling excitedly at her dress. 'Come. Come . . .'

Mei-ling smiled, her face full of regret. 'I'm sorry, Mike,' she whispered. Then she took Pepe's hand.

Mike watched her walk across to join the other refugees. 'I'll see you as soon as I can,' he called after her.

This is ridiculous, he thought. I'm head-over-heels in love with the woman and I haven't even kissed her yet.

The night before, with the permission of the captain, Mike had sent a ship-to-shore radio message to Chuck Baldwin to let him know he was still alive and that he might encounter a little difficulty in getting ashore. Chuck understood the problems and the fact too that – as far as the CIA were concerned – the less publicity the better. So the necessary arrangements were made.

The crew of the *Asia Windward* were persuaded that while they were in Hong Kong they should say nothing to the press or immigration and later that morning, after the refugees had been placed on board a ferry to take them to a quarantine camp on Lantau Island, Mike was brought quietly ashore as a member of the crew.

His British passport, or the remnants of it, had been reduced to the texture of stone-washed denim. But it sufficed – just – and when Mike eventually emerged from the immigration building, Chuck Baldwin was waiting.

Mike heard the voice first. 'You crazy bastard, what have you been up to?' Then he saw the stocky, grey-haired American striding towards him, his windcheater flapping around that solid sandbag of a torso. 'You had me half-scared to death. Until I received your radio message last night, I thought you were history.'

Mike concurred. 'There were times when I thought the same.'

Chuck Baldwin was laughing, an expression of pure relief. 'From the garbled messages we've been getting out of the British Embassy in Hanoi, it seems the Vietnamese are blaming you for everything – the cost of living, genocide, you name it! What were you up to there? Jeez, it's good to see you. Just don't scare the shit out of me like that again. I'm getting too old to take the strain.'

They climbed into the back of a waiting consular car and drove out of the terminal towards the Cross Harbour Tunnel in Tsim Sha Tsui.

'Okay,' said Chuck Baldwin. 'If you feel like talking, what really happened in Vietnam?'

Mike gave a tired smile. 'You're going to think I'm crazy, Chuck. Maybe I am. The more I think about it, the more crazy it all sounds. But do me a favour will you, hear me out first.'

Chuck Baldwin said nothing, simply nodded.

And Mike began.

They had reached Mike's apartment in Deep Water Bay – a full hour's drive – before he had finished his story and it took another forty or fifty minutes to repeat it slowly, step by step, as Chuck Baldwin took notes.

Finally, when Mike had exhausted his memory of events, he dropped into an easy chair, stretched out his long legs and said, 'So, what do you think?'

Chuck Baldwin walked to the bay window that looked down over the small nine-hole golf course wedged in between the hills. 'As you said, it's crazy. Incredible . . . maybe too incredible, I just don't know.'

Mike went through to the kitchen. There were some cans of beer in the fridge and he cracked two open, returning to the lounge. 'You had to be there, Chuck, you had to see the look in his eyes. Tang was telling the truth, I'd stake my life on it.'

'That's exactly what you did – and you damn near lost.'

'Why would he want to make up a story like that? And

he named names, Chuck – Blackmore, his old section head. Chan Chi-Wai, the Triad.'

'There must be ten thousand Vietnamese who can name somebody in the CIA, somebody who they had connections with during the war.'

'But I keep telling you, Tang wasn't Vietnamese, he was American.'

'How can you be so sure of that?'

'Please, Chuck, give me some credit – '

'You were bouncing along that track in the middle of the night. The guy was Chinese. You were in shock, you admit it yourself. Okay, so he spoke English with an American accent. Do you know how long we were in Vietnam? Over ten years.'

Mike picked up the ring that lay on the coffee table. In the daylight he could see how worn it was; old grubby gold, grimed with sweat and dirt. 'So what about this?' he asked, holding it up.

Chuck Baldwin drank his beer from the can. 'So what does it prove?'

'That there was a group called the Phoenix Pact.'

'Does it? Or simply that he had a ring with a phoenix on it?'

'Oh for chrissake!'

'A man jumps out of the bushes and tells you about a doomsday weapon – let's face it, you're going to be sceptical.'

'So who's crazy, him or me?'

'How can you trust anybody in a situation like that?'

'I don't say trust him, all I say is check him out. He knew all about the junk. He knew I was involved with the diving team. How?'

'Because you were the only Europeans in a radius of about three hundred miles.'

'But we'd been there a few hours, that's all. We hadn't even started diving yet. I'm sorry, Chuck, bush telegraph doesn't work that fast.'

Chuck Baldwin finished his beer, squashing the empty can in his fist. He stared fixedly out towards the sea and tried to explain. 'Do you have any idea, Mike, how many South Vietnamese officers were imprisoned after the fall of Saigon? Do you have any conception of how they were treated, starved, tortured, brain-washed? What do you think eighteen years in prison does to a man? What kind of madness does it instil? The past becomes the present. They begin to live in a world of their own. They dream of how things could have been so different, how they could have been the victors . . . if we'd just had a nuclear bomb, oh Jesus, man, we could have blown them all to hell.'

'Okay,' said Mike, 'for the moment let's say that Tang was one of these guys, gone crazy in the head. That's what the Vietnamese officer, Nguyen, said he was – some kind of schizophrenic. Okay, so that explains Tang. But how do you explain the questions I was asked by Nguyen?'

Chuck Baldwin looked at him, beginning to understand.

Mike paced the carpet. 'Nguyen specifically asked me a number of questions – if Tang had spoken about the sunken junk, if he had spoken about weapons, about some secret pact. But why? If they were just the ramblings of some madman, why bother? It would have been a joke, something for us to laugh about. But believe me, Nguyen wasn't laughing. And the telling fact – the one thing that convinces me – is that every question he asked mirrored everything Tang had told me. How do you explain that?'

'I don't.'

'No, because somewhere there Tang was telling me the truth. Exaggerated maybe, out of kilter, all twisted and turned – but the truth, Chuck, still the truth.'

Chuck Baldwin went through to the kitchen to get the last two beers. 'Okay,' he said, tossing one to Mike, 'if there was a weapon on that junk, why didn't Tang tell you what kind it was? A doomsday weapon, he said, like it's something out of science fiction. But what kind of doomsday weapon? A nuclear warhead? Poison gas? What? If he knew so much about the junk, why didn't he tell you?'

All Mike could do was shrug.

'And if the Vietnamese or the Russians – or whoever – wanted to raise it, why wait nearly twenty years? How do you explain that?'

'I don't.'

'They've had Tang since the Vietnam War. Or that's the impression he gave. And why use outsiders? Why not raise it themselves?'

'We're talking about a five minute helter-skelter ride with both of us scared to death,' said Mike lamely. 'It's not the best environment for tying up loose ends.'

'I'm talking about more than loose ends, Mike. If this was a court of law, would you be satisfied beyond a reasonable doubt on Tang's evidence alone?'

Mike didn't disguise his disappointment. 'So what do you intend to do?'

Chuck Baldwin turned to him and there was a wry smile on his face. 'I intend to do exactly what you suggested – check him out.'

Chuck Baldwin left at six that evening. An hour later Mike drove to Repulse Bay in the small BMW he kept, had dinner at a little Cantonese restaurant on the beach-front, drank a bottle of Chinese white wine and by eight thirty was back at the front door of his apartment ready

257

to sleep a full twenty-four hours. But, as he put the key in the lock, he heard the persistent ring of the telephone and knew intuitively who it had to be.

Rakosi sounded as if he was about to throw a fit. 'How could you do this to me? What possessed you?'

'Look, Joe, I'm dead on my feet. Can't we discuss this some other time?'

'Sure, no problem,' said Rakosi, his voice dripping sarcasm. 'We've just blown the biggest arms deal of the decade but what the hell. Easy come, easy go, hey, Mike? Just so long as it doesn't offend your moral sensibilities.'

Mike had been expecting a tirade and wasn't prepared to argue, not at this time. 'Let's talk about this tomorrow . . .'

'Where in the hell do you think I am? I'm in Bangkok trying to sort out the mess you've created. And first thing tomorrow I fly to Mozambique. So tomorrow won't do – '

Mike let out his breath. 'Look, Joe, I'm sorry it all turned so sour . . .'

'But you were meant to be such a whiz kid in the field. The man who could deal with any situation.'

'Believe it or not, Joe, I was trying to save my life.'

'You get involved with some ex-goon from the South Vietnamese Army, of course they're going to ask you questions. But what do you do? You panic, you bolt. You turn a minor incident into an international drama.'

'Where did you get this crap from?' asked Mike.

'I have my sources,' said Rakosi guardedly.

'And you're not prepared to listen to my side first?'

'There could have been a fortune in this if you hadn't blown it. Now all we've got is the gold.'

'What gold? Don't delude yourself, Joe, you'll never see any gold.'

Rakosi was contemptuous. 'So you're giving up on that too, are you?'

Mike tried to keep his patience. 'Stop and think a second, Joe. It's not just me . . . Mozambique, Vietnam, it's all been a disaster. Don't you see it? Delacroix, and whoever he's representing, they're leading you by the nose.'

'What are you trying to suggest here, some kind of conspiracy?'

'Trust me, Joe. Please, just this once – accept my word.'

'It's you, you're the one who has brought this on us, not Delacroix!'

'Just listen will you! Stop for a second and think instead of charging like a bull at a gate. Don't you understand what I'm trying to say to you? You've got to pull out now while you've got the chance. Cut your losses. Airlift Seager and his team out as soon as possible. Once and for all, cut yourself free of Delacroix.'

'Why? Tell me one good reason why?'

Mike hesitated. If he told Rakosi about Tang, he knew what his reaction would be. But what other choice did he have? They were partners. Somehow he had to convince Joe they were heading for disaster. 'Let me tell you what really happened in Vietnam,' he said. 'Let me tell you about that escaped convict, Joe . . .'

As briefly as possible, sketching over a lot of the detail, he explained to Rakosi what had happened that night. And ended by saying, 'Tang was American, Joe. Ex-CIA, that's what he told me. And he knew all about the junk, he knew what it contained.'

'American?' Rakosi gave a bitter laugh. 'Oh come on, Mike, you don't buy that missing-in-action bullshit do you? American prisoners still there eighteen years after the war?'

'Tang spoke to me, Joe. I know what I know.'

'Okay, assuming you're right for a second, what did this American – this CIA agent – tell you was in the junk?'

'Some kind of weapon.'

'What, a bomb?' Rakosi started to laugh. 'I'm a businessman, Mike, I make deals. All right, some may involve a little dirty money. But salvaging bombs off the bottom of the sea? Why would the Hungarians want me to do that? They've got enough bloody bombs of their own. Fancy cars, that's what they want, Jaguars and shiny red Mustangs – and even fancier women. They want money, Mike, hard currency. Swiss francs and Japanese yen. They want me to line their fat little nests for them, not blow up the world. What do you think Delacroix is, some kind of Red Army anarchist? He used to be a Jesuit priest. He lives in Fribourg for chrissake! Have you been there?'

Mike tried to contain his anger. 'I'm not suggesting Delacroix is a terrorist. But what do you know about him, Joe? What do you know about any of them? If only half of what Tang told me is the truth, then there's no gold. And that means you're being used, Joe.'

'You keep using that word – used, used – but for what?'

'I don't know!' Mike was shouting down the line now. 'Christ, do we have to know everything before we act? The whole thing stinks. Isn't that enough?'

But Rakosi was boiling with temper too. 'You say I'm being used, pulled along by the nose – okay, maybe I am. In business people use each other every day. That's the name of the game. But you're worse because you've been made a fool of, Mike, treated like an idiot. You've bought a load of gobbledegook off a lunatic and it's cost us both a fortune. But that's as far as it goes. Seager and his team are going to stay in Vietnam. Because there's gold on that junk, Mike, I don't care what you say. And I need it – both of us do!'

And, before Mike could answer, the phone was slammed down.

Before he had picked up the telephone, Mike had been asleep on his feet. But he couldn't sleep – not now. All he could do was lie on his bed and stare up at the ceiling, his mind a raging battlefield of doubts and fears and uncertainties.

Earlier that day on the *Asia Windward* he had been so certain in his mind that Tang had been sane . . . haunted, yes, compelling, trembling on a knife edge, but a man who knew what he was saying and understood its implications. Now, however, he couldn't be so sure.

Chuck Baldwin was right. A lot of things didn't add up, too many things. But Chuck at least, despite his scepticism, was willing to check out Tang's story.

Rakosi, on the other hand, was deaf to everything he said. Mike knew that from the moment Rakosi had accepted the Mozambique deal, the first strands of some kind of web had been flung around him. And it wasn't just business – gold and currency – as Rakosi liked to think. It was more sinister than that. But Mike had warned him in the very beginning – that December day in London in the restaurant along the Thames – and now he had warned him again. What more could he do?

And, as sheer exhaustion, a fatigue that went to the marrow of his bones, finally forced him into sleep, he dreamt of Mei-ling.

It was midnight, Hong Kong time – eleven in the morning in Langley, Virginia – when Chuck Baldwin despatched the secret cypher message to CIA Headquarters. It was marked for the attention of the Chief of Operations, Far East Sector, and within the hour James Dexter had it on his desk.

Although Baldwin had expressed certain reservations, it was clear he placed a lot of credence in Keats' wild story. If there was, in fact, such a man as Ricky Tang and if he was telling anywhere near half the truth, Dexter knew that the implications could be serious, very serious indeed. And dropping everything, he went down to the archives in the basement of the building to the special section that guarded top-secret material.

It took a time to dig out the material. It meant going back nearly two decades. But Tang's name was there all right: TANG Pak-sui k.a. Larry Tang, born Honolulu, 23. 9. 45. He was an American, born and bred, just as Keats had said. But even more disturbing was the fact that his personal file was cross-indexed with another operational file that bore the title:

THE PHOENIX PACT (Final Report)

So Keats hadn't fled from shadows of his own making. The Vietnamese had wanted to kill him. Damn sure they had. And, with his unlit pipe clenched between his teeth, James Dexter hunched down in front of the viewing screen to study the microfilmed papers.

The year was 1968. He had been a law professor then at the State University of New York; a bright young liberal, one of America's best, exempted from military service. 1968 . . . half a million troops in Vietnam, the Tet Offensive, Khe Sanh, the year of the great protest marches. Bobby Kennedy assassinated and Martin Luther King too. The year America was divided unto itself. A year of drugs and bitterness and blood on the streets. The year of the Phoenix Pact.

James Dexter, a humourless man at the best of times, sat grim-faced, disbelieving, as he read document after document. Then, still in the gloomy hush of the archives, he telephoned the office of the Director himself. 'I have to speak to him urgently,' he said to his secretary. 'No, tomorrow won't do, I must see him now.'

It was Kirilenko who conveyed the news, speaking by telephone on secure means. 'Keats made it back to Hong Kong,' he said in a slow, heavy voice.

Nguyen was silent for a time, digesting the news. Then he answered. 'So what do we do?'

'We spoke about the possibility before. There's been no change. We continue as planned.'

'For how long?'

'As long as necessary.'

But Nguyen, an unwilling accomplice in the first place, was beginning to feel the pressures. 'It's getting too dangerous, Grigori. By now the CIA must know what we're trying to do. Anything could happen. We can't be sure they won't act. Another three days, that's all I can allow.'

'That's unreasonable, Xuan, you've got to give the divers more time.'

But Nguyen was adamant. 'Three days, no more. If nothing is found by then, I'm aborting the operation.'

Mike Keats awoke suddenly, sunlight streaming through the window onto his face. But, as he showered and dressed, he was aware of a strange sensation in the pit of his stomach; not an unpleasant feeling, but something difficult to describe . . . a sense of anticipation.

There was no food in the kitchen, just a couple of six-week-old yoghurts in the back of the fridge with their tin foil lids ominously bulging. Hey ho, the domestic life of a bachelor, he thought, as he made himself a cup of black instant coffee. And the thought of a future like this appealed to him as much as the rest of his life in solitary confinement.

Leaving the apartment, he flagged down a taxi, still aware of the sensation. It was puzzling. A nervous excitement, a prodding by the subconscious. And slowly, as the taxi drove down Stubbs Road into Wanchai, Mike began to understand the significance of it. What was it that Pascal, the French philosopher, had said? It was one of the few quotations he remembered from an undistinguished career at school: *le coeur a ses raisons que le raison ne connait pas* . . . the heart has its reasons which the reason does not know of. Yes, he thought, that was exactly how he felt.

As always, the traffic through Wanchai was nose to tail with minibuses and double-deckers, cement mixers and little Japanese cars edging along between the taxis, all of them travelling at a mile an hour. Mike wanted time to think, to walk through the streets and be part of the bustle. So he stopped the taxi on Queens Road East and jumped out.

Crossing the road, he made his way down towards Johnston Road. He had to walk in the street because the pavement was filled with dai pai dongs, the cooked food stalls where workers sat on fold-up stools drinking tea and eating unmentionable things. A group of construction workers, already grey from cement dust, were playing mahjong at one table, clacking and banging the tiles, laughing and shouting. Further on, housewives were bargaining for fish still so fresh they flip-flopped on

264

the hawkers' carts. The sing-song blare of Cantonese pop came out of shop doorways. Everywhere there was noise, women gesticulating, car horns hooting. The Cantonese were the Italians of China, just as emotional and every bit as vibrant.

As Mike strolled along under the neon signs and the laundry hanging from bamboo poles, there was a smile on his face. He felt good. Hong Kong: borrowed place, borrowed time. But it lived, it was full of hope and humour. It reflected everything he felt. And standing there on the corner of Johnston Road, with the old wooden trams rattling by, he made his decision.

It took two hours to get to Chi Ma Wan quarantine camp, catching the ferry to Lantau Island and then a taxi to the camp itself. The place was run by the Correctional Services Department – the prisons – and looked like a barracks. It took Mike another hour to obtain permission to see Mei-ling. Nobody was difficult, just slow. But he would have waited a week if necessary.

She emerged from one of the long blockhouses with a member of the camp's staff. She knew it had to be him and the moment she saw him, her eyes lit up.

Mike couldn't believe how beautiful she was; beauty in its simplest form, unadorned, as fresh as morning. He took her hand and together they walked across the concrete parade ground, along the wire-mesh fence to a single stone bench. It stood in the shade of a banyan tree where some wild, sulphur-white cockatoos were perched. Mei-ling sat but he remained standing.

'How are they treating you?' he asked.

'They're very kind.'

'You look rested.'

'It's a dream come true for us.'

'Even in this place?'

'Even here.'

'And Pepe?'

'He's been given a football. So the world's a wonderful place for him too.'

'I'm pleased.' Mike smiled, lost for words, desperately trying to summon up the courage. 'I've got something to ask you . . .'

She looked up at him.

Mike hesitated. 'Will you marry me?' he asked.

Her eyes widened, filled with surprise. She went to speak but, just as he had been lost for words a few seconds before, now she was too.

Mike waited, his heart thudding in his chest. He could see that Mei-ling was filled with confusion.

'Why are you asking me?' she said in a voice that trembled.

And suddenly, where before he had been groping for words, now they came strong and true. 'Because I love you,' he said. 'Because I want to spend the rest of my life with you. Because we've been through hell and water – literally – and I know you're the only woman I'll ever be happy with. Because the thought of losing you tears me apart. That's why.'

The words took her breath away. But she was still uncertain. 'I'm just so terrified you're doing this because you feel sorry for me . . .'

'Sorry for you?' Mike was amazed, almost angry. 'Why should I feel sorry for you? That's the last thing I feel. In ninety days you'll be out of here, on your way to America. You're young, you're a doctor. To hell with it,' he said, laughing. 'You're better qualified than I am!'

Then Mei-ling rose up from the stone bench, a quivering smile on her lips, and there were tears sparkling in her almond eyes. 'Oh yes, Mike,' she said, almost inaudibly. 'Oh yes.'

'You'll marry me?'

And she said a little louder, 'Of course I will.'

And they both stood there looking at each other, their faces filled with expectation.

And it was probably the happiest moment of his life.

If they were going to get married, the first priority was to get Mei-ling out of the camp. But it didn't matter who he saw, how much he pleaded and cajoled, the law allowed no discretion. Mei-ling would have to remain there until the wedding. She would even have to be escorted to the service by members of the Correctional Services Department. Very well, thought Mike, if that's the way it had to be, they'd get married immediately.

But it seemed that even getting married in Hong Kong posed a problem. The rule book said that seventeen days' notice had to be given, seventeen days kicking their heels while a piece of paper hung on a notice board gathering dust in some government hallway.

And that's when Mike's war began. Poring through the statute books, he discovered what looked like a loophole. The Marriage Ordinance stated that the Chief Registrar could, when he saw fit, grant a special licence dispensing with notice entirely.

So Mike insisted on seeing him – not tomorrow, not the day after. Now. The Chief Registrar, a vapid-faced Chinese gentleman who looked as if he hadn't seen the sun in years, asked Mike, without a trace of humour, if he intended to die within the next week. Otherwise special dispensation could not be granted. That was the only grounds he allowed.

But Mike wasn't prepared to take no for an answer. By

nature he wasn't a pusher but if he had to push and threaten until they shoved him in jail, he'd do it.

Mei-ling, he said, was a refugee, a qualified doctor, a woman who could be doing good work in the community. The two of them had just survived the most harrowing ordeal at sea. He was a businessman with an impeccable reputation, a Hong Kong resident. They loved each other and wanted to be married at the first opportunity. But now it seemed she would have to languish in a camp because certain civil servants didn't have the courage to exercise the discretion they had been invested with in the public good. Mike wondered – out loud – what the newspapers would make of it. Then he asked the Chief Registrar for the spelling of his name.

It was nine o'clock that night before Mike managed to track down Chuck Baldwin who was at the Consulate working late. 'I'd like to ask a special favour, Chuck.'

'Sure, shoot – '

'Would you mind being my best man?'

'Your best man?' He started laughing. 'I had no idea you were even involved with anybody. But sure, of course, I'd be delighted. Who is the lady?'

Mike explained.

'Kind of sudden, isn't it?'

'More sudden than you think.'

'Why? When's the big day?'

'Tomorrow,' said Mike.

They were married in a small room of the City Hall on the waterfront.

Mike and Chuck were waiting when Mei-ling arrived escorted by two women officers of the Correctional Services Department. In the rush, Mike hadn't been able to get across to the camp on Lantau. But the female staff at the camp had found her a simple white cotton dress and white shoes which she wore with a quiet grace.

And Mike would not have asked for it any other way. For as she entered the room, he seemed to see and comprehend everything that made her the woman he loved. The bleakness of life that had made her strong as only victims can be strong. The oppression that had taught her compassion. Her innate love for people and above all for children. Her gentleness. And in the synthesis of all these things an abiding beauty that was timeless.

She stood side by side with Mike, barely coming up to his shoulder, as the short, simple ceremony took place.

Chuck Baldwin stood to one side. Privately he had had grave reservations about the marriage. He had seen too many romances like this born out of hard times, bloodshed and war. And had seen too many of them die on the rocks of peace. He was a cynical man. But even he was captivated.

Afterwards, free of the escorting officers, with a marriage certificate and Mei-ling's Hong Kong residence permit in hand, the three of them walked across to the Mandarin Hotel for an early dinner in a private room.

Mike had suggested to Mei-ling that they spend the night in the hotel. By some accounts it was the best hotel in the world and they would take the very best suite. But Mei-ling wanted nothing more than to return to his apartment, to be in a place which was his. Rich hotels meant nothing to her. But a home, a place she could share with him, was something else entirely.

There was wine waiting in the apartment when they arrived. Mei-ling bathed, laughing at all the soaps and shampoos – ten different kinds at least – that Mike had bought to try and please her. Then, when she was dry, and her nutmeg skin was scented, she came to him wearing just a towel.

Mike let it slip from her body and heard himself gasp as he beheld her nakedness. Gently, he lifted her up and laid her on the bed. Her breasts were small, softly rounded. Moonlight shone through the window and on the sheets she was luminously pale . . . tapering curves, slender thighs, small bare feet. Mei-ling turned her head in profile, reaching out gracefully to beckon him. And when he pressed his lips against her skin, he heard her sigh with pleasure. They made love then, slowly, as if they had the whole of eternity to please each other, the long arch of his back joined to her honeyed loins.

Afterwards they drank wine and talked and laughed and forgot everything in the world except their togetherness. For a long time they lay in each other's arms until slowly the passion grew in them again. Then he began to caress her as a man might caress a jewel too precious to believe, wide-eyed, hesitant, fascinated by every curve and rich shadow.

But when he came in her the second time it was with a power that dominated them both. Mei-ling had never known such a need before. And he bore down upon her until it seemed their bodies had melted into one. And she clung to him, to the browned athletic body, until, with a final cry, it was finished.

There were no words to describe it. Mei-ling lay beneath him, her slender body damp with perspiration. She gazed up at him, touching his face, letting the tips of her fingers smooth the beard, and she knew that she would love him until the day she died.

*   *   *

Joe Rakosi knew nothing of the wedding. He was in Maputo with Simpson, his London manager, ensuring that the second shipment – twenty million dollars' worth, including military radio equipment, American wheat and engine spares for Mozambique's existing fleet of Western vehicles – didn't meet the fate of the first. Mike had sent a telegram but it got no further than the Maputo post office where it lay gathering mould.

This time, however, the arrival of the aid shipment ran smoothly. It was landed, cleared through Customs and officially handed over to a representative of the government. Even the Hungarian Ambassador attended the function, which was held on a hot, sticky morning. There were smiles all round, platitudes about socialist solidarity, photographs, the buzz of mosquitoes and warm champagne. And then, thank God, the second shipment was off Rakosi's hands and payment was guaranteed.

That left just one more shipment, already on the high seas, due in Maputo in ten days' time. Once that was handed over, the final fifteen million US dollars would be paid. In the end result – provided there were no more hitches – he would have broken even; nothing to congratulate himself on but, considering the initial disaster, it could have been a lot worse, thought Rakosi.

James Dexter had to wait forty-eight hours before the Director referred back to him. It was late afternoon, the first day of March. Virginia was gripped with unseasonal snows when he received the call in his office. 'I think we'd better talk,' said Thomas Delaney. And five minutes later Dexter was ushered into his office.

Tom Delaney had aged ten years in the past few months. The radium treatment seemed to have shrivelled him. The cancer was incurable, Delaney accepted that now. He was trying desperately to keep a grip on the Agency's affairs in these last few days before his successor took over. But it was a losing battle. He was a man facing death, tired and old and terrified what history would make of him.

'I have studied the papers,' said Delaney in his slow Georgia drawl. 'I have consulted the experts. I am advised, Jim, that when the junk went down it was most severely damaged. The chances of anybody – or anything – surviving unscathed were a thousand to one.'

James Dexter chewed at his unlit pipe. 'Tang survived.'

'But that junk has been on the bottom for eighteen years, Jim . . . subject to currents and tides. The container must have been damaged, at least to some extent, the casing split or cracked. Water must have seeped in. Rust must have started its work. In short, Jim, I am assured there's no danger.'

'But how confident can you be in that assessment?'

Delaney was tap-tapping his old tortoise-shell glasses on the desk top. 'We're talking about an unstable substance, Jim, untested and volatile. I am assured that within ten years, let alone eighteen, it would have lost its lethal properties.'

'So you are satisfied?'

'Yes, I am.'

The Director had the long, sad face of a bloodhound, heavily wrinkled with pouches under his eyes. He was a dishevelled figure, his white hair unbrushed, brows furrowed. His suits were always too baggy. In that regard he was a figure of amusement in the Agency. But appearances were deceiving. Delaney was a brilliant man, James Dexter recognised that, and a thorough one too. Accordingly, he was prepared to abide by his assessment.

'What do you wish me to do? he asked.

'Keep an eye on the situation. See if the divers find anything. The chances are they won't. But if they do, follow it up. Maintain a low profile though. We don't want to be tripping over our own feet.'

Blizzard-blown snow crackled against Delaney's window and he swivelled his chair so that he could look out. 'I hate these kind of matters, Jim . . . dealing with agents who have gone off the rails, even if it is ancient history now. At one time they were good men. They did a fine job in the field under trying conditions. Did you know that Tang had the Silver Star? And we left the poor bastard to rot. That was one hell of a decision.'

'What Tang and the others attempted to do was no better than terrorism,' said Dexter stiffly.

Delaney gave a grudging nod. 'You're right of course. But I can't help thinking . . .'

Dexter, however, had no such qualms. 'If the Phoenix Pact had become public knowledge. If it had ever leaked out what means they attempted to use . . .'

'Which brings us on to the matter of Mr Keats,' said Delaney. 'What in your opinion would happen if the truth about the Phoenix Pact was to get out now, eighteen years later? Could it still do us harm?'

'Incalculable harm.' Dexter lit his pipe, a reflex action when he became involved in heated matters, and there was soon the sweet smell of tobacco in the room. 'For a start, we'd be crucified in the UN. The Russians would have a field day. It would destroy our credibility and brand us as war criminals. The CIA itself would be castigated as an outfit of pathological lunatics bent on destroying the world. We could take years to recover . . . if ever.'

Delaney gave a dry nod, letting out his breath. 'An apocalyptic vision, Jim. But an accurate one, I think. So you can imagine that we can't have Mr Keats spreading the gospel. It could place us in a difficult position. Tang still has relatives in Hawaii. They were told he was killed in action. But if they ever heard, if the press got hold of Keats' story, if we started being badgered with questions . . . well, the rest speaks for itself.'

Dexter sucked methodically at his pipe. 'So Mr Keats must be persuaded Tang was not telling the truth.'

Delaney picked up the slim file of papers on his desk. 'Baldwin's report suggests that Keats harbours certain doubts already. I think we should confirm those doubts.'

'So what do you propose?' asked Dexter.

'Tang gave Keats certain instructions.'

'Yes, to contact his old section head.'

'Earl Blackmore?'

'That's right. But Blackmore is – '

Delaney held up his hand. 'Blackmore is a central figure, Jim. He's a man who can confirm or destroy Tang's credibility. He's a very important man to us.'

James Dexter gave a rare smile. 'So what action should I take?'

'Put Mr Blackmore on a plane,' said Delaney. 'Let him have a few days in Hong Kong.'

For nine days they had been diving. But doing it the orthodox way with grid searches, shot lines and charts was getting them nowhere. So Podge and Patti Seager relied on their instincts instead and let themselves be carried by the underwater tide, drifting they hoped where the broken remains of the wreck may have drifted eighteen years before.

They had been down forty minutes, keeping themselves

stable with slow fin strokes, but they had seen nothing, not so much as a tin can. Shafts of diffused sunlight, silvery blue in the turquoise deep, illuminated the rocks and coral. Podge Seager's pressure gauge was hovering dangerously close to the red. It was time to surface. He turned to Patti to signal his intention.

And it was then he saw it . . .

At first glance it resembled the rib cage of some animal. Curved bones jutted up from a bed of cabbage-green kelp. But, as he swam closer, Seager saw that the bones were made of iron. Excitedly, he signalled to his wife, forgetting the problems of air supply, and she finned in towards him.

At close quarters they could both see that the iron ribs were in fact twisted iron girders that bled rust like coppery lava. They were part of some machine, some engine that must have been subjected to violent, explosive forces. Podge Seager swam on and found more fragments on the far side of the kelp bed, jagged chunks lying like shrapnel on the bed of the estuary, even some worm-eaten wood from the hull. It was as if a bomb had hit it.

And that's exactly what they had been told. The junk they were seeking had been bombed by accident and sent to the bottom. They were looking for the remnants of a wreck that had been blown apart.

Nodding his head vigorously, Podge Seager pointed up to the surface. Their exact location had to be fixed, indicated by a buoy and marked on the charts. They had found it. At long bloody last the wreck was theirs! Breaking the surface, they shouted out the good news. One of the inflatable boats roared across. They changed cylinders quickly and down they went again.

If parts of the engine were there then the gold – much heavier than iron – had to be in the near vicinity. So the two of them commenced a circular search, using the iron girders that jutted up from the kelp bed as the centre of the circle, slowly widening the circumference.

And suddenly there it was . . . all alone, isolated, blue metal in blue water. They stared at it a long time because it was like nothing they had ever imagined. They had been expecting to find iron boxes bleeding rust, a debris of containers that had been blown apart and scattered across the rocky floor. But this – this was extraordinary.

It was shaped like a coffin, a huge one. It had to be at least fifteen feet long and six feet deep. Silt had gathered at the base and barnacles had encrusted themselves in the wedges and grooves. There was rust, yes, but otherwise no sign of damage at all.

Podge Seager signalled to his wife and they surfaced again. Podge asked for his camera, the special one that he kept with his private gear. Then the husband and wife team swam back down. Podge took six photographs of the metal container, one of them with Patti swimming next to it to give some indication of scale. Then they both surfaced for the final time that day.

But when their heads broke the surface fifteen or so feet from the nearest boat, the earlier look of jubilation had left their faces to be replaced by an air of grim puzzlement.

Patti turned to her husband, treading water. 'I don't know what that thing is,' she said. 'But it spooks the hell out of me.'

Nguyen received the news with grim stoicism like a general told of a military disaster. 'Is the container intact?'

'It appears to be so, yeah.'

'Airtight?'

Podge was perplexed by Nguyen's attitude. According to his information, Nguyen was going to be taking his share of the gold. And to ask whether the container was airtight, that was a strange damn question.

'Well?'

'I can't be sure. It doesn't look damaged. I can't say any more than that.' Gold didn't rust, it didn't oxidise in sea water. So what did it matter if it was airtight or not?

Nguyen stared out across the estuary. 'How long will it take you to raise it?'

'We'll have to get some idea of the weight first, take measurements and then calculate the best way to use the air bags. Forty-eight hours, I reckon.'

'Have you taken any photographs?'

Another strange question, thought Seager. 'No, not yet,' he said. 'Why, would you like me to take some?'

Nguyen didn't look at him. 'I would rather you didn't. You understand the confidential nature of this project. Photographs are evidence we don't need.'

'Yeah, I understand.'

Nguyen gave a curt nod. 'Then I expect you to start planning your lifting operations first thing in the morning. The quicker this is done, the quicker we can all be gone.' And, with his hands behind his back, his shoulders hunched, he strode away.

From the first day Podge Seager had always been aware of guards around the camp. Whether they were there to keep intruders out or to keep them isolated, he was never quite sure. But in the past they had always kept their distance, shadowy figures in the trees. That night, however, for the first time, they came right into the camp, patrolling past the tents and lifting the flaps to stare in.

'I feel like a prisoner,' said Patti nervously. 'What have we been dragged into here? Do you think there's gold in that container?'

'To hell there is,' said her husband.

'Then why didn't Chuck Baldwin warn us?'

'Maybe Chuck didn't know . . .' Podge Seager lay on his camp bed pretending to read a paperback novel but in the folds of the book lay his passport; plastic-covered royal blue, with the Australian coat of arms on the front cover. Turning to the inside pages, he carefully lifted the plastic sheeting that held down his photograph and then, with a pair of tweezers, placed a set of microdot negatives behind the photograph itself.

His wife saw what he was doing and was frightened. 'We're taking a terrible risk. Is it necessary?'

'Yeah, I think it is,' said Podge. He completed the work, sealing down the photograph and plastic sheet then dropping his passport into the canvas bag that contained the rest of their documents. 'I've got bad vibes about that container,' he muttered, 'very bad vibes indeed.'

By five that evening Mikhail Kazakov had received news of the discovery and immediately telephoned Moscow. 'The bird has been found,' he said, straining to control his glee.

'There were fears its wing might be broken,' Kirilenko replied, without emotion.

'Preliminary reports suggest it's fit and strong.'

'But you will check on that personally?'

'Naturally.'

'And make the necessary preparations.'

'Everything will be done as planned.'

'Good. Please keep me informed.'

The Deputy Director of the GRU replaced the receiver and with a sense of deep satisfaction lit himself a cigarette.

There was a reception that night in the Ukraina Hotel. It was for the delegates to an international conference on population control. Under normal circumstances Kirilenko would never have bothered to attend such a function. He disliked clutching a drink and making small talk with people whose names he couldn't remember. But this time there was a purpose to be served.

He arrived purposefully late, at a time when the alcohol would be making itself felt. He was in his full dress uniform and it was snowing when he climbed stiffly from the chauffeur-driven Chaika. One of the Russian organisers met him at the entrance. 'Good evening, Comrade General. May I be of assistance?'

Kirilenko held up his hand, indicating that he would mingle on his own. As expected, the place was unbearably crowded, a crush of bodies worse than rush hour on the metro. The majority of the delegates were drunk already . . . which was the reason most of them had come to the conference in the first place, thought Kirilenko cynically.

Across by the buffet table he found his target. He was with a group of African delegates, all laughing loudly as they swapped jokes in heavily-accented English, swilling back the imported whisky and wolfing caviar as if it was sandwich spread. Kirilenko waited until the man was on the edge of the group, facing in his direction, then he stepped forward. 'Mr Malimbi, I believe?'

The African was smiling fatly when he turned his attention to the stern figure in the uniform of a Soviet general. 'You're not a delegate are you?' he said drunkenly. 'I thought the military had their own way of dealing with population control.' And he laughed loudly, full of inebriated raucousness.

Kirilenko noticed that the buttons on the man's waist-coat were about to burst. He enjoyed good living. He wondered if he would enjoy the heart attack as much. 'You are Mr Malimbi of the Kenya Government?'

The man gave a glassy-eyed nod. 'Amon Malimbi, yes, that's me, Minister of Economic Development.'

'I do apologise for the inconvenience,' said Kirilenko with the barest deference, 'but I wonder if we might have a word in private.'

It was Mike's first day back at the Good Hope offices, back into the harness of Deputy Chairman again, when Chuck Baldwin telephoned. 'So how's married life?' he asked.

'Bloody marvellous,' said Mike. 'You should try it.'

'I did – twice. The first couple of days were great for me too.'

'You're a cynical bastard,' said Mike, laughing. 'So why are you phoning, is it social or business?'

'Strictly business,' said Chuck Baldwin in a serious tone. 'It's to do with Ricky Tang.'

Mike waited.

'You said that Tang wanted a message passed on to his old section leader . . .'

'That's right – Earl Blackmore.'

'Well, Blackmore arrived in town today. Washington organised it so the two of you could talk.'

'Fine by me,' said Mike.

'Are you free for lunch?'

'Sorry, I'm meeting Mei-ling.'

There was a chuckle at the other end of the line. 'I should have realised. But how about a drink this evening before you fly back to the love nest?'

'I should be free about six,' said Mike.

'Fine, we'll be in the Dragon Boat Bar at the Hilton.'

It was a high-pressure day. With Rakosi away, Mike was the one who had to liaise with the office managers, making the final decisions on a hundred and one matters that piled up over the past weeks and by six that evening he was still heavily involved. It looked like being a late night and he was about to contact Chuck Baldwin to arrange another time, when Joe Rakosi telephoned. He was in London, he said, finalising the Mozambique contract.

His animosity came over the line like a cold wind. Their conversation was sharp, monosyllabic; putting queries and answering them. Nothing was said, not directly that is, but Mike could sense a major confrontation brewing. In a way he was relieved. It was time to make the break. He and Rakosi were like oil and water.

'What's this rumour I hear about you getting married?' asked Rakosi gruffly.

'I sent a telegram to Maputo. Didn't you receive it?'

'I received nothing.'

'Yes, it's true. I got married a couple of days ago.'

Rakosi grunted in surprise. 'So who is she? Bloody quick wasn't it? Where did she spring from?'

'Her name's Mei-ling.'

'Hong Kong Chinese?'

'No, Vietnamese.'

'You married a refugee? One of those women off the boat?'

'Yes, Joe,' Mike answered evenly, refusing to be riled. 'One of those women off the boat . . .'

He could hear Rakosi sucking in his breath. 'I suppose you know what you're doing. Although on the basis of some of your decisions recently – '

Mike cut him short, his voice sharp as a razor's edge. 'Don't make assumptions, Joe. Meet her first.'

'Yeah, well . . .' said Rakosi grudgingly. 'I hope you're both happy.'

And he rang off.

Mike sat for a moment holding the receiver in his hand. If Rakosi had been there – face to face – he would have hit the bastard. Then he thought: no, I'm not going to let you get to me. You're not worth it. And, leaving the files on the desk, he headed for the Hilton.

He found Chuck Baldwin sitting with a big, heavily-built man of about fifty dressed like a tourist in a bright yellow golf shirt and one of those tartan-patterned jackets that Americans favour.

Earl Blackmore had a hearty handshake and a likeable smile. 'It's been close to twenty years since I was last in Hong Kong,' he said with a slow, easy-going drawl. 'And the place sure has changed, I'll tell you that. Manhattan and Chinatown all rolled into one. Great place though, just love it. Having myself half a dozen suits tailor made – forty-eight hours from the first pin to the final fitting. You might have all them skyscrapers now but the little sweat-shops are still the same.'

Mike ordered a round of drinks. After his telephone conversation with Rakosi, he needed one.

Blackmore said he had left the Agency fifteen years ago and had been in the poultry business since that time: day-old chicks, eggs, broilers, that sort of thing. It had been a small business when he had started. 'Just me and one very keen cockerel,' he said. But since then it had grown into one of the biggest poultry businesses in New Jersey.

Blackmore was a good raconteur and they had talked for forty minutes or more before Mike was able to bring up the subject of Ricky Tang.

THE PHOENIX PACT

'What was he like?' Blackmore considered his words carefully before answering. 'You want the honest truth, Mike, no punches pulled? I'll tell you . . . I always thought Ricky was a mite too smart for his own good. An opportunist, if you know what I mean. There was always a bit of the snake-oil salesman in him.'

Mike didn't comment. Blackmore had obviously been well briefed. 'Tang said you were his section head.'

'Yep, Ricky worked under me for two years. We were part of the biggest Agency-conceived operation of the war,' said Blackmore. 'The aim was to get out there in the boondocks and crush the network that Charlie relied on for his food, his money, his recruits. Play Charlie at his own game, that was the philosophy. And I must tell you, Mike, it was effective, very effective indeed. The anti-war guys back home didn't like it too much. "Mass murder", that's what they labelled it. Sure it was. We were taking out twenty thousand Vietcong organisers and tax collectors a year. It was messy kind of work and it put a strain on us all. But it worked, that's what counted. And Ricky, despite his flaws, was a top operator.'

'I remember reading about the operation,' said Mike. 'What was it called again?'

Blackmore drained his bourbon. 'It was named after that mythical Vietnamese bird, Chinese too, the one that never dies . . . Op Phoenix, we called it.'

'That's what Tang had on his ring,' interjected Chuck Baldwin, 'a phoenix.'

'We gave them to the whole team,' said Blackmore casually, 'kind of a memento.'

'It was an interesting design,' said Mike. 'Do you remember who drew it?'

Blackmore was evasive. 'Just some guy.'

'Why the dragon?'

Blackmore smiled. 'Oh hell, Asia and dragons . . . they go together, I suppose. Like eggs and bacon.' And he laughed.

'When did you last see Tang?' asked Mike.

'That would be back in '74, about a year before the fall of Saigon.'

'Was he still working for the Agency?'

'Not at that time, no. It seemed he was doing some undercover work for the South Vietnamese but his main source of income was the black market. And a little dabbling in drugs. Like I said, Ricky was an opportunist.'

'He spoke surprisingly good English.'

'Yeah, strangest thing that, Ricky was a great linguist. Spoke fluent Vietnamese, Mandarin and English. He had lived in Hawaii as a kid, that's what he told me. You know what Chinese are like with their extended families.'

Chuck Baldwin ordered a further round of drinks.

Blackmore was beginning to look flushed, consuming his bourbons like water. 'Chuck told me about this message Tang gave you – they're raising the Phoenix. As fascinating as it sounds, Mike, I must tell you that I don't have the first notion what it means.'

'It related to a junk sunk off the coast of North Vietnam.'

'We never operated that far north, not when I was with Ricky. And we certainly never used junks.'

'What about the Phoenix Pact? Mean anything to you?'

'Nope, not a thing.'

Mike glanced at his watch. It was well after eight. 'I'm sorry, gentlemen,' he said. 'But I have to leave you.'

Earl Blackmore got up, shaking his hand. 'It's been a real pleasure, Mike. If you're ever in New Jersey, look me up, you hear. Damn shame about poor old Ricky.'

'Yes,' said Mike, 'a damn shame . . .' He walked down through the lobby and out into the night. Earl Blackmore was an amiable guy. But when it came to Ricky Tang, he was lying through his teeth.

Podge Seager and his divers had no problem raising the container from the sea bed. Slung under two air bags, it ascended slowly and smoothly to the surface and was then winched aboard an old riverboat that Nguyen had commandeered for the purpose.

Now that it was out of the water, Seager noticed a number of gouges and indentations on the rusted exterior. And, wiping away the slime, he saw a long splayed crack at the back. So it hadn't escaped totally unscathed. Nor, as Nguyen had hoped, was it airtight.

While the rest of the diving team returned to camp, Podge and Patti remained on board the riverboat which chugged half a mile or more up the estuary, turning into a reed-choked channel towards a cluster of teak sheds on the bank. There was an old jetty where Nguyen and a squad of armed soldiers were waiting. The riverboat tied up alongside.

'What are all the soldiers for?' whispered Patti nervously.

Her husband said nothing. But he was filled with foreboding. They stepped onto the jetty and immediately the soldiers came forward. 'What's going on here?' demanded Seager. 'Get your bloody hands off me!'

'Don't argue,' said Nguyen in an icy voice.

Flanked by the troops, Podge and Patti Seager were led to an isolated shed. Nguyen indicated that they should go inside and followed them. He shut the door, leaving the soldiers outside to act as guards.

Nguyen sat atop some sacks of rice, one foot up on a

cask. He regarded the two Australians for a moment and then said in a flat voice, 'We know you are CIA agents.'

Patti Seager went ashen. But her husband showed no reaction, just stared into Nguyen's eyes.

'We know you helped the Americans with the 1983 invasion of Grenada.'

'Bullshit.'

'We also know that you are in our country at the behest of the CIA.'

'You people are paranoid.'

Nguyen stood up, shifting the cask with his foot. A swarm of cockroaches and silverfish scurried out from underneath it. 'We are satisfied with the accuracy of our information,' he said.

'Then there's no point in denying this garbage,' Podge Seager replied. 'You've obviously made up your mind. So what do you intend doing with us?'

'I intend to deport you.'

Outwardly, Seager maintained his stony expression but he was almost dizzy with relief. Considering the alternatives, being deported was a pleasure. 'What about the others?' he asked. 'Are they supposed to be CIA agents too?'

'You came in as one group,' said Nguyen, 'you will leave as one. A telegram has already been sent to the air charter company that brought you to Vietnam requesting it to collect you. Until then you will remain in custody.'

'All of us?'

'All of you.'

'What about our equipment?'

'You can take that with you.' Nguyen smiled sardonically. 'Of course, as for any share of the gold, you understand that's forfeit.'

'That goes without saying,' said Podge Seager with a

defiant, facetious smile and thought to himself: you asshole, what damn gold?

Later that same afternoon in Hong Kong, Chuck Baldwin left the US Consulate, crossed the steep road that ran down into Central and entered St John's Building. He took the lift to the seventh floor, walked through the glass doors that bore the words: Good Hope Group, and asked the pretty Chinese receptionist if he could see Mr Keats.

Mike Keats came out to meet him. 'Come on through, Chuck. Do you want some coffee?'

'Nothing thanks, I won't keep you a moment.'

Mike's office – smaller than Rakosi's – nevertheless had a stunning view down over the graphite waters of Hong Kong harbour.

'So what's the news?' asked Mike. 'Good or bad?'

Chuck Baldwin tossed the photostat copy of a telex across the desk. 'Bloody marvellous,' he said with a look of obvious relief. 'Larry Pike sent it from Bangkok. You don't have to worry about Tang anymore . . . go on, read it, you'll see what I mean.'

Mike picked up the telex:

URGENT REQUEST RECEIVED FROM PODGE SEAGER TO UPLIFT TEAM AND EQUIPMENT. I WILL PILOT AIR CHARTER DC8 INTO VIETNAM TOMORROW, ETA HANOI 1500 HRS. APPEARS ESTUARY DIVE DREW A BLANK. SEAGER'S MESSAGE READS: 'NOTHING FOUND. SEARCH ABANDONED.'

He read it a second time and then with a long exhalation of breath, let it slip from his fingers onto the desk. 'Thank God for that,' he said.

'Hallelujah,' echoed Chuck.

'So whatever went to the bottom is still down there.'

Chuck Baldwin nodded. 'And it doesn't matter a damn if Tang was a prophet or a nutcase. It's irrelevant now.'

Mike flopped back in his chair, folding his arms behind his head. 'I tell you, Chuck, I was becoming obsessive about it.'

'Put it down to experience, Mike. I'm flying to Bangkok in the morning to debrief Podge and Patti Seager – dot the i's and cross the t's – and after that it goes straight into the mental file marked bad memories.'

'How long will you be away?'

'Not long, just a couple of days.'

'When you get back, come around and have some dinner.'

'Are you and Mei-ling getting out of the hay long enough to entertain guests?'

Mike grinned. 'Occasionally.'

'Okay then, it's a date.'

'But no shop talk,' said Mike. 'Not a word about Tang's phoenix.'

And Chuck Baldwin began to laugh. 'Never heard of the bird!'

Mikhail Kazakov, wearing the uniform of a captain in the GRU, was waiting at Hanoi Airport when the convoy arrived. He saw the four lorries drive through the gates and pull up beside a limewashed cell block. Orders were barked and the members of the diving team jumped down from the front vehicle. There were six of them led by a short tubby man, suntanned and balding. That had to be

Seager, the one they called Podge. And with him – the only female in the group – was a tall, strikingly blond woman; Patti, his wife. The group stood by the vehicle for a few moments, unsure of themselves, until they were led to the cell block where they would be held until departure.

Kazakov waited until he saw the door of the block slammed shut then he walked across to the hangar where the lorries containing the diving equipment had been driven. The drivers had parked their vehicles inside the hangar and, after the long haul up from the coast, had gone off for their midday meal. The place was deserted. Mikhail Kazakov, normally such a nervous man, smiled to himself . . . he had all the time in the world.

At three that afternoon the DC-8 freighter, with Larry Pike at the controls, touched down and taxied to the hangar. The lorries emerged and, under the supervision of the aircraft's loadmaster, all the diving equipment – the generators and compressors, the rigid-hull inflatables, the outboard motors and camping gear – was stashed aboard. It took more than an hour to calculate the cargo's centre of gravity and properly secure it with netting. But by four thirty the DC-8 was ready to make the seventy-minute return flight to Bangkok.

Podge Seager led the divers from the cell block out onto the tarmac and, with soldiers encircling them, climbed aboard. Nobody said a word. Tight-lipped, Seager and his wife sat on the fold-down seat next to the galley while the other four climbed onto the freight, finding themselves comfortable positions. The cargo door was closed. The engines started up and slowly the aircraft began to move.

When it reached the end of the runway, there was a long, heart-stopping pause with a great deal of radio talk coming from the cockpit. Anything could still happen. They could be yanked off the plane and thrown back into prison, they all knew it. Patti squeezed her husband's hand, too frightened to say anything.

But then, with a shriek of engines, the aircraft began to lumber down the runway and the moment they felt it lift off, the moment they knew they were airborne, the entire diving team let out a wild whoop of joy.

'That's the worst package holiday I've been on in my entire bloody life,' said Drongo Hunter, the team's mechanic. 'And as for the hotel staff – un-bloody speakable!'

They were all laughing now, jubilant to be out of the place. The loadmaster, an Aussie too, pulled out the Fosters from the galley fridge and for the first time in days Podge and Patti Seager could relax.

'You're never going to get me into one of these situations again,' Patti said. 'That's it, absolutely the last time.'

Podge smiled; all dimples and middle-aged mischief. 'But the money's so good, pet.'

'You know what you can do with your money – '

'What a shame, I thought we could spend it instead.' And, before she could push him off the seat, he had grabbed her around the shoulders and was kissing her in a movie matinee embrace while the others let out a chorus of catcalls.

When the beers were finished and the DC-8 was nearing its cruising altitude of thirty-one thousand feet, the loadmaster tapped Seager on the shoulder. 'The pilot would like a word . . .'

There were three crew in the cockpit; the pilot, co-pilot and flight engineer. As Podge and Patti Seager opened the door, Larry Pike turned his head around. 'Hi,' he said.

'How are you doing? I'm Chuck's partner.'

'Bloody pleased to be out of that place,' said Podge Seager.

'I bet you are. Just a pity that you didn't find anything. All a waste of time.'

'We found something all right,' said Seager. 'Fact is, we found more than we bargained for.'

'But your telegram said – '

'What telegram?'

'The one calling us in, the one that said you had abandoned the search.'

'Abandoned it? Listen, sport – '

But the explosion obliterated his words.

Podge Seager felt it more than heard it – a tidal wave of concussion that smashed against his back, hurling him and Patti forward so that they collided with the flight engineer, all three of them thrown to the floor in a bruising tangle of limbs. And as he struggled to get up, blood streaming from his nose, Seager felt the first icy blast of outside air.

'Christ, what's happened?' screamed Larry Pike.

'We're decompressing!' shouted the co-pilot.

'Oxygen masks! I can't hold her straight!' Larry Pike was struggling with the controls, his face drained of blood as he screamed at Seager above the howling noise of the wind. 'There are two seats next to you. Use the masks there, quick!'

The sudden decompression turned the atmosphere into a blizzard-blown vacuum. Gasping for breath, Podge Seager grabbed one of the masks from where it was clipped above the seat, holding it hard against Patti's face while she sucked in deep. Then, as she grabbed the other one, he pushed the rubber over his own mouth, his lungs heaving for the air.

'I'm making an emergency descent!' shouted Larry Pike.

'What in the hell's happened in the back there?'

Podge Seager was still too stunned – like a boxer pummelled to the canvas – to appreciate the full gravity of their situation. But, as he fumbled to strap himself into his seat, he glanced back through the open cockpit door and the terrifying immensity of it hit him . . .

The whole cargo door – twelve foot across – was gone, ripped away from the fuselage. The noise inside the cockpit was deafening but out there it was indescribable. And everything was moving. The cargo, ton upon ton of it, was being inexorably sucked towards the open door, gyrating under its netting as if it was alive, shuddering and rising and breaking apart.

With the wind beating at his face, Seager looked desperately for his divers. But he could only see two of them. The other two and the loadmaster were gone. Then he saw Drongo Hunter, saw him clinging despairingly to the last tatters of netting and knew he was only seconds away from being sucked out through the gaping hole too. He turned, screaming at Larry Pike, 'You've got to do something! He's going to die!' But Pike couldn't even hear him.

Seager unstrapped the safety belt, lurching to his feet, trying to barge his way out through the cockpit door, but the flight engineer grabbed him, wrenching him back. 'There's nothing you can do! They're finished!'

Podge Seager could hear the co-pilot shouting. 'Mayday! Mayday! We've got an explosion on board! Mayday!' But his eyes were fixed on Drongo Hunter, mesmerised as he watched his fingers slowly torn from the netting. Hunter's legs were being pounded against the jagged edges of the gaping hole in the fuselage. Blood was sprayed all over his body, a great blizzard of it. Hunter opened his mouth in a silent scream – and was sucked into oblivion.

With its engines screaming, the DC–8 made a half turn and plummeted into a dive. Podge Seager was thrown back into his chair while Patti, shouting incoherently, tried to strap him in.

Above the terrible noise, a new sound was suddenly heard, the sound of a bell ringing. 'It's the number two engine! We've got a fire warning on number two!' shouted the flight engineer. He pushed the fire shut-off lever fully forward. Then, working like a robot on pure reflexes, he wrenched at the fire extinguisher lever.

They were down to twenty thousand feet and the plane was shuddering in every rivet. The co-pilot swung around in his seat. 'What's happening? What's happening?'

And the fire light went out.

Sweat was sluicing down the flight engineer's cheeks. 'The fire's out,' he said. 'Thank God for that.'

'We're on three engines,' said the co-pilot, his voice cracking.

Larry Pike replied in a dull, dazed voice. 'I'm going to have to land. I've got no choice. I'm going to have to bring her in.' He was terrified that the aircraft would break up in the air. He knew the immense strain it was taking.

Podge Seager couldn't believe what was happening to them. 'What was it, a bomb?'

The co-pilot was still calling on the international distress frequency. 'Mayday! Mayday!' And giving their position. 'The cargo door has gone. We're landing now. I repeat, landing now. Our cargo door has gone. Mayday! Mayday!'

Podge Seager felt Patti's hand clinging to his. He turned his head one last time, staring back through the cockpit door into the devastation of the fuselage. There was only one of his divers left there now – Joe Giles, face purple, eyes as blank as stone, his body bouncing lifelessly up and down where it was caught in the netting. He had died of oxygen starvation.

They were down to five thousand feet. But the terrain beneath them gave little hope. The jungle-clad mountains seemed to stretch on into eternity, nothing but jagged cliffs, granite peaks and serpentine rivers as green as jade.

But then Larry Pike suddenly shouted, 'I see it! There to starboard!' It was a long narrow valley, the slopes thickly jungled. But the base of it at least – for three or four hundred metres – was grassy and open. Larry Pike swung the crippled aircraft around, lining it up, and said almost beneath his breath, 'Give me fifteen flap.'

The co-pilot obeyed.

'Twenty-five flap . . . and gear down.'

The three green lights came on indicating that the undercarriage was down and locked. 'Spoilers armed!' was his next command.

Larry Pike knew what he had to do – drop down and plough through the tree tops close to the grassy area so that when he hit the open ground he could use the full length of it, every precious foot. 'Thirty-five flap!' he shouted. And then – with just a second or two's pause – he shouted again. 'Full flaps now!'

Now it was up to him and him alone.

He was dragging the plane in at ten knots below final approach speed, trying to land as slowly as possible. The tops of the trees were getting closer and closer.

Behind him, still clutching her husband's hand, Patti Seager closed her eyes and began praying. 'Our Father . . .'

The DC-8 hit the tops of the trees with a great

screeching noise as if the underbelly had been torn away. Then it pancaked down, hitting the ground at a hundred and twenty-five knots – a hundred and fifty miles an hour – ninety tons of aircraft and freight literally ploughing up the soil.

Larry Pike was standing on the brakes now, teeth gritted, screaming. 'Fire shut-off levers fully forward!'

Thrown around in his seat, the flight engineer reached for the lever to cut off fuel to the engines. But at that moment – totally unseen – they hit a small stream which ran across the valley and he was thrown into the panel in front of him, his head splitting open.

The DC-8 slewed around, its undercarriage ripped away. But it didn't stop. There was just too much momentum, too much speed, and it careened on. Larry Pike saw the trees looming towards him, a great wall of vegetation. He knew they were still doing seventy or eighty knots. There was no way they could stop, just no way . . .

He had often wondered what he would feel like if this moment ever came. And he was surprised. He felt nothing at all, just a kind of resignation. It was a damn good try, he thought. No pilot could have done better.

And they hit the trees.

High on a mountain track above the valley a young hill tribesman and his wife saw it all. They saw the aircraft land, they witnessed it crash into the trees. They saw the wings cleave off and the long fuselage break in two. Then, to the sound of a dull, distant boom, they saw one of the wings explode.

The fire quickly spread, engulfing the fuselage, and within minutes a pall of black smoke had risen hundreds of feet into the sky, as high as they were even, a memorial of wind and ash that marked the grave.

They were simple folk and there was nothing they could do. They waited a time, helplessly watching, but there appeared to be no survivors. So they turned away and continued their journey in silence along the high contour lines.

Two hours later, towards evening, when the sky was washed with a gentle pink and the horizon had become a smoky mauve, they looked up and saw the speck of another aircraft following the same path as its doomed predecessor, flying south towards Bangkok.

They could not see, of course, but this aircraft was smaller, an ancient Dakota, its fuselage bearing the green and gold markings of an air cargo company called Mekong Charters. And the cargo it carried consisted of just one item; a large wooden crate more than fifteen feet long with no markings upon it, no writing, no indication at all of what it contained.

It was nearly midnight when the persistent chirping of the telephone woke him. Mike groped for it on the bedside table.

It was Chuck Baldwin on the line. 'Did I wake you?'

'It's all right, no problem.'

Chuck Baldwin's voice was tight, his manner terse. 'I'm in Bangkok,' he said. 'I thought you should know . . . it's about the aircraft bringing Podge Seager and his team from Vietnam . . .'

'What about it?'

'It's gone down, Mike, it's crashed in the mountains.'

It took a couple of moments for Mike to take it in. 'Oh my God,' he murmured. 'The one Larry Pike was flying?'

'Yeah, Larry was the pilot.' Chuck Baldwin spoke in a low, flat voice trying to control his emotions. 'The wreck has been spotted north near the Thai border.'

'Any news on survivors?'

'They're all dead, Mike. None of them made it.'

Mike didn't know what to say. The words dried in his mouth. All he could mutter was . . . 'But what happened? What made it go down?'

'It's too early to say. I'm flying up there tomorrow morning. I want to see for myself.' Chuck Baldwin fell silent for a few seconds. Then he said in a hard voice that brooked no doubts, 'But I'll tell you one thing – it wasn't pilot error. Larry Pike was one of the best damn pilots I've ever known. This was no accident, Mike. You know it and I know it. And some bastard is going to pay.'

After Chuck had rung off, Mike sat on the edge of the bed while Mei-ling made coffee. There was no way he could sleep, not now. Everything inside was churning. Chuck was right – pilot error, engine failure . . . it was too glib, too coincidental. So nothing has ended, he thought. It just gets worse. And he could almost sense Ricky Tang, like a pale ghost, at his shoulder.

There was no more fire, no more smoke. The wreck of the DC–8 lay scattered along the valley floor broken into a thousand pieces.

Off to one side, on a small hillock, they had placed the bodies – the ones they had been able to find – in an orderly row, each one covered with a white sheet. Larry Pike lay there; Podge and Patti Seager too. Chuck Baldwin had grown old with death . . . Vietnam, the Middle East, Angola, Chile . . . he knew the smell of it, the look of it, the final emptiness of flesh without a soul. But he and Larry Pike had been together for the past ten years. They had been friends, partners. They had worked together, got drunk together. And he couldn't bear to look, not even at the sheets. He was sick of it all, sick to the stomach.

For the better part of that day he searched the wreckage, picking his way patiently through the twisted metal and shattered cargo until eventually he found the canvas sports bag. It was badly burnt and the plastic zip had fused together. So he had to cut it open with a knife. Inside he found what remained of two passports. The fire had done its work on them too. The blue plastic covers had bubbled and melted like cheese.

He didn't hold out much hope. Even if Podge Seager had hidden any microfilm, it would almost certainly have been destroyed. But Chuck Baldwin had learnt long ago that to hope against hope was often the only way. And odds, even of a thousand to one, sometimes paid off. So when he left the crash site that afternoon, he carried the two passports with him and later that night, when he caught the Northwest Orient flight to Washington DC, they lay in his briefcase, each one carefully sealed in its own polythene bag.

For Mikhail Kazakov, getting into Thailand was not a simple matter. The country was anti-Communist, pro-West, and it was essential that he hide his true identity.

That was why, when he left Hanoi, he flew first to Burma, a socialist country friendly to the USSR. He arrived in Rangoon as a Russian citizen, dossing down for the night in a small, seedy hotel near the Sule Pagoda. Burma was a shambles, a country closed for decades to the outside world; backward and torpid with an ill-educated bureaucracy – the ideal place to change identity. And the following evening, when Kazakov drove out to Rangoon airport, he carried a West German passport in the name of Pieter Beckers.

No questions were asked. His passport was stamped and two hours later he stepped off the plane in Bangkok.

He spent the night at the Erawan, a middle-range hotel that had seen better days, and the next morning at eight he was waiting on the main steps when Jean-Paul Delacroix drove up in a hired Mercedes.

Delacroix drove south. Bangkok over the years had mushroomed into such an endless urban sprawl that it took more than an hour to get out onto the open road that led down to Cha Aam.

Delacroix and Kazakov had never met before and from the beginning Kazakov was wary of the Swiss financier, unable to make up his mind what he really was and what he only seemed to be.

'Did you have any problems with Customs?' he asked.

An ironic smile played on Delacroix's lips. 'Not after we agreed the amount of the bribes.'

Kazakov sneered. 'Typical of a capitalist country.'

Delacroix laughed. 'Don't be so smug, my friend. Communists take bribes too. The only difference is, they're prepared to sell themselves cheaper.'

Kazakov folded his arms, staring morosely at the road ahead. The remark was typical of a Western capitalist, he thought. 'Where's the container now?' he asked.

'It's in the factory.'

'And the special equipment, did that arrive?'

'Yes, it's there.'

'All of it? Are you sure? The equipment is critical.'

'I'm a thorough man, Mikhail.'

'I can't work without that equipment.'

'Trust me.'

Kazakov had no choice in the matter. But trusting him and liking him were two different matters. Delacroix was altogether too smooth. Kazakov felt uncouth in his presence, as rough as a peasant.

'How much do you know about this operation?' he

asked cockily, attempting to illustrate that he was the man in charge and Delacroix simply the helper.

'As much as I need to know,' Delacroix replied evenly.

'But don't you wonder what it's all about? Where it's all leading?'

'Not one bit.'

'Why not?'

Delacroix cast him a quick, disdainful look. 'You're an officer in intelligence. I'm surprised you ask.'

The remark stung. Kazakov took out some chewing gum from his pocket. He liked Western chewing gum. 'I don't know why,' he said, 'but you don't fit the image I had of you.'

'What image is that?'

'More committed, more of a radical.'

Delacroix gave a condescending smile. 'And how do radicals look?'

'You should know. From what I understand, you were one twenty years ago. A disaffected priest hiding out in a Nicaraguan slum.'

'That was twenty years ago . . .'

'My uncle says you had deserted the Jesuit seminary where you were teaching . . .'

'Yes, he's right.'

'He says you were openly preaching revolution . . . giving communion to thieves and prostitutes during the day and at night smuggling guns to communist guerrillas.' He laughed. 'I can't imagine you with a Kalashnikov under your cassock.'

'Don't mock it, my friend,' said Delacroix, without changing the even tone of his voice. 'I was very good at what I did.'

'Guns though . . . for a priest.'

Delacroix gave the slightest shrug. 'Tyranny and guns,

the one follows the other. Christ whipped the money lenders out of the temple.'

'A little different from shooting fascists.'

'The one is simply an extension of the other.'

In a way, Kazakov had to admire him. 'I'm surprised the military didn't assassinate you.'

'They nearly did. It was your uncle who warned me.'

Kazakov looked him up and down. 'And now you're a capitalist.'

Delacroix smiled. But there was no mirth in it. 'Money is power, my friend. And it is only with power that the world can be changed.'

They had been driving for over two hours now and swung off the main road, heading inland. The country-side was flat and marshy; strata of green, the lime of young rice shoots against the darker olive green of broken shrub and bamboo. They drove through a small farming village, the houses built on stilts. Smoke drifted through the trees. An old Mazda truck stood rusting under a mango tree. And then they were onto the cinder track that led to the deserted factory.

'How much further?' asked Kazakov.

'Just a couple more minutes.'

Kazakov felt his stomach knot. 'When we get there, take me to where the crate is stored. Show me the equipment and then leave.'

They rounded a corner in the road and Kazakov saw the factory ahead. It had been well chosen, he had to give Delacroix that; isolated, ramshackle, surrounded by a concrete wall. So this was it, he thought . . . the first physical encounter.

The shed stood alone at the back of the factory, a large whitewashed structure with no windows, just one high fan light and double wooden doors. It was like an execution shed, thought Kazakov, as if he expected to find a gallows inside.

With Delacroix's assistance, the padlock was opened, the chains were removed and he entered the place alone, closing the doors behind him. It was hot and airless inside. Dust lay thick on the rafters and thick on the concrete floor.

A door led off to a small room at the side. Near the door were half a dozen wire-mesh cages and he could just make out the small, humped shapes of cane rats inside them, scurrying back and forth.

But Kazakov's attention was focused on the wooden crate that stood in the middle of the bare concrete floor. He stared at it for a long time, uncertain, a little afraid. Then, tentatively, he approached. He took a deep breath, picked up a sharp-edged crowbar and began to work.

He opened the crate, splintering the wood. He gashed the palm of his hand on a nail so that the blood ran between his fingers. But, wincing from the pain, he continued until the crate had been totally dismantled. Sweating badly – part exertion, part fear – he pulled away the canvas covering that had been placed around the container. And there it stood.

In the gloom of the shed it looked disappointing, like an old boiler that had been left to rust in some backyard. Nervously, he touched the metal. It was rough with corrosion. Bright orange-brown rust came off on his fingertips. He examined the casing, noting the gouges, the pockmarks and the one long crack that ran at least an inch deep. The container casing had been badly damaged. But it was no worse than expected.

It took a lot of effort to break the seals which had rusted solid. He worked for an hour, the ringing of his hammer sounding like rifle shots that sent the cane rats in their cages into a squealing, pink-eyed frenzy. Eventually, however, he was able to prise off the lid and beneath it he found insulating material, six inches thick, stinking of slime and decay. Using a knife, he hacked it away, slowly revealing the second, inner casing.

And it was untouched, perfect . . . fully airtight. As he gazed down at the smooth, onyx-black surface, Kazakov experienced a fierce surge of triumph. After all the months of planning, after the sleepless nights and the constant living on his nerves, there it was before him – the affirmation of their faith.

Although Kazakov would never admit it, there were times when he had harboured the gravest doubts. But Kirilenko, he knew, had always been so certain that the second, inner container would be intact. He had never wavered in that belief, not even with the passing of eighteen years.

But then Kirilenko had been with Tang in the very beginning. He had been the one to clip the electrodes to his testicles and to puncture them into the small of his back near the spine. He had been the one to inject the sodium pentathol, to listen to the shrieks and the babbling and the howls of defiance . . . and finally to obtain the full, unvarnished truth, the saga of the Phoenix Pact from its inception to its end. And, despite his understanding with the Vietnamese that no records would be kept, he had been the one to secretly retain a transcript of those interrogations . . . transcripts which Kazakov had read time and again:

Q: You said you took extra precautions?
A: Yes, yes.
Q: Why?

A: We were terrified, that's why.

Q: Terrified of what?

A: That something would happen . . . that the junk would hit rough weather, that there'd be a leakage and it would kill us all.

Q: So what was done?
(No response)

Q: It's such a pity, you invite pain.

A: Please God, no, don't press that switch.

Q: Then tell me.

A: We built an outer container.

Q: Airtight too?

A: Yes, yes, airtight.

Q: What was it made of?

A: Some metal, I don't know.
(Electric charge)
No, no, no, please.
(Intermittent screams, no words discernible)
Please, oh mother of mercy, I'll tell you everything. But I just don't know.

Q: Then what do you know?

A: It was thick. Two inches. In parts even thicker. Thick as armour plating, especially designed.

Q: How was the container secured in the hold?

A: I'm so tired, please. I hurt so bad.

Q: How was it secured?

A: It was wedged in tight with ballast. Sandbags all around it. Even sandbags on top.

Q: So that would have given it extra protection?
(No response)

Q: So unless it received a direct hit, it could be there now at the bottom of the estuary, still intact, still airtight? What do you say to that?

A: (Barely audible) Find out for yourself, you
bastard . . .

It had taken eighteen years, thought Kazakov, but in
the end they had found out. And Kirilenko's supposition
had been right. Wiping the sweat from his forehead, he
turned away from the container and walked towards the
small room that led off the shed. His feeling of nervousness increased, a tight, trembling kernel of it in his gut.
Because now the dangerous part began.

There was a large suitcase inside the room and, just as
Delacroix had promised, everything was there. Kazakov
carefully checked each item and then, struggling with the
cumbersomeness of it all, he began to dress.

The first item he put on was a rubberised suit that went
from his neck to his ankles. Then rubber boots and surgical gloves and finally a respirator, a gas mask that covered
his whole head, the front of it protruding into a long
metallic snout. He checked that the respirator worked,
hearing the slow exhalation and inhalation of his breath,
and then, walking slowly, resembling some weird, robotic
creature, he re-entered the shed.

It was not difficult to open the airtight seals of the
inner casket. All it took was a couple of taps from the
hammer and he heard the soft *whoosh* of air filling a
vacuum. But the lid was heavy, lined with lead,
and he had to use both hands. He took a deep breath,
prepared himself and then eased it up. At ninety degrees
the hinges clicked tight and the lid stood on its own.

Kazakov took half a step back, looking down through
the perspex goggles. And there it was, exactly as Tang
had said . . . undisturbed, untouched, untarnished. It
could have been placed there yesterday.

It all looked so innocent, he thought. But that was the

terrible, insidious power of it. The victims would be stricken without ever knowing they were under attack. They would die without knowing and those who buried them would perish in ignorance too. The ultimate weapon, the invisible victory . . .

He picked up the first small box, holding it up to the light. It contained morphine tablets. But others held penicillin and antibiotics. There was powder for jungle rashes, ointments and unctions and antiseptics. There were field dressings and prophylactics . . . everything, in fact, that a soldier in the field might need.

That was it, that was the ultimate weapon, no more than a simple batch of medicines. They looked like nothing, thought Kazakov. Who would ever suspect? Who would ever believe they could destroy the world?

FOUR

Washington DC

Chuck Baldwin had heard the rumours of course. The Director was a sick man, they said, with only a few months to live. But seeing him for the first time in three years, sitting across a desk and talking to the man, he was appalled by the ravages of his illness. Tom Delaney had shrunk into himself, hollow-cheeked and hunched. He had lost at least fifty pounds. He looked tired and dispirited.

In the past Delaney may have resembled an absent-minded professor . . . odd socks, crumpled suits, forgetting people's names . . . but he had been almost universally respected. Agents in the field, cynical men at the best of times, had a lot of time for him. 'Balls of iron', that's what they used to say about him. But not if they could see him now, thought Chuck. Tom Delaney held one of the most powerful positions in the United States but the cancer had reduced him to a shell, just a parody of himself.

Delaney gave him a baleful glare and reached for a glass of water. 'I know how you feel, Chuck. Losing a partner has to be a terrible thing. A man dies violently, it's natural to look for culprits, to start dreaming up conspiracies. But we've got to be hard-assed about this. Objective.'

Chuck Baldwin didn't reply. The suggestion was

insulting. He glanced across at James Dexter, the only other man in the room. Dexter was worried too, Chuck could see it. He knew there was more to the crash than bad luck or bad flying. Then why didn't he say something? Why didn't he use his influence? But Dexter just sat there, puffing methodically at his unlit pipe. He was a creature of the system, a good headquarters man. He didn't contradict superiors.

Delaney gave a dry cough, covering his mouth. 'I hate to see good men lost. But, as much as I sympathise, Chuck, there's no evidence that the DC-8 was brought down by sabotage, none at all.'

'With all due respect, I disagree.'

'Then enlighten us,' said Delaney with condescending sarcasm. 'What have we missed?'

'The first mayday call was quite clear. It said there had been an explosion on board.'

'So?'

Chuck hesitated before stating the obvious. 'Bombs cause explosions.'

'So do a thousand other things,' snapped Delaney. 'Almost anything gives in the air – snaps, breaks – and you're going to get a loud bang. But listen to what was said after that . . .' With palsied fingers, he opened a buff-coloured file. 'Yes, here it is – and I quote: ''The cargo door has gone. We're landing now. I repeat, the cargo door has gone.'' '

'Of course it had gone,' said Chuck. 'It had been blown away.'

Delaney's white head jerked up. 'Where do you get that from?'

'I think it's a fair enough supposition, Tom,' said Dexter, intervening for the first time.

Delaney grunted, swallowing more water.

'Supposition, yes – that's all it is. The mayday calls take us nowhere. We're not able to assume anything, not until we have the black box analysis.'

'And how long will that take?' asked Chuck.

Delaney muttered to himself. 'Maybe three weeks, a month.'

Chuck gave a cynical laugh. 'We could have World War Three by then.'

'There, you see! What sort of remark is that?' Delaney was opening and shutting his mouth like a fish. 'I told you, Chuck, you're all screwed up about this thing.'

Chuck wanted to grab Delaney by the lapels and shake him. But instead he took a deep breath and tried to state his position as logically as possible. 'That DC-8 was effectively under charter to the CIA, flying into a country that's paranoid about Americans. The pilot was an agent and two of the divers had done extensive work for us in the past. We have evidence to suggest the possibility – and I won't put it any higher than that – of an explosion on board. In those circumstances, Mr Director, I believe we're obliged to investigate the probability of hostile action.'

'Investigate? Of course we're going to investigate,' muttered Delaney. 'But we're not going to charge off like the Seventh Cavalry looking for some conspiracy that doesn't exist. America has had too many damn Custers.' He removed his tortoise-shell glasses, tapping them on the desk. 'Fact and fiction, Chuck – our job is to separate the two. That's the function of intelligence.'

'Which is done by investigating every possibility at the earliest possible time,' said Chuck quietly.

Delaney rose angrily from his chair. 'You think we're slouching on this?'

Chuck looked him straight in the face. 'Yes I do.'

Delaney coughed sputum into a handkerchief. 'Everybody is a goddam Custer. Just blow the bugle and charge in . . .'

'We have sufficient cause,' said Chuck.

'Oh do we? Then tell me, what did the forensic analysis of those passports reveal?'

'They were too badly burnt.'

'That's not an answer! Did analysis reveal any microscopic trace of microfilm, any trace at all?'

'And I've told you, they were too badly burnt.'

'Then is there anything to suggest that Seager didn't send that telegram from Vietnam?'

'That begs the question – '

'Is there any contradictory evidence?'

'It's just a telegram. Anybody could have sent it.'

'Nothing found, search abandoned – that's what it said.' Delaney was breathing hard, in short, dry gasps. 'A diving team goes into Vietnam. It finds nothing, it learns nothing. Why blow the poor bastards out of the sky?'

'Because it did find something, that's why.'

'But you've got no proof of that.'

'Oh for chrissake!' said Chuck, exploding. 'I'm not a damn trial attorney, I'm an intelligence agent. I'm not talking about proof, I'm talking about suspicion, gut feeling. Instinct. I'm talking about the tools of our trade.'

Delaney stared at him, coughed once and then sat back in his chair. 'Gut feelings, huh?' And he grunted. 'Like I said, it's too damn easy to dream up conspiracies.'

They were going around in circles.

'Sitting where I sit, I have a clearer picture than you,' said Delaney. 'That's something you're just going to have to stomach, Chuck. So from now on you leave this matter to us. That's an order, you understand? You keep right out of it.'

Chuck Baldwin got up from his chair. He looked at Delaney and the image that filled his mind was of Nero fiddling while Rome burnt to the ground. You jerk, he thought. Then he turned on his heels and marched straight out.

After he had gone, Delaney sat hunched in his chair and brooded. 'Five years I've been in this seat, Jim. The goddam job has killed me. But I've tried to make the Agency something America can be proud of, you know that, not just a bunch of smart-asses financing coups, thinking they're above the law. And to hell with it, I'm not going to have us self-destructing now. The Phoenix Pact is ancient history and that's where it's going to stay. I'm not going to have some renegade ghosts undo all the good work you and I have done.'

James Dexter made no comment.

'If there was some genuine threat that would be different. But there's no evidence of that . . . none . . . none.' He was silent for a time. Then he asked, 'What do our intelligence sources in Hanoi have to say?'

'It's very low-grade stuff, Tom – '

'I know that damn it! What do they say?'

Dexter remained impassive. He had always held Delaney in the highest admiration. But the man was losing his grip. 'The diving team was arrested.'

'Why?'

'Alleged Agency connections.'

'No other reason?'

'None that we know of.'

'That's no reason to blow them out of the sky. They'd do what everybody else does, the same as we do with their agents – deport them.'

Dexter lit his pipe.

'What about the dive itself?'

'We've had nothing. But if they were looking for germ warfare pathogens, it would be kept top secret of course.'

Delaney began to polish his glasses. 'Even if the stuff was found it would be useless. That's what the scientists assure us, Jim. And we've got to go by their advice.'

Dexter frowned.

'Even if it is virulent, where does that take us? We know the Vietnamese have got their own biological warfare capabilities. They've been using anthrax in Cambodia for the past couple of years. The minute germ warfare was outlawed in the late sixties, every country in the world got in on the act. There's nothing like banning a weapon to make people aware of its possibilities. As for the Soviets – they're years ahead of us.'

Dexter smiled thinly.

'So where's the point in salvaging some eighteen-year-old wreck to get something they already have? Does it make any sense to you, any sense at all?'

'None,' said James Dexter. But that's what worried him most.

Chuck Baldwin had started on the beers at eight, graduated to scotch and by ten thirty that night was in some nameless bar, red-eyed, introverted and blind-angry drunk. Five years to retirement, he thought morosely, and he was still being treated like a pawn in some damn game; shoved from square to square, blindly obeying orders.

Leaving CIA Headquarters that afternoon, he had been collared by a balding minion from Personnel. 'Effective now,' the man had said, 'you're on three weeks vacation. Have a nice trip. Oh yeah, and while you're sunning yourself in Florida, learn some German – your next posting is Berlin.'

Screwed up or not, Delaney didn't waste time. Berlin, shit, the paperwork must have been completed before he got out of the elevator. The orders were loud and clear – forget about the Vietnam operation, toe the line, don't ask any more questions. But Delaney was sick – sick in the body, sick in the head – and it was wrong to listen to such a man.

Every bit of evidence screamed out that the DC-8 had been sabotaged. Either Delaney was just too sick, too tired to deal with it, or it was a cover-up. Either way, the whole thing stank.

To hell with it, thought Chuck. If Delaney was too sick and frightened to act, he would act for him. Because one thing was certain – he wasn't going to forget about the Vietnam operation, he wasn't going to toe the line and from tomorrow morning – hang-over permitting – he was going to start asking every question in the book.

As much as he begrudged it, Mikhail Kazakov had to admit that Delacroix had acted with typical Swiss effeciency. Within hours of receiving his inventory of all the drugs, dressings, powders and ointments found in the container, Delacroix had contacted Bangkok suppliers and ordered – cash in advance – large quantities of the very same or almost identical items.

The object of the exercise was simple . . . to mix contaminated items with new ones, bulking out the supply to ensure that most but not every person who took an anti-biotic or dressed a raw wound would die. That way the lethal effects would appear to be haphazard – in the beginning at least – more in keeping with a natural catastrophe than a man-made one. And that way too the root cause of it all would be impossible to detect.

But mixing the old and the new meant a complete

313

repacking. And that in turn meant that new boxes and labels, cellophane packets, bottles, syringes, even new instructions printed in Arabic lettering were required.

So Delacroix had contacted two separate companies in Bangkok which had agreed to print and supply the necessary packaging. Kazakov had worried that printing the names and logos of international corporations might be risky. But Delacroix knew better. The printers, he said, would be unconcerned. And he was right. Their managers simply assumed that cheap pharmaceutical substitutes were being produced, no different from fake watches, cameras, computer parts and a hundred other items that pretended to be what they weren't. Delacroix had paid top prices with no invoice required. In the Far East that carried the implied condition that no questions would be asked.

But while all the necessary materials could be obtained from outside, the job of physically mixing the contaminated and uncontaminated products would have to be done at the factory – and that's where the critical danger lay. A job for peasants, thought Kazakov.

Delacroix had purchased the necessary machinery and calculated that half a dozen women from the local village could complete the work within three days. The factory caretaker, Pansomchit, had put out the word and six women had been signed up within the morning. As soon as the goods were delivered, they would commence work; the quicker it was done, the bigger their bonus.

Kazakov should have been delighted with the progress but he was a bundle of nerves, plagued with uncertainty. And that night, when he telephoned Kirilenko, he spelt out why. 'The rats are still alive,' he said, unable to conceal his alarm. 'Not one of them is dead yet.'

The old General remained unconcerned. 'Patience,

Misha, patience. Every man and beast is different. Some take hours, some take days, the stronger ones a week or more. Obviously Thai rats are resilient. What's important now is to be prepared.'

From where he sat in the Russian Embassy, Kirilenko had a fine view out over the roof tops of Damascus. He had imagined it would be warm at least in the Middle East but there was a bitter wind coming down from the Golan Heights.

When Kazakov had been in Vietnam, calls to Moscow by secure means from the Soviet Embassy had been possible. But now that he was in Thailand working under an assumed name, all such calls would have to be on an open line and Kirilenko knew only too well the dangers involved. That was why he had taken the opportunity to visit Syria to confer with his counterparts in military intelligence there. Calls to Damascus could be made freely from Thailand and here in the embassy he had secure means to receive them without any questions asked.

'Is everything arranged?' he enquired.

'Yes, everything.'

'When do you expect delivery of the items?'

'Within the next forty-eight hours.'

'How long will the work at the factory take?'

'According to Delacroix, no more than three days.'

'So in less than a week it can be accomplished?'

'If the rats die – '

'That's good, very good. Better than I had hoped. And Jean-Paul, is he still with you or has he completed his work?'

'He flew back to Switzerland last night.'

'To see our mutual friend, I presume?'

'It was time for the garrotte, that's the expression he used.'

315

Kirilenko laughed quietly. 'An interesting man, isn't he, Misha?'

Kazakov said nothing.

'You didn't take to him?'

'Not much.'

'Why, did he disturb you?'

'If you want the truth, yes, he did.'

'He disturbs me too, Misha, he always has . . . a man of the world, a man of the spirit, a capitalist, a communist, a Christian, a spy. Which is the mask and which is the real face?' Kirilenko chuckled. 'But then the Roman Catholics themselves used to say it, Misha – if there's dirty work to be done, always choose a Jesuit.'

It was a crisp March morning, frosty and bright. After the sapping humidity of Thailand, the cold air invigorated him. Delacroix had been to an early Mass at the College St Michel and came walking down through Fribourg's ancient streets. What lay ahead, he thought, required the benefit of a mass.

He was due to meet Joe Rakosi that morning. The purpose, ostensibly, was to settle the Mozambique finances but a far wider confrontation was inevitable. He knew what to expect. Rakosi was not a difficult man to read. After the disastrous failure of the Vietnam project – at least what he perceived as its disastrous failure – Rakosi would be angry and suspicious. No doubt he would make accusations that he had been cheated. And, of course, he was right.

There was no way Rakosi could be enticed further with airy promises of extravagant profits and the abiding gratitude of certain anonymous officials in the Hungarian Government. That might have worked in the beginning but by now they had lost all credibility. While, on paper at least, the Mozambique contract looked like breaking even, the costs of the Vietnam project had soared to nearly a million dollars.

If Rakosi had any sense at all, he would cut his losses and get out now. Only fools persisted with disasters. And Rakosi, despite his shortcomings, was no fool. Hence the inevitable confrontation. Because Delacroix's instructions were explicit – there was still more work for Rakosi to do.

When he climbed the stairs to his office, he was surprised to find Rakosi already waiting in reception, wrapped in an overcoat and looking cold and tired. He must have left Geneva at the crack of dawn. 'Good morning, Joe. Did you have a good trip?'

Rakosi got up from his chair. He was in a fighting mood. 'What happened in Vietnam?' he demanded.

Delacroix gave a sad shrug. 'What can I say? It was a terrible accident, an absolute tragedy . . .'

'I'm not talking about the plane crash. Why did you pull the divers out so early and without any reference to me?'

'I didn't pull them out, Joe. They were deported.'

'Deported? What in the hell for?'

'They were CIA, you knew that.'

'But I thought you had this thing sewn up?'

'There's only so much I can do.'

'Bullshit! This is some kind of set-up.'

Delacroix gave an embarrassed smile. 'I think we should talk in my office, Joe. It's more private.'

'It's a con, that's what it is.'

Delacroix left him, walking through to his office.

But Rakosi barged after him. 'The whole damn thing's a con!'

'Would you like some coffee, Joe?'

'No, I don't want any coffee. What I want is some answers. Do you know how much this little jaunt in Vietnam has cost me?'

Delacroix smiled without humour. 'I keep the accounts, remember.'

Marching across to the window, Rakosi glared out for a moment and then swung around, raising one finger like an angry politician. 'I did everything I could with that Vietnam project. You can't blame me if the gold wasn't found.'

'Nobody is blaming you, Joe.'

'I know you, I know the way you operate.'

'What is that supposed to imply?'

'I'm due my money on the Mozambique contract – '

'Don't worry, you'll receive your money.'

Rakosi looked surprised. 'Okay. Good,' he said. 'Then that's settled. I'm pleased.'

Delacroix gave a sharp smile. 'As always of course there are a couple of ancillary matters . . .'

The look of surprise turned to instant suspicion. 'What sort of matters?'

'They're of small moment, Joe.'

'Nothing with you is of small moment. What are they connected with . . . Mozambique? Vietnam?'

'Neither.'

'Then forget it! I don't want to be involved anymore, is that clear? All I want is the money that's due to me.'

'Budapest still has great faith in you, Joe.'

'You can tell Budapest to go suck!'

Delacroix assumed a mournful look. 'I can understand you're disappointed, Joe. And I can appreciate you might wish to sever ties. But I'm afraid it's not as simple as that.'

'It's every bit as simple – watch me. The last goods

have been delivered to Mozambique. Read your contract, Jean-Paul, the one you shoved down my throat last time. You'll see that the final payment is due in forty-eight hours' time. Fifteen million dollars, not a penny less – payment in full into my London bank.'

Delacroix sat very still. 'I don't think I've made myself clear, Joe. You see, these additional matters are not discretionary.'

'What's that supposed to mean?'

And Delacroix said in a hard voice, 'It means you have no choice in the matter.'

Rakosi started to laugh. But it died in his throat. He could see that Delacroix was deadly serious. 'I don't believe this, you're threatening me – like some cheap gangster.'

'Let's rather say I'm warning you, Joe.'

Rakosi swallowed. His voice was suddenly hoarse. 'All right, what are these additional matters?'

Delacroix paused a moment as if considering the best way to express himself. 'We would like you to do certain things for us in Afghanistan.'

Rakosi's mouth fell slack. 'Oh no,' he muttered, backing away. 'I don't want anything to do with it. Budapest, Moscow . . . oh no, no, this stinks.'

'You'll be in no danger.'

Rakosi's eyes were bulging. 'You want me to work against the Mujahedin, that's it, isn't it? You want me to get involved in espionage of some kind. Who in the hell are you? You're an agent, aren't you, a communist agent.'

Delacroix smiled. 'Don't be so melodramatic, Joe. I'm not an agent and I'm not talking about espionage. It's business, that's all.'

'Yeah, I know your type of business. Mike warned me. Why in the hell I didn't listen. . . .'

'All you have to do is sign some documents, make a business trip or two. No harm will be done.'

'I'm not working against the Mujahedin. I'm not stabbing them in the back. I have some principles, damn you.'

Delacroix smiled. 'Simmer down, Joe, please, you're getting over-emotional.'

Rakosi was shaking his head. 'There's no way you're getting me involved in this, no way . . .'

'But I'm afraid you're already involved. You have been for months.'

'I'm a businessman, that's all – '

'But that's all I'm talking about, Joe, a little business.'

'You're just dragging me in deeper, I know you.'

'Please, Joe, why don't we sit and talk? Let me explain – '

'Forget it,' muttered Rakosi, his cheeks burnt a bright, shocked crimson. 'You keep your murky bloody dealings to yourself. All I want is my money – just as the contract says.'

Delacroix sighed. 'But I am trying to explain to you, Joe . . .'

'And don't think you can blackmail me by holding it back. I'm not a total cretin. You might sucker me once but not twice. Contingency plans have been made this time, alternative finance is available if necessary. And if you or the Hungarians hold back, I'll sue you to kingdom come. That's not a threat, that's a promise. And this time I'll win. I'm not frightened of you, Jean-Paul. You want a fight, you'll damn well get one!' And, slamming the door behind him, Rakosi stormed out.

Delacroix walked to the window and stood watching Rakosi as he bullocked down the narrow street past the little boutiques and the poster shops. 'Oh, Joe, Joe, my friend,' he said out loud. 'What am I going to do with you?'

Chuck Baldwin could count his assets on the fingers of one hand . . . an original Roy Lichtenstein painting which neither of his ex-wives had known about; some moth-eaten furniture which neither had wanted, a rusty old Chev and a clapboard farmhouse on two acres of woodland which was mortgaged to the hilt.

The farmhouse wasn't much but it was a roof at least and the following morning, head pounding from his hang-over, Chuck stocked up with frozen hamburger patties, broccoli and beer, climbed into the Chevvy and drove due south towards the Potomac. He reached the place at noon, fed the chickens, took some aspirin and started to do a little investigating of his own.

Earl Blackmore – Ricky Tang's old section head, the New Jersey poultry man – was the first lead. Chuck had always been suspicious but, with what he knew now, he realised that Blackmore's story to them in Hong Kong had been sheer invention, a pack of lies. But why? What was he hiding? And just what was the truth?

The New Jersey business directory listed more than fifty poultry producers. But one stood out as the obvious choice – Blackie's Day Old Chicks. And, sitting cross-legged on the floor, chewing raw broccoli, Chuck Baldwin made the call.

A female receptionist answered. 'Hi, Blackie's Day Old Chicks – sunshine with a chirp.'

Chuck nearly burst out laughing. Sunshine with a chirp! 'I'd like to speak to Mr Blackmore please, Mr Earl Blackmore.'

There was the faintest pause. 'I'm terribly sorry, sir, but Mr Blackmore is dead.'

Chuck was shocked. 'What happened?'

Another pause. 'A heart attack, I think.'

My damn luck, he thought. 'When was this? I saw him only a few weeks ago.'

The receptionist hesitated. 'I don't think that can be right, sir.'

'Why not?'

'Mr Blackmore has been dead ten years now.'

It was six thirty am and Mike had just finished showering, when the call came through. It was Rakosi telephoning from London. And he was clearly drunk.

'I'm with a lady friend,' he said, slurring his words. 'We've had an evening out. But I thought I'd tell you, Mike – before I do battle between the sheets – that this morning I cut all ties with Delacroix. He and the Hungarians – my Magyar cousins, the little shits – are history. I'm following your advice, several months too late, but I'm following it all the same.'

'Why, what happened?' asked Mike bluntly.

'You can't trust any of them.'

'Was there anything specific?'

'Slimy bastards, that's all . . .'

'What about the financial side? Have you disentangled yourself?'

But Rakosi slurred on. 'I'm in London just a couple more days, Mike. Then I'm coming back to Hong Kong. And we're going to have a party, what do you say to that? We're going to have a celebration, Mike – for you and Mei-Ling.'

Mike said nothing. Last time they had spoken, Rakosi had been contemptuous of the marriage. Maybe Rakosi could swing his moods in a moment but for him it wasn't that easy.

Through the haze of his liquor, Rakosi sensed the hostility. 'Look, I'm sorry. Last time we spoke I was in a foul mood, under a lot of stress, you know how it is.'

'Yeah, Joe, I understand.' There was no point in arguing with a drunk.

Rakosi seemed relieved. 'So Mei-ling is a refugee. Incredible. But you couldn't have done better, Mike. Hell, what am I? I'm no different. Family 387, that's what they called us in that Austrian camp when we got out of Hungary. And I was 387, little three in brackets. Cute name for a kid, hey?' He laughed; a tired sound like a gramophone winding down. 'So you tell Mei-ling from me, tell her that refugees are the best. And do you know why, Mike? Because we come up from the bottom, that's why.'

'Okay, I'll tell her, Joe.'

'You're a mate, Mike, you know that.'

'Sure.'

'I'm beginning to learn you can't trust anybody in the world these days . . . except you, old friend, except you.' There was some kind of shout in the background and then Rakosi said, 'I'm sorry, the lady needs me. Duty calls.' And with a vulgar, we're-all-boys-together kind of chortle, he rang off.

'What was all that about?' asked Mei-ling when Mike put down the phone.

'A kind of peace pact.'

She smiled, obviously pleased.

'It also seems that Joe has broken with Delacroix.'

'But isn't that what you've been urging him to do?'

'Yes it is.'

'Then what's the problem? You don't look too happy about it.'

Mike gave a small, dubious shrug. 'There's more to it

than Joe is admitting. That's what worries me. He was drunk but not that drunk. He was hiding something. I'd be happier if I knew what the consequences are likely to be.'

And within the hour he had his answer. Mike was always one of the first into the office but this morning Lawrence Yau, his senior manager, was already there waiting for him. 'What is it?' asked Mike.

'Have you read *The South China Morning Post* this morning, the business section?'

'Not yet, why?'

'I suggest you do,' said Yau in a grave voice. He held out the paper for Mike to see and there it was, splashed in bold headlines across the front page:

RAKOSI NAMED IN INSIDER TRADING SCANDAL

New York special investigators have named Josef Rakosi, the Hong Kong based entrepreneur and arms dealer, as the man behind a multi-million-dollar insider trading deal which went badly wrong. Instead of making millions, say investigators, Rakosi and his associates precipitated a panic which saw share prices collapse in forty-eight hours of Wall Street bedlam.

Theodore Snow, Executive Vice President of Oiltec, the corporation whose shares went on a bull rampage and then lost ninety per cent of their value in a matter of hours, was arrested late yesterday at his Fifth Avenue apartment. It is understood that a warrant has been issued for Rakosi's arrest but can only be served if he sets foot in America.

Advisors close to the Hungarian-born high flier say that this latest scandal comes on top of a stormy year. Rakosi is rumoured to have lost millions in an abortive 'Aid for Africa' contract which could result in even further losses.

A Swiss financier with close business ties said yesterday, 'Rakosi specialises in high-risk ventures. A man like that keeps his creditors nervous at the best of times. But with losses piling up, they are rapidly losing faith.'

Mike didn't need to read any further. Stony-faced, he turned to Lawrence Yau. 'Get hold of the accountants. Set up an emergency meeting. I'm going to need a full breakdown of our finances, company by company. Drop everything else. That's priority number one. And I want a list of major creditors too – what we owe them and when.'

'Do you think it's going to be bad?' asked Yau.

'This is Hong Kong,' said Mike grimly. 'You tell me.'

Hong Kong was founded for one reason only: trade. That's all it had ever possessed, the people to make things quicker, cheaper, better. Hong Kong's real heroes had never been movie stars or sportsmen. It was the Shanghai tycoons who bedded the movie actresses, they were the ones to be envious of. Stockmarket moguls taking millions in bribes, that's where the real news lay. And that's why the Rakosi scandal was already old news by eight am. But, ironically, the one person for whom the news had the greatest personal significance almost missed it entirely . . .

Tina Wai had a fashion shoot in Singapore. She had been out late the previous evening and, as always, it was a frantic rush to get ready and get to the airport . . . a running breakfast of black coffee, no sweeteners, and half a grapefruit; checking that she had her passport and air ticket, trying to put on some make-up before the taxi arrived.

The only reason she opened the newspaper at all was to check the exchange rate on the Singapore dollar because she needed to buy some at Kai Tak. But, when she did so and saw the headlines, suddenly there was no more rush, no more scramble – her attention was perfectly focused.

It had been over six months since that August morning when Tina had fled half hysterical from Joe Rakosi's apartment; more than half a year to make a new life for herself. And she had done well, very well indeed. She was in constant demand and travelled the world. But time hadn't healed the pain. Just seeing Rakosi's name in print or hearing it spoken out loud brought the bitterness flooding back.

Sitting at the table in her tiny kitchen, she began to read the article and, as she did so, a look of deep-set satisfaction came to her face. She knew the source of the Oiltec story. She knew what had led to the arrest warrants being issued in New York and that gratified her. So there was some justice in the world after all. But it was not enough. It couldn't end there.

Because she knew Joe Rakosi. He had the lives of a cat. Somehow, before the creditors bankrupted him, he would negotiate his way out of the trap. Unless of course . . . and suddenly, in a moment of inspiration, it was all there before her – so obvious, so simple.

It was no secret in financial circles that Trident, Rakosi's arms-dealing company, was the most profitable in the entire Good Hope Group. And it was no secret either that the man responsible for that was Mike Keats.

But, if Mike Keats were to resign, if he were to disassociate himself from Rakosi, turn his back on him now when the Good Hope Group needed him most and walk out, if there was a split in top-level management at this critical time . . . Tina smiled . . . then it would take a miracle to keep Rakosi alive.

It was a pity, she thought, that a nice man like Mike Keats should have to be subjected to the pain. But the world was full of victims. She was one herself.

Tina went through to the bedroom and opened the bedside drawer where she kept a few papers, name cards and keys. At the back was a single cassette tape. She picked it up, holding it in her hand for a moment, lost in her thoughts. Then, as if breaking out of a dream, she dropped it in her handbag, grabbed her suitcase and made her way downstairs.

A quarter of an hour later she was dropped outside St John's Building. She made her way up to the seventh floor where she had been so many times before and entered the offices of the Good Hope Group. The receptionist was new, a young Chinese girl called Gladys Chiu. Tina explained that she had to see Mike Keats immediately. It was an important matter, she said.

The receptionist apologised. Mr Keats had left a couple of minutes ago. He had urgent meetings and would be gone for the rest of the morning. But perhaps somebody else could help?

No, said Tina, it was a private matter. She asked the receptionist for some paper and scribbled a hurried note. Then she wrapped it around the cassette tape, put both into an envelope and sealed it. 'I have to fly out of Hong Kong. I'll be gone for three days. Can you ensure Mr Keats gets this today?'

'I'll put it into his basket,' said Gladys.

'No, I'd rather you handed it to him personally. It's very important. And it must be today.'

'Very well. I'll give it to him the minute he gets back.'

'Thank you.' Tina Wai was satisfied. There was nothing more she could do. Now it was in the lap of the gods.

Mike telephoned Joe Rakosi from the accountants' offices. In London it was 3.20 am and Rakosi had had a long, debauched night. But he was awake in a moment, sitting bolt upright in bed, stunned by the news. 'What are you talking about, a warrant for my arrest? I don't believe this. It's Snow, it has to be. The stupid bastard – ' While the woman Rakosi had bedded, a Mayfair hooker, groaned in her sleep, he stumbled naked from the bed, fumbling for his robe. 'Has the article appeared anywhere else?'

'Not that we know of, just Hong Kong,' said Mike. 'I'm sure we can contain the damage, Joe. It's just a question of acting fast. I've set up an emergency meeting with the Hongkong and Shanghai Bank people for an hour's time.'

'Yeah, good, good. That's the way. Keep the lid on it,' mumbled Rakosi in a cold sweat. 'A warrant for my arrest . . . it's unbelievable. Why are they trying to assassinate me like this, Mike? Who put them up to it?'

But the answer was all too obvious. It was Delacroix. Rakosi slumped down on the edge of the bed. It was uncanny. Delacroix seemed to know every move he had ever made. Who was he for God's sake? What did he want from him?

'Look, Joe, I'm going to have to ring off. We're under a lot of pressure here.'

'Sure, sure,' mumbled Rakosi, hardly listening. 'I know I can rely on you, Mike.'

When the phone was replaced, Rakosi began to pace the hotel room. He had never been hit so hard and so publicly before and for a time he was emotionally paralysed. But then slowly he began to shake himself free of it. He had boxed his way out of tight corners before, he said to himself, and he would do it again.

Morning came, grey and cloudy with intermittent drizzle. The hooker who had spent the night in his bed woke up. She wanted room service to bring up breakfast, but Rakosi paid her and got her out of the place. She could eat her breakfast elsewhere.

After she had gone, Rakosi showered and dressed slowly like a soldier preparing for battle. He was still in a state of shock, there was no denying it, but the initial fear and humiliation had transformed itself now into a boiling rage. And when, on the stroke of ten, he marched into his Holborn offices he was ready to fight the world.

He strode straight through reception to Simpson's office. 'Delacroix was meant to pay the fifteen million this morning. Has it been received?'

'I'm afraid not,' said Simpson solemnly.

Rakosi took a deep breath. 'So that puts it beyond doubt. The bastard wants a fight. All right, let's give him one.' And, picking up Simpson's telephone, he spoke to the receptionist. 'Get me Delacroix in Fribourg.'

The receptionist sounded puzzled. 'I'm sorry?'

'What's the matter? You've got him enough times before.'

'But he's here,' said the receptionist. 'Mr Delacroix is sitting right here in front of me.'

Rakosi wanted to deal with Delacroix on home ground and he was standing behind his desk, arms folded, with a look of Churchillian defiance when the Swiss financier entered his office. 'You couldn't wait, could you? You had to fly across to gloat.'

Delacroix smiled. 'I tried to warn you, Joe.'

'So who was it? Who told you about Oiltec?'

'You know I can't tell you that.'

'The sanctity of the confessional; I'm surprised. I didn't think defrocked priests cared that much!'

And for the first time that Rakosi could remember, Delacroix visibly reacted. His jaw tightened, the smile became a grimace. 'Let me put it this way, Joe – hell hath no fury like a woman scorned.'

Rakosi's mouth fell open. 'Tina . . .' he said in a voice of dull realisation. 'So it was Tina Wai.'

Delacroix sat in one of the plush blue velvet chairs; relaxed, totally in command again.

'How did you get to her?' Rakosi mumbled.

Delacroix gave the ghost of a shrug. 'Old lovers, Joe, women betrayed . . . there's nothing very original in seeking them out.'

Rakosi looked sick. 'So all these months you've been digging into my past, shovelling for dirt.'

'Sometimes it is necessary.'

'What sort of man are you, for God's sake?'

'A very thorough one, Joe.'

Rakosi grunted, getting up from his chair and striding across to the window. He looked out at the rain. 'The American thing is a temporary set-back, that's all. The lawyers will sort it out. The same as your failure to pay the fifteen million. That was stupid. You can't hurt me that easy. I told you in Fribourg that I had made contingency plans. So I can live without your money, Jean-Paul – long enough anyway to pull you screaming and kicking into court.'

Delacroix sighed as if the ill feeling between them was

lamentable. 'I have to tell you, Joe, that the Hungarians suspect there may have been certain . . . how can I express it? . . . certain malpractices in fulfilling the Mozambique contract.'

Rakosi swung on him. 'What in the hell are you talking about?'

'To be blunt, they suspect you may have received secret commissions from the suppliers.'

'You've got no proof of that!'

'Your past behaviour does indicate it, Joe.'

'What past behaviour?'

'There is the Oiltec matter.'

'That's insider trading. It's irrelevant.'

'But it does indicate a pattern of corrupt conduct.'

'Bullshit!' Rakosi's cheeks had reddened. 'You've got no proof of corruption – '

And Delacroix said, almost sadly, 'But I'm afraid we do, Joe.'

Rakosi stopped, caught in mid-breath, lost for words. 'I don't believe you . . .' he murmured. But it was without conviction.

Delacroix rose from his chair, removed a folded paper from his jacket pocket and placed it on the desk. 'It's only a photostat copy. But no doubt you will recognise the signature.'

For a moment Rakosi held back as if afraid to touch it. Then, with a clumsy grab, he picked it up and began to read:

> I, Amon Malimbi, Minister of Economic
> Development in the Government of Kenya,
> do hereby make oath and say:

Rakosi's eyes darted down the page until he reached the signature. Then, as if the arm holding the paper had lost all its strength, it flopped down into his lap. 'Is there anything you don't know?' he murmured.

Delacroix spoke quietly and sympathetically like a psychiatrist with his patient. 'The Kenya chemical plant was a large, international project, Joe. You know as well as I do that ninety per cent of these contracts are corrupt.'

Rakosi sat staring out of the window with vacant eyes. 'How did you get Malimbi to sign?'

'Once we had the affidavits of the German and Italian suppliers, it was not difficult.'

There was a long silence. Then Rakosi asked, 'So what do you intend to do now?'

Delacroix spelt it out like a doctor explaining a diagnosis. 'Corruption in Kenya carries a maximum jail sentence of twenty years, Joe. And the Kenyans will extradite you from wherever you are. You won't be safe here in England, you won't be safe in Hong Kong. Imagine twenty years in an African jail. All the Kenyans need is the evidence.'

Rakosi looked shattered. 'You'd give it to them too.'

'If you forced our hand, Joe, yes we would. But it doesn't have to come to that. It's not our aim to ruin you – just the opposite. You can still come out of this on the winning side.'

Rakosi's voice was thin and feeble. 'What do you want from me?'

And Delacroix replied softly. 'A little co-operation, Joe, that's all.'

Grigori Kirilenko disliked Syria. The people were surly and money-grabbing while Damascus itself was a dirty city devoid of any redeeming features except its antiquity. Consequently, waiting inside the Soviet Embassy was more a relief than a burden.

He was having an early lunch that day when a member of the embassy staff came into the dining room. 'Excuse me, Comrade General, it is a long-distance call – Thailand.' Kirilenko followed the man to the communication room, picking up the telephone receiver.

It was Kazakov on the line and he was barely able to conceal his glee. 'They're dead,' he exclaimed. 'All the rats are dead!'

It is nineteen hours' flying time from Washington DC to Hong Kong; nineteen hours watching in-flight movies and drinking beer. Chuck Baldwin hated air travel at the best of times and when he landed at Kai Tak at five thirty that evening he looked as if he hadn't slept in a week. But there was no time to worry about jet lag. Every hour counted. And, after he had cleared Customs, he took a taxi direct to Mike's office.

Mike himself had had a harassing day and looked drawn and pale when they met.

'We have to talk,' said Chuck.

'Ricky Tang?'

'Yeah, Ricky Tang.'

Mike nodded. 'Okay,' he said wearily. 'It's been a bitch of a day anyway. I'm pleased to get out of here. What do you say to dinner at the apartment?'

'Great.'

'Mei-Ling will be pleased to see you.'

Mike threw a few papers into his briefcase and he and Chuck walked out. 'I'm on my way home,' said Mike to the receptionist. 'I'll see you in the morning.'

'Goodnight, Mr Keats,' she replied. Then, suddenly remembering, she called out to him. 'Oh, there's an envelope here for you.'

Mike turned at the glass doors. 'I'm sorry, it will just have to wait.'

'But the lady said it was urgent.'

'Everything today has been urgent. Remind me in the morning.'

He and Chuck caught the lift down to the ground floor, coming out onto Garden Road. The roads were crowded at this time of night; four lanes thick, crawling along bumper to bumper. Together they walked down the hill towards the Hilton parking garage.

'So what did you find out in the States?' asked Mike.

'Remember Blackmore?'

'Sure, the chicken man. What about him?'

'He died ten years ago.'

Mike said nothing, not immediately. At first he was shocked by the news, then bewildered, then suspicious . . . until finally it began to make sense. 'Are you saying that the CIA – your own organisation – sent an impersonator to try and convince us Tang was just a crook, some crazy con artist?'

'It looks that way.'

'But why?'

'What other reason can there be? You were right, Mike, Ricky Tang was telling the truth – and they don't want the truth made public.'

Mike took a deep breath. 'So what Ricky Tang said about some kind of doomsday weapon . . .'

Chuck nodded gravely. 'That's what it's all about.'

'But the telegram you showed me, it said that the divers found nothing – '

'Like hell they didn't,' said Chuck in a hard, flat voice. 'They found it, they raised it. And then they were blown out of the sky. That telegram was a fraud, Mike, it had to be.'

By now Mike was thoroughly alarmed. 'But if we're talking about some kind of doomsday weapon, why won't the CIA take any action? It was their own weapon, for God's sake! They must understand the dangers involved.'

All Chuck could do was shrug. 'I've tried to gain access to the old records, whatever there is on the Phoenix Pact, Tang, Blackmore. But they've blocked me, Mike. I can't get near them.'

'But there has to be some reason,' said Mike, desperately searching for a rational explanation. 'The CIA wouldn't let some doomsday weapon loose on the world.'

'Wouldn't they?' said Chuck with deep cynicism.

'Okay,' said Mike, agitated now. 'Let's assume the weapon has been raised. Let's assume it still works. That doesn't mean it's going to be used. The world is full of doomsday weapons, Chuck, weapons that would boggle our minds. Half the countries in the world stockpile them.'

'Countries, yes . . .' said Chuck.

Mike frowned. 'What do you mean by that?'

'Okay, you tell me . . . what country, what duly constituted government, needs to bring in a team of commercial divers – foreigners at that – feed them some horse shit about gold bullion and then get them to do a dive like this? Lichtenstein maybe. Andorra. But Vietnam has its own divers, Mike, its own experts, men it can control. It doesn't need outsiders. There's one thing you can be certain of, whoever is behind this, it's not the Vietnamese Government.'

'Then who is behind it?'

'What was it that Rakosi told you . . . about this corrupt deal Delacroix had set up for him, this link with Hungary?'

'He said there were two parties behind it, a high-ranking official in the Hungarian Government and some

335

Vietnamese general. They were the ones who knew about the gold and wanted it raised.'

'Yeah, that's probably closer to the truth,' said Chuck. 'Except delete "gold" and insert the word "weapon". Think about it for a second, Mike . . . it has to be people with enough political clout to get the divers into Vietnam in the first place and then get them clearance to undertake the dive.'

'Okay, so it has to be somebody powerful, somebody senior in the Hanoi regime.'

'That's it – somebody who can work the system from inside. But take it one step further. Who would be interested in a doomsday weapon, who would want to make use of it?'

'The military? Maybe the secret service?'

'Yeah, it has to be.'

'Some army faction perhaps?'

'It's logical isn't it . . .'

'Working on their own?'

'Maybe . . . or maybe with a group of outsiders.'

'Who?'

'Who would be prepared to use a doomsday weapon for their own ends? Take your pick . . . the KGB, Palestinian terrorists, the IRA, the Japanese Red Army, Sikh extremists. The world is a screwed-up place, Mike.'

'My God,' said Mike beneath his breath. 'So what are we talking about here?'

Chuck cast him a hard look. 'It's got to be some faction in Vietnam, probably military. It's either working for its own ends or it's collaborating with outsiders. But whichever way, common sense dictates that it's got to be a lunatic fringe, a bunch of madmen. And it's part of the definition, Mike – madmen don't care what risks they take . . . or how many people they destroy.'

*   *   *

For both of them now the moral imperatives were compelling. Privately, of course, each of them considered the alternatives. The easiest way out was to find some excuse . . . it wasn't their business, it should be left to others. But there was no way they could wash their hands of it now. It was too late. They were in too deep. Whatever the consequences, whatever the risks, they would see it through to the end.

Mei-Ling had supper waiting for them when they got back to the apartment. In Chuck's eyes she looked more beautiful than ever; serene and graceful and, as he said when he kissed her, 'sexy as hell!'

From the time Mike had first confided in her aboard the refugee boat, Mei-Ling had known about Ricky Tang and the Phoenix Pact. And she had always been prepared to believe. Because for her there was no debate about men in power being inherently rational. They, more than anybody, she said, were capable of insane acts – Americans, Vietnamese, it didn't matter who. Because power, like a drug, deluded them. In Cambodia, on Vietnam's border, men who had trained at the Sorbonne in Paris, cultured men who could recite Rousseau and cry at a Bach fugue, had swept the cities of every inhabitant and murdered over three million people. That was an insanity that defied imagination. And it was planned in a committee room, bloodless and dry. It was done in the name of logic.

So for Mei-Ling, no matter how wildly far-fetched Ricky Tang's allegations might have sounded, she could accept they were not far-fetched at all.

They ate supper quickly and then, with a pot of black coffee on the table, the three of them sat to work out the avenues of investigation left open to them . . .

From what little they knew, Delacroix was the man behind the Vietnam operation. So it was vital that

Delacroix's background be investigated and his movements traced. Did he have genuine connections with the Hungarians? If so, did they extend to other Warsaw Pact countries, all the way to the Kremlin perhaps? What was he, just a financier or something more? It was work for researchers, the rabbits back at Langley, and Chuck still had enough friends to co-ordinate it for him. It might take a few days, he said, but he had been promised results.

But if Delacroix was the man behind the Vietnam operation, Joe Rakosi – innocent or not – had been used as the front. The question was, to what extent? Mike knew that he had met Delacroix in Thailand. He knew that monies had been sent to Bangkok. Why? For what purpose? Mike didn't know of any legitimate business interests they had in that country. So it was agreed that he would do a little digging through the business papers, following the transfer of monies from account to account.

Which just left Chan Chi-wai . . . Chan, the office bearer in the Wo Shing Wo, the man who Ricky Tang had said had given him the ring inscribed with the phoenix. Until now, in the rush of events, Chan had been forgotten. But if, after all these years, he was still alive and if he could be persuaded to talk, he perhaps, more than anybody, could lead them to the heart of the matter.

It was a hazy blue morning, warm and humid: the morning of the second day.

The six women from the village worked in one of the old storage sheds. The windows had been sealed and the doors bolted. Each of them wore a surgical smock, rubber gloves and a surgical face mask. For hygiene purposes, Kazakov had explained. An air conditioner had been installed but it was only powerful enough to take the edge off the heat. But the women were happy enough.

The work was easier than bending all day in the paddy fields and the pay was good.

So they gossiped and giggled and got on with the job. They put new labels on the tins of powder, on the ointments and dressings. They took the drugs out of their packets, mixing the old with the new and then re-packing them together. They sealed the packets and put them into boxes.

Perhaps if they had been more sophisticated they might have been suspicious. But they were peasant women, the wives and daughters of local farmers. They knew nothing about manufacturing. When they finished, there would be nothing to talk about, no rumours to spread. Work was work, tedious and time-consuming, whether it was packing pills or washing laundry at the river's edge. A simple, unquestioning workforce was vital to the project. But it presented its own special problems too . . .

Using the caretaker, Pansomchit, as his interpreter, Kazakov had explained to the women how important it was for them to be scrupulously hygienic. They had to wear rubber gloves at all times. They could only take off their face masks outside the shed. But, although they were peasants, the women could see easily enough what they were dealing with – pills and ointments, that's all. They had all been sick at one time and had been prescribed drugs themselves. They had handled them with no ill effect then and had been cured soon enough.

Consequently, when the heat became too much, a couple of the women took off their face masks. A couple more found that they couldn't handle the drugs in their clumsy rubber gloves and took them off too. They knew it was against instructions but they could get the work done more quickly that way. And the quicker they finished, the bigger the bonus they received.

If Kazakov had seen it, of course, he would have done something. That's why he was meant to be there – to supervise the work. But Mikhail Kazakov was not a brave man; he suffered from dreams, and when the work was in progress, when the medicines were being handled, he stayed well clear.

Chan Chi-wai . . . one man's name, a common one at that, and the knowledge that eighteen years ago he had held some kind of rank in the Wo Shing Wo Triad Society. That's all they had. Chuck Baldwin was normally a confident man but this time it was hard to be optimistic.

The Triads – the Tongs, as they were also known – were Chinese secret societies. At one time, back in the seventeenth century, they had been formed as nationalist groups to overthrow the foreign Manchu Dynasty but had quickly degenerated into criminal gangs . . . whorehouse keepers, racketeers, loan sharks, drug traffickers. Whether they called themselves the Sun Yee On, the Wo Shing Wo or the 14K, they were just thugs under another name. Less than three years after Hong Kong had been ceded to Britain back in 1842, the Triads had been outlawed. The standard punishment in those days had been branding under the left arm, imprisonment for three years and then deportation. But the Triads thrived.

Like the Cosa Nostra their members were initiated in secret ceremonies. And, as always, the myth consumed reality. A few of the societies were highly structured but most were no more than housing estate gangs; petty criminals using the mystique to their own advantage. Most secret ceremonies took place in stone cottages on Hong Kong hillsides, a couple of fifteen-year-olds beheading a cockerel, drinking each other's urine and going through a mumbo-jumbo of Ming poems.

And like all criminal gangs, they were riven with strife. Even within the same societies, different groups fought each other. Bloody chopper attacks – isolating an opponent and then hacking him to death – were commonplace. So the leadership, especially at the lower levels, was fluid and behind the veil of Triad secrecy it was often impossible to discover who held the throne at any one time and who was just a pretender.

But Chuck knew that if anybody had an accurate record, it would be the organisation most closely involved in combating the Triads – the Royal Hong Kong Police.

Police forces, however, did not freely divulge their intelligence. Every request from an outside agency had to be routed through formal channels, vetted and then approved. That could take days, precious time lost, unless there was some way of cutting through the red tape – which was why Chuck went direct to Bill Martin.

Bill, an FBI agent, held the post of Legal Liaison Officer with the US Consulate. He dealt on an everyday basis with the Hong Kong Police and had, as he expressed it, 'good comms with the guys'. Bill was a big talker, known in the Consulate as motor-mouth. But this time he was as good as his word. All it took was one phone call to Interpol Bureau and within the hour Chuck had received an invitation to the offices of Criminal Intelligence at Police Headquarters. He took a taxi to Arsenal Street and by eleven fifteen was drinking coffee with the officer in charge, Len Scally.

Scally had a file in front of him. 'Chan Chi-wai has had Wo Shing Wo connections since he was a babe in arms,' he said.

'So he's still alive?'

'Very much so.'

'Still in Hong Kong?'

'And thriving,' said Scally who was from Donegal and didn't believe in treating life too seriously. 'One way or the other we've known about Chan since the Second World War. He started off life brown-nosing the Japs when they occupied Hong Kong, working for the Kempatai, their secret police. He should have been hanged in '45 but the only witnesses we had were either dead or Japanese or both. A lucky man is Mr Chan. Arrested thirteen times, only convicted once – and then he flew out some QC from London and wriggled off the hook on appeal.'

'How is he today, still active in the Wo Shing Wo?'

'Difficult to say. Maybe behind the scenes. But on the surface he's a very proper gentleman now. Lives on the Peak, plays tennis with the Taipans. Only shits gold bricks.'

Chuck grinned. 'You mean he's wealthy?'

Scally gave an envious laugh. 'As the old joke goes, he wrote a cheque once that was so big the bank bounced.'

'How did he make his bread?'

'Drugs mainly . . . in the early days at least. He did some smuggling on his own but most of the time he acted as broker between the suppliers in Laos and the buyers on the West Coast. Over the last ten years, however, he's been more proper than a parson at Sunday service. Property, shipping, toy factories, electronics. Ratbag to merchant prince.'

'Do you know what position he held in the Wo Shing Wo back in '68?' asked Chuck.

Scally scanned through an index on the inside cover of the file. 'Seems he was a big fish even back then. Yeah, the top man in fact – the Dragon Head himself.'

Chuck Baldwin shook his head. So in every respect Chan was a force to be reckoned with. It wasn't going to

be easy. 'What personal information have you got on
him?' he asked. 'Family, that sort of thing?'

Scally checked his papers. 'He's a widower, just one
daughter, Pui-Wah . . . Teresa is her Western name.
She's a professional violinist, played for the Chicago
Symphony for a couple of years. Married to a doctor now
and living in California.'

'Any grandchildren?'

'Yes, three. Chan obviously dotes on the family. His
travel record shows he's over in the States four or five
times a year.'

'Thanks,' said Chuck. 'I owe you one. You've given
me everything I need.'

And within the hour he was back at the US Consulate
checking through the Immigration files.

For Mike Keats it had been a crisis-ridden morning. Constantly on the telephone back and forth between the
accountants and the bankers and then into meetings
trying to cobble together any financial package that
would keep the creditors at bay. Proving Good Hope's
viability did little. The newspaper article, like a torpedo,
had blown a great hole below the water line and the creditors were terrified of going down with the ship.

Attempts had been made all morning to contact Joe
Rakosi in London but without success. Mike had spoken
to Simpson. 'Where in the hell is he?'

But Simpson didn't know. He had left the morning
before with Delacroix and hadn't been seen since, that's
all he could say.

So the decisions were left to Mike and by mid afternoon
the point of no return had been reached. If the major
creditor, the Hongkong and Shanghai Bank, accepted the
package, they would limp into port. If not, they turned

keel up and sank. One phone call would decide it. There was nothing to do but wait.

Mike was in his office, exhausted, past the point of caring, when Lawrence Yau came in and placed a sheaf of computer printouts on his desk. 'What are these?' he asked, so preoccupied with the crisis at hand that everything else had been forgotten.

'You wanted a full breakdown of our Thailand connections,' said Lawrence Yau.

'Oh yes, thanks.' Mike picked up the printouts and began to read through them. What there was was mostly history . . . a syndicated loan involving two Thai banks that had been signed eighteen months earlier, a feasibility study on the building of a resort hotel on Phuket that had never got past the planning stages. But there was one item that disturbed him and he ringed it in red. 'Get me the file on this will you.'

Yau looked over his shoulder. 'I'm sorry, that's all there is.'

'But there has to be a file of some kind.'

'I checked it personally,' said Yau. 'There are no documents that I can find.'

'Oriental Ventures, isn't that one of our shelf companies?'

Yau nodded.

'Then what's it doing leasing factory premises way down near Cha-Aam?'

Yau had no idea.

Mike studied the printout. It indicated that the lease was for six months only, strangely short. And the reason for taking it out was stated in one line: the manufacture and export of wood-block flooring.

Mike knew that Joe Rakosi involved himself compulsively in all sorts of commercial schemes. But he also knew that Rakosi never went into anything blind. He was too thorough, too shrewd. There would always be files containing feasibility studies, financial reports, correspondence and telexes. But according to Yau there was nothing; no file, no papers, just this one cryptic entry in the computer that gave details of the lease and stated that the original documents were held by the Thai Danu Bank, Patpong Road, Bangkok.

'Have you checked to see if we've made any lease payments?' asked Mike.

'There was just one payment of two hundred thousand US to the Thai Danu Bank. That was three weeks ago,' said Yau.

'And after that?'

'Nothing.'

Mike stared down at the printout. It was wrong, all wrong. Rakosi made million-dollar decisions on the turn. But he was meticulous with the paper work. And every cent was accounted for. So why not this time? He slumped back in his chair, eyes closed, rubbing his forehead with his fingers. There had to be a rational explanation, he thought. Because if not . . .

Shaking his head, he got up from the chair. No, he thought, Joe wouldn't knowingly get himself involved. He played hard and fast, he bent the rules. But there was a boundary to every man's conscience and there was no way he would ally himself with murderers.

An hour later, at five o'clock, Mike received the telex. It was from Switzerland and read:

COMPROMISE REACHED WITH DELACROIX. TEN OF THE FINAL FIFTEEN MILLION WILL BE RELEASED

IMMEDIATELY. THE BALANCE TO BE
PAID WITHIN THIRTY DAYS. ADVISE
BANKS THAT DELACROIX HAS ALSO
BROKERED FIVE YEAR LOAN TO THE
GOOD HOPE GROUP OF FIFTY MIL-
LION US. TROUBLES OVER, MIKE.
LOOKS LIKE PLAIN SAILING AGAIN.
WILL TAKE ABOUT TEN DAYS TO
CONCLUDE MATTERS HERE IN
EUROPE. THANKS FOR HOLDING THE
FORT.
JOE.

Mike called Lawrence Yau through to his office to give
him the good news, then telephoned the accountants who
would relay the information to the bank and the other
creditors.

As he sat in his office, he could hear Yau passing the
news to the other staff; he could hear their relieved banter
in Cantonese and the loud laughter. Mike was relieved
too, there was no doubt about it – on one level. But on
another he was deeply troubled.

Rakosi had always made a great thing about personal
contact in business. It was typical of him. 'Don't send
messages on bits of paper,' he always said. 'Get the guy
on the phone. Go into his office and thrash it out eyeball
to eyeball.' Rakosi would telephone from the North Pole
if he could, rather than send a telex. So why hadn't he
telephoned this time? Why just a piece of paper?

Mike tried contacting Switzerland to speak to Rakosi
himself but the receptionist at Delacroix's office said that
both men had gone. No, she said, they wouldn't be in
tomorrow. They had business elsewhere.

Now Mike was convinced. Rakosi was avoiding him.

But why? And at whose behest, he wondered, his own or Delacroix's?

At eight o'clock that night Mike finally snapped his brief-case shut and climbed wearily from his chair.

He paused a second at his window. Hong Kong was dazzling at night, a universe of lights and neon signs that ran along the waterfront from Central all the way to Causeway Bay. Ferries like fireflies floated on the harbour and beyond were the million and one lights of Kowloon, a sea of electric brilliance set against the black mantle of the mountains, the nine dragons – Gau Loong – that gave Kowloon its name. This was his town. The bank was happy, the creditors had pulled back. The crisis was over.

He picked up the phone, dialling the apartment. Mei-ling answered.

'I love you,' he said.

'When are you coming home?'

'Right now.'

'How has it gone today?' she asked tentatively.

'We live to fight another day.'

'The joys of capitalism.'

'I need it like a hole in the head,' he said.

She laughed softly. 'Don't be long.'

'Half an hour at the most, I promise.'

Switching out the light in his office, Mike closed the door behind him and walked through to reception.

Gladys, the young receptionist, was still on duty, hold-ing her post with the diligence of a Roman guard. 'Mr Baldwin telephoned. He said he was seeing Mr Chan Chi-wai tonight and he would phone you in the morning.'

'Thanks,' said Mike. 'And thanks for staying so late. It's been a hectic day.'

She smiled brightly. 'There's also the envelope, Mr Keats, the one I told you about last night. It's the one from the lady. She did say it was urgent.'

'Oh yes, I'd forgotten.' Mike took it from her, recognising Tina Wai's neat, script-like handwriting. The envelope contained something solid, the size and shape of a cassette.

He took the elevator down to street level, walking across Garden Road and down to the Hilton parking garage. As he got into his car, he dropped his briefcase onto the front passenger's seat. The envelope puzzled him. He hadn't heard from Tina in a long time, not since she and Joe Rakosi had broken up. All he knew was that it had been a bitter parting of the ways. So he didn't expect her to be saying anything too complimentary. Retrieving the envelope from the briefcase, he tore it open and saw that there was a letter inside folded around a cassette tape.

Mike assumed that both the letter and the tape had to relate to some incident in her relationship with Rakosi; other insider trading deals perhaps, Rakosi's many sharp and crooked moves. But not for one second, as he unfolded the letter, did he dream they could refer to him. Nor have such devastating consequences. . .

> Dear Mike,
>   I had hoped to find you in the office so that I could tell you this personally. It is so difficult for me to find the right words in English. You see, it concerns Jackie's suicide.
>   I know you loved each other very much and I know how terrible it is to open old wounds. But what choice do I have? Please believe me, Mike, I am doing this for you. I have just read about Joe in the newspaper. The business is

going to be in great jeopardy now and I know you will be dragged down with him unless you understand the true situation.

I have always admired your loyalty. Even Joe said that when you make a friend, you will walk through fire for him. But loyalty is one thing, Mike, blindness is another. It's time you understood what sort of man Joe Rakosi really is. Because if you stay loyal to him it will be suicide, no different from Jackie's tragic end. Because, you see, Jackie made the same mistake as you.

When you were away in Afghanistan and her new business was in such terrible trouble, she went to Joe. He was meant to be your friend, your partner, the one person who could help. But what did he do? He betrayed her. I can't explain in words, Mike, but listen to the tape, it will prove everything I say. I promise that it's genuine. This is not some terrible sick joke.

It humiliates me to admit it but I have to make you understand. Because I know, you see, I know from my own experience that Joe liked to record his exploits in bed. It was a sick fetish he had.

Never trust him, Mike, no matter what he does or says. He has no conscience. He uses people. The morning after he had invited Jackie to his apartment, I found the tape. I made a copy and I have kept it ever since. Listen to it, Mike, I beg you. Don't be blinded anymore. Because Joe Rakosi is responsible. He is the one who pushed Jackie over the edge.

Mike picked up the cassette, letting it rest in the palm of his hand. He didn't understand fully what Tina had been saying, he could only guess at something monstrous that would be heard. And yet somehow, deep down inside him, he was not surprised. It was as if all his doubts and suspicions, all those months of naivety had been leading to this one moment. The truth had always been there for him to see. All he had to do was open his eyes and look. Well, now his eyes would be opened for him.

Mike placed the tape into the car's radio-cassette. Then, like a man raising a revolver to his temple, he slowly turned the knob that would make it play . . .

Chan Chi-wai, the Dragon Head, had his residence on the Peak, up there at the top of the mountain with Hong Kong's colonial elite. The Chief Justice's official residence was immediately below his – below, Chuck Baldwin noted with wry amusement. Chan would gain great face from that.

There was a March mist on the Peak, warm as blood, thick and so wet that the walls dripped humidity. He arrived five minutes before the appointed hour, driving through the electronically operated iron gates and parking his hired Toyota on the concrete forecourt next to the obligatory gold Rolls Royce.

Chan's mansion was a gloomy, Gothic-style building with leaded windows and vaulted arches. Like a boys' boarding school, he thought; a ten-year-old's nightmare. The entrance was flanked by statues of Chinese lion dogs, their faces grimaced into a ritual growl. A Chinese manservant came to the door, then led Chuck through to the library. Without a word being said, cognac was poured from a crystal decanter and handed to him. Then the servant slipped away.

The library was not so much a repository for books as a place to display precious things: Chinese antiquities . . . vases and scrolls, paintings and tomb figurines. On one wall was a painting of a horse, one of those squat, thick-bodied animals that the Mongols had ridden out of the Gobi Desert. It was masterfully drawn, powerful and yet evoked with a fine lyrical quality.

'It was painted during the T'ang Dynasty,' said a thin, reedy voice at the door. 'It possesses a great inner vitality. It is one of my favourites.'

Chuck Baldwin turned to see Chan enter the library. He was tall but thin, sallow-faced, humourless, dressed in a dark business suit. His hair was brushed straight back, oiled down, and greying a little at the temples. Chuck's abiding impression was of the businessman, not the gangster. He was the essence of the wealthy banker; conservative, cautious, features chiselled with responsibility.

They shook hands. Chan's grip was limp and boney; bird-like.

'It's very good of you to see me at such short notice,' said Chuck. A little deference, he thought, would do no harm.

Chan pointed to another painting. 'That is by Ma Yuan,' he said. 'So simple, don't you agree, just a bare willow and distant mountains. And yet such grace. It dates back to the thirteenth century, to the time of the Sung Dynasty.'

'It's very beautiful,' said Chuck, thinking to himself: amazing what drug money can buy.

Chan poured himself a cognac. If his guest was drinking, he would drink too. Although it was obvious from the way he pecked at the liquor that he had little time for it. 'When you telephoned from the American Consulate, Mr Baldwin, you said I could be of assistance to you. A matter of historical importance was how you expressed it.'

His English was good; fluent and precise with hardly a trace of his Cantonese origins. Clearly, whatever Chan did, he did well.

Chuck considered his words carefully. 'I would like to make it clear from the outset, Mr Chan, that anything you tell me tonight is off the record.'

A shadow fell across Chan's face. Guarantees like that were a portent of trouble. 'Who do you represent at the Consulate?' he asked with a marked tone of hostility.

Chuck looked him full in the face. 'The CIA.'

The shadow darkened. 'And how do you think I can possibly help you?'

Chuck savoured his cognac; probably fifty years old, he thought, and fifty bucks a swallow too. He smiled. 'It concerns a group of Americans you worked with back in 1968. They were CIA too, a very special little group. I'm sure you remember them, Mr Chan. They called themselves the Phoenix Pact.'

Chan said nothing but the barest stiffening of the jawline was answer enough.

'You helped them with an operation into North Vietnam,' Chuck continued. 'You provided a junk and a crew.'

Chan sniffed as if there was a bad odour in the room. 'I'm afraid I don't remember any of this. I think you must have the wrong man.'

Chuck admired a delicate blue-and-white porcelain Ming vase. 'No, it was definitely you, Mr Chan. You see, the crew of that junk was all Wo Shing Wo.'

Chan stiffened. The imperious look became calculating, almost reptilian. 'I think you should leave, Mr Baldwin.'

'But you've been in the Wo Shing Wo since you were a boy,' said Chuck casually.

Chan's face was pinched and ashen. 'Triad societies are illegal in Hong Kong. Are you suggesting I am a criminal?'

Chuck gave an easy grin. 'Come on, Mr Chan, I'm not a policeman. I want some information, that's all. You could be the grand wizard of the Ku Klux Klan for all I care.'

'Leave,' said Chan with an icy hiss. 'Leave now.'

Chuck turned his attention to a small tomb figurine that stood on top of the grand piano. 'Our records show that you have a daughter living in California, Mr Chan. Orange County, Los Angeles.'

They shared a long silence. Chan's eyelids flickered but otherwise there was no acknowledgement.

'Our records also show that you visit her several times a year. She is your only child. It would be a pity if those visits became impossible.'

Chan sat in a leather chair. The lamplight next to it turned his skin into the texture of old parchment. 'That is so crude, Mr Baldwin.'

Chuck agreed. 'Unfortunately some matters don't allow us the luxury of finesse, Mr Chan.'

'My daughter can come to Hong Kong as many times as she likes. You can't stop that.'

'Your daughter has a husband, Mr Chan, a doctor with a busy practice. Your daughter has children. They have school to attend.'

'Do you think I have no influence in your country?'

'I'm sure you have a great deal of influence, Mr Chan. Money buys friends, especially in America. But money doesn't buy everything. Once it's on the records that you are a high-ranking Triad, a trafficker in narcotics, then all the friends in the world won't help you.'

Chan was immobile, barely breathing.

'I know how much your daughter and your grandchildren mean to you,' said Chuck with an air of amiable sympathy. 'Your daughter is a violinist and from what I understand, a good one too. You intend flying to America to listen to her play next month. Why make problems for yourself? Why put your future visits at risk? You're not a young man anymore. You have all these paintings and statues and they're fine. But they're just things. Consider what's really important in your life . . . your family, your flesh and blood.'

'How did you get to me?' asked Chan in a whisper.

Chuck sipped his cognac. 'I'm not at liberty to divulge that. Just as I wouldn't be at liberty to divulge any information you gave me.' He grinned, knowing that it was a cheap shot.

But it worked.

'Are you able to guarantee that my travel rights to America will not be impeded?' asked Chan.

'Not by the CIA they won't.'

'By the Immigration Authorities?'

'I know that you're a Triad,' said Chuck casually. 'But it need go no further. Does that answer your question?'

There was a long silence as Chan considered his options. Prudence had made him a survivor. 'You don't require me to put my name to any document?'

'No document at all.'

Chan pondered the problem, swallowing his cognac too quickly and wincing as it burnt his throat. He stood up from his chair, showing no emotion. Then he said in a business-like voice, 'Very well, Mr Baldwin, what is it you want to know?'

*　　*　　*

Chan had a remarkable memory for events. Or perhaps, more correctly, the events themselves were so remarkable that they remained indelible. He had been dealing in the opium trade since the early Sixties, he said, building his supply lines into the West Coast cities of the United States: San Francisco, Los Angeles, San Diego. Then, in January of 1968, he was approached by a Laotian contact who had links with Hanoi and from that time on he began to obtain his supplies from North Vietnam.

It was in March of '68 – the year of the monkey – that he despatched his first two junks from Hong Kong to North Vietnam, sailing them under the flag of Red China. He shipped general trade goods . . . machine spares, yarn, electronics . . . anything that could turn a profit. But his main cargo, hidden deep in the holds, was something far more valuable. It was gold. And in return for the bullion, he received heroin; already refined and packed . . . number four heroin, the mixture most prized on the American market.

'I dealt with agents of the North Vietnamese Government,' said Chan. 'Their rationale was simple – if the heroin was being smuggled into the United States to be consumed by young men of military age then the drug was a weapon of national liberation. I remember one of them telling me – "The Yankees bomb our children and we pump white powder into their children's veins." '

Chan smiled darkly. 'Although, of course, we knew that the Vietnamese would have auctioned their souls for hard currency. It was the gold, that was the real reason. But for me the business was easy. It was discreet and lucrative. My junks sailed the route for six months without any trouble . . .' His voice trailed away. 'But then, in July I was visited by an American.'

'Who was that?' asked Chuck.

'His name was Earl Blackmore. He was from the CIA, just like you. And, just like you, Mr Baldwin, he came at me, clanking and roaring, with all the subtlety of a tank.'

Chan explained how he and Blackmore had met at the Peninsula Hotel on the Kowloon side that hot summer's evening. 'It was amazing really. Blackmore knew everything about my trade with North Vietnam. He was a very big man, with a big chin and a black moustache, like a Mexican bandit. Dealing in drugs in such circumstances, he said, obtaining them from the North Vietnamese and smuggling them into America, made me an enemy agent. And that made me liable to assassination. In short, he said, he had every right to kill me there and then. As he put it in his American way, to spill my guts all over the carpet.'

There was the ghost of a smile on his face. 'It was just posturing of course. What he really wanted was my cooperation. He directed me to continue shipping general goods to North Vietnam as a cover for the gold bullion. But he told me I should widen the trade to include an extra class of goods . . .'

'What were they?'

'Pharmaceuticals.'

Chuck was amazed. 'You mean medicines, drugs?'

'Yes, exactly that.'

It was the very last thing Chuck Baldwin had expected. But he didn't question it further, just sat there listening.

Chan paused a moment and then continued, 'Blackmore said he would supply the goods. All I had to do was arrange the deal with my Laotian contact. So that's exactly what I did. I knew, of course, that the pharmaceuticals would be tampered with in some way and that concerned me. But what choice did I have? Blackmore, quite literally, had a gun at my head.'

Now Chuck was beginning to piece it together. It hadn't been a bomb at all, a tactical nuclear weapon. Christ alive, he thought – it had been germ warfare! And suddenly it all made sense . . . the Black Death, a plague sweeping the length and breadth of North Vietnam, destroying everything that American bombs couldn't touch, decimating the people, shattering their will. And suddenly too he began to realise why Tom Delaney was so determined that the Phoenix Pact should remain hidden. Because if that ever got out, if the world ever knew . . .

Chan recounted how he had met with his Laotian contact in a Wanchai teahouse, explaining to the man that he had come into possession of a large consignment of Swiss and West German pharmaceutical products especially packaged for military use. An inventory had been supplied. They had drunk tea, bargained and agreed a price. And ten days later confirmation had been received that the goods should be shipped.

Chan had been at the airport when the full consignment of medical supplies arrived on board an Air America McDonnell Douglas DC-8. Blackmore had rented a godown in the New Territories near the Tai Po Market and the supplies, packed into a large metal container, were taken direct from the airport to that warehouse to be stored until the junk's departure.

'So you say the medical supplies came from the US, not Europe?'

'I have no idea where they originated,' said Chan. 'It was not my concern. But that aircraft had flown from America, I know that, from a military base somewhere in Maryland.'

He went on to explain that from the outset Blackmore had insisted that, when the junk sailed, there must be two of his men on board. They were to ensure that the operation ran smoothly and that they weren't betrayed. The two men arrived in Hong Kong on the same Air America DC-8 that carried the medical supplies. 'One was called Tang,' Chan remembered. 'Good looking, very strong. The other was older, fatter, less impressive. They were both fluent in Cantonese although their accents were American. But, of course, the Vietnamese would not have noticed that.'

'What were they like together?' asked Chuck.

Chan thought back. 'Very secretive, obsessively so. And tensions ran high in those few days. They argued a great deal among themselves. One of them, maybe two, wanted to abort the mission. I could hear them shouting at each other. I was the only one they trusted. I rented a small house for them out in the New Territories near Tai Po. And that's where they stayed, drinking and arguing, until the day the junk sailed.'

'So they did sail?'

'Oh yes, they sailed. How do you Americans express it? The hawks won over the doves. There was a typhoon warning but they were determined to take the risk.'

'What was the next you heard?'

'About a week later I was visited by Blackmore. He looked distraught. He informed me that the junk had gone down.'

'Did he tell you how?'

'It must have been the typhoon.'

'Nobody told you that the junk had been attacked?'

Chan looked genuinely surprised. 'Blackmore said nothing. I had always assumed it had been lost in the storm.'

'You never advised the North Vietnamese that the cargo was contaminated?'

'I considered it,' said Chan.

'But?'

'But the risk was too great. It's wiser to placate the dragon at your door, Mr Baldwin, than the dragon on the far side of the hill.'

'So what did you do?'

Chan gave a condescending smile. 'I continued to trade. For me personally the Vietnam War was a time of much opportunity.'

Yeah, I bet it was, thought Chuck as he looked around at the objets d'art on display in the room. Reaching into the pocket of his windcheater, he took out Ricky Tang's gold signet ring and handed it to Chan. 'Do you recognise that?'

Chan studied it for a moment with a vague air of disdain. Then he nodded. 'Yes, it was Blackmore's idea. He loved badges, medals, that sort of thing. It was Blackmore who spoke about a ring, some symbol to bind them together. He asked if I could have it made for them.' He turned the ring in his fingers, peering at it. 'Yes, that was Blackmore's design . . . the phoenix clutching the Vietnamese dragon in its talons. Very dramatic, very American.'

'So it was Blackmore who gave out the rings, not you?'

Chan shook his head. 'No . . . once the rings had been made, I decided that they should be my gift. On the night before the junk sailed I went to the house and gave one to each man. It was a matter of face, you see, a sign of generosity. In any event, there were only four rings.'

Chuck looked up. 'Four? Are you certain of that?'

'Yes, I remember quite clearly. There were four.'

Chuck sat on the edge of his seat, counting off the names. 'One went to Blackmore, right?'

Chan nodded.

'One went to Tang and one to the other crew member, the fat one?'

'Yes,' said Chan. 'But there was a fourth man too.'

'Where did he come from?'

'He flew in on the same Air America flight. He was the man who dealt with the technical side of their business, a scientist of some kind.'

'Old, young?'

'In his late forties . . .'

'Older than the others?'

'Oh yes. He was the father of the group. I had a lot of sympathy for him at the time. I remember him well . . . a small man, very sad. I saw tears in his eyes on many occasions. He was very confused, full of doubts.'

'But he was a scientist, you say?'

'That's right.'

'Do you remember his name?'

And for the first time Chan gave a small, dry laugh. 'As the father of a violinist, how could I forget? It was most surprising, even the initials were the same. Yes, Mr Baldwin, I remember his name – it was William Arnold Mozart.'

As Chuck Baldwin hurried out of the house, apocalyptic visions filled his mind; deserted towns, empty villages, not a thing alive, not even a bird in the trees, just the drone of flies and the sweet, gagging smell of a world destroyed. 'Damn you, Delaney,' he cursed as he swung out of Chan's gates. 'Damn you to hell!'

With his yellow fog lights on full, Chuck careened down the precipitous switchbacks of Magazine Gap Road, down through the jungle-warm mist to the US Consulate at the foot of the Peak. The Toyota's brakes were visibly smoking as he climbed out and ran in through the rear entrance of the building up to the communications room.

He checked his watch, calculating the time zone difference. It was just eight thirty am in Virginia. But James Dexter got to the office early every morning to read the overnight despatches. Dexter was a conscientious man, a man of principle. Dexter went to church on Sundays. He never blasphemed. So damn easy, thought Chuck Baldwin, when you're a million miles away from the shit and the blood and the death. But let's see shall we, let's see what you're made of when you've got to put your ass on the line.

The surprise in Dexter's voice was undisguised. 'What are you doing in Hong Kong? You're in grave breach of orders – '

'I know about Blackmore.'

There was an abrupt silence.

'How could you have done this?' said Chuck, trying to keep his rage under control. 'I mean, for God's sake, Dexter, you know what's at stake.'

'You were told to leave this thing alone, Chuck.'

'To hell with that.'

'Believe me, the decision was taken in the best interests of national security.'

'National security? Christ, we're talking about germ warfare here! We're talking about some plague that could be used against America.'

'Where did you find out about that? Who told you?'

'Chan Chi-wai – remember him? He's the one who supplied the junk and the crew. Bloody hell, Dexter, how did you expect to keep this under wraps?'

'You have to appreciate that there were high reasons of state, Chuck. Tom Delaney didn't make the decision lightly.'

'For Pete's sake, Jim, stop trying to defend the indefensible! Delaney didn't want a scandal destroying his last days as Director, that's all it was. You knew he was wrong, you just didn't have the guts to say so.'

'That's not true . . .'

'You've been living in Delaney's shadow since I've known you.'

Dexter sighed. Every word was hitting home. 'You must remember that all this happened nearly twenty years ago . . .'

'What do you think we're dealing with here, some crappy little covert plan to poison Fidel Castro's cigars that we can hush up without any problems? This may have started twenty years ago but it's only finishing now – and it could just end by killing a few hundred thousand people!'

Dexter was flustered now, backing off but still trying to defend his previous inaction. 'We've been assured those pathogens could have no effect, not after eighteen years at the bottom of the sea.'

'How can you be certain of that?'

'It's a scientific evaluation.'

'And what if the scientists are wrong?'

There was no answer.

Chuck waited a moment, then he said in a low voice, 'Please, Jim, you've got to help us.'

There was a short sigh from the other end of the line. 'But I don't have the authority, Chuck, you know that. You know my position. Delaney has given specific instructions – '

'Forget Delaney's instructions! He's dying, Jim. It's a terrible thing, but it's a fact, and his mind is going.'

'But I'm betraying the man.'

'You're doing what's right.'

Dexter was wavering. Deep down in his heart he knew the course he had to take. All he needed was the final push.

Chuck spoke quietly now and rationally. 'Your scientific evaluations are guesswork at best, Jim. What if they're wrong? What happens if a plague breaks out, anywhere in the world . . . Britain, Israel, South East Asia, the US itself . . . thousands, maybe hundreds of thousands killed. What are you going to do when this whole thing blows up in your face? Plead superior orders?'

'How would they trace it back to the Agency?'

'How do you think?'

'You wouldn't betray us?'

'For this I would.'

'You'd never be forgiven.'

'I couldn't give a damn.'

There was an enduring silence.

'Please, Jim, don't do this to yourself,' said Chuck. 'In a few months Tom Delaney will be dead and you'll be left to take the blame. Do what's right. Don't just blindly follow the system.'

There was a moment's hesitation, a short exhalation of breath. Then James Dexter said, 'Damn you, Baldwin.'

'So are you going to help?'

'Yes . . . as far as I can.'

Chuck clenched his fist in triumph.

'But don't expect me to try and convince Delaney. It's impossible. Whatever we do, it's got to be without his knowledge.'

'Okay,' said Chuck. 'The first thing we have to know is what pathogens the Phoenix Pact hi-jacked. What are we talking about here, Jim . . . Q fever, anthrax, encephalitis? Are there any vaccines that can fight it?'

'I just don't know.'

'But you had access to the secret files, there must have been something – '

'There was nothing, no details at all. Don't you think I looked? All the papers talked about were "biological capabilities". That's it – corporate double-talk.'

'Then how do we get access to the information?'

'It's virtually impossible. Whatever the Phoenix Pact got their hands on – and I don't know how they did it – must have been new, totally new, beyond the ordinary classifications of secrecy. Without Delaney's help it could take us forever to find out.'

'Maybe not,' said Chuck. 'There is one man. If we can trace him – and if he's still alive.'

'But who? There were no other names I found in the files.'

'Then he obviously escaped from the net,' said Chuck. 'But he was in the Phoenix Pact, there's no doubt about it.'

'Okay, then give me the name. I'll check it out.'

'It's Mozart – as in the composer – William Arnold . . . and he's a scientist of some kind.'

The first feeling was one of disbelief. Somehow he had misinterpreted it all, the sounds and the voices. It couldn't be Joe Rakosi saying those things. It was impossible. No, no, he had got it all wrong. Mike's fingers moved to play the tape again to prove to himself . . . but he couldn't do it. And he let out a small cry of anguish.

As the numbed disbelief diminished, he tried for a few faltering seconds to cling to rationality. How did he deal with this thing? What steps did he take to verify it? But the shock and the pain were just too much. There was a great burning inside of him. He could hardly breathe. He grabbed the wheel of the car until his knuckles went white. Then he began to pound his hands against it. He wanted to scream. 'Oh God,' he sobbed. 'How could he have done this?' Because Rakosi had betrayed him, betrayed him in a way that was beyond comprehension. Mike took a deep breath, trying to control himself. But all he could hear was Jackie's voice; child-like and terrified and totally alone.

For an hour or longer he sat in the car, his emotions swinging wildly from a fierce desire to get straight onto a plane, find Rakosi and kill him, to a paralysed sense of impotence. Eventually he knew he must drive home, he couldn't sit there all night, and, with a long, deep sigh, he switched on the ignition, driving slowly out onto Cotton Tree Drive and up the hill.

When he stepped into the apartment, Mei-ling could see at once that something was dreadfully wrong. But she didn't push him. Mike said he was sorry but he couldn't eat. He sat on the sofa drinking whisky and listening to music and Mei-ling waited until he was ready, until he was able to sit quietly, speaking from the heart, and tell her the story . . .

He told her how he and Jackie had met and fallen in love. He told her how they gone into business together but how, from the very beginning, the business had been plagued with financial troubles forcing him to undertake one last weapons deal – the trip to Afghanistan. He told her about that desperate telegram calling him back and how he found Jackie lying comatose in the apartment; the panic and horror of it all as he tried to keep her alive, the wail of the ambulance siren, the stomach pump and the drips. And then how Rakosi himself had come to the hospital ward, mouthing words of comfort . . . his good friend, his partner, shocked to the core by the turn of events. And how finally, tonight, he had received the tape and had sat in the car listening to those sounds . . . sick, perverted, gloating . . . until he thought they would tear him apart.

As he finished, there were unashamed tears spilling down his cheeks; heartbroken tears for Jackie, tears of impotent rage for himself. 'He gets away with everything,' he said in a voice filled with bitterness. 'Is he going to get away with this too?'

Mei-ling had no answer. All she could do was take his hand to try and comfort him.

Mike bit at his lip, tears shining on his face. 'You know what he said to me when we last spoke on the telephone? "I'm beginning to learn you can't trust anybody in the world" – those were his exact words – "except you, old friend." Ironic, isn't it? From him, of all people.'

Mei-ling got up, walking to the far side of the room. Sometimes, she knew, the greatest comfort came in simply speaking the facts. She turned to face Mike. 'Now at least you know what sort of man he is. It's just as this woman Tina Wai says in her letter, Rakosi has no conscience, he uses people. Think about it, think about how he has used you. He sent you to Vietnam. Why? What was really behind it? Just how deeply is he involved with this man Delacroix? You can't trust him, darling, you can't trust him in anything.'

Mike slowly nodded. 'Yes, I know . . .' He fell silent for a time and then he said, 'There's a factory in Thailand that he rented a few weeks ago. He moved quarter of a million to a Bangkok bank too, apparently in connection with it all. But there's no file, no business papers, nothing. That's not like Rakosi, not unless he's hiding something.'

'Where's Rakosi now?' asked Mei-ling.

'He's with Delacroix.'

'Where?'

'I don't know. He's reached some financial compromise with him. I received a telex to that effect this afternoon. But I haven't been able to contact him.'

'And you knew nothing about this factory in Thailand?'

'Not a thing.'

'Then we must check it out,' said Mei-ling.

'How do we do that? Try and contact Rakosi?'

'No, that's the last thing we do,' she said. 'That will only serve to warn him – and Delacroix too. No, we fly to Thailand, Mike. We see for ourselves. And we do it tomorrow.'

Once the decision was made, once they knew the immediate course ahead, they sat and talked for a long time and it was only in the early hours that they retired to bed. By then, for Mike, the full heat of the catharsis had been spent. The glowing ashes of his pain remained of course; they would remain for months. But now at least he knew what must be done.

They lay for a time in each other's arms knowing that, above all else, they had each other. And then they made love. Mei-ling caressed him and showed him the sweet grace of it all. There was no dominance, no force, it was done gently with the slow, lovely rhythm of a poem. She said nothing. But her meaning was clear . . . don't become embittered, my darling, don't think that everything must be crude and ugly. Here, with the two of us, love is what love should be.

And when eventually Mike fell asleep, there were no dreams, just a long, healing oblivion.

At eight thirty the following morning, as they were having breakfast, Chuck Baldwin arrived. Mei-ling gave him coffee and toast and he sat at the table. It was clear he had

367

news, important news. But he wanted to hear from them first, to put it all into context.

When Mike told him about the recent lease of the factory in Thailand, Chuck's rumpled features clouded with concern. 'Yes, they'd need a place,' he said. 'They'd have to have one. It fits in.' He looked across at Mike and said briskly, 'Can you check it out, go there personally?'

'We're flying to Thailand today,' said Mike. 'The earliest available flight is late afternoon. We'll hire a car in Bangkok and drive down first thing tomorrow morning.'

'Okay,' said Chuck. He turned to Mei-ling. 'Are you going?'

'If I can organise travel papers, yes . . .'

'Good, I think it's important you go. If you have problems travelling on your Hong Kong identity document, contact me, I'll organise something on the turn.'

Mike was alarmed. 'Why's it so important?' he asked.

'Because she's a doctor,' said Chuck.

'What's that got to do with it?' asked Mei-ling. 'I thought we were talking about a military weapon of some sort.'

'Yes,' said Chuck, 'that's exactly what we're talking about.'

Kazakov was pleased. The village women had completed their work half a day ahead of schedule. Everything had been repacked, resealed and relabelled. The boxes were neatly stacked now in the main warehouse, ready for collection, each bearing the warning : MEDICAL SUPPLIES. HANDLE WITH CARE.

It had gone without a hitch. Kazakov calculated the bonuses due to the women and then asked Pansomchit to call them to be paid. But when they came, small, slender, brown-skinned women, coyly queuing, Kazakov saw that there were only five. 'One is missing,' he said.

'She's not well,' said Pansomchit.

Kazakov felt his pulse begin to race. 'What's the matter with her?' he asked.

Pansomchit spoke to one of the women in Thai and then turned back to Kazakov, speaking in English. 'She has had fever and some chills . . . coughing a little blood, they say.'

Kazakov felt weak. 'Where is the woman now?'

'Back in the village.'

'Are they going to call a doctor?'

Pansomchit shrugged. It was a matter of little concern to him. 'The nearest doctor is a hundred kilometres away.'

Kazakov's innards had turned to ice. He was gripped by panic. The temptation to flee the place there and then was overwhelming.

Pansomchit looked quizzically at him. 'Are you all right? You have gone very pale.'

'It's all right,' said Kazakov in a dry, jerky voice, not daring to look at him. 'Just a touch of the sun . . . here, you hand out the money. It's all marked. I need to go and sit down.' And, turning on his heels, he walked away as quickly as he could. Tomorrow morning couldn't come quick enough, he thought.

Mike and Mei-ling flew to Thailand that afternoon, arriving in Bangkok at four. They drove straight to the Thai Danu Bank on Patpong Road and uplifted the original lease agreement. The lease gave the name of the landlord and, with the help of bank officials, they were able to contact him.

The landlord said that the factory was an old sugar

mill. He had no idea what it was being used for now that it was leased and he didn't care. He had received the full six months' rental in advance, that's all that mattered to him. However, he agreed to meet them at the Oriental Hotel to give them a map of how to reach the place and that night, at eight, the map was handed over.

Mike and Mei-ling hired a chauffeur-driven car, arranging to be picked up at seven am. Then – as they had agreed – they telephoned Chuck Baldwin in Hong Kong to let him know that they had obtained directions and would be at the factory in the morning.

After dinner they had coffee on the elegant veranda overlooking the Chao Phya River where great writers like Somerset Maugham and Joseph Conrad had sat before them. The river was a brilliant sight, an immense waterway, high with muddy water, along which the long-tailed speedboats cut a silver wake. At any other time they would have marvelled at it all but tonight they were lost in their own thoughts.

They went to bed early, tossing and turning, and at three am Mike was awake, standing on the balcony looking out over the endless rooftops of the city. Mei-ling climbed from bed and came to join him, slipping her arm around his waist. Neither of them could sleep – not after Chuck Baldwin's revelations.

Another man who couldn't sleep that night was Mikhail Kazakov but for a different reason. For him it was a matter of personal, private terror. And an hour after dawn, bleary-eyed and haggard, he was waiting at the factory gates when the lorry arrived.

After the boxes had been loaded, Kazakov said a perfunctory goodbye to Pansomchit, walking quickly away to avoid shaking hands, and climbed into his car ensuring that the windows were closed. He hadn't asked about the condition of the sick woman. He hadn't dared. All that mattered was getting out of the place.

The road back to Bangkok was filled with lorries carrying everything from teak wood to sacks of salt. As with everything in Thailand, they were brightly painted like circus trucks; ancient most of them, bouncing and clattering along the two-lane highway in an endless procession.

At about nine o'clock, shaking off his fear now and beginning to drowse behind the wheel, Kazakov noticed a metallic-grey Mercedes approach him as it drove south. He saw the chauffeur in his blue serge and, looking into the back seat, caught a glimpse of the two passengers as the car sped past. But a glimpse was all he needed – he would remember Mike Keats until the day he died.

Pansomchit, the caretaker, was sitting on the veranda of his small house, frankly delighted to have everybody gone and the factory to himself again, when the Mercedes drew up at the main gate. He saw a tall, dark, bearded man get out, joined by a good-looking Chinese woman. 'Can I help you?' he called out.

'Yes, good morning,' said Mike. 'I'm with Oriental Ventures – '

It meant nothing to Pansomchit.

'The company that has leased the factory premises.'

'Then you're too late,' said the Thai. 'You've just missed him.'

Mike stopped in his tracks. 'Missed who?'

Pansomchit was puzzled. 'The German of course, Beckers. Isn't he with you?'

Mike's face was a mask. 'When did he leave?'

Pansomchit glanced at his watch. 'Two or three hours

ago. He went up with the lorry that took all the stuff.'

Mei-ling drew closer. 'Do you mean the medicines?'

'Yes, that's right.'

Mike and Mei-ling glanced at each other. Their worst fears had just been confirmed.

Pansomchit sensed something was wrong. 'Why, what's the matter?' he asked.

'Are any of the medicines still here?' asked Mei-ling.

'No, nothing. The whole lot was loaded and shipped out.'

'Nothing at all?'

'No, Mr Beckers was very particular about that.'

'What sort of work was being done here?' asked Mike.

'I'm just the caretaker,' said Pansomchit evasively. 'It's your company that rented the place. You should know.'

'There must have been some workers hired,' said Mei-ling. 'Where are they now?'

'They're back in the village.'

'Could you take us to them?'

Pansomchit was reluctant. Why should he go running around the countryside for a couple of strangers, foreigners too?

'We'll pay you,' said Mike.

'How much?'

'A thousand baht.'

Pansomchit climbed sluggishly to his feet, tucking his shirt into his trousers. 'All right,' he said. 'But I'm not taking you to the sick one – '

It was as if he had just uttered the most terrible blasphemy. Mike and Mei-ling froze, staring at him. They were lost for words. Then Mei-ling asked in a low voice, 'How bad is she?'

Pansomchit was flustered now. 'I don't know . . .

some fever, coughing up blood. Whatever it is, I don't want to catch it.'

'When did she fall ill?'

'Just yesterday . . .'

'After she had been working with the medicines?'

'Yes. Why? Look, if there's a problem, you've got to tell me. I've been here too, you know.'

'Then you're going to have to see a doctor,' said Mei-ling in a voice that brooked no dissent, 'you and every-body else who has worked here.'

From a man content to put his feet up and contemplate a few weeks of sunny idleness, Pansomchit had been transformed into a quaking casualty filled with the fear of God. 'What's this all about?' he bleated as he was bustled into the front passenger's seat of the Mercedes. 'I've never felt better in my life. I'm fine, I promise you . . .'

'I'm sure you are,' said Mei-ling reassuringly. 'It's a precaution, that's all.'

They reached the village in a couple of minutes, pulling up in front of a traditional Thai farmhouse. It was built on stilts, its walls made of weathered teak, with a low thatched roof.

'That's where she lives,' said Pansomchit.

Mei-ling took her black medical bag out of the boot. She could see the farmer standing under the house where the great clay pots that held the drinking water were stored. She turned and spoke to Pansomchit. 'I'd like you to come inside and act as my interpreter.'

'Oh no,' said the caretaker, shrinking away. 'I'm not going in there. You can go, you're a doctor . . . but not me.'

'Then at least explain to the husband who I am and why I am here.'

Pansomchit was prepared to do that – but only from a

safe distance. Standing close to the Mercedes, as if somehow the vehicle would protect him, he shouted across to the farmer and the man shouted back saying that his wife was alone in the house. Everybody else, his children, his sister and mother, had left.

'It seems I'll have to find her on my own,' said Mei-ling.

'Are you sure you're going to be all right?' asked Mike, equally concerned.

She smiled up at him. 'The woman is ill, Mike. I'm a doctor.'

'Be careful,' he whispered.

Mei-ling nodded. Then she stepped across the broken ground and climbed the wooden steps into the dwelling.

She found the woman in a small back room. She lay on a low wooden bed, covered in a sweat-drenched sheet. Nobody had brought her food or water. Fear was a powerful thing. Kneeling next to the bed, Mei-ling felt for her pulse. It was still feebly fluttering – just. Her blood pressure was right down. She was rapidly sinking into a coma. Her eyes were red, her face purplish and congested. The tongue was coated with mucus. The woman coughed and fresh blood came up, pinkish and frothy. She was haemorrhaging from the lungs. There was nothing that could be done for her, not here.

Walking back out into the sunlight, Mei-ling saw that a crowd had gathered around the Mercedes . . . farmers and their wives, old women and children.

As soon as he saw her, Mike came hurrying across. 'How is she?' he asked.

'She's bad, I'm afraid, desperately ill. She needs hospitalisation immediately. You're going to have to take her.'

'Any idea what she's suffering from?'

'I can't be sure, not without tests . . .'

'But assuming we're talking about germ warfare agents, about bacteria of some kind, what then?'

'It's possible,' she said hesitantly. 'The symptoms appear to fit.'

'What?' he asked. 'What could it appear to be?'

'But it's a guess, Mike, that's all, just a guess.'

'I don't care. Just give me some idea of what we're up against here.'

'All right,' she murmured. 'If it's a bacterium, then possibly, just possibly, it could be pasteurella pestis. It's been tested in the past, I know that. Experiments have been done on it.'

'But what is it?'

She looked into his eyes. 'You would know it as the bubonic plague.'

He went pale. 'The Black Death?'

'Yes,' she said in a dry voice. 'The Black Death.'

For a moment or two he was lost for words, his whole body washed with a sudden, irrational fear. Then, with a nod, he said, 'All right, so what do we do?'

'You must drive her to hospital now, get her into a quarantine ward.'

'What about you?'

'I'll stay here,' she said. 'There could be more sick.'

'But if it's that infectious – ' and his eyes were begging her.

Mei-ling squeezed his hand. 'Don't worry, nothing is going to happen to me. But, until help arrives, Mike, this is my place.'

It was amazing how calmly and confidently she took command. Gathering the villagers around her, using Pansomchit as an interpreter, she explained that the sick woman may have contracted her illness by handling certain substances at the factory. There was nothing to be alarmed about, she said. But, for safety's sake, she wanted all the women who had worked at the factory to remain on their own – in quarantine – just until medical help arrived and they could be properly checked. In fact, everybody who had had physical contact with the women should stay in the village.

Listening to her speak, Mike was afraid that the villagers would panic, especially when one woman who had worked at the factory came forward, weeping, saying that she felt sick and feverish. Suddenly there was fear in everybody's eyes, made even worse when a second woman complained that she had been vomiting all night.

But Mei-ling acted quickly and surely. She knew how the Thais revered age and brought forward the village elder, a farmer who must have been all of eighty years old. She urged him to speak to his people, to convince them that there was no reason to panic. She would remain here in the village, she said, attending to anybody who didn't feel well, while her husband took the sick woman, the one in the farmhouse, to hospital. Then, to show that she herself was not afraid, she went down to the two women who had complained of illness, speaking quietly and reassuringly to them both.

The moment of crisis had passed. The villagers would do as Mei-ling wished.

A crude stretcher was made and four of the farmers carried the woman out, laying her in the back of the Mercedes.

Mei-ling took Mike to one side. 'There's nothing you can do for her, just get to the hospital as quick as you can. To be safe, don't touch her. Just let her lie.'

'What do I say when I get to the hospital?'

'Tell them about the factory. Tell them about the possibility of a viral infection of some kind. Tell them it could be highly contagious. But don't start talking about germ warfare, not immediately. It's a country hospital. They'll think you're mad. Later, when you can get to somebody senior, do it then. But what's vital is that the police cordon off the village. It must be quarantined and it must be done today.' She reached up to kiss his cheek. 'Hurry,' she said. 'Every minute counts.'

Mike climbed into the front passenger's seat with the Thai chauffeur driving. As the vehicle set off, he glanced back and saw Mei-ling wave. And he knew that he had never loved her more – or feared for her more – than he did at that moment.

They drove at breakneck speed. But the nearest hospital was a hundred kilometres away and the journey still took two hours along the dirt roads while the woman lying on the back seat burnt up with fever.

As they came in through the hospital gates, tyres squealing, Mike glanced back at the woman for the hundredth time and knew immediately. Because suddenly there was an immutable stillness about her. She was beyond help now.

Mike was badly shaken. Twenty-four hours ago she had been fit and well, a hard-working housewife looking to earn a little extra money to help her family. My God, he thought, what sort of virus can it be that kills somebody in just a day?

There were only three doctors at the hospital, all overworked. The woman was certified dead so there was no rush, that was their initial reaction. They had other matters to attend to: babies being born, victims from a car crash to be operated upon. But Mike kept at them, harrying them down the corridors and in their surgeries until he was able to convince them of the urgency of the matter.

The dead woman was examined more closely . . . and then they understood. Yes they said, shocked, that is what it could well be: the bubonic plague.

After that, in their own way, they acted quickly and efficiently. The local police were sent to cordon off the village and factory while an emergency call was put through to Army Headquarters in Bangkok. In matters like this, said the chief doctor, the Thai army was often used, especially in the remoter areas, as they had the men and equipment to cope with outbreaks of contagious disease. An urgent autopsy would also be required on the body of the dead woman to ascertain the cause of death. The army would attend to that too, flying down one of their forensic pathologists.

So at last, to Mike's immense relief, things began to happen . . .

By mid afternoon police had cordoned off the village, keeping everybody in and all traffic out. Pansomchit had been interviewed and confirmed that the man who was in charge of the recent work at the factory was a European, a West German by the name of Pieter Beckers. The medical supplies had been loaded onto a lorry just that morning, said Pansomchit, and taken to Bangkok. Beckers had followed the lorry in a private car. But Pansomchit had never been told where the supplies were being taken. No, he said, he couldn't remember the name of the trucking company. Nor were there any records kept. That wasn't his concern. He was just the caretaker. Beckers kept all the papers.

Police nation-wide were given a description of Beckers and told to arrest him on sight. Interpol was requested to put out a red alert for his apprehension wherever he might be found. But it was too late.

It was only at eight o'clock that night, checking

through the various passenger lists at Bangkok Airport, that the police came across his name. Beckers had flown out of Thailand at midday; destination, Burma. An urgent request was made to the police in Rangoon to track him down but, despite the fact that the Burmese had a record of Beckers' arrival, they were unable to find the man. Eventually, both they and the Thai police came to the conclusion that Beckers had been travelling under an assumed name and must have switched identities inside Burma before flying out again.

There were never too many Europeans travelling through Burma and the immigration authorities there did remember a podgy-faced, sandy-haired man flying out that same day to Hanoi. But when they checked the records, they found that he was not a West German, he was a Russian. His name was Mikhail Kazakov, some kind of government official. Burma, an isolated state, heavily reliant on the USSR, decided it would not be prudent to take the matter further.

As for the medical supplies, it proved impossible to track them down. The name of the trucking company was not known. There were no invoices, receipts, shipping orders or consignment notes. It wasn't even known if they were being kept in the country or transported out by air, sea, road or rail. Bangkok Airport was checked as being the most likely point of departure but no pharmaceutical supplies could be found nor was there any record of them being air freighted out that day. In fact, while the cargo-holding areas at the airport were being searched, the medical supplies were on the back of a lorry clattering along the open road.

Following one of the basic rules of security – that you never go out the way you came in – Jean-Paul Delacroix had arranged for the supplies to be delivered to a small

Bangkok trucking company and then, as a matter of urgency, driven south again, back through Cha-Aam, right past the hopital where Mike was waiting, and over the border into the Islamic republic of Malaysia. The supplies would be delivered to the airport in Kuala Lumpur at six the following morning and by ten would be loaded aboard a chartered Boeing 707 bound for Peshawar in Northern Pakistan.

The supplies – at Rakosi's cost – would form part of a much larger consignment . . . clothing, footwear, blankets, canned fruit . . . all of it labelled as 'refugee aid'. Most of the aid was destined for the hundreds of thousands of refugees who lived in squatter villages along the border. But, first and foremost, the recipients were to be Farouq Mohammadi's Mujahedin.

In Mike Keats' mind there was no more room for doubt – Joe Rakosi had played an integral part not only in salvaging the biological warfare agents from the sunken junk but also in having them repacked at the factory and then shipped on. Whether he knew all the facts or whether it was a case of moral complicity, Rakosi was guilty of a crime beyond comprehension.

The only question now was where those medical supplies were destined. And if Rakosi had played such a crucial role in the earlier part of the operation, Mike was convinced that somewhere in his business records – somewhere among the papers of the Good Hope Group – lay the answer.

Lawrence Yau was senior manager in the Good Hope Group, their top administrator. If anybody could find the answer among the thousands of files and computer records, it was him. And it was Lawrence Yau who Mike telephoned first. 'I have to know,' he said, 'and I have to know as a matter of utmost urgency – have we sold pharmaceuticals to anybody, anywhere in the world, in the past six months?'

Yau was emphatic. 'We don't deal in pharmaceuticals, Mr Keats. We never have.'

'Could we have been involved in some joint venture?'

'Nothing that I can recall.'

'Please, Lawrence, this is literally a matter of life and death. Check it out for me, will you?'

'Of course.'

'Anything that you can find – I don't care how small or how indirect – anything at all on the manufacture, sale or shipment of drugs.'

'When do you require the information?' asked Yau.

'Within twenty-four hours,' said Mike. 'Sooner if you can.'

As soon as he had finished his call to Yau, Mike telephoned the US Consulate in Hong Kong to speak to Chuck Baldwin.

'What did you find at the factory?' asked Chuck, clearly anxious.

'We arrived too late,' said Mike. 'The stuff was gone. But we've been left with the effects.'

'Oh Christ. How bad?'

Mike grunted. 'It's a nightmare . . . and it looks like getting worse.'

Chuck listened in grim silence as Mike told him everything. 'But you say they've cordoned off the village, they've isolated everybody?'

'Now they have, yes. But God knows who went in and out before we got there. There's one death at the moment and two women sick. Tomorrow there could be twenty, thirty . . . and how do they fight it, Chuck? What vaccines do they use? For God's sake, you've got to be able to convince Delaney now!'

'The woman who died, do you know her cause of death?'

'No, of course not, not until the autopsy has been done.'

'So what we've got so far is one death – from unknown causes. No contaminated medicines, no pathology reports.'

'But the facts speak for themselves!'

'I'm sorry, Mike, it's just not enough to convince a man like Delaney to put the reputation of the CIA at risk. He's obsessed, you know that.'

'So what are we meant to do? Mei-ling is out there in the village. All I keep thinking is, my God, maybe she's been infected herself. And I tell you, Chuck, it terrifies me.'

'You've just got to hang in, Mike. Because we're getting there – Dexter thinks he may have found Mozart.'

'Thank God for that. Where is he?'

'All Dexter knows so far is that he's in India, a missionary of some kind. But he's checking with contacts in New Delhi. By tomorrow, he says, we should have enough to track him down.'

'Who is going to confront him?'

'We both are,' said Chuck. 'Dexter has authorised the hire of a business jet.' He gave a mirthless laugh. 'Amazing isn't it, I can get all the money I need, just no f-ing information!'

'What's your schedule?' asked Mike.

'I'm flying out of Hong Kong in a couple of hours' time. I'll be night stopping in Bangkok. Which hotel can I contact you at?'

'The Oriental.'

'Okay, meet me in the lobby there at five am. We'll fly to India together.'

It wasn't until after dark that Mike managed to speak to Mei-ling on the police radio net.

She sounded tired but full of spirit. 'You must go,' she said. 'There's nothing you can do here in Thailand.'

'What about you?' he asked.

'At least here I'm doing what I'm trained to do. I'll be fine, don't worry.'

'How are the two women?'

'They're critical. I don't know if they'll make it through the night.'

'The same symptoms?'

'No,' said Mei-ling, 'that's the strange thing. If they all had bubonic plague or similar symptoms, I could understand it. But one of them has typhoid while the other has viral hepatitis. They don't have to be fatal diseases, not with modern medicine. But nothing we can do seems to be helping. They just don't seem to have the strength to hold on.'

'Don't take any risks,' said Mike, 'please.'

'No more than I have to,' she replied.

'I'll arrange for money to be left for you at the Oriental.'

'Don't worry about me . . .'

'I'm worried sick about you,' he said. 'And I will be until this whole damn thing is over.'

Grigori Kirilenko made an intimidating figure. A tall tree of a man, dressed in a military greatcoat, with general's insignia of rank, he was waiting at Sheremetievo Airport, when Kazakov returned from Hanoi. The two men embraced, Russian style, gave each other brisk greetings and then walked out onto the snow-dusted steps to wait for Kirilenko's Chaika limousine.

'Enjoy Moscow while you can,' said the General. 'You only have twenty-four hours. This time tomorrow you fly to Kabul. I have arranged a temporary attachment to the 210th Spetsnaz as an intelligence officer. You'll be operating near the Pakistan border north of Chitral.'

'Farouq Mohammadi's area of infiltration?'

'We have to ensure that the Phoenix is given a clear, free flight into the heartland, Misha. That was always your final task.'

Kazakov understood. But the prospect of being in the front line again filled him with a dull, sapping fear. 'I had hoped there would be a little more resolve in the Party Presidium by now,' he said limply.

Kirilenko snorted in disgust. 'Resolve? Of course there's resolve – to accept defeat.'

'But we still have more than a hundred thousand troops in Afghanistan.'

'For how long, tell me that? There will be diplomatic manoeuvres of course and grand declarations. But in the end it will be the same kind of tawdry performance that the Americans put on when they scurried out of Vietnam. Unless we do something, Misha – you and I – Russia is beaten.'

Kazakov turned up his collar against the raw, gusting wind. 'I just worry that we're doing too little too late. Whether the risks are worth it . . .'

Kirilenko glared at him like a hawk focusing on a mouse. 'What happened to you in the Far East? You talk like a defeatist. The Afghans are primitive people. Set a plague loose among them, decimate their bandit gangs with dysentery and cholera, have their children shrivelling in the womb, then soon enough they'll be saying that Allah has deserted them. And without their God, they're nothing.'

'But you say the decision has already been made to pull out.'

'Because the Kremlin can see no prospect of winning. But show our brave generals twenty thousand dead Afghans, show them a stricken people, Misha, and then see how rapidly they change their minds.'

'And what if our own troops are infected?'

'We've discussed that before. Why are you suddenly querying everything? In any war there must be casualties. A soldier who perishes from typhus is no less a hero than one who is shot through the heart. In any event, it won't take long for the General Staff in Kabul to realise that it's dealing with a form of biological warfare and then the necessary steps will be taken to protect our men.' Kirilenko took a deep breath, enjoying the icy air. 'And once it has been learnt that this biological warfare is a botched attempt by the CIA to decimate Russian troops . . . ah, Misha, then see how our Russian resolve is stiffened.'

Kazakov was openly alarmed. 'But couldn't that be dangerous? I mean, if there's a close check . . .'

'At the right time, Misha, when tempers are high and when the facts have been sufficiently blurred, then we'll feed the General Staff with the information.'

'That worries me . . .'

'Everything worries you. Catching a cold worries you! Consider it a moment. What other choice do we have? Virulent, man-made bacteria don't spring out of the earth like grass. There has to be an aggressor. And the aggressor in this case has to be the CIA. It's their style to use some cheap Hong Kong arms dealer as their front man. Rakosi and his partner Keats have CIA contacts, there's ample evidence of that . . . and Rakosi is going to be there when the bandit, Mohammadi, receives the contaminated medicines – all the evidence we need, final and conclusive.'

Despite himself, Kazakov had to smile. 'You've arranged to have Rakosi at the Afghan border?'

'Shaking hands with the dushmen and smiling from ear to ear,' said Kirilenko. The Chaika limousine drew up and he opened the back door. 'So you see, Misha, there's no question of the Phoenix being too little too late. Just the opposite. You and I are going to turn history on its head.'

Joe Rakosi was pacing the room like a caged tiger. 'How long are we going to be holed up in this bloody place?' he asked.

Delacroix didn't bother to look up from his book. 'Don't you enjoy the view?'

'I've been staring at the Matterhorn for the past twenty-four hours. A mountain is a mountain . . . a pile of rock.'

'Then read, listen to some music. There is a wonderful version of Gounod's *Faust* – '

Rakosi swilled the ice around in the bottom of his whisky glass. 'When are we going to eat?'

'In half an hour.'

The telephone rang and Delacroix went through to the bedroom of the chalet to answer it. He was gone just a minute before he returned with a fixed smile on his face. 'It seems, Joe, that the waiting is over. We fly out tomorrow morning.'

'Just a public relations exercise, that's it?'

'That's it, Joe. Fly in by helicopter, shake a few hands,

accept a few grateful thanks. Then it's over and the world goes back to normal again.'

Rakosi grunted. 'Yeah,' he said.

They were cruising at thirty thousand feet over the Bay of Bengal and scheduled to land in Hyderabad when the pilot of their chartered Gulfstream received the radio message from Dexter saying they should change course and touch down at Bombay.

Two and a half hours later, after they had landed and were making their way through immigration control, a middle-aged man in an open neck shirt came over, smiling broadly. 'My name is Vijay,' he said. 'I will be your driver.' He handed Chuck a folded piece of paper and there was the address they had been waiting for:

Dr William Arnold Mozart,
All Souls Mission Hospital,
Shahapur Junction,
Bhiwandi.

'How far away is this place?' asked Chuck.

Vijay beamed. 'Oh, not too far, sir, just north a little. We'll be there very soon, you'll see.'

The journey took four hours, away from the sea into the agricultural heartland. But that included the time it took to replace a punctured tyre and follow a bullock cart the last half mile along a winding avenue of jacaranda trees that led up to the mission.

It was a Roman Catholic establishment, a hospital, school and orphanage run by the White Fathers. They came across a priest in a small office near the entrance and asked if they could speak to Dr Mozart. 'Ah yes,' said the priest, a Frenchman, 'he is in the ward down the passage. You should find him there.'

They entered the ward cautiously, their footsteps ringing on the highly polished concrete. There were no beds as such, just cots, each with its own mosquito net, at least fifty down either wall. The patients, old and young, lay silently watching the two intruders. A couple of Indian orderlies went about their business of folding sheets.

And then Mike and Chuck saw him. They walked a little closer. 'Dr Mozart?'

The man bent over the cot straightened up and turned. 'Yes, can I help you?' he asked with a quizzical look.

The first impression was one of frailty, a little sparrow of a man who couldn't have weighed much more than a hundred pounds. He wore glasses perched on the end of his nose, giving him a vague professorial look, and was almost totally bald except for a few wisps of brown hair blown out behind each ear. The clothes he wore, a white cotton shirt and grey trousers, seemed to hang off him as if they were two sizes too big. But his handshake was strong enough and his voice was firm.

'We're sorry to disturb you,' said Chuck. 'But it's an important matter. Do you have anywhere we can talk in private?'

The quizzical look turned to one of concern. But he smiled and said chirpily in a strong Indiana accent, 'I've got an office at the end there. How private it is . . . well, that's another matter.'

He led them past the silent, wide-eyed patients to a small room at the far end of the ward. There was a scrubbed wooden table under the window and four wooden chairs. Mike noticed the crucifix on the wall. But otherwise there was no decoration. The room smelt of disinfectant.

Mozart lit a cigarette. 'Even missionaries are allowed the occasional vice,' he said.

Mike and Chuck smiled politely.

Mozart waited. 'You said it was an important matter?'

Chuck Baldwin searched for a way to begin. There was a moment's awkward silence. Then he asked, 'Have you ever heard of an organisation called the Phoenix Pact?'

Mozart's mouth fell open. 'Where are you from? Who are you with?' he asked in a hollow, hushed voice.

'I'm with the CIA,' said Chuck.

And Mike added, 'Please, Doctor, you must help us.'

Mozart seemed to have aged ten years in a matter of seconds. 'I always knew this day would come,' he murmured. 'I've prayed and hoped. But I always knew.' He looked directly at Chuck. 'What has happened?' he asked.

'Somebody has salvaged the container from the junk. They've raised it off the estuary bed.'

'But nothing would be left, not now,' said Mozart, visibly trembling. 'I was told the junk had been destroyed, totally destroyed!'

Chuck's features were hard-set. 'Whoever told you that was wrong. We know the medicines were still within the container when they were raised. We know they were taken to a particular place in Thailand to be repacked and relabelled. And we know that at least half the women who handled those drugs have fallen critically ill.'

'Ill, you say? How quickly did it happen?'

'In under twenty-four hours.'

'All the same symptoms?'

'No.'

For a moment they thought Mozart might faint. He closed his eyes, rolling his head. 'Oh God forgive me,' he prayed.

'You've got to tell us what sort of bacteria we're dealing with,' said Mike. 'What sort of vaccine is needed?

There's one woman dead already and there could be hundreds more.'

'But there is no vaccine,' said Mozart in an almost inaudible whisper. 'That's the terrible thing. There's nothing to help them.' And, his face full of anguish, he fell to his knees on the concrete floor, clasping his hands.

Chuck Baldwin, however, had no time for sympathy. At this moment guilt was a luxury they couldn't afford. 'Then tell us,' he said in a hard voice, 'tell us what this is all about. Give us some idea what we're dealing with.'

Mozart climbed shakily to his feet. 'Can we walk?' he murmured. 'I need the air . . .'

He led them out of the office, through a small door and into a terraced garden. A couple of old men squatted a distance away weeding the lawn. The earth was red and the air was heavy with the scent of frangipani. Mozart walked across to a bench that stood in the speckled shade of a flame tree and sat, staring down at the ground between his feet.

Mike and Chuck waited.

'It was in 1967 that I commenced work at the US Army Biological Warfare Laboratory at Fort Dettrick in Maryland,' he said. 'My field was genetics. In layman's language, I was exploring the possibilities of Crick and Watson's discovery of the double helix structure of DNA . . . the molecule that controls heredity.'

'Tinkering with the genetic code?' said Chuck Baldwin harshly.

He didn't look up. 'Yes, you could put it that way.' He sniffed, wiping his eyes, and continued. 'I was just one of a team and our team was working in conjunction with others, the microbiologists. They were studying two things, a bacterium called V23 which destroys the body's immunity system – its defence against disease – and a toxin called T2.'

'T2, what's that?' asked Chuck.

'It's a fungal growth, a kind of penicillin. It was first discovered in Russia in the 1930s on poorly stored grain. Except penicillin hears you. T2 is lethal.'

'So there were three separate areas of research, is that what you're saying?' asked Mike.

'Separate?' Mozart had a far-away, haunted look in his eyes. 'Separate, yes, to begin with . . . but we were all aiming towards one thing, you see, and then in early '68 we stumbled across it.'

'And what was that?' asked Chuck.

Mozart looked up at him, his eyes red-rimmed. 'We called it SP,' he said. 'But the military men, the gung-ho ones, simply called it the super germ.' He got up from the bench and walked quickly away. 'The super germ . . . it sounds like something out of a comic book, doesn't it, some concoction boiled up in a test tube by a bunch of goofy high school kids. But believe me, that's the last thing it was.'

'What are its effects?' asked Mike.

'SP attacks the body's hereditary strengths, wiping them out in a matter of hours. The body is rendered defenceless to even the smallest infection.'

'So the common cold?'

'Could be fatal and probably would be,' said Mozart, 'in that it would lead rapidly to other conditions . . . pneumonia, viral fever. But it goes further than that. Because – how can I explain it? – you have to appreciate that the frenzied destruction of the body's immune system not only renders the body defenceless but actually makes it a magnet for infection of every kind. Usually the victim will be struck down within days, hours even . . .'

'But surely there must be some kind of vaccine?' said Chuck. 'I thought you bastards were meant to ensure you had the vaccine before you start experimenting?'

'That's what the newspapers are told, yes. But there was nothing, no vaccine, not back in '68. We discovered the disease but not the cure.'

'Okay, if there's no cure, how high is the fatality rate?' asked Mike.

'We estimated about seventy per cent.'

'Men, women and children?'

'Everybody.'

Mike took a deep breath. It appalled him. 'So, if the body's natural immunity is destroyed, people won't die of just one disease,' he said. 'Anthrax, for example, or green monkey disease?'

Mozart shook his head. 'No, they'll die of pneumonia, viral hepatitis, typhus, typhoid. The victim quite literally sucks infection out of the air. That's what SP stands for, you see – the Spectrum Plague.'

'Cute,' said Chuck, trying to control his sense of outrage, 'really fucking cute . . .'

Mike felt the same; the nightmare vision grew more horrifying every second. But survival was all that counted and there had to be some way of lessening the impact. 'If there's no vaccine that you know of and if the fatality rate is seventy per cent, how do we prevent the disease being passed?' he asked.

'There's only one way,' said Mozart. 'You have to cut off all human contact with infected victims. That's what made SP a feasible biological weapon. We were able to define the casualties, protect our own men. SP isn't like a poisonous gas that blows back in your face. To pass it, somehow it has to be ingested into the body or mingled with body fluids.'

Mike was beginning to see some hope. 'So it has to be eaten, you mean, swallowed in some way or transmitted through sexual intercourse?'

'Yes, that of course. But remember, we're talking about virulent bacteria. Drinking from the same cup could be sufficient, even letting infected blood fall onto your hand. In the field, with soldiers drinking and eating out of the same mess tins, their bodies touching, sweat mingling – in a situation like that the bacteria would spread quicker than any plague you could imagine. As I said, there's only one way – that's an absolute quarantine.'

Mike accepted his advice. What other choice did he have? 'There's a telephone in your office,' he said. 'I have to phone Thailand.'

'Yes, use it of course,' said Mozart, hurrying with them back into the building. 'But the exchange system in Bhiwandi is very antiquated. I'm afraid it might take a time.' As soon as they reached his small, sparse office, Mozart contacted the local exchange and was informed there could be anything up to an hour's delay. There was nothing to do but wait.

Three enamel mugs of tea were brought and Mozart lit another cigarette, puffing nervously.

'Tell me,' said Chuck, 'what brought you to a place like this?'

'Don't you know?'

'The Phoenix Pact?'

'Some deeds require a life's penance.'

'That sounds very noble,' said Chuck with undisguised scepticism. 'But you're a thinking man. How could you have become involved with a bunch of renegade lunatics like that in the first place? They were madmen, they had to be – '

393

'Of course they were,' said Mozart in a slow, passive voice. 'It's a cliché, I know, but war breeds madness, especially a war that you are losing. You must understand how we felt at that time . . . our boys were dying out there in the jungles and the paddy fields, thousands of them with no effect. We made Vietnam a war of contrition, blood for blood. We were playing the communist game, just as they wanted it played. America's strength lay in its technology. I was a scientist, I knew the sort of weapons we could marshal. And yet we were bogged down there, losing a war we could win, watching our boys die for nothing.' With trembling lips, Mozart took a deep draw on his cigarette. 'I'm not excusing what we tried to do. I think back now and I shudder. But at the time, that's the way we thought.'

'But why you?' asked Chuck. 'You were in the States the whole time, working nine to five in some white-tiled lab.'

'Why me?' Mozart gave a sad smile. 'Why me . . .?' He reached into the drawer of his desk, taking out a wallet, and from the wallet he took out a small photograph. 'I still carry it,' he said and his eyes were suddenly sparkling with tears. 'James Eldridge . . . Jimmy, my only son.'

Mike took it from him. It showed the head and shoulders of a young man in Marine dress uniform, a lieutenant. It was a sturdy mid-Western face, blue-eyed and full of optimism. Born in the USA, proud and strong, ready to do and die for his country. How common that look used to be, he thought. How rare it was today.

'He was just twenty-two when that photograph was taken,' said Mozart. 'It had to be the Marines, he said. He wasn't interested in the army or the air force, the "non essential personnel" as the Marines called them. He wanted to be out there with the best.' His lower lip trembled as he tried to control his emotion. 'Because he was the best himself, you see, the very best. Brave, loving . . . do you have any idea what it's like to lose your only son? God made that the worst pain of all.' He tried to laugh then, embarrassed at the wetness on his cheeks, and blurted out, 'You must think I'm very foolish after all these years.'

There was nothing Mike and Chuck could say.

Mozart retrieved the photograph, replacing it reverently into his wallet. 'Jimmy had been four months with the 26th Marines at the Khe Sanh Combat Base besieged by the North Vietnamese. His commanding officer said he was one of the finest officers he had. It was the last morning of his tour. Would you believe that? He was waiting on the edge of the airstrip when the shells came in . . .' He tried to continue but the words were stifled. A tear dribbled down his cheek.

There was a moment's awkward silence. Then Chuck asked him, 'Blackmore was obviously the motivating force behind the Phoenix Pact. But how did he get to you?'

'Earl Blackmore and I grew up together in Indiana,' said Mozart. 'He was on leave from Vietnam and in the week after Jimmy was buried we talked a great deal. In his own way, he was just as embittered as I was. Because nothing mattered for me then, you see. I was mad with grief. All I wanted was revenge – revenge against the whole world. I didn't care how, or who died.' He sighed and then said in a low voice, 'So I agreed to join him.'

'So it was you who decided to use SP?'

Mozart nodded. 'The final tests on it had been completed the day my son was killed. We were celebrating when I received the news. At times like that, when your mind's unbalanced, you look for every sign, you read symbols into every coincidence. God had decreed it, that's what I thought. There it was – the means of my vengeance.'

The telephone jangled on the table and they were through to the hospital at Cha-Aam. The line was bad but Mozart was able to explain what had to be done. A second woman, he learnt, had died but the third, although critical, was in a stable condition and, as yet, nobody else had fallen ill.

When he put down the telephone, Mozart looked considerably relieved. 'With luck – and God willing – the plague will be contained.'

But for Chuck Baldwin it wasn't that easy. 'In Thailand maybe,' he retorted, still smouldering with rage. 'But there's an entire shipment somewhere out there, enough to wipe out half the world, and we haven't a clue where it is. All we can be certain of is that the men who control it are lunatics too and – just like you, doctor – they intend to use it.' He climbed to his feet. 'Come,' he said gruffly to Mike, 'we've got to get back to Bombay. I've got a number of calls to make and it'll take forever on this Stone Age exchange.'

Mozart accompanied them out to the car; an old man crushed by his past.

'There's one final thing,' said Chuck as he was about to climb into the car. 'We know the junk was attacked and sunk. But what was it, pure chance or design? Did the North Vietnamese find out on their own or did somebody within the Pact tell them?'

'It was somebody within the Pact,' said Mozart.

Chuck studied his face. 'It was you, wasn't it?'

'Yes, it was me. But the North Vietnamese were never involved. They knew nothing, not until after the junk had been sent to the bottom.'

'So you never dealt with them?'

'Never.'

'Nor the Russians?'

'No.'

'Then the fighter bombers that attacked it – ?'

'They were navy Phantoms . . . American aircraft.'

'Americans killing Americans, how did you organise that?'

'I had nothing to do with the sinking of the junk, I knew nothing about it, not until after. But when I was in Hong Kong, I made the decision. I knew the Phoenix had to be stopped but I couldn't convince the others. So I had to do it on my own. There were a couple of occasions when I managed to get out of the apartment where we were hiding. I had to organise a special outer casing for the container. And I used those times to contact a CIA agent that I had dealt with in Washington.'

'What was the deal?' asked Chuck.

'In exchange for not mentioning me at all, for letting me walk clear without my name appearing in any documents, I told him everything I knew about the Phoenix Pact . . . the date the junk was going to sail, its course and what it was carrying.'

'What happened to Blackmore?'

'He was dismissed,' said Mozart. 'But they couldn't send him to jail. They didn't want the Phoenix Pact to be known, not ever. So they gave him some money, half a million or so, and Blackmore started a business somewhere.'

Chuck Baldwin spat into the red dust. 'Who says crime doesn't pay?' He turned to Mozart. 'And you walked away from it all too, no money maybe, but the slate wiped clean. Tell me, who was this Good Samaritan?'

'I had dealt with him at Fort Dettrick,' said Mozart.

'That's why I contacted him. His name was Tom Delaney.'

Driving back to Bombay, Mike and Chuck found themselves in the disturbing position of having learnt almost everything and achieved virtually nothing. Mozart may have spelt out in graphic terms the devastating power of SP. He may have answered questions about the past. But, in the context of the present crisis, the past meant nothing.

Who had possession of the contaminated medical supplies now? Where were they hidden? And when were they going to be used? Those were the vital questions. And they remained unanswered. Chuck summed up their shared aggravation. 'North, south, east, west – we don't even know which goddam continent they're on!'

The road north to Chitral was as old as history itself. Alexander the Great had passed along it under the gaze of the barren mountains, marching his troops across the arid nothingness of this roof to the world. The Mongols had swarmed along it and today it remained as bleak and desolate, the glaciers just as daunting. The only difference was the presence of a tarred road – of sorts – and along it in the cold, thin air of that late afternoon, a convoy of three trucks could be seen.

They had journeyed all the way from Peshawar and would reach Chitral shortly before dusk. There were guards sitting on each truck, tucked in among the boxes and the canvas, bearded Afghans with rifles, because the trucks carried a precious cargo . . . supplies for Farouq Mohammadi's fighting men. And tomorrow, in the pale light of dawn, they would be carried across the border into the high reaches of the Hindu Kush.

There were boxes containing many things: khaki clothing, footwear, belts and pouches. And in addition – perhaps most precious of all – there were medical supplies that had been flown from the Far East.

From his room in the Taj Mahal Hotel, Chuck Baldwin telephoned Washington DC. James Dexter was in his office and listened without comment as Chuck recounted what he had learnt from Mozart at the Mission of All Souls.

'So what do you suggest now?' he asked.

'First, we have to find out if a vaccine has been developed. That way at least, if the plague suddenly hits us, we'll know how to handle it. You've got no choice, Jim, you're going to have confront Delaney. And he's going to have to start giving some answers. Goddam it, he was the one who gave Mozart immunity in the first place!'

'I'm afraid it may be too late for Tom Delaney . . .'

'What do you mean?'

'He collapsed this morning at home. They don't hold out much hope.'

'Then you're going to have to contact the biologicial warfare people direct – spell it out to them. To hell with secrecy, there's a catastrophe staring us in the face. They're going to have to do something and they're going to have to do it fast!'

Dexter understood the proportions of the crisis only too well. 'All right,' he said quietly. 'I'll get on to it now.'

'What about Thailand?' asked Chuck. 'Have the police got anything more on the medical supplies?'

'There's just no trace.'

'What about this man Beckers?'

'Nothing on him either.'

Chuck Baldwin gave an angry grunt of frustration.

'We're getting nowhere. We're just chasing our tails here.'

Dexter said nothing. 'Can I contact you at the hotel?' he asked.

'Yeah,' said Chuck, dispirited. 'I'll be waiting. I've got nowhere else to go.'

As he put down the telephone, Mike came through from the adjacent room.

'Thought I'd get drunk,' said Chuck, going to the room fridge and taking out a bottle of local beer. 'Do something constructive.'

'So you got nothing from the States?'

'Nothing at all. What about you?'

Mike took a beer too, retrieving a glass from the bathroom and pulling off the hygiene wrapping. 'I managed to get through to Switzerland and speak to Delacroix's secretary.'

'Any joy?'

'She says Rakosi and Delacroix are still away on business. It could be the North Pole, it could be Timbuktu, she's just not talking.'

'Did you speak to your manager, Yau?'

Mike flopped back on the bed. 'He's been through every record, every file, every bit of paper he can find. But he tells me he's found nothing.'

'Can you rely on him?'

'One hundred per cent,' said Mike. 'He said he worked until after midnight last night and I believe him. He's still looking now, double-checking. If he finds anything, he says he'll come back to me.'

Chuck walked over to the window, gazing disconsolately along the Colaba waterfront. 'I've never felt more useless in my life,' he said. 'We've got the Black Death on our doorstep and we're sitting here warming our asses.'

'So what do we do?' asked Mike.

Chuck swilled back his beer. 'What can we do? We sit tight and pray.'

It took more than three hours for Mike to track her down, switching long-distance calls from one number to another. But eventually he caught her as she came into the hospital at Cha-Aam. 'How are you?' he asked, his anxiety obvious.

'I'm fine,' said Mei-ling buoyantly, 'just fine. We think the third woman, the one with hepatitis, is going to make it.'

'But I want to know about you. How are you feeling?'

She laughed. 'Don't worry, darling. I'm as strong as a horse.'

And Mike could breathe again.

'Nobody else has fallen ill,' she said, 'not so far. I think we might have got here early enough to contain it.'

'That's good,' he said.

'You found Mozart?'

'Yes, we did.'

'And the shipment that left the factory here, is there any news on that?'

Mike gave a frustrated sigh. 'None at all. It's like looking for a needle in a haystack.'

With the thoroughness for which the Swiss are renowned, Delacroix had arranged everything. Only the timing had been left to Kirilenko. And, as it transpired, that too was perfect.

After landing in Islamabad, Rakosi and Delacroix flew north over the arid brown plains to the city of Peshawar, touching down in the mid-afternoon. And it was there – to Rakosi's astonishment – that they boarded a privately

chartered Bell JetRanger helicopter to take them north
into the moutains to Chitral. The cost would be crippling,
Rakosi knew it and inwardly he railed, but what could he
do? Until this thing was over, he was Delacroix's hostage.
Everything he had ever built in his life, everything he
hoped for, rested on his compliance. All he could do was
grit his teeth and bear it.

They landed at Chitral at five that evening and were
met on the wind-blown airstrip by the short, dumpy
figure of Halima flanked by two bodyguards. Bustling
over, unveiled, she greeted Joe Rakosi effusively. 'We've
never met,' she said. 'But I feel as if I know you. Mike has
been a good friend to us.'

Rakosi smiled dutifully. 'Yeah, well, Mike has always
been committed to your cause.'

And Delacroix, introducing himself, added smoothly,
'It was Mike Keats who motivated Joe in the first place.
You can't just take, you must also give. It's a philosophy
Joe subscribes to a hundred per cent.'

Halima gave a brown, wrinkled smile. 'Your
generosity has been outstanding. And to have you here
with us expresses your solidarity better than any words.'

It was all bullshit, Rakosi knew. Just platitudes and
pretty words. The sooner this thing was done with, the
sooner he was out of here, the better.

'Joe would like to visit a number of refugee camps,'
said Delacroix, 'especially the clinics . . . to get a better
understanding of how the Good Hope Group can help.'

'That's all been arranged.'

'Because, of course, the supplies flown in from
Malaysia will be for the refugee families too. The trucks
on the road are just the advance guard bringing essentials
for the Mujahedin.'

'You have a very full schedule in the morning,' said

Halima. 'Much more than could normally be achieved. But with this – ' she pointed excitedly at the helicopter as if it was some bright new toy – 'with this it will be simple.'

'Limited time demands it,' said Delacroix. 'The pressures of business elsewhere . . . I'm sure you understand.'

Halima spoke to the Pathan pilot in rapid Pashtu and then turned back to Rakosi and Delacroix. 'The pilot says you flew over three trucks a little way back on the road. Those will be the ones. Come, we should hurry if you wish to be there. The helicopter will be quickest.'

'Then climb in,' said Rakosi perfunctorily. And, bending under the rotors, he opened the rear passenger door of the white and royal blue machine and climbed in next to her.

Standing back a little, Delacroix noticed that a scattering of onlookers had been attracted by the arrival of the civilian helicopter, an unusual sight in these far-flung, poverty-stricken reaches. Good, he thought, it was exactly the attention he had hoped to receive. Because Kirilenko had briefed him carefully . . .

The Afghan border swarmed with spies: devious adventurers representing KHAD, the secret service of the Russian-backed government in Kabul, Pakistani police agents with multiple allegiances, part KGB, part CIA, competing Afghan guerrilla groups, arms dealers and drug dealers and among them all, a scattering of independents who peddled their intelligence like pots and pans along the roadside. 'Don't be alarmed,' Kirilenko had said. 'With so many different factions, it is like a second-rate comic opera. But they will serve their purpose. All we need, you see, Jean-Paul, is for word to filter back . . . word that Rakosi – the philanthropist – has flown into Chitral.'

* * *

403

Michael Hartmann

Dusk was descending in a pearl-grey haze as the helicopter curled around the barren mountains, in and out of the clouds, flying north west along the border. They were just ten minutes out from Chitral when Halima pointed down to a cluster of white tents set amid the mountainside terraces. It was Farouq Mohammadi's staging area, his last camp this side of the border. The JetRanger landed, setting its white-painted skids on the stony summit of a hill, and Farouq Mohammadi himself, a tall man, brown and handsome, wearing a camouflaged battle jacket, climbed the slope to meet them.

There were formal greetings, handshakes, smiles and much green tea and, when the three trucks arrived an hour later, their radiators gushing steam, Joe Rakosi was present to watch the goods being unloaded.

As the boxes marked MEDICAL SUPPLIES. HANDLE WITH CARE were unpacked and their contents placed into leather pouches that the donkeys would carry across the border, Delacroix took a couple of photographs of the work being done. As soon as they saw the camera, the Mujahedin gathered around Rakosi, posing gallantly like Edwardian military men. And one of them even, holding a box of drugs in his left hand, clasped Rakosi's hand with his right. It couldn't have been better if it was rehearsed, thought Delacroix.

Darkness fell quickly; moonless and silent except for the cold whisper of the wind. A meal was cooked of vegetables fried in dough. It was agreed that they would bed down for the night with the Mujahedin – comrades together – and be there at dawn to watch them depart.

When they finished the beers, Mike and Chuck Baldwin had opened a bottle of scotch and then sat in the hotel room watching Bombay television and waiting. They had nothing else to do.

Around midnight, James Dexter had telephoned from Washington. By putting his reputation on the line and threatening a lot of people, he had obtained the information they wanted on SP. But it wasn't good. SP, he said, had proved too unstable, too contagious. It was no longer part of the US Army's CBW arsenal. It had been disposed of, poured down some bottomless hole in the Rocky Mountains ten years ago.

'What about the vaccine?' Chuck had asked.

And Dexter had replied, 'Nobody thought it necessary to develop a vaccine for a weapon that didn't exist anymore.'

'So there's none?'

'Not at this time.'

'How long would it take to develop one?'

'A year, maybe two.'

'By which time half the world could be dead.'

'If the plague ever struck, yes . . .'

'Have you approached the Russians?'

'Indirectly, yes.'

'And?'

'They're unable to help us.'

'What about the Vietnamese?'

'The same thing.'

'Christ alive, Jim, what are we going to do?'

But Dexter had no answer, nobody had. So they sat there and flattened the scotch, waiting for some call out of nowhere that they knew would never come. Then, at two in the morning, frustrated, maudlin, blind-terrified drunk, they both crawled into bed. They had reached a dead end.

When Joe Rakosi awoke, dawn was the thinnest smudge of gold leaf on the blue-black aurora of the mountain peaks. It was cold and softly drizzling, dark and still. He stood outside his tent watching the horses and the donkeys being loaded, hearing the sharp ring of their hooves on the stones. The Mujahedin worked in silence, some still draped in their blankets and he saw Delacroix among them, helping to check the straps and buckles on the animals. 'So you're a boy scout as well are you?' he said with a sneer.

But the Swiss financier refused to rise to the bait. 'Just making myself useful,' he answered.

Farouq Mohammadi came across to say goodbye, shaking their hands, thanking them again for their support. Then he led his scouts up into the arid mountain pass until he was lost from view. The Mujahedin fell into line, setting off after him. They were the advance guard, one hundred men with fifty beasts of burden.

As he watched them depart, Joe Rakosi was troubled by conscience. There was no way he could delude himself. The facts were clear. Somehow, in the supplies that had been donated to the Mujahedin – supplies donated in the name of the Good Hope Group – lay the seeds of these men's destruction. He knew that the horses and mules didn't carry a hope of life. Whatever they carried was poisoned . . . just how he didn't dare contemplate. He knew too that from the earliest days, from his first meeting with Delacroix, he had been used as a pawn in some complex game to bring it about. Mike Keats had been right. The whole thing had stunk from the beginning. But there was no purpose in regrets, not now.

Joe Rakosi wished there was some way he could warn them. He had nothing against the Mujahedin. In many ways he admired them. They were honest men fighting for their country. But to try and do so, with Delacroix at his shoulder, would place everything he had ever worked for – his buinesses, his wealth, his future – in dire jeopardy. And Joe Rakosi had learnt a long time back, as a terrified young boy fleeing Hungary, that only one thing mattered in life . . . personal survival.

The call came through at seven am, jarring him awake. Mike groped for the telephone on his bedside table. 'Yes, what is it?'

It was Lawrence Yau on the line, telephoning from Hong Kong.

'Have you found anything?' asked Mike, his head thick from the night's heavy drinking.

'Nothing to do with any sale or purchase of medicines, no,' said Yau. 'But there is one thing I've come across that's puzzling.'

Mike sat up. 'What is it?'

'It's a letter addressed personally to Mr Rakosi. It came in the mail this morning. but it's not marked private or confidential so naturally his secretary opened it.'

'Where's it from?' asked Mike. 'Who sent it?'

'It's from London,' said Yau, 'from the secretary of that trust you helped to set up, the Malik Gailani Trust. Do you remember it?'

Mike was already clambering out of bed, his heart thudding in his chest. 'What does it say? Quick, tell me.'

'Let me find the relevant part . . . ah, yes, here it is,' said Yau. 'It reads as follows: ''While, as you say, the Good Hope Group may have profited in the supply of arms to the Afghan freedom movement, nevertheless your generosity in donating such a substantial consignment of medicines to the fighting men – ''.'

'My God,' said Mike, 'that's it! When was that letter posted from London?'

'Just three days ago. Does it help?' asked Yau uncertainly.

'Yes, Lawrence, yes it does . . . thank you.' Mike stood for a moment, paralysed by the revelation. He had a sudden dreadful image of Halima and Farouq Mohammadi lying among the stones of the Hindu Kush coughing up blood, their faces pale as death. Then shaking himself out of his torpor, he said a hurried goodbye to Yau, put down the phone and ran to Chuck Baldwin's room.

Chuck opened his door, bleary-eyed. 'What's up?' he asked in a croaky voice.

'I know where the medical supplies have been sent,' said Mike. 'Why didn't we think of it sooner? It was staring us in the face. The Russians in North Vietnam, the Russians in Kabul – '

'Afghanistan?'

'Yes, Chuck – Afghanistan!'

Time was critical, they knew it. Two things had to be done. First, they had to contact Halima to warn her and then they had to get up to the border themselves. So, while Chuck made hurried arrangements for the flight, Mike tried to telephone Chitral.

It took him nearly an hour to get through, by which time Chuck was pacing the carpet ready to leave for the airport, but eventually a young girl answered in broken English.

No, she said, Halima was not there. She would not be back until the early afternoon. She was escorting two visitors; important men, foreigners.

Intuitively, Mike knew. 'Does one of them have ginger hair – red?'

'Yes,' said the girl. 'Red.'

Mike looked up at Chuck. 'Rakosi's there in Chitral, the bastard's there now!'

'Ask her about the medical supplies,' said Chuck. 'Have they received any? What's happened to them?'

Mike put the questions.

But the girl hesitated, frightened to answer in case she was breaching security.

'I'm trying to help you!' shouted Mike. 'Those medical supplies are bad. They'll kill people. They mustn't be used. Do you understand me? They're poisonous.'

'Poisonous?' stuttered the girl.

'Yes, poisonous! Tell Halima that Mike Keats telephoned. Have you got that name? Write it down. Tell her that I'm flying to Chitral immediately.' He turned to Chuck again. 'How long's our flight?'

'We leave here at ten. Estimate two and a half or three hours' flying time. There's no time difference between here and Pakistan. So you can reckon on landing about twelve thirty.'

'We'll be landing in Chitral before one o'clock,' said Mike to the girl. 'Tell Halima to meet us at the airport. But most important of all, the medicines must not be used, they must not be touched in any way. That's vital. Do you understand?'

'Yes, yes . . .' The implications of it all had reduced the girl to a state of shocked idiocy but one thing was beyond doubt in her mind – the medicines were fatal.

Grabbing his overnight bag, Mike followed Chuck down to the lobby. Their bills had been paid and Vijay was waiting with the car. They had an hour and a half to drive the eighteen miles to Santa Cruz Airport, clear Immigration and be airborne.

Tired and frightened, having marched half the night in a cold, drenching rain, Mikhail Kazakov sat huddled in a cleft of rock with his Kalashnikov across his knees. From where he sat, he had a panoramic view that stretched the full length of the valley as far as the distant, mist-shrouded mountains that marked the Pakistan border.

There were a hundred different routes that Mohammadi's dushmen could take and this was just one of them. But, if Delacroix had done his job, the Spetsnaz radio operator and cipher clerk huddled together under a groundsheet would soon start to receive the regular bleep-bleep of a radio signal – a signal sent out by a small trans-mitter hidden among the supplies that the dushmen carried. And, just as an aircraft beamed in on such a sig-nal to find its landing ground, so Kazakov and his platoon would cut across the mountain watersheds to home in on Mohammadi's men.

Not that Kazakov had any intention of ambushing them – just the opposite. It was his sole task to ensure that the bandit column was not bombed or raided by any other Russian or Afghan force. Like a good shepherd, thought Kazakov with sardonic humour, it was his job to bring the little lambs home.

Like royalty on a tour, Joe Rakosi had smiled and waved his way through a countless succession of foul-smelling tents, houses and mud-walled clinics. He had accepted grateful thanks for his beneficence from Mujahedin with their legs blown off, children with diarrhoea and begging females clucking unintelligibly behind black veils. He had inspected operating theatres in which he wouldn't dare have his nails cut, latrine pits and grubby little schools run by ignorant mullahs. And by midday, punch-drunk, all he wanted to do was fly back to Chitral, have a hot bath and get out of Pakistan as soon as he could.

'One Afghan in three has been killed, maimed or is living as a refugee because of the Russian invasion,' said

Halima as they walked to the waiting JetRanger.

'You need to see with your own eyes,' said Delacroix who appeared to be genuinely grieved.

But Rakosi's initial concern had evaporated. He was a frightened man who just wanted to be rid of it all. 'Where to now?' he asked.

'I'm afraid we have to return to Chitral,' said Halima.

Thank God for that, he thought. The purgatory was nearly over.

His sergeant, an animal of a man who relished these miserable conditions, tapped Kazakov on the shoulder. 'The radio operator is getting something.'

Kazakov could see the radio operator huddled beneath his groundsheet with a large grin on his face. Through his earphones the man could hear the persistent bleep-bleep now as clear as the call of a bird. 'They are to our west,' he said. 'And close.'

Kazakov hurriedly consulted his map. There was a village due west, too small to have a name. The sergeant estimated that it was no more than twenty minutes' march away. 'Easy,' he said.

Muscles aching, Kazakov climbed to his feet. 'Then let's take a look,' he said.

They had been airborne for more than three hours. The Gulfstream II was one of the fastest executive jets in the air, cruising at five hundred and eighty miles an hour. But, having taken off late to begin with, thunderstorms over the Gulf of Cambay had pushed them out over the Arabian Sea and since then they had been battling fierce headwinds all the way. And now, as they began their approach run into Chitral, heavy rain began to fall.

'Our bloody luck,' said Chuck Baldwin with pent-up

frustration. 'First, we're late and now we're going to be washed out.'

But luck – good or bad – can change in an instant and, as they stepped from the Gulfstream after landing, it suddenly went their way.

They were walking towards the small airport building, their passports ready, when Mike heard the sound of approaching rotors. He half turned, looking over his shoulder and saw the helicopter coming in. He called to Chuck, 'That's a Bell JetRanger, civilian not military. What's it doing up here?'

They both turned, watching it hover and then settle on the tarmac fifty yards away. Mike caught a glimpse of a thick-set figure in the back, a blur of gingery hair. 'Christ, it's Joe Rakosi, I can see him there in the back,' he said. 'And there's Halima with him.'

Rakosi climbed from the helicopter, head hunched down into his anorak, striding towards the airport building to get out of the rain.

Mike began to run, shouting above the gust of the wind, 'Joe, it's me! Stop!'

Rakosi heard him and spun around, a look of astonishment – and guilt – on his face. 'Mike, what on earth are you doing here?'

Mike stopped a couple of feet in front of him. 'You bastard,' he hissed, wanting nothing more than to swing out a fist and lay him flat. 'Do you know what you've done? Do you have any comprehension – ?'

Rakosi was stupefied. 'What are you talking about?'

Mike grabbed him by the collar of his anorak. 'The medical supplies, where are they? What have you done with them?'

Rakosi tried to push himself away. 'What's got into you? Are you crazy?'

Mike saw Halima come bustling across, delighted to see him. But the second he spoke, the smile faded from her face.

'The medical supplies that were brought in for the Mujahedin,' he said. 'You've got to tell me, what's happened to them? Have they been used?'

'Why, what's wrong?' she asked nervously. There was an anger on Mike's face that she had never witnessed before.

'They've been poisoned, that's what's wrong!' Mike was twisting the collar of Rakosi's anorak, garrotting him. 'They contain germ warfare bacteria. If they're used, they'll start a plague that could be impossible to stop.'

Halima stood rooted, unable to believe what she was hearing.

Mike turned on Rakosi. 'You murdering bastard, I should kill you right here!'

Rakosi was squirming, trying to struggle free. 'Please, Mike, this is crazy. What do you mean, germ warfare? I don't know what you're talking about.'

Mike saw a second man with wind-blown chestnut hair – obviously Delacroix – backing away from the group, looking for an escape route. 'Hey!' he shouted. 'You, stop!' But Delacroix turned his back and began to stride out, half-running, towards the airport building.

Mike let go of Rakosi. 'Try and run, you bastard, and I promise, I'll kill you.' He took a step, ready to pursue Delacroix when he heard Chuck questioning Halima; short, concise, rational questions that cut through the confusion and anger of the moment, getting to the heart of the problem. Delacroix, he knew, would have to wait. There were more immediate problems.

'Tell us,' said Chuck, blinking against the slanting bite

of the rain. 'Have you received any medical supplies?'

'Yes,' said Halima.

'When?'

'Only last night.'

'Where are they now?'

'They were given to Mohammadi and his men.'

'Have they crossed the border yet?'

'This morning, yes, just after dawn.'

Chuck glanced down at his watch. 'Seven, eight hours ago, is that right?'

She nodded.

'How far would he get in that time?'

Halima was bewildered. 'Eight or nine miles . . .'

'Ten at the outside,' said Mike. 'It's a hard climb and he must have pack animals with him.'

Chuck Baldwin was trying to put it all together. 'You're a pilot, Mike. If we took the JetRanger, the chopper there, how long would it take to catch him?'

'But Mohammadi could have crossed the border at a hundred different places, Chuck. We could be criss-crossing the mountains for hours – '

'I know the route he's taken,' said Halima.

Chuck could have kissed her. 'Could you show us from the air?'

'Yes, I think so. Yes, yes, I'm sure I can.'

Chuck turned to Mike again. 'Okay, if we know the route and assuming we're able to take the chopper – how long?'

'Depends on the terrain. But, once we're over the border, ten minutes, maybe quarter of an hour – if we can find him.'

'In and out,' said Chuck. 'What other choice have we got?'

Mike looked across at the helicopter that stood

glistening in the rain. It had been four years since he had flown one and he had never been in a JetRanger in his life before. But his inexperience with the machine was nothing compared to the risks involved in crossing the border. The frontier area was crawling with Russian and Afghan government troops. Once they were in Afghan airspace – civilian or not – no questions would be asked. If the Russians had a chance, they would blow them straight out of the sky.

But if they did nothing, if they followed the rules, if they remained here in Chitral, what then? The result was inevitable. 'All right,' he said. 'Let's do it.'

'Do you know how to fly this thing?'

'I'll learn.'

Chuck gave him a sudden grin. He took Halima by the arm. 'Get into the front passenger's seat,' he said. 'You'll have to direct Mike.'

Halima swung around. But, as she did so, the Pathan pilot who had witnessed most of the conversation blocked her way. 'This is against the law,' he said with squeaky pomposity. 'You have no right to take my helicopter.'

Chuck bore down on him. 'I'm sorry, buddy, this thing is way out of your league. Just let us pass. We'll explain later.'

'It's illegal to cross the border,' protested the pilot. 'You can't do this.' And, chest out, he stepped defiantly in Chuck's way.

Chuck shook his head. 'Bloody fool – ' And, before the pilot could blink, he had sent his right fist clubbing into the man's jaw.

The pilot threw his arms out, toppled backwards and slipped on the wet tarmac, cracking his head, his cap rolling away.

'Okay, quick,' said Chuck, 'before we get half the airport staff trying to stop us.'

Mike grabbed hold of Rakosi again. 'You're coming too, you bastard.'

'Across the Afghan border, are you mad?' Rakosi flailed out his arms, trying to struggle free.

'You've got some questions to answer.'

'I told you, I don't know anything about medical supplies. Please, Mike!'

'What else have you poisoned? Foodstuffs, clothing? You don't just walk away from this, not this time – not like everything else!' And, twisting his arm up behind his back with such force that Rakosi yelled, Mike frog-marched him to the helicopter where Chuck Baldwin grabbed him and hauled him in.

Mike climbed into the pilot's seat, staring at the panel. He was stiff with nerves. It was a half-hour round flight, maximum – if they made it – so he didn't have to worry too much about fuel. But what was the start sequence?

'Come on, buddy,' muttered Chuck behind him. 'Let's go, let's go.'

Mike saw the Pathan pilot staggering to his feet, clutching his jaw, and then begin to run towards the airport building. He looked back at the control panel again. He had to do this on memory and hunch. All right, he thought . . .

Battery switch on, fuel booster pump on, throttle closed. He pressed the starter button and heard the engine begin to wind up. Now he had to wait – precious seconds lost – before he was able to open the throttle to flight idle. But good, good, it was working. Holding the starter button down, watching the temperatures rise, he released the starter at fifty-eight per cent. He wound on the throttle to full power, waited a moment, bleeped up and then loosened the frictions. 'We're on our way!' he shouted and the JetRanger lifted like a bird into the sky.

Standing to one side of the airport building, Delacroix peered through the rain as the little helicopter with its teardrop fuselage arced away to the north and was lost in the mist.

Normally so much in command, never caught by surprise, he was still shaking from the confrontation. Keats had spoken about germ warfare, about plagues, and that had jolted him. He had always known he was dealing in death but, deluding himself perhaps, had never conceived that anything so indiscriminate as a plague would be used . . . men, women, children, even the cattle in the field; innocent and guilty alike. Kirilenko had always assured him – it had been their unwritten bond – that whatever was done, no matter what the price in blood, it was ultimately for the best, the least possible harm to the fewest souls for the greatest possible good. But, if what Keats had said was true, then Kirilenko had broken that covenant and could never be trusted again.

Delacroix was breathing hard, like a man out of breath. 'My God, oh my God, please forgive me . . .' he muttered. 'I should have seen, I should have known. It was all there before me.' And, mumbling to himself, staring at the ground, he stumbled into the building to try and board the next flight out.

A sudden burst of rain caught the column as it toiled up a long, slippery ascent towards the village. But the Mujahedin marched on, in and out of the restless mists, prodding their pack horses along the shale-black trail.

The village was little more than a warren of mud and straw huts set above a river, a gloomy beehive of desolate

417

buildings that ran up and over a mountain spur. Close to the river, there was a stony pasture in which a few goats grazed. But in general it was a poverty-stricken hamlet made insignificant by the towering razor-back ridges behind it from where small waterfalls, ribbons of bright water, came splashing down.

Clothed in an old and ratty blanket, the village priest, the mullah, came to greet Farouq Mohammadi and tell him that his people knew of no Nikolais operating in the area.

Farouq was pleased. This particular village had always been of great assistance to him and, for that, it had suffered in the past. The Russians had bombed it more than once, using yellow gases that made people cough up their lungs. 'Are there any sick in the village?' he asked.

'There are always sick,' said the mullah, not a well man himself. 'Why do you ask?'

'Because this time we have medicines. This time we have men who are trained to heal the sick. You have helped us in the past. This time let us help you.'

Although the mullah was steeped in the ways of Islam, he understood the blessings of modern medicine. So he called the men from their huts and the women too and they gathered their children about them.

Farouq was first and foremost a soldier, not a man to be caught unawares. Before anything was done, therefore, he put his men into a broad defensive perimeter, digging in a couple of mortars and sending a few of his more agile troops to scale the rocky cliffs where they could keep watch.

There was an ancient walnut tree in the centre of the village with the mosque nearby; an open space where the clinic could be held. Farouq placed two of his medics

there and, satisfied that the village was protected, stood
contentedly by as the sick lined up to be treated.

The rain passed and for a few minutes the sun appeared like
a watery orb between the shifting clouds. High up, five
hundred feet or more above the village where the wind
moaned, Mikhail Kazakov crawled on his belly across a
wet, mossy ledge and looked down. He could see the
dushmen spreading out around the village; a couple setting
up a machine gun post, three or four more climbing the
black crags with their rifles slung over their backs. They
were stopping. But why?

He took out his binoculars, adjusted them and looked
down again. In the centre of the village, close to the little
mosque, a line was forming. Mothers were holding their
babies, solemn fathers standing further back with their
sons. A couple of the bandits pulled a heavily-laden don-
key into the square. Then he saw that the first person in the
line, a small girl, stepped forward and one of the bandits
lifted her onto his knee. There was some brief conversation
before the girl tilted her head back and the bandit used his
fingers to open her one eye, leaning close to examine it.

Kazakov smiled to himself; a smirk that puckered his
podgy features. So that's why they had stopped. They were
treating the sick. He imagined a succession of such villages, a succession of such clinics with snivelling infants
and clucking females. It was just as Kirilenko had predicted. And all he had to do was sit and watch.

The JetRanger came out of the rain into a burst of silver
sunlight. Fifty feet below them was the river they had followed from the border, a snowy tumult of water that cas-
caded over rapids, while towering up on either side were the
seemingly sheer faces of the cliffs.

Up there, to the right, in among the crevices and crags and the wind-blown thickets of bamboo, ran the trail that Farouq and his men had taken. But Halima could see no sign of them. 'They must be further along,' she said, 'nearer to the village.'

They followed the river around a tight S-bend, the roar of the water crushing the resonant throb of the helicopter's engines. A wooden bridge loomed up, lichen-green with age, and, without warning, Mike banked the chopper to clear it.

Behind him, Rakosi groaned, his belly in his mouth. 'I swear to God, Mike, I never knew the medicines contained anything like you say.'

'But you knew it was something.'

'But nothing like this, I promise!' For the first time Rakosi was terrified, blabbering like a child, not just for his money, his future. This time his life was at stake.

'You knew people were going to die,' said Chuck, his voice as flat as a hangman's. 'It doesn't matter how.'

Rakosi was appealing to everybody in a high-pitched, pleading whine. 'What choice did I have? Please, Mike, you know how I've battled all these years. How could I lose it all? I was being blackmailed. You've got to see my side!'

'But you were prepared to kill people – '

'I wasn't going to kill anybody. I didn't know!'

'Leave him to Farouq,' said Halima, her voice bereft of pity. 'The Mujahedin understand justice.'

Rakosi almost gagged. 'Please, Mike, you've got to help me . . .'

Mike was staring ahead at the rushing waters of the river. 'Why?' he demanded.

'You're my friend,' Rakosi blubbered, 'the only one.'

'What have you ever done for me as a friend?'

'I've never let you down, Mike, never.'

'Don't lie to me, Joe. It's too late for lies.'

'But I swear to God!'

The moment was right, Mike knew it. This was when he had to tell Rakosi; accuse him to his face. You raped Jackie. You waited until I was gone and then you raped her. Just when she needed someone so desperately, you destroyed her. So don't talk to me about friendship, you bastard. You killed the woman I loved. All the words were formed in his mind and now in this shuddering helicopter – in front of witnesses – he was going to speak them. But, before the words would come, Halima suddenly pointed across in front of him and exclaimed, 'There, do you see it? There's the village. I can see horses too. Farouq is there.'

The moment had passed. Buffeted by swirling down-draughts, concentrating on more immediate problems, Mike brought the JetRanger into a hover and searched for a spot to land.

Kazakov heard it first, that distinctive chopping sound made by rotor blades. But he thought it had to be a Russian helicopter, nothing else was possible. Gripping the edge of the ledge, he stared down towards the rushing river and, gawking in astonishment, saw it appear.

It was small, one of those American helicopters that civilians used, like a tiny blue and white toy. And instinctively he knew it had to be Keats. Nobody else would take such an insane risk. Keats had been to the factory at Cha-Aam, Keats had learnt about the repacking of the medicines and the woman falling sick. Only Keats truly understood what was at stake.

From an assurance of victory, Kazakov was suddenly staring defeat in the eyes. Scrambling back from the ledge, he yelled to his sergeant. 'Call for air assistance. There's a bandit helicopter below us. It can't possibly be ours. It must have crossed the border.'

The sergeant looked sceptical.

'Look for yourself!'

The sergeant did so, letting out a grunt of surprise.

'It has to be intercepted!' shouted Kazakov. 'We must have our own helicopters patrolling in the area. Hurry, man, do it now. Call them in!' Dizzy with shock, he stared down at the distant river, watching the JetRanger as it hovered so close to the mud houses that its downdraught whipped at the thatch, sending it scattering into the air like chaff. The pilot was looking for somewhere to touch down. Yes, it had to be Keats.

Lifting a little, the helicopter cut back on itself and flew to the edge of the village. Kazakov watched it settle down behind an overhang of cliff – and then it disappeared from view. There was no way they could destroy it with rifle or machine gun fire, not from their present position.

But what did he do? How did he stop them destroying the medicines?

As the JetRanger had passed over the mud houses, Chuck Baldwin had seen the villagers scatter from the square in fright, thinking they must be Russian. But he had caught a glimpse of open boxes too and yelled at Mike, 'They're holding a clinic down there! They're dispensing the medicines!'

As the skids touched the ground, Chuck was out of the chopper and running, almost bowling Farouq over in his haste. Halima was only a step or two behind and, as Farouq stood, amazed, she explained in Pashtu why they had been forced to fly across the border.

'Hurry,' said Chuck. 'There are people taking those medicines – taking them now!'

There was a rapid crossfire of questions and answers and, his face very gaunt, Farouq led them at a sprint towards the village square.

As they reached it, Halima saw one of the medics and called to him in Pashtu. Chuck didn't understand the words but he knew what they had to mean. Had he given out any medicines? If so, to whom?

Perplexed by the sudden arrival of the helicopter – an amazing event in itself – and now these questions about such an innocent thing as prescribing some medicines, the medic stuttered that yes there was one child, a girl with eye trouble. He had given her ointment.

'Where is she?' asked Halima.

The medic looked around. But everything was confusion. He couldn't see her.

The old mullah was there, waiting for attention himself, and Halima fired questions at him. Which child was it? Which house did she live in? Where was she hiding?

Then Chuck saw the girl. She was seated on a wooden stool in a lane on the far side of the square. She had her head bent back so that her long black hair fell almost to her waist and she was looking upwards, about to squeeze ointment into her eye. Chuck knew no Pashtu so he couldn't shout a warning – all he could do was run.

Pushing the mullah aside, scattering a couple of wet dogs, he sprinted across the square, barging people aside, and charged into the lane. The girl looked up at the last moment but by then Chuck had launched himself into a full-length dive and, as he crashed past her into the mud, one hand slapped the tube of ointment from her fingers. The girl was knocked from her stool back into the wall of her house and, terrified, let out a wail. But Chuck grabbed her, taking her pretty moon-shaped face into his hands. She stared at him as if he was some monster, tears welling. But her eyes were clear. There was no ointment on her cheeks. And, with a sob of relief, as if it was his own child, Chuck pulled her to him.

'Is she all right?' asked Halima, running over.

'She'll be fine,' Chuck replied, hugging her tight. 'Just fine.'

They had been seconds away from their first death. But unless all the medical supplies were destroyed immediately, right here in the village, Halima knew that next time they wouldn't be so lucky. She turned to the mullah. 'Do you have any oil or gasoline in the village, anything that can be used to start a fire?'

The mullah shook his head. 'We have no tractors, we have no engines. Why do we need gasoline?'

'Then bring wood,' said Halima. 'Bring it here to the square. Get everybody doing it. Go, quick!'

The old mullah tugged his beard, looking upwards at the soft drizzle falling. 'The wood will be wet,' he said.

'There's dry kindling in the houses.'

'But they need it for their cooking – '

'Their lives are more important!' shouted Halima. 'Now bring it!'

And, his eyes popping in astonishment – that a mere woman should address him so – the mullah scuttled off to do her bidding.

Through the drifting clouds and drizzle, Kazakov saw the bonfire being set in the village square. Lifting the binoculars to his eyes and scanning across the rooftops, he saw the bandits unpacking the horses and the donkeys, working like men possessed. Within minutes it would be destroyed, everything he and Kirilenko had striven all these months to achieve.

Then, at his shoulder, he heard his sergeant say, 'A helicopter has been diverted. It's on its way.'

'How far out is it?'

'They estimate five minutes. Do you want troop reinforcements too?'

'No,' said Kazakov, flustered. 'No, don't do that!' While something had to be done to prevent the dushmen destroying the medicines, it would be a hundred times worse to have Russian troops arrive – troops not under his control – and confiscate them. 'No,' he said, dry-mouthed, in a ludicrous lie. 'We are Spetsnaz. We can handle this ourselves.'

And in truth, Kazakov was beginning to grope towards a solution to his problem. Sometimes, in trying to win hearts and minds, Spetsnaz troops attended to the sick in isolated villages, leaving medicines for them. So why not do it with the medicines that were down in the village? Why not do Mohammadi's job for him? If he could keep the bandits pinned down for five minutes – just until the helicopter arrived and they scattered – then he and his men could gather up the medical supplies at their leisure.

Yes, he thought, with sudden courage, it was the only way; crude but equally effective. If the turn of events had prevented Mohammadi spreading the plague, they would do it for him. He called the sergeant. 'Get the men ready to open fire,' he commanded. 'Let's teach these scum a lesson.'

The first sharp chatter of machine-gun fire sent them sprawling for cover. Fire raked the village, puncturing the mud walls, spurting up the black mud. Then, with a long arcing whistle, the mortar shells began to land. The

425

panic was total. Women screamed, searching for their children. One of the thatched roofs caught fire. A shell landed on the roof of the mosque, exploding inside. The mullah ran across the square, shouting incoherently, trying to pull open the door to get inside his beloved building. But a burst of fire hit him and he toppled down, nerves still working, his old legs drumming the mud as he died.

It took only a few moments to realise that the fire was coming from high above them, from concealed positions along the tops of the ridges, and it was concentrated on the village square.

'There must be thirty or more of them up there,' said Chuck. 'A full platoon . . .'

'They'll be calling in air support,' said Farouq, very matter-of-fact. 'You can expect helicopter gunships any moment now.'

'Christ,' muttered Chuck. He was silent for a moment, working out the options. Then he asked, 'Do you have any of the back-pack missiles that Mike sold you, any of the Grails?'

Farouq smiled, showing his teeth. 'On the edge of the village, with the horses, that's where you'll find them.'

And, with a quick, almost boyish grin, Chuck darted away along the mud wall towards the place where he had seen the horses tethered.

But, while Chuck Baldwin and Mohammadi had been considering the immediate problems of defence, Halima's thoughts were on the contaminated medicines still and she was at her wits' end. The centre of the small square was pockmarked with rifle fire. 'We'll never be able to get near to the fire,' she said. 'And we can't leave them here.'

'Fly them out,' said Mike. 'It's the only way.'

'Is your helicopter hidden from the ridges?'

Mike nodded.

'Then yes, you're right, Salesman. It is the only way.'

'If we can just get the supplies into it – '

But Halima was obsessed with worry. 'What happens if you don't make it to the border? What happens if you're hit and have to land?'

'Give me a phosphorus grenade,' Mike replied. 'I'll fire the stuff if I have to, burn the supplies and the chopper with it.'

'We have the grenades,' said Farouq.

'There's no other way,' said Mike to Halima. 'It's the only chance we have. Trust me.'

Halima tried to smile to show she had always trusted him and still did. Left here in the village, the contaminated supplies could start a plague that would destroy Afghanistan.

'Very well,' said Farouq calmly. 'Let's begin. We'll set up a chain of men, passing the medicines from hand to hand.' Then he smiled. 'You had better get to your helicopter, Salesman, we are returning the goods – substandard merchandise.'

And even Halima laughed.

Grabbing a canvas satchel full of field dressings, Mike crouched in the shelter of a mud wall. He looked up at the towering ridges from where the Russians were firing down upon them. The rain was coming again, heavier this time. Thick clouds were closing in. Good, he thought, at least it gave them some cover.

He was about to run, bent almost double, when, a couple of feet in front of him, huddled against the wall, he saw Joe Rakosi. 'Grab some of the supplies,' he said. 'Help us!'

Rakosi, who had been hiding his head in his arms,

looked up. There was dribble coming down from his mouth. A mortar exploded nearby, spraying them both with grit and he let out a small cry.

'Come on,' said Mike, angrily. 'Get up.'

But Rakosi cowered away from him, shaking his head. 'We're going to die,' he kept saying over and over. 'We're all going to die.'

Chuck Baldwin saw it coming along the river, blurred at first like some great fish looming out of salt grey waters. It was a big bastard, cumbersome and ugly. From its snout he could see the antenna of its heavy machine gun and from its two stub wings the bulbous outlines of its rocket pods. It was a Hind-D, as good as anything ever made.

Chuck had found a high spot, a cleft in the monolithic slab of the mountain, and had wedged himself into it beneath an overhang. His feet were secure, his body well set and he had left enough room behind him for the back blast. The SA-7 Grail rested firmly on his shoulder, tucked against his chin. He had already taken the first pressure on the trigger and breathed slowly, evenly, as he waited for the red light to turn green indicating that the seeker had locked itself on to the target.

For over twenty years he had trained others in the use of weapons like this. He had smuggled them by sea, parachuted them in by night. He had risked his life for them countless times. And now for the first time – when it counted most – he was about to use one himself. He felt calm, almost detached, his finger crooked around the trigger.

He saw the Hind-D swivel on its axis, turning towards the village. He heard the heavy chatter of its machine gun and knew that any second now it would let loose with a salvo of rockets. 'Just stay there,' he whispered. 'Stay there.' And in that instant the light turned green. Chuck took a final breath, whispered a prayer – and squeezed the trigger.

The blast from the launcher jarred his whole body, almost dislodging him. But there was no way the Hind-D could avoid being hit. It was trapped there, he knew it. And when he heard the concussive boom of the five and a half pound warhead hitting its turboshaft engines, he let out a shout of triumph.

He saw the big gunship spin around, belching black smoke. It tried to head off, back along the river, but its engines had been crippled and it was on fire. Chuck saw the rotors suddenly cut, saw it veer wildly to the left, coughing like a beast mortally wounded, and then, turning over on itself, it smashed into the foot of the cliff, white water drowning the crew.

Crawling out of cover, stepping over the mutilated corpse of a woman who had been hit by heavy-calibre machine-gun fire from the Hind-D, Mike heard the distant, final splutter of its engines and knew that it was down. Thank God, he thought, now work could resume again.

The back of the JetRanger was full up to the roof with a mass of canvas satchels and bags, boxes and packets – anything at all that might contain medical supplies. And still more was coming. It wasn't the weight of it, that didn't worry him – the JetRanger could take over a thousand pounds – it was the sheer bulk of it all. He took another rain-drenched box from a young, wounded Mujahedin, pushing it high into the back. When is it going to stop? he thought.

Then, from the relative safety of the nearest hut, he saw Halima signalling to him and scrambled across to her.

'Everything has been given to you,' she said. 'There's no more.'

'Are you sure?'

'Yes, that's it.' She was panting, not from fear so much as pure physical exertion. 'We haven't had time to sort anything. Every container that looked like it might have drugs has been given to you.'

A mortar shell whined overhead followed by a long stream of red tracer. But, with the Russian helicopter down, the firing from the ridges was becoming more sporadic.

Halima looked across at the JetRanger, sheltered against the cliff face, and a wry smile came to her wrinkled face. 'There's only room for two, I see.'

Mike said nothing. With every sack and bag, the dilemma had grown more pressing. There was simply no way he could fly out the same number of people he had flown in.

Halima squeezed his hand. 'Don't worry about me,' she said. 'I walked every step of the way from Qishlaq Imir with you and I can do it again. I'll stay with Farouq.'

For a few seconds the rain ceased and they saw Chuck Baldwin come staggering down the rocky incline, dragging an olive-green missile launcher. As he drew closer, they saw that blood was spreading across his rain-soaked windcheater. His face was grey with shock as he flopped down next to them. 'Bloody shrapnel. Caught me in the rib cage,' he said.

'Let me see,' said Halima. She opened his anorak and shirt and saw where the flesh had been ripped open to the bone. It was a jagged wound, bleeding profusely, dangerously close to the heart.

Grimacing, Chuck tried to make a joke of it. 'No problems, a couple of morphine tablets from the chopper there and I'll be fine.'

But Halima wasn't laughing. 'He's not going to be able to walk out of here,' she said to Mike. 'You must take him with you. He's your one passenger.' Tearing a strip from her dress, she pushed the wet cloth against Chuck's wound as a temporary dressing, closing his windcheater. 'Now go, hurry!' she urged them both. 'You must get away.'

Taking Chuck under the arm, Mike helped him into the JetRanger and then clambered into the pilot's seat. As the rain beat against the cockpit, he commenced start procedures, hearing the loud whine of the rotors as they began to turn.

More tracer arced over the village, burning into the waters of the river. Once they were airborne and pulled away from the cliff face, Mike estimated that there would be a period of ten seconds during which they would be in full view of the Russians high on the ridge; ten seconds to run the gauntlet.

He dropped his head, studying the gauges on the panel as he bleeped up the power, ready to lift off. He looked up, turning to Chuck – and there, beating at the perspex, was Joe Rakosi.

Half-mad with fear, Rakosi wrenched open Chuck Baldwin's door and was screaming above the engine's roar, 'You've got to take me! You can't leave me here!'

Mike shook his head. 'There's no room. You know why we're doing this. Stay with the Mujahedin. They'll take you back across the border.'

Panic-stricken, in a frenzy now, Rakosi tried to claw his way into the cockpit, grabbing for sacks of the contaminated supplies in an effort to hurl them out. Chuck tried to stop him but was too weak.

Mike knew there was only one way to do it and, reaching across Chuck Baldwin's body, punched Rakosi hard in the face. He felt the nose break, cartilage give, and saw the blood spurt down Rakosi's chin.

Rakosi staggered back, the rain splashing the blood down over his chest like watery wine. But it wasn't the pain that had rocked him, it was the sheer, stunned disbelief. 'How can you do this?' he whimpered, his legs giving under him.

Mike glared at him. 'How could you do it to Jackie, you bastard?'

Rakosi's bloodied lips fell slack. 'Jackie?'

'I heard the tape, the one you recorded that night – the night you raped her.'

Through Rakosi's mad terror, a kind of recognition dawned. 'But how . . .?'

'Tina Wai,' said Mike. 'She found it. You murdered her, Joe, you murdered Jackie. Oh you bastard . . .'

He reached across again to push Rakosi back but, before he could do it, Chuck Baldwin had kicked out with his foot sending Rakosi sprawling into the mud. 'Now let's get the hell out of here!'

Mike nodded. It was done. And, teeth gritted, he lifted the JetRanger into the air. He rose ten feet, pulling away from the cliff face. But something was wrong, he could sense it. The helicopter was slewing out over the river directly into the line of the Russian fire. Bullets punched through the fuselage. The perspex shattered just behind Chuck's head. Struggling with the controls, however, Mike didn't appreciate the obvious until he heard Chuck bellowing, 'The bastard is hanging onto the skids!'

Halima saw it all happen. She saw Rakosi lifted into the air, clinging desperately to the skids. She heard the sudden intense rattle of fire from the ridge high above them and knew that the Russians were concentrating on the helicopter, trying to bring it down. For her it was not a question of justice or revenge. For her only one thing mattered – obliterating the obscenity of those contaminated medicines, wiping them from the face of the earth. And Rakosi, a bullock of a man dragging himself beneath the helicopter, was threatening a million lives. Farouq was crouched next to her, cradling his Kalashnikov. Halima spoke only two words. 'Kill him,' she said.

Mike felt the JetRanger buck in the air as if a weight had been lifted from it.

'He's dropped,' said Chuck.

But more bullets were finding their mark, punching into the fuselage. Mike brought the chopper hard down, clinging as close as he could to the wall of the ravine, and, just a foot or two above the rushing spring waters, sped away down the river.

Dimly, in the far periphery of his vision, he glimpsed a broken body on the rocks . . . wasted flesh, a wasted life. But he felt nothing. Rakosi had finally paid his debts, that was all he could think.

They turned the bend in the river and, as they came clear of the Russian guns, Chuck said, 'Ten minutes to the border.' Then he grinned. 'Do you serve coffee on this flight?'

Mike smiled but said nothing, concentrating on keeping the crippled chopper in the air. He knew it had been hit, certainly in the tank because the fuel gauge was dropping dramatically. But where else he couldn't be sure.

The simplest and quickest way back was the way they had come in, along the river, and that's the route he took. But, after a couple of minutes he was beginning to regret the decision. Glancing at the warning lights on the panel, he saw that the transmission pressure gauge was dropping while the transmission temperature was alarmingly high. 'We must have taken shots in the gearbox,' he said.

Chuck looked at his watch. 'Just keep her flying, Mike. We're half way there.'

The fuel tank was nearly empty. Twisting his head, Mike could see avgas spraying out behind them. The transmission pressure had dropped to zero which meant that the main transmission was burning up. Any second now and it could seize entirely. 'I've got to land, Chuck,' he said, falsely calm. 'We're not going to make it.'

Chuck nodded, suddenly grim. 'But where?'

The mountain walls rose sheer on either side of the river. Mike considered trying to fly up and over them. But, if the transmission seized, they would smash into the cliff walls and drop into the river like a stone. There was only one way. And they had to do it now. He turned his head towards Chuck. 'You're going to have to jump.'

Chuck stared at him as if he had lost his mind. 'How high are we?'

'Fifty feet. You'll be okay. I'll hold her steady.' Mike brought the JetRanger into the hover, holding it over the water.

'But what about you?' shouted Chuck.

'I'll jump after you. Now go!'

'What about the supplies?'

Mike pulled a phosphorus grenade from his jacket pocket, a round olive-green tin. 'I'll burn them. Now jump!'

Chuck opened the door, cold wind beating at his face. He stared down at the boiling white waters. 'God, I hate heights,' he muttered. Then he threw himself clear.

The chopper rocked violently but Mike compensated, dipping the nose so that he could see Chuck hit the water and disappear beneath the swirling foam. For what seemed like minutes he was lost, then, arms thrust out above him, he broke the surface and struck out for the bank. Mike saw him wave. He was okay.

Now, somehow, without killing himself, he had to get out too. The first step was to tighten the frictions, making the controls as stiff as possible so that when he jumped, the chopper wouldn't turn straight on itself and drop out of the sky, catching him before he got clear. But choppers were such unstable, unpredictable animals that, even with the frictions as tight as he could make them, he just didn't know what would occur.

Sweat was sluicing down his cheeks as he tightened the collective friction with his left hand then the cyclic friction between his legs. Now came the critical part . . .

Preparing himself, Mike took his feet off the pedals, coming up into a crouch on his seat and wedging open the door with his shoulder. The chopper held steady. Mike didn't dare breathe. Now, he thought, now – and he pulled the pin from the phosphorus grenade, dropping it at his feet. He had just three seconds.

As he leaned further out of the door, the frozen wind battering his arms, the chopper began to yaw and he lost his balance. He hesitated, half in, half out. The grenade was rolling towards him – and, in a tangle of arms and legs, he fell.

He saw the water coming up to meet him, thought: thank God there are no rocks. Then he felt the sensation of impact – like smashing into a concrete wall – and down he went, down through the icy waters until his legs buckled under him as he dug into the gravel on the river bed. He wallowed a second, dazed, but then, using his arms, pulled for the surface. The current was strong, pushing him and twisting him. He was sucking in water.

But, as he broke the surface, gasping for air, his first

Michael Hartmann

and only thought was the helicopter. Looking up, he saw it arcing slowly away towards the cliffs on the far side of the river. The phosphorous grenade had exploded and the JetRanger was wreathed in brilliant white smoke that trailed behind it like a huge cloud of powder. There was a crevice in the mountain face from where a small waterfall dropped hundreds of feet into the river and the JetRanger made unerringly for it.

Mike saw it hit, seeming to implode between the sharp sides of the crevice. Black, oily smoke belched out, staining the pure white of the phosphorus while chunks of the fuselage, thrown out by the explosion, cartwheeled lazily through the air. Mike expected to see the wreck fall away from the face of the rock but it remained there, held tight, burning fiercely.

Struggling against the rushing current, Mike swam for the pebbled riverbank where Chuck was waiting. Chuck saw him and, lying on a spray-lashed rock, his face grimaced with pain, he reached out to take Mike's hand. 'Grab for it, grab for it,' he said. And, with a final tug, hauled him ashore.

Then they stood together, saying nothing, just gazing across the river at that burning machine wedged into the mountain face. Nothing, they knew, could survive the conflagration. The smoke rose high, brown now, smudging the sky. Chuck gave the slightest nod, a kind of grin, as if to say: we did it, Mike, we did it.

Then, shivering from the bitter cold of the water, the two of them turned their backs on the funeral pyre and, helping each other as best they could, limped painfully towards freedom.

Epilogue

'History is a selfish bitch. Confide in her too closely and one day she'll destroy you. We've weathered the storm, casualties have been minimal. Of course you must guard for the future, Jim, but leave it at that. You'll get nothing out of the Russians, you'll get nothing out of the Vietnamese. I doubt you'll get much out of that Swiss banker, Delacroix. So leave it. There are some events that should never see the light of day.' Those were Tom Delaney's words, spoken from his hospital bed when James Dexter informed him of the final outcome. And Dexter, still the disciple, acted upon them.

In Thailand, because of Mei-ling's prompt work, there had been only two deaths, not enough on their own to prove that the victims had been infected with biological warfare bacteria. One had admittedly died of the bubonic plague but isolated outbreaks of it were not unknown in South East Asia, while the other had succumbed to typhoid, a common enough disease in remote rural areas. There was talk of course . . . rumours, as there always are. But the army officer tasked with the investigation, a man trained at West Point, found that both deaths were due to natural causes and the affair was quickly forgotten.

In Afghanistan, of course, it was more difficult to sweep it away. But in the ensuing weeks a number of eminent physicians visited Peshawar to assure the

Mujahedin leadership that nothing sinister had occurred. The medicines had been tainted, yes, but not by germ warfare bacteria. That unfortunate impression had been the result of garbled communications, very understandable in moments of high crisis. In fact, there had been a regrettable but totally innocent act of negligence in the manufacture of the pharmaceuticals. Certain poisonous substances had been misapplied. It had been a freak accident, said the physicians, and one which would never occur again.

Both Halima and Farouq Mohammadi, who had survived the battle at the river and returned to Pakistan, were dubious at first. But, 'for the good of the service and America's reputation', Chuck Baldwin had been convinced not to persist with his allegations about the Phoenix Pact and, when he visited Peshawar, he was able to allay their fears.

In any event, supplied openly again with US Stinger missiles and other arms, the Mujahedin leadership had no cause to doubt their good friends in the CIA. What was done was done, they said.

Even the possible diplomatic embarrassment of Joe Rakosi's death in Afghanistan was neatly handled. His body was conveyed back across the border by a Mujahedin commando and, after an 'arranged' autopsy, his death was publicly attributed to an air accident that had occurred near Chitral in poor weather conditions while he had been visiting refugee camps in the area.

Mike Keats and Mei-ling knew the truth of course. But they agreed with Chuck Baldwin that there was no point – in the face of a barrage of denials – in trying to tell the world how close it had come to being swept by a man-made plague for which there was no vaccine. The bacteria had been destroyed, that was all that mattered. They had done their job.

Mike Keats, as he had promised himself, never dealt in arms of war again. With Joe Rakosi's passing, the Good Hope Group was liquidated – dust to dust, even in commerce – and Mike accepted the position of executive director with a large air cargo company operating out of Hong Kong. He and Mei-ling have twin boys now, both of them as dark and devilish as gypsies. They travel a great deal, especially to the south of France where they own a ramshackle old farmhouse in the hills of the Dordogne, and both have found a contentment in their lives that had eluded them in the past. They talk of the Phoenix Pact, of course, but never to third parties. It is a secret they share with Chuck Baldwin, the godfather to both their sons, a secret the three of them will carry to their graves.

The only person troubled by the burden of his knowledge was Dr William Arnold Mozart of All Souls Mission. But he died suddenly before he could speak to the press. Nobody thought it strange. He was into his seventies and known to suffer from a weak heart. So prayers were said and he was buried according to Roman Catholic ritual in the mission grounds, resting in peace at last.

In the final analysis, therefore, just as Tom Delaney had decreed, the Phoenix Pact never saw the light of day. James Dexter may have lived in Delaney's shadow but he had learnt his lessons well and executed the cover-up with admirable efficiency. What deaths there had been went into the history books as isolated incidents, attributable to natural causes or tragic accidents. Men and women had perished in an event that had never occurred. But, as Dexter himself said, it was a small price to pay to maintain the integrity of an organisation vital to the protection of world freedom.

On the Russian side, Mikhail Kazakov received a decoration for his gallantry in action against the dushmen at the river. But it wasn't enough to dispel his fears that the real truth might still emerge and for the next six months he lived in a state of perpetual terror, haunted by nightmares of the furnace doors. He had no need for concern, of course, and later that year he was appointed to an administrative post at GRU Headquarters in Moscow, a sedentary life shuffling papers for which, in all honesty, he is best suited. He is married now to a round, compliant woman from Estonia who openly adores him. He has nothing to prove to himself anymore and it is only rarely, late at night, that he remembers back to that conspiracy which he and Kirilenko created, and the dreams return.

Jean-Paul Delacroix refused to do any further work for Kirilenko or his successor. Profoundly disillusioned, he cut all ties with the Soviets, realising that they had always promised a false Eden. Six months after he had fled Chitral, one early autumn morning as a light drizzle fell, he walked up to the chapel in the College St Michel, prayed for a time, and then shot himself through the heart. He gave no forewarning to his friends or family and left no written reasons behind. He died as he had lived, in the folds of an enigma.

As for Kirilenko himself, he was 'retired' later that year, a dinosaur who had outlived his usefulness in the new, open society of the Soviet Union. Bitter and abandoned, he took up permanent residence in his country dacha and continues to live there, a lonely man who sits at night and listens to the howling of the wolves.

But when he is deep in his cups, muzzy with vodka, he still goes over the plan that so nearly worked, still analyses it, step by patient step . . .

The Mozambique segment had worked perfectly. He had held out the bait of a legitimate contract and then used it to place Rakosi under his power, to half cripple him financially, knowing that the man – obsessed by money – would do anything to stave off the collapse of his burgeoning business empire. And once Kirilenko had him financially captive, just as he knew he would, Rakosi had grabbed at the escape route offered by Vietnam, especially when – in return for raising the gold – he had been tempted with that glittering jewel in the crown . . . the opportunity to buy the vast stockpile of weapons America had left behind.

Just as there had been no gold, of course, so there had been no weapons – at least not for sale to Rakosi. Vietnam was a ruse, a mirage of greed. And it so nearly worked.

The plan had been simple . . . Keats was to be kept at the coast with the diving team on the assurance that, as soon as the gold bullion was raised, he would be shown the weapons. Then, the day the container was raised from the estuary bed, he would have been arrested, accused of having CIA connections and deported aboard the same aircraft that had taken the divers out, the same one that had plunged to its destruction after a mid-air explosion.

So what had gone wrong? It was such a little thing. But with such great consequences.

Ricky Tang, after eighteen long years of deprivation, a skeleton of a man, brought down to the coast to point out the landmarks upon which he had taken his bearings of the wreck, had managed to escape. Nobody knew exactly how . . . a guard dozing off for a second or turning to talk to one of his comrades about a woman . . . an act so inconsequential that it was forgotten almost before it was completed.

And yet, as a result of it, Tang had managed to warn Keats, and Keats had believed him, fleeing Vietnam with the torch of that belief. And it was Keats, at the very last minute, in the final soaring wing bursts of the bird, who had brought the phoenix down.

So thus it is, when he is drunk on vodka, that the old General does not dwell on the grand global sweep of events, but rather on that one simple irony . . . that history was changed and a country lost because, after eighteen years of captivity, one half-starved man was allowed to slip away into the night.